T0017253

Singing of Mount Abora.
Could I revive within me
Her symphony and song,
To such a deep delight 'twould win me,
That with music loud and long,
I would build that dome in air,
That sunny dome! those caves of ice!
And all who heard should see them there,
And all should cry, Beware! Beware!
His flashing eyes, his floating hair!
Weave a circle round him thrice,
And close your eyes with holy dread:
For he on honey-dew hath fed,
And drank the milk of Paradise.

Handwritten comment on 'Kubla Khan' by Samuel Taylor Coleridge,
by permission of the Master and Fellows of Jesus College, Cambridge.

The Second Person from Porlock

DENNIS HAMLEY

Fairlight Books

First published by Fairlight Books 2021
This paperback edition first published by Fairlight Books 2022

Fairlight Books
Summertown Pavilion, 18–24 Middle Way, Oxford, OX2 7LG

A CIP catalogue record for this book is available from the
British Library

1 2 3 4 5 6 7 8 9 10

ISBN 978-1-914148-02-6

www.fairlightbooks.com

Printed and bound in Great Britain

Designed by Leo Nickolls

For my wonderful wife Kay
who eased me gently away
from all my avoidance strategies.

Overture

Siracusa, October 1804

...a damsel bright
Drest in a silken robe of white
That shadowy in the moonlight shone:
The neck that made that white robe wan,

Her stately neck, and arms were bare;
Her blue-veined feet unsandal'd were,
And wildly glittered here and there
The gems entangled in her hair.
I guess 'twas frightful there to see
A lady so richly clad as she—
Beautiful exceedingly!

My sire is of a noble line,
And my name is Geraldine.

—'Christabel', Samuel Taylor Coleridge

A man walks alone down a green lane lined with poplar trees. Their heady resinous smell and the scent of flowers on each side of the lane almost make him swoon. Cicadas singing their song of procreation tease his ears.

The lane is in Sicily, in Siracusa on the south-east coast. As he walks, a two-thousand-year history of heroes and great battles walks with him, the temples of Athena, Apollo, Zeus, the fort of Euryalus, the Grecian amphitheatre that Aeschylus, Sophocles and Euripides knew – for all this is what has brought him here. But it is not what detains him.

The year is 1804, the month October. The Mediterranean is a dangerous place. Warring fleets seek each other out to kill and destroy. But here all is calm, clear, a peaceful, azure evening. The green lane leads to the opera house. The man is going to the opera and his heart beats fast.

Come closer: you will see that he is in his early thirties, his hair dark and thick, his features firm and striking despite the slight puffiness of his face. He radiates health and well-being, yet something about his slightly shambling gait might make you suspect he is not always – or even often – like this. Come very close indeed – no, he won't notice you, he is preoccupied with his own thoughts – and you'll see his dark eyes dance and glitter with delighted anticipation. Every sense is alive: his imagination is working vividly. Perhaps too vividly. There is pleasurable discomfort in his loins and ecstatic, fevered visions of bliss in his mind, perhaps very near now because if not tonight they will never be brought into life.

But look again and you'll realise that a war goes on inside him. Despite his sparkling eyes, his brow is lined: his thoughts are hobbled by a great weight. This longed-for prospect of delight runs hard against some heavy rock, some strong-built dam, deep in his mind. Temptation is ahead, severe, alluring. Yield and it will

8

damn him. He prays for strength to withstand this temptation: failing that, wit to avoid it. Yet he knows that neither strength nor wit can help him: he needs a different order of miracle.

Perhaps he shouldn't, this perfect October evening, be going alone to the opera. But he has to, he knows he has to.

This man is Samuel Taylor Coleridge. He is thirty-two years old, a poet who has already made a revolution in how his art is created, a thinker yet to make a revolution in how it is understood. For the last months he has been personal secretary to the Governor of Malta, Admiral Sir Alexander Ball. Sometimes he cannot believe what lucky chance gave him that job, nor that, for now anyway, he is an unlikely but important cog in the great machine waging war for Britain against Napoleon Bonaparte. The Admiral has sent him on a mission to Sicily and he is staying with the British Resident and his wife in Siracusa.

But he's not thinking of war now – at least, not one fought with ships and cannon. Music echoes through his mind. A soprano voice of surpassing beauty and clarity sings. 'Amo te solo' – 'I love you alone'. This melody, those words, that voice, once heard, spread like a warming flame through the town: sober citizens and urchins sing them. But those words, he tells himself, were not sung for them. Tonight, he goes again to where he first heard them. The heavenly, soaring voice of a beautiful, bewitching woman, singing – an alarming intuition says – only for him. His intuition must have been right. Why else would he be walking up the green lane to the opera house?

But consider. Back home are a wife and three children. The children at least are very dear to him. There is another woman, too. He tells himself he loves her with an aching, passionate, useless love. Until these last weeks her image has taken up every waking hour – and hours of sleep as well – and his memories have made him sweat with longing. And something else. He is a poet:

often he finds himself writing verses which strangely forecast his own fortunes. He remembers (how can he forget, for his words and rhythms are always with him?) his own creation:

Behold! her bosom and half her side—

A sight to dream of, not to tell!

Oh shield her! shield sweet Christabel!

But perhaps the one to be shielded is not Christabel. Maybe it is he, Samuel Taylor Coleridge, as he walks up the green lane to meet this magical, beautiful creature with the bewitching voice.

Tread carefully, Mr Coleridge, lest she is a reincarnation of your own ominous Geraldine.

You will soon know. Every step you take towards the opera house brings you nearer to yet another defining struggle in your chaotic life.

PART I

Chapter 1

The Discovery

Cambridge, April 1824

In an inauspicious hour I left the friendly cloisters and happy grove of quiet, ever honoured Jesus College, Cambridge.
—*Biographia Literaria*, Samuel Taylor Coleridge

The Old Library of Jesus College, Cambridge is a place of secrets. Handsome bookstacks are connected to the roof beams by wooden balusters and arranged in bays, each illuminated by a stained-glass window bearing a scroll proclaiming the subject of the books housed – *Physic, Canon Law, Civil Law, Theology*. An early cataloguing system?

The year is 1824 and this is the only library in the college. On an April evening, still cold and strangely dark after a hard winter, a few shivering readers huddle over the tables in flickering candlelight. Soon the library will close for the night, before evensong in Chapel and dinner in Hall. A library clerk, George Scrivener by name, is browsing the shelves. As well as a clerk, he is an undergraduate. He came up to Jesus College from the grammar school in Hertford as a sizar, meaning free board and lodging from the college, but in return he had to work. He blesses his good fortune in being a library clerk. Some sizars are servants to rich fellow commoners, including some who are not above inflicting pointless humiliation on them. Scrivener knows who they are.

As he congratulates himself, not for the first time, on his luck, something makes him look up to a high, almost inaccessible shelf lined with very old books, published through four centuries, from the fourteenth to the eighteenth. They stand monolithic, forbidding, daring the reader to open them.

Scrivener has never even tried. He has presumed that they are packed tightly together. But now he notices this might not be so.

He finds a stepladder to investigate. He sees a thin glint coming from between the two largest and most forbidding books. Even as he watches, it seems to glow with a soft brown light. A reflection from the flickering candlelight?

Mystified, he climbs the stepladder. Yes, sandwiched between these mighty volumes is a very thin book. The cover is marbled blue and brown. It contains three poems by Samuel Taylor Coleridge. He was an undergraduate at the college thirty years ago. His career there courted notoriety rather than glory. He, too, was a sizar and had been a library clerk.

But before Scrivener opens the book, watch him pause and wonder – *why should it glow? Is it a beacon?*

*

Scrivener skimmed the poems, vowing to read them attentively later. 'Kubla Khan', 'Christabel', 'The Pains of Sleep'. Of course, he knew 'The Ancient Mariner', which Mr Coleridge had published with Mr Wordsworth in *Lyrical Ballads*: who did not? But the others were new to him. 'Christabel' – a wild, romantic story and, he noticed, unfinished. 'The Pains of Sleep' – he shivered as he read, for it spoke of agonies and horrors in the loneliest hours of the night, surely the work of a tortured soul. And 'Kubla Khan' – like a dream, hypnotic: he almost swayed to its subtle rhythms.

Then he stopped short. His eyes widened, first in surprise, then horror, then surpassing interest. Underneath 'Kubla Khan' was a comment pencilled in an angular hand.

The writer of the above had much better have kept his sleeping thoughts to himself, for they are, if possible, worse than his waking ones.

His first thought was as conscientious library clerk. *Defacing precious books is an offence and a disgrace.* The second was as embryo critic. *What an elegant sentence, expressing a trenchant thought memorably.* The third was the earnest scholar. *What does it mean?* The fourth was obvious to the assiduous investigator. *Who did this terrible thing?*

The college Fellow in charge of the library was at his desk reading a much older, bulkier book. He was Scrivener's moral tutor, *in loco parentis*, a title Scrivener found deeply ironic. Scrivener scurried up the library holding the book open. 'Dr Vavasour, sir,' he whispered urgently. 'See here.'

Dr Vavasour looked at the pencilled scrawl. His mouth pursed with anger. 'This is disgraceful. What barbarian has dared to despoil one of my books?'

Scrivener knew that Dr Vavasour felt towards his library books much as the conscientious gardener does towards his flowers. He felt the guilt of the insecure person who fears unjust blame. But Dr Vavasour knew his library clerk better than that.

'Surely no undergraduate would write such words,' he said, with unaccustomed forcefulness. 'Mr Coleridge is too much admired by the young. He is one of the *moderns*.' He almost spat the last word. Modernity was obviously anathema to him.

'Though I admire Mr Coleridge, I prefer Lord Byron and Mr Shelley,' said Scrivener.

Dr Vavasour looked at him over his spectacles. 'As to poetry, Mr Scrivener, you would do well to confine yourself to Ovid and Horace.'

'But, sir, who would cast such a slur on one whose works are so fine?'

For the first time Scrivener noticed two words printed above the inscription. *Perfect nonsense.* Surely a contradiction in terms. Ignore it.

Dr Vavasour peered at the handwriting. If not an undergraduate, then who? The college Fellows were fond of writing tetchy memoranda to each other: he knew their hands well. This belonged to none of them. Some older Fellows still remembered Mr Coleridge and the disgraceful scene in the Senate House during the trial for sedition of William Frend, sometime Fellow of the college. How he fled from Cambridge and his debts and enlisted in the 15th Light Dragoon Guards under an assumed name, only released because the army deemed him insane and his brother paid them a great deal of money. And how drink, opium, a penchant for whoring and a talent for laziness approaching genius had ruined a promising mind.

Yes, several colleagues could have written such a vituperative comment.

But the handwriting was stiff, angular, nothing like that of any of his colleagues.

Dr Vavasour had a strange thought. *Why did I not know about this already?* Then another. *I do not remember seeing this book before.* 'Leave it with me, Mr Scrivener,' he said. 'I will not stand for spoliation of my books, even if I agree with the sentiment expressed.' He found the accessions list to look for the date the college received the book. He found none. So how had this book slipped unnoticed onto the shelves?

'I must get to the bottom of this,' he muttered.

But though his enquiries were exhaustive, he never did.

*

Scrivener's rooms were on First Court, directly opposite the gatehouse and the library. After dinner in Hall he returned to them, lit candles, stoked up the fire and sat at his small desk to think.

He knew he was no genius. Back in Hertford they thought him a brilliant young fellow. Many had sympathy as well as admiration for what he had achieved. His parents had died before he was ten and he lived with his uncle, a strict and unforgiving guardian. Nobody visited the dark, gloomy house in Bengeo, at the top of Port Hill. Uncle and nephew were locked in what seemed to Scrivener akin to a prisoner–warder relationship. Each day led to a night of captivity and silence. Coming to Cambridge meant release from Plato's shadow-cave into the sunlight, to spend life contemplating the Form of the Good. Or so he hoped. Hope born to die. Cambridge was an extraordinary place where he had found out what real brilliance was. He had also found extremes of stupidity, drunkenness and sheer bloody-mindedness which he had never dreamt of. Sometimes, he was puzzled to note, all four co-existed seamlessly within the same person.

Could Mr Coleridge have been like that? Surely not. Everyone knew that his one-time friend Mr Wordsworth, at Cambridge some years before Mr Coleridge came up to Jesus, certainly wasn't. People at St John's College now regarded Mr Wordsworth as one of their brightest sons. Most at Jesus who remembered him personally seemed to have nothing good to say about Mr Coleridge. Except, grudgingly and infrequently, that he was a fine poet, excellent critic and could have been a great scholar.

Still, Mr Coleridge did have debts at Cambridge; he drank too much, took opium and was not above dalliance with ladies of the night. Scrivener shuddered to think what they would say in Hertford if he were guilty of such practices. He knew that Mr Coleridge had written poetry at Cambridge and won the prize for Greek verse. He felt a twinge of shame at the ineptitude of his own efforts to win the same prize.

Scrivener so wanted to be a poet. He had been working on a poem only that morning. Should he carry on with it? He found the sheet of scribbled-on paper and reread what he had jotted down.

'Lines Written on Jesus Green'
As through the dusky silence of the groves,
Through tiny valleys and past green retreats,
With easeful ripple flows the shining stream
Along its hidden course,
So flows my Life, unnoticed in the throng
Of chattering seekers-out of worldly fame,
Always the observer, never the observed,
And thus...

And thus – what? He threw the paper on the desk and covered it with books so nobody should see it. The encounter in the library had unsettled him.

Always the observer, never the observed. Yes, that was his trouble. He must not let this place overwhelm him but be positive in all he did. He sometimes wondered whether anyone else even knew he was there. He certainly hadn't made a single friend. No, he must burn this lame verse and never write such self-pitying rubbish again. And then he would...

Yes, what? His mind was a blank.

Then he remembered the pencilled comments on 'Kubla Khan'.

The writer of the above had much better have kept his sleeping thoughts to himself, for they are, if possible, worse than his waking ones.

He wrote it down. How terse. How economical. How precise. Might he be the first person to have read the sentence since it was written? Was that important?

Yes. Was he *meant* to see it? He must be, else why the brown glow? Did it concern him in some way? How? Sleeping thoughts? Waking thoughts? Was 'Kubla Khan' a sleeping thought?

Scrivener had read Mr de Quincey's book *Confessions of an English Opium Eater*, published two years before. It was all the rage, in Cambridge as everywhere else. It said that opium caused dreams more vivid, real and wonderful than anything in ordinary life. This thrilled others; it frightened him.

Did the mysterious defacer mean that 'Kubla Khan' was an opium dream? The poem's words danced hypnotically through his brain, the visions of the Abyssinian maid with her dulcimer and the poet with flashing eyes and floating hair (*Beware! beware!* – sonorous bells in his mind) were so vivid, real, wonderful – and, yes, *frightening.*

He was about to throw the paper into the waste basket. But the strange thought of a moment ago became a conviction. *He was meant to see it.* It contained a message on which he must act.

What could it be? He peered at the words and said them aloud several times. Once, in case of some hidden code, he said them backwards. But they stayed as they were: no secrets there.

It was time for sleep. He undressed, put on his nightshirt, climbed into bed and blew out the candle.

But his mind wouldn't stop working. There was something strange and puzzling about the sentence, which had to be considered seriously. He sat up, relit the candle and examined it again. Dr Vavasour had said '...*even if the sentiment is one with which I agree*'.

What sentiment was that? The writer seemed no friend to Coleridge. He must hate his dissolute habits and see him as a charlatan whose poetry was fit only for burning. No wonder Dr Vavasour agreed.

But, as Scrivener silently rehearsed the sentence yet again, he fancied he found another tone. These weren't the words of a baleful critic. There was something wry, even cheerful about them, a good-natured comment despite its obvious meaning.

And something else. Dr Vavasour had no need to tell Scrivener to confine himself to Ovid and Horace. To study them and their like in

Latin and Greek was his reason for being in Cambridge. He knew about poetic scansion. Anapests and dactyls were his meat and drink. He saw how superbly the sentence was constructed, how the two words 'sleeping' and 'waking' were opposed not merely in meaning but also in their placing. The rhythmic structure threw the main stress on each, making the sentence finely balanced. Was that important?

Well, no, not necessarily, he thought. It was just a sentence and the meaning alone dictated the emphasis. The stresses came naturally. They were part of language's power to make the meanings. The writer need not have consciously designed it. But wait. What if he wrote the sentence out himself, as though he was composing it for the first time?

He slipped out of bed, shivering in his thin nightshirt, sat again at the table and took pen and paper.

Writing the sentence down as if it were a poem, he mouthed the words:

The writer of the above
Had much better have kept
His sleeping thoughts to himself,
For they are, if possible, worse
Than his waking ones.

There. The sentence naturally fell into a four-line stanza, culminating in a five-syllabled final flourish. The rhythm was perfect. Look where the natural stresses were.

The <u>wri</u>-ter of the a-<u>bove</u>
Had <u>much</u> better have <u>kept</u>
His <u>sleep</u>-ing thoughts to him-<u>self</u>,
For they <u>are</u>, if possible, <u>worse</u>
Than his <u>wak</u>-ing ones.

Perfect. A jaunty, regular rhythm such as you might find in a trivial ballad or comic song, with a shorter line at the end to make a good finish. Add, say, '*have* <u>been</u>' and the line would be finished. But the words would be redundant and the whole sentence would be weakened.

This rhythm would never appear in the serious classical poems with which he spent most of his time. Lines with the same rhythm crept in to his mind:

<u>Hey</u>, *diddly*-<u>dee</u>,

A <u>poet's</u> *life for* <u>me</u>.

That second line surprised him. What made him write *poet's*? He could have written *farmer's*. Or even *actor's*. Or, God save the mark, *student's*. They would be better, because the hard consonants separating each syllable would define the rhythm more sharply. But his mind seemed to write *poet's* for him.

He knew why. It was almost instinctive. Oh, if only a poet's life *could* be his. But, unless he sold every poem he wrote, how would he live? For someone from his class in life, a degree led either into the Church as vicar of a living in the college's gift, probably a remote windswept village in the Fens, or long years teaching Latin and Greek to unwilling boys banished by their parents when they were eight into the care of a probably sadistic headmaster. No bishoprics for the likes of him, no parliamentary seats elected by landowners rich enough to vote, nor the power of life and death given to a judge. These were for the fellow commoners, if they had to work at all. Years of boring drudgery awaited his sort.

Yet what if he *could* be a poet? He might attain fame, praise and the satisfaction of completing works in words which would live for ever. He remembered the lame rhyme with its tired old sentiments lying on his table. He would do better. He would use the best examples, study them closely, find how these poets worked their magic, emulate them and be better than Mr Wordsworth, Mr Southey, Mr Keats, Mr Shelley.

But what about Mr Coleridge? Scrivener forgot the preference for Lord Byron and Mr Shelley that he had confessed to Dr Vavasour. For here, attached to a poem written by his new hero, was a strange, gnomic statement surely meant for him alone. Was it encouragement?

Or, a doubting voice in his mind said, a warning? It didn't matter. The message was clear. Henceforth, Mr Coleridge would be his guide and mentor.

He turned back to his rhythmic rearrangement of the sentence, read it aloud again and frowned.

No, this was not a serious rhythm. Was the writer making a private joke? Or trivialising 'Kubla Khan' and making fun of the poet?

Whichever it was, this was no accident: the writer knew about poetry. He might be a poet himself – and one who did not like Mr Coleridge. Who could it be?

Well, that was interesting. But he was no nearer knowing why this sentence had affected him so much. Except that it brought him to a great decision and action stretching him to a cloud of unknowing, which, until that evening, he had never imagined.

He climbed into bed and blew out the candle.

He had not chosen the book. The book had chosen him. Why? So he would see the inscription?

When he finally slept at three in the morning, the strange, angular handwriting crawled across the page and mocked him in his dreams. When he woke, his head ached and the puzzling words were still there.

Chapter 2

The Haunter

Highgate, April 1824

Now wherefore stopp'st thou me?
—'The Rime of the Ancient Mariner', Samuel Taylor Coleridge

Samuel Taylor Coleridge had seen a ghost. He wasn't surprised. He had grown up with tales of ghosts and let supernatural experiences into his poems so vivid that they became a part of him. They strode through his dreams, sometimes enlightening, usually stoking depths of fear. So the figure dogging his footsteps was not a surprise.

He hated being called 'Samuel'. He was 'Mr Coleridge' to the world and 'STC' to his friends. Sarah Fricker, his long-estranged wife, who suffered so much through his weaknesses which, though he tried, he could do nothing about, had her own name for him. 'Esteesee.' There were ghosts enough in his life already. And now, here was a new ghost.

Coleridge was looking for opium. He had been alive for more than fifty years and had been slave to it for half of them. He walked from Moreton House, Dr Gillman's substantial residence in which he lodged, crossed Highgate High Street, turned right and came to Dunn's chemist's on the corner of Townsend's Yard. Backsliding again. Dr Gillman had given him a home specifically to shake off this opium habit. Not so much a lodger as an unreliable patient with a need for secrecy. He went cautiously, one eye open for spies who might report to the good doctor.

Inside Dunn's, he negotiated with the apprentice behind the counter and produced three shillings, the price of a four-ounce bottle of laudanum with an extra infusion of opium, from his secret cache of money. He proffered them and the apprentice put them in the cash box and smiled smugly.

'Can I interest you in some of our special stock, reserved for connoisseurs?' he said. 'Kendal Black Drop, straight from the Lakes?'

For a moment Coleridge was tempted. He remembered Kendal Black Drop from when he lived in Keswick. It was murderously strong and had brought him low. He lived with the consequences. But a secret store of an ordinary strength, plus a slight, by his standards, strengthening, could surely do no harm. Cure with Dr Gillman was a slow process, with occasional backsliding.

Coleridge muttered his farewells and the apprentice watched him go, with a secret but pleasing feeling of power over this strange man from Dr Gillman's house. Some said he was a great genius and others a wretched opium eater. To the apprentice, he was just another customer.

Outside the shop, there was the new ghost again. A tall, dark-haired youth, slightly olive-skinned. He looked faintly familiar. Was he Dr Gillman's spy? Intuition said he wasn't.

This was the fifth time in two days. This man-boy had watched him yesterday on his morning walk on Hampstead Heath and outside Dr Gillman's house during the evening. Coleridge saw him through the window, standing on the pavement, motionless as a statue. Twenty minutes later Coleridge had looked again. The man-boy still watched. Coleridge pushed up the sash window to ask what he wanted. However, in the instant between undoing the catch and pushing the window up with the scrawking sound of wood on wood the revenant had disappeared. Remembering the ghost of Hamlet's father, he could not help saying aloud:

'*At the sound it shrunk in haste away*
And vanished from my sight.'

A fitting reaction. In a lecture on Shakespeare, he once said, 'I have a smack of Hamlet myself, if I may say so?'

Almost as if it said, 'Yes, you may,' here was the revenant again.

Something about this young man disturbed him. What was it?

He looks like a son. Ridiculous. Every man was a son, just as every woman was a daughter.

Coleridge knew about sons. He and Sarah had produced two of them. Both were here in Highgate. There was once a third, but such bad memories lie deep, to erupt only in moments of despair.

He had a daughter, too, another Sara, in whom he took unalloyed delight even though he had barely ever seen her. But oh! the two sons he had: what doubts, what frustrations, what anguish. Both were in their twenties. The younger, Derwent, whose name recalled happier days in the Lakes, was in Highgate, having come down from Cambridge. It was not a social visit. He had brought typhus, rampant in his college, St John's. Coleridge called him home. Now he lay isolated in a room at the top of the house next door, in a fever which might yet kill him. Coleridge kept vigil at his bedside every night. He knew about fevers. He had done this before. He could never forget.

The eldest, Hartley, was here also, which was a rarity. Hartley. His firstborn, in whom he had placed such hope, whose rare talent he divined early and sought to foster. His '*little child*', his '*limber elf*'. Hartley would be a great poet, and Coleridge's life's mission was to make him so.

But he had failed. Must flaws in one generation be passed to the next? Plump, good-natured Derwent was free of them. Wiry, dark-bearded Hartley was not. But his weakness was not for opium. He drank.

He had survived at Merton College in Oxford long enough to take his degree. But Merton was an easy-going, tolerant place. His father had been so proud when his son was elected to a fellowship at Oriel College. Sadly, however, Oriel was the soberest, most austere college in Oxford with Fellows both stern and religious. If Hartley had stayed at Merton, or, better still, joined hedonist, high-living Christ Church over the road, he might have done better.

The fearsome Provost of Oriel, Dr Copleston, was deaf to Coleridge's pleadings. Drunkenness and keeping low company meant there was no place for Hartley at Oriel. His fellowship was taken away. The disgrace hit Coleridge hard.

But now, after years of wandering and sometimes teaching, Hartley was home, ostensibly to help look after Derwent.

There was little sign of that. Hartley's personal habits and incompetence enraged Mrs Gillman, and Coleridge was saddened by his uncooperative sullenness.

'*How sharper than a serpent's tooth it is to have a thankless child*,' he said aloud as he crossed Highgate High Street and people stopped to listen to him.

It could not continue. Each day saw the connection between father and son dwindle to the weakness of a spider's thread.

*

By mid-afternoon, Coleridge was home. He climbed the stairs to his room and sat down at his desk. A cold feeling spread through him. Derwent was being watched over by a nurse. His responsibility was to see him through the night.

Was this revenant a more reliable version of Hartley? Something unearthly was happening. Was this man-boy one of the Eumenides, the Furies bent on revenge? Revenge for what? His mind swarmed with possibilities. But the name also stood for 'the kindly ones'. Perhaps the revenant might bring good news.

Yes, the man-boy looked slightly familiar. But the remembrance was so faint that it may as well not be there.

But it was, it was.

At least he had opium, which he intended to use the moment he could. He opened the laudanum, sniffed the so-familiar smell, lifted the window to clear the odour away, sealed the bottle and, instead of hiding it so that Dr Gillman, his wife or servant would find it, slipped it in his pocket.

Chapter 3

The Pest House

How long in that same fit I lay,
I have not to declare
—'The Rime of the Ancient Mariner', Samuel Taylor Coleridge

Eight o'clock. Coleridge opened the front door of Moreton House and looked cautiously out. The revenant was gone.

Relieved, he padded softly to the house next door and tugged at the bell-pull. No answer. He was about to pull it again when, with a squeal of sliding bolts, the door was opened by a housemaid.

'Good evening, Mr Coleridge, are you here to see your son? The nurse left half an hour ago.'

'I was detained,' he replied.

Without answering, she led him upstairs, stopped outside a closed door and went down again without a word.

He stood trembling. *You cannot fear to see your own son.* But he *was* afraid, as he was whenever he stood here. With an effort of will he made himself knock at the door. Then he listened.

No sound. He opened the door. The blinds were down: the room was dark. A single bed was placed opposite the door. Someone slept in it. Coleridge crossed the room and looked down on the sleeping body.

'Derwent?' he whispered.

No reaction. Breath racked out of the body like sandpaper over rough wood. Coleridge sat on the chair next to his son, who had a fever that was likely to kill him.

He should not have done what came next. He intended the laudanum for when his vigil ended. But the compulsion seized him. He unstopped the bottle and took four drops. Even as the drops passed comfortably down he knew he was abusing his responsibility.

The tortured breathing continued. Nothing changed. He waited.

Then something did change, suddenly and shockingly.

*

He is awake on a dark night in February 1794. The heat and smell of human sweat, piss and shit are overpowering. On a low bed covered with filthy sheets a man lies sleeping. His breathing is shallow, snatched, loud and liquid. His nightshirt is soiled. His face and body are covered in scabs.

'Oh, my dear son!' Coleridge cries aloud.

But this is not Derwent. A soldier's tunic is draped over the back of a chair by the bed. Why is he wearing a uniform?

Memory strikes like a blow in the face. He is in the 15th Light Dragoons. He has run away from Cambridge. He is still STC, but different. Silas Tomkyn Comberbache. It isn't funny now. He is the worst soldier in the world. His arse is blistered from his efforts to ride a horse. His body throbs from bruises after many fallings-off. He is looking after a man with smallpox in the pest house, because this is all the army could find that he can do. With luck they may die together.

He sponges the sick man's brow. 'Courage, my friend. Your sickness will pass. You will laugh again soon.' But encouragement is futile in this stinkhole.

The day dies. The room grows even hotter. It is difficult even to breathe. The air seemingly crawls with long-legged, writhing creatures which reach chokingly down his throat. The sick man moans, then shouts, wordless like a trapped animal. His back arches suddenly, as if snatched by an invisible bird of prey. His face runs with sweat: the bedsheets are soaked. The man struggles convulsively, then is still. The ragged breathing starts again, weaker now.

Throughout the night, screams and convulsive shocks recur. Each time, Coleridge holds his patient down, then relaxes when the fit is over. He grows tired. A worthless sleep with no sustenance takes him. Creatures of the night beset him round. Claws, teeth, foul breath, reduce him even in oblivion to whimpering fear.

At some time – he cannot tell when – the unconscious man's breathing becomes more regular, like ordinary sleep. Coleridge is not fooled. This has happened before, but by morning the fever has returned. Coleridge lies down on his own narrow, hard bed and his thoughts take over, like waves beating on eroding cliffs. Night images, death images, swirl round him. He lies, breath suspended, in dreadful fear. He is wrapped in guilt for acts done and undone, and – please merciful God – never to be done.

The night passes slowly. As light dawns his cry fills the pest house. 'God help me! It is my fault that I am here. I bring my sorrows on myself.' He knows that he is waiting for death, because after such a life as his, it cannot be long delayed. But the sun rises in a clear, cold sky. A lightness in the air speaks of spring and better times. It even penetrates into the pest house. His night fears lighten.

There is stirring in the bed, snorting and gasping. The sick man opens his eyes, thrashes around as if not sure where he is, or why, then tentatively sits up.

'Fuckin' 'ell,' he says. 'What the fuck's wrong with me?'

'My dear comrade,' Coleridge cries. 'You have been through the travails of the dying. You have journeyed through your own purgatory. You join us in the land of the whole and the healthy. You have triumphed, and I have triumphed with you.'

The bowl of cold, congealed stew, stale loaf and bucket of water are still there, untouched. He thrusts them under the sick man's nose. 'Here, take some bread and stew, for now you must regain your strength.'

'Fuckin' army bread and stew?' says the sick man. 'Fuck that.'
'Water, then?' says Coleridge.

'All right, mate. I en't 'alf got a fuckin' thirst on me.' The man takes the bucket and slurps noisily. 'I'd rather have a quart o' beer, though. Fuck that purga-whatever-it-fuckin'-is you said I've been to,' he says. 'What the fuck's been wrong wi' me?'

And suddenly Coleridge is light-hearted. He has given life back to this man he doesn't even know. All will be well.

*

Now he was back, out of his dream, if dream it was. For he was still watching over a fevered soul. Derwent's breathing had not changed.

Oh my son.

Derwent suddenly moved convulsively and his eyes opened. His forehead was beaded with sweat. Coleridge poured water from a jug on the table, lifted Derwent by the shoulders and held the glass to his lips.

'Come, my dear son,' he said softly. 'Sip this. It will cool you.'

Derwent tried to swallow but spluttered and water dribbled from his mouth. Coleridge laid his son down gently. Derwent's eyes closed and the stertorous breathing returned.

Where is Hartley? Why are my two sons so different?

And the third son? What of dear dead Berkeley, the son he never met? Now grief triumphed as slumber took hold, the Eumenides continued their revenge and led him back to surely the worst thing even he had ever done.

Chapter 4

Sarah

My genial spirits fail;
And what can these avail
To lift the smothering weight from off my breast?
It were a vain endeavour,
Though I should gaze for ever
On that green light that lingers in the west:
I may not hope from outward Forms to win
The passion and the life, whose fountains are within.

—'Dejection: An Ode', Samuel Taylor Coleridge

It is July 1799. He has been ten months in Germany with William and his sister Dorothy. Sarah, pregnant, was left behind in Nether Stowey. And now he is home.

He takes a deep breath and opens the door. Sarah will run to him, throw her arms round his neck in joy and all will be well. Won't it?

Nobody comes. He calls softly, 'Sarah?'

The silence sits like a stone. Then a small voice from the scullery says, 'In here.'

Hesitantly, he looks round the door. Sarah sits in a wooden chair. Hartley sits on her lap. Her arms are protectively wrapped round the little boy. Her face is turned away.

'Sarah, I'm home,' he says.

'So I see,' she answers, still not looking at him.

'I'm here, to share in our grief and help you in this hour of sorrow,' he says tentatively.

Now she turns round. 'That hour of sorrow was six months ago,' she hisses savagely. 'You were not here.'

'But I had my work to finish. I was bound by promises.'

'Like the promises you made to the Wordsworths?'

'But we had so much to write, such great matters to discuss. Besides, I left them in Germany.'

'What use is that to me?' says Sarah.

'Sarah, why are you so cold to me now I have returned to be with you in this time of trial? I expected welcome and love, such as I bring you.'

This rouses Sarah to real anger. 'Before the three of you left here you were inseparable. You walked with them all over the Quantocks. And you never took me. I stayed in this mean little cottage alone with one child and pregnant with another.'

'But Hartley...'

'Don't use Hartley as an excuse. You knew I was pregnant. A proper husband would not have left me. But you were too selfish, too thoughtless even for it to cross your mind.'

She stands up, turns away from him and puts Hartley down. 'Run away into the garden,' she whispers. 'You'll see your father later.' Hartley, frightened, does as he is told.

Sarah's face is lined, deathly pale, her eyes sunken and dark-rimmed. She looks thirty years older than when he left.

'Your beautiful hair...' he starts. With an almost shocking movement, she digs her hands into it and snatches it away.

'A wig,' he gasps.

'Yes,' she says. The vindictiveness stings like a whip. 'See what's left.' Her scalp is half bare. Clumps of hair, colourless and dead, sprout from it, as easy to pull off as the wig had been.

'But you've been looked after,' he cries defensively. 'I made arrangements.'

'You don't know what I've been through,' she answers hotly. Her eyes glint with distaste. 'After Berkeley died I was ill. Doctor Lewis said I was having a breakdown. I lost my hair.' She looks at him narrowly. 'Tom Poole next door was very good to me. My sister Edith stayed. She helped me as only a sister can. But she's not happy either. She married a man as selfish as you are. I need my sister. I want you and Robert Southey reconciled.'

'Not Southey,' says Coleridge stubbornly. 'He abused my "Mariner" in the public prints. We cannot be friends any more.'

'Oh yes you can,' says Sarah grimly. 'You weren't here when I needed you most.'

'No, I forbid it,' cries Coleridge.

'You will be his friend again.' Sarah speaks with steely resolution. 'Why should I care a jot about you? Even when I wrote begging you to return you didn't care to answer for another six months. What sort of a man are you?'

What sort indeed? And now the real question shows itself. What am I? A husband, a father, a provider? Or a poet, a philosopher, whose every thought matters more than domestic duty in the great scheme of things?

A man's voice calls from the front room. 'What shall I do with these boxes, sir?'

'One moment,' Coleridge replies.

'Oh, see to your precious boxes,' says Sarah.

Soon the boxes are stowed away and the carrier has departed. Coleridge sidles back into the scullery.

'Go away,' Sarah says.

Miserably, he trails into the garden. Who is he? What is he? What ought he to be? Then he sees Hartley, healthy, bubbling *with joy, running into his arms. He clasps the little boy to his chest and thinks,* The answer is clear before me.

Yet somehow it still isn't. All that night, as Sarah, her back to him, sleeps fitfully, he wrestles with it until his brain seems to burst and he gets up to mix a draught of laudanum. The inevitable nightmare and horror sweeps in so that when he wakes he is dizzy and constipated like a stone. Yes, he will try to be a dutiful husband. Hartley needs him – and he needs Hartley. But he can't stay here. He has *to be with the Wordsworths.*

For a few precious months in Germany with them he was living again, no cares, no responsibilities. It meant everything to him. The memories unwind: the beauties of Hamburg, an unforgettable Christmas in Ratzeburg, disinterested study and constant lionising at the university in Göttingen, good fellowship and Gothic folklore in the Harz mountains.

He puts that on one side of the scales. On the other he places the misery in the house he should love above all else. He sees the dregs of a once idyllic life with Sarah congeal at the bottom of the glass. He watches one tray of the scales outweigh the other and conviction steals over him.

He will be gone again soon. And next time something final might happen.

*

The vision was gone and Derwent's breathing rasped again.

Oh Sarah, what happened to us? Even as he asked, he was somewhere which at first he did not recognise. With him was Sarah, young, beautiful, ecstatic. As, he told himself, was he. Even through his misery, he could remember the feeling of ecstasy they shared in being together.

*

The day dawns bright and clear. It is 4 October 1795. It is their wedding day, in St Mary Redcliffe church, Bristol. After the ceremony the couple sweep into the little cottage they have taken in Clevedon. Sarah points to an object hanging outside the bedroom window. 'Esteesee,' she says. 'What is that?'

'An aeolian harp, my love. It will catch the wind's song, the music of nature, the voice of God himself.'

Sarah ventures into the scullery. 'Esteesee,' she says. 'Where is the kettle?'

'Oh,' says Coleridge. 'I forgot we needed a kettle.'

'And saucepans. And plates. And cups. Where are the forks? Where the spoons, the knives?'

'What do such things matter to us, dear Sarah?'

'There's no dustpan, no brush, to keep our house clean.'

'But dear Sarah, it can't be dirty. We've only just walked in.'

'Esteesee, we can't make a drink. Even if we had food, we couldn't cook it.'

'Dearest Sarah, why do we need these things? We're married. We're here, alone, together in our own place. We have each other now and that's enough. Oh, and our aeolian harp to fill us with the witchery of elves.'

Sarah sits down in the only chair in the cottage and laughs until tears pour out of her eyes. Then she stands, folds her arms round his ample body and looks up at him. Her eyes sparkle with joy. His heart leaps and the dreadful phrase 'I will do my duty' seems to flame and burn to ash.

'Yes, my own Esteesee,' she murmurs. 'You're right. That is all we need.'

Ten minutes later she says, 'Esteesee, we'll need food and furniture, whatever you say.'

'Very well,' Coleridge replies. 'I'll send to Cottle to get them. As my publisher, it's his duty. Perhaps I'll write him a poem for nothing.'

At least there is a bed. Soon they are in it and thus begins a night of joy in which he knows his Sarah and she him. He kisses and caresses her lithe body and thrusts and thrusts and she receives, gasps and clasps. The aeolian harp at the window chimes in time to their mutual rhythm and they are in tune with wind and sky and the great principle of nature itself. When they wake to a fine autumn morning, he says aloud, 'I wish this moment would last for ever.'

*

But of course it didn't, because that moment never truly arrived in the first place. He woke not to an idyllic cottage but a sickroom in Highgate. His memories were now of recrimination and a night of failure and shame. Instead of the witchery of elves, the aeolian harp sent discordant noises as if the missing pots and pans were clashed by simple-minded demons. When morning came they avoided each other's eyes, Sarah to hide frustration, disappointment and, yes, contempt, and he to conceal bitter humiliation.

Which of these two versions was real? Either? Or neither? Here in the sickroom, he seemed to remember both equally vividly. *My curse is a mind which combines total recall of long ago with confusion about its reality.*

But now, as his mind cleared for a moment, he could admit it fully and finally. He had knowingly done a foolish, irresponsible thing. He had married in an emotional frenzy, not on account of Sarah herself, though she was integral to it. He had been blinded by a wonderful mirage, of which Sarah was but a part. As he waited for Derwent's nurse to arrive and the day to begin, he found himself reaching in his mind back to the roots of this great illusion.

SARAH

I should have seen the signs. It all seemed so wonderful at the start. Sister Edith and Southey, myself and Esteesee, pioneers in the great adventure. A double wedding in St Mary Redcliffe. Then Esteesee fell out with Southey; there would be no double wedding after all – and even then I did not see the consequences.

I was so very happy as we left the church to go to our little cottage in Clevedon. The aeolian harp seemed such a wonderfully romantic instrument. I was charmed. But there was no food, no crockery, no cutlery, no plates. The aeolian harp was suddenly ludicrous and I had the first ominous presentiment. My paragon of genius seemed to think that the rules of ordinary life did not apply to him.

And then to the wedding night itself. It was not unpleasant but neither was it ecstatic. There was something odd about it. Before we finally slept I knew what it was. When it came to the crux, he was afraid of me. I made a rule I would keep to. Never be afraid of him.

The day dawned bright and clear and for the moment I forgot my night thoughts. Life would go on. I remembered Mary Wollstonecraft. A wife should be her husband's friend.

Yes, we would be friends. I would share in his great work. I would be his helpmeet. We would be a team.

Chapter 5

Southey

Yet will I love to follow that sweet dream,
Where Susquehannah pours his untamed stream...
　　　　　　—'Monody on the Death of Chatterton',
　　　　　　　　　　　　Samuel Taylor Coleridge

This next encounter was of such crucial importance in his life that Coleridge saw it in a different way from all the others. He remembered it as if he were an actor in a play and knew his part perfectly. So did the others, but he could not hear them and had to put words into their mouths. But this meeting had such consequences. It led straight to the sorry situation which had shaped the rest of his life and he needed to understand it after all these years, because so far he never had.

He had left the army and returned to the college determined to work hard so as not to be sent down. He was gated for ninety days, which meant he could not go outside the college. This was not a punishment. He was supremely happy. He explored the wide grounds, the pastures, the streams, the woods and began to find a poetic voice. And he worked hard. So what could possibly have gone wrong?

*

Term ends and he is free. He leaves Cambridge on a sunny June morning in May 1794. He will never return. Like most of the young, he is fired by the French Revolution. The end of aristocracy, the rule of the people. He must explore the country, to find out how the people who will be made free are living their oppressed lives now. He must meet like-minded men who wish to join in the battle, prepared to stand up against accusations of treachery and sedition. He needs a companion. Joseph Hucks, another undergraduate, is ideal, stolid, unimaginative, a foot soldier in the coming struggle. Coleridge's heart swells with expectation as they stride westward. This is a journey to great things.

First they come to Oxford and University College to see Bob Allen, his old school friend. A hearty reunion. He forgets about poor lonely Hucks, miserable in the corner.

Bob asks if Sam still scribbles away at verse. There's another scribbler here he might like to meet, he tells him. 'He's a bit of a revolutionary like you, Sam. Chap called Robert Southey.'

When he is with old school friends, he expects to be called Sam and doesn't mind a bit.

So they walk off to Balliol College, Hucks trailing behind, and find, in rooms too close to the privies for Sam's liking, Southey himself.

The moment he sees him, he knows this encounter is important. He sees a tall man with a lean face which speaks of strength and power. A staunch ally in the struggle.

'We shall meet enemies in the struggle,' says Sam. 'A few broken heads might change their minds.'

Southey says Sam's a man after his own heart. He swears death to all kings and princes and Sam laughs with pleasure. 'Our benighted country needs revolution,' he says.

Southey shakes his head. He fears it may never have one. Even the peasantry seems content with its lot. If only they knew what glories their brothers in France have gained.

'If only,' Coleridge agrees.

Southey says great decisions must be made. Will Coleridge join with him and friends in an expedition to America, where luminaries exiled for sedition are working out new ways to live in freedom and fulfilment, far from the constrictions of life at home? There is a place, a heaven for dreamers, to which those refugees have escaped. It is in Pennsylvania, where the eastern branch of the River Susquehanna meets the western and they join in a broad stream. An easy climate, fertile land, fish in the rivers, game in the woods. Life will be good and humankind can start again.

'We shall go,' says Coleridge.

Southey tells him that Joseph Priestley, scientist and philosopher, is there already. Neither have met him, but they know his story. He questioned the government and the Church and was reviled as a seditionist. His home and laboratory in Birmingham were burned down by a mob. He fled with his family to the great New World to start again.

'We'll take like-minded friends and bring greetings to the good Priestley,' says Coleridge. 'In America we shall make our own community. All decisions will be shared and everything held in common. Honest labour will clear our minds and purify our feelings. Our poetry shall sing songs finer than gold.'

He will never forget Southey's reply. When in the future he comes to consider it, he wonders whether Southey means pleasure or an intimation of doubt to come. Is it suspiciously enthusiastic? 'By God, Coleridge, you really mean it.'

'Of course I do,' Coleridge replies.

Southey says they'll lead honest, hard-working lives. They'll be kings over the earth, the soil, plants, beasts, birds and fish, because nature will fill them with her harmony.

Coleridge doesn't at once realise what an unsuitable word 'harmony' is. 'Kings' means the opposite, whether of countries or nature. But what Southey says next is music to his ears. 'And we'll cultivate lives of the mind. We'll write poetry, philosophy, make scientific discoveries. The achievements of one will be the achievements of all.'

They look at each other, fired by their eloquence.

They go on talking day after day.

Coleridge invents a name. 'We shall call our society...' He paused. Then, 'Pantisocracy. The society which governs itself. We are all Pantisocrats now.'

Then Southey says – and this Coleridge remembers all too clearly – 'Of course, we shall take our womenfolk.'

'What womenfolk?' he asks.

'Oh, I forget,' Southey replies. The first snap since they met. 'You've no need of the sort of womenfolk I have in mind.'

'Not so,' Coleridge retorts indignantly. 'There's a girl in London for whom I have the tenderest regard. But she's promised to another.'

'I don't believe you,' Southey replies. 'On your own admission you've been with whores.'

'What womenfolk?' Coleridge repeats stubbornly.

What womenfolk indeed.

*

He woke suddenly. He remembered his dream, and now recalled its consequences.

He remembered that Southey returned to Bristol to his friends, Robert Lovell, close friend and Balliol man, and the Fricker sisters, Sarah, Edith and Mary. He should have known that the scheme to them was simply a nice idea and not the great hope for mankind, as Coleridge had assumed.

Coleridge and Hucks continued through Wales. Coleridge harangued Welshmen in taverns about revolution and was either cheered or threatened. Hucks had soon had enough of this and in Welshpool he said farewell and went home. Coleridge, ready for new adventures, turned south again to Bristol and the wellsprings of Pantisocracy.

He lodged with Southey in Lovell's house and was introduced to the Fricker sisters. Edith was engaged to Southey; Mary was to marry Lovell. As he was introduced to Sarah, Coleridge realised what Southey meant by 'womenfolk'.

Sarah was small, with lustrous brown hair, a handsome face and a dazzling smile. He tried to dazzle her in return with brilliant talk. She remained stubbornly undazzled as she made up her mind about him.

At last it seemed he had passed the examination. Soon they were talking freely together. When the evening was over, Coleridge knew that something exciting had happened.

Before he slept, he realised what it was. Edith would accompany Southey to America and Mary with Lovell. Who would he be with?

Sarah. It had to be. A perfect symmetry. Three married couples, six pioneers and seekers of an ideal, secure in their mission. Three poets and philosophers, three devoted helpmeets, united in love and devotion to a Platonic form of the good.

Yes, now he could sleep soundly, secure in his destiny.

*

But it was not possible. There was another with whom he told himself he was in love; Mary Evans, sister of his schoolfriend Tom Evans. Had he declared himself to her? No. In Wales he looked out of the window one morning and saw Mary Evans coming out of church with her sister. Why had he felt such shock? He had not seen her since he had fled into the army.

He hurried out of Wrexham almost in panic. Later, in 'The Sigh', he wrote:

Thy image may not banish'd be –
Still, Mary! still I pine for thee.

Then he heard that Mary was engaged already. Now he had a new compulsion. Marrying Sarah. For love? He would try to make it so. But, deep down, ran the doubt that it might be for duty.

He recalled a letter he had written to Southey in the first flush of Pantisocracy. He remembered every word.

Miss Fricker! Yes – Southey – you are right – Even Love is the creature of strong Motive – I certainly love her. I think of her incessantly & with unspeakable tenderness – with that inward melting away of Soul that Symptomizes it. Pantisocracy – O I shall have such a scheme of it.

Those were not a lover's words. They reeked of hypocrisy. True love was for its own sake. He had merely sought a partner for Pantisocracy. And that hadn't lasted long. Long before they should have set off for America, Lovell died, Mary Fricker broke down with grief and Edith was bereft. Southey changed his mind. So Coleridge was left with no Pantisocracy and a woman he had made promises to, which he knew he could not keep.

That was over twenty years ago, twenty years before this sickroom. He recalled the women he had been involved with. Mary Evans, but only in his head; Sarah, with a sort of love but also shame and guilt; Asra, his name for another Sara because he feared mixing them up. For her, he told himself his passion was far above physical love. And then that strange episode in Sicily. No, he wouldn't think of that. Let it stay buried deep, lest it led to conclusions he dared not contemplate. And then he remembered his own creation. *Geraldine.*

She had first come to life in 'Christabel'. Who, *what*, was she? She had emerged from recesses deep in his mind which he feared to investigate. Best not think of her now. But he could not help it. Had he met her in Sicily, disguised as an opera singer? Or was she Asra, that once-beloved phantom? Protean opposites, yet united in his private fantasies.

Morning was here, bright and sunny, belying his mood. He had better get up and face it. Derwent slept. The nurse would soon be here.

Chapter 6

A Desertion

The sage, the poet, lives for all mankind,
As long as truth is true, or beauty fair.
The soul that ever sought its God to find
Has found Him now – no matter how, or where.
Yet can I not but mourn because he died
That was my father, should have been my guide.

—'Written on the Anniversary of Our Father's Death',
Hartley Coleridge

Next morning, a bright, sunny July day. Coleridge's vigil was over. He had managed a few hours of sleep after his painful memories.

Hartley was already at breakfast. The atmosphere was fraught. His son ate porridge, head low, arm curled round the bowl like a schoolboy hiding his work. Mrs Gillman was seething. *What has Hartley done now? Ann will not speak out while I'm here.*

'Hartley,' he said with forced jollity. 'It's a fine, fresh day. Let's take a turn in the city. Good clean air in our lungs.'

'London streets stink,' Hartley muttered.

'We won't walk the streets,' said Coleridge.

'I have writing to do,' said his son.

'I, too,' said Coleridge. 'I have a lecture to prepare. But it's a fine day and it would be a pity to waste it. Perhaps this afternoon?'

Hartley fixed his father with a strange, ambiguous look. There was a tense silence. Coleridge counted the seconds. Eight. Each one hung in the air like a hovering hawk. Then Hartley muttered almost inaudibly, 'If you say so.'

*

The day was warm. They walked over Hampstead Heath to Parliament Hill and looked over the towers of London towards the Thames. Neither had spoken since they left Moreton House.

Hartley was looking straight ahead. Coleridge glanced sideways at him. His face was reddened and coarsened by drink. His once thin, sharp features were almost puffy. The struggle with Copleston to keep Hartley at Oriel had been doomed from the start.

One morning many years before, when he and Sarah lived in Greta Hall, he had looked through his study window at the mountains and fells outside: Scafell. Skiddaw, Helvellyn, Blencathra, Cat Bells on the opposite side of calm, blue Derwentwater.

Hartley was there, too, and Coleridge was happy as he played lovingly with him. He observed his reactions, gloried in seeing an imagination developing from simple beginnings. The boy would be a greater scholar and poet than his father.

One particular memory made him smile. He would remind his son of it now. They would relive those precious seconds and all would be well again.

'Hartley, do you remember when we lived in Keswick amidst the lakes, in a house called Greta Hall?'

Hartley grunted.

'And how outside the great bow window of my study the fells and mountains stood like tents pitched by giants?'

Silence.

'And how you were looking at the same mountains, but in a mirror on the opposite wall?'

Silence again. Coleridge ploughed on. 'And then you looked out through the window and asked: "Will yon mountains always be?" A delightful child's question but with a profundity you could not begin to see.'

Still silence.

'"Well," I answered, "they will last for as long as the mountains in the looking glass will. So are they the same mountains?"

'"Of course they are," you said.

'"How can that be?" I asked you. "The mountains are outside the window."

'"I see that," you answered. "But they're still in the looking glass."

'"So which are the real mountains?" I asked you and you said, "Both."

'"But Hartley," I said, "there's only one real set of mountains and they are outside the window."

'This was a hard conundrum. "Think carefully, my son," I said. "You are close to the secret of poetry." And you asked me what I meant. "Poetry is all around you, Hartley," I replied. "In your child's way you know this, you are open to it, you see it fresh and new. But you don't *realise* it and even if you did, you could never explain it. It's beyond a child's understanding."

'"I still don't know what you mean, Father," you said, and I replied, "Of course you don't, my dear son. But one day, my Hartley, you'll know the difference between object and image and how one is the lifeblood of the other and at the root of all poetry. You'll be a better poet than ever your father was." Do you remember that day, Hartley?'

Even as he spoke, he knew this precious moment was gone.

Another silence.

At length, Hartley spoke. A gruff monosyllable.

'No.'

They walked on. Hartley led the way, as if on some urgent expedition. Coleridge followed. They left the heath and were back in the streets.

'The streets still stink,' Hartley said.

Coleridge caught up with him. 'Shall we go back?' he said.

'No,' said his son and kept on walking. At length, he stopped, and said, 'I have friends who live nearby. I owe them money. I must honour my debt.'

'Of course,' Coleridge replied.

A tense silence.

'But I have no money,' said Hartley at last.

'I see,' said Coleridge.

Another silence. Then, 'Would you lend me some?'

This was new to Coleridge. Usually, *he* was both borrower and debtor. But he had no doubt about what to do. *Of course I will.* But the only money he had with him was a two-pound note for his next opium purchase. The choice was bitter, but he knew what it had to be.

He took the note from his pocket and handed it to Hartley. 'Will this suffice?' he said.

Hartley looked at it suspiciously. 'It is for my friends to decide,' he said at last. He slipped it into a pocket. 'Thank you,' he added, grudgingly.

'This is a loan, isn't it, Hartley?' Coleridge asked.

His son did not answer directly. 'I'll meet you at six o'clock.'

'Where?' said Coleridge.

'There's a shop in York Street which sells sweets and the like. We'll meet outside it.'

He turned on his heel and walked away.

'Hartley,' Coleridge called, in sudden panic. 'Remember. *Six*. I'll be there.'

Hartley looked back. A terrible certainty smothered Coleridge. His son's face seemed to dissolve behind suddenly flowing tears.

He wiped them away and looked again. Hartley had disappeared. Coleridge knew he would not see him again. Nevertheless, he would wait.

The hours passed. Six o'clock came and went. His hopeless vigil was over. Grief overwhelmed him.

Then his heart leapt. Someone stood beside him. Had Hartley repented? Coleridge turned with a cry of joy.

But it was not his son. It was the revenant.

*

The pang more sharp than all. This, his most profound loss, lay like a cancerous tumour. Soon he would write about it, a poem dragged out of his mind over weeks, every thought a struggle, every word wrenched out of deep places best not explored.

Ah! he is gone, and yet will not depart!—
Is with me still, yet I from him exil'd!
For still there lives within my secret heart
The magic image of the magic Child.

Chapter 7

Humiliation

Cambridge, April 1824

Work without Hope draws nectar in a sieve,
And Hope without an object cannot live.
— 'Work Without Hope', Samuel Taylor Coleridge

Scrivener was unwell. He slept fitfully and woke at seven meaning to prepare for a tutorial. Instead he fell into a shallow, unsatisfying doze, waking at ten, dizzy. Last night's ardour was gone.

What next? As a sizar he would get short shrift if he slackened. His task was to make an adequate translation from Virgil's *Aeneid* Book 8. He sat at his table, opened his text, sharpened a pencil – and then could not write a single word.

His head ached. The words which kept him awake returned, a chorus he no longer wished to sing.

The writer of the above...

He still felt those words were directed at him. Today, they mocked him. He would never have fantastic opium-induced dreams. A poor student who might have bitten off more than he could chew by coming here could never afford to.

He looked through the window at deserted First Court. The real scholars were at work, the gentlemen were sleeping off the night's debauch. He alone in the university was not doing what he had come for.

Last night's mist had lifted. The day was fair. A weak sun shone. A hint of spring.

Suddenly energised, he dressed, struggled into his threadbare overcoat, donned his black undergraduate gown and stole downstairs. He turned left into Pump Court, which was still being built, and sidled out of the college by the rear entrance, as if creeping close to the wall might make him less observable. He crossed Jesus Green and Midsomer Common to Bridge Street, turned left, walked to the bridge over the river and looked down at the water flowing underneath.

The sun was bright now. The water sparkled and the ducks made him obscurely happy. Snowdrops showed and daffodils budded. Cambridge was coming alive. Perhaps his heart might lighten.

No. Something stubborn was determined to make him miserable.

He walked on until he came to Magdalene College.

Opposite stood the Pickerel, the oldest alehouse in Cambridge. Though it was against his principles he felt an urge to go in. He crossed the road and entered through the open door. The dark brown panelling and heavy beams made it a gloomy place. Smells of stale beer and roasting hops from the brewhouse assaulted his nostrils.

The public bar was empty apart from a group of noisy townsmen sitting close to the fire. The braying laugh of Magdalene students sounded from the saloon bar. He would keep out of their way. A thin-faced, dark-haired man wearing a white apron stood behind the bar polishing a glass.

'Ah,' he said. 'Another young gentleman from the university, I see.'

Scrivener, unused to being called a young gentleman, looked round to see who the barman meant. Realising it was him, he checked the remark for irony. But he hardly needed to. The sneer still on the man's face clearly told him. There are none so quick to show contempt as a servant seeing one of their own in a place beyond his station in life.

Had Mr Coleridge been to the Pickerel? Would he be sneered at? No, Scrivener thought. Coleridge's father was both vicar of Ottery St Mary in Devon and headmaster of the local school.

'What will you have, young sir?' asked the barman.

Scrivener was startled. He hadn't expected to make a decision. He nearly asked for a glass of water. But no, perhaps not. 'A small measure of your best ale from the barrel,' he said.

He felt dizzy. Never before had any alcoholic liquid passed his lips.

'Small, you say?' said the barman as if he had never heard such a request before. 'Not a quart? Not even a pint? You're very unlike most young gentlemen who come here.'

Drink a whole quart? Scrivener shuddered. 'A pint will do.'

'Mild or bitter?'

Well, mild of course. The thought of 'bitter' made his stomach curl.

The barman drew the pint and slammed the tankard down so that drops flew over the rim.

'Twopence,' he said.

Scrivener searched and found two farthings, one ha'penny and a penny. The barman scooped them up, shoved them in the cash pot and then intervened in a heated argument between students and townsfolk, not to quieten them but to take their orders.

Scrivener sipped the brown liquid. If this were mild, he shuddered to think of the bitter. He endured two mouthfuls, felt the slight kick of a first taste of alcohol, resolved it would be the last and slipped out unnoticed. He did not see the barman return and swallow the rest in two gulps. Nor did he notice the tall young man with an olive complexion that suggested warmer climes, who had quietly entered.

He needed to walk. Anywhere, it did not matter. He stepped down to the river path crowded with townsfolk and carefree undergraduates. He turned east. The other way would take him to the Backs and looks of pity from grinning undergraduates and their womenfolk. He set off eastwards towards Fen Ditton, Waterbeach and Clayhithe, where the paths were empty and he could be at peace.

As he walked the breeze ruffled the water and the sun freckled the surface with sharp points of shifting light. Ducks and coots fussed close by the banks and a long procession of swans swam proudly past. Scrivener felt almost at peace with the world. He even started composing verse.

But he soon stopped. *Poetry is not for the likes of people such as me.*

He sauntered on, almost happily, for nearly a mile seeing no more signs of humanity, for which he felt heartily glad, until he spotted five men approaching. He saw their clothes and heard their voices. His spirits sank at the sound, especially the laughter. That strange braying quality he feared so much.

To his horror, he recognised two of them. The Honourable Mr Copperthwaite-Smirke and Viscount Bonewood. Fellow commoners of Jesus College, feared by sizars unfortunate enough to serve them. He had never seen the other three, but would bet money, if he had any, that they were fellow commoners from other colleges.

He tried to dodge out of sight in the bushes. Too late.

'Ah,' cried Copperthwaite-Smirke. 'Who have we here?'

'A creature not fit for the university,' said Viscount Bonewood. 'We should be rid of him.'

'A scullion, I presume,' said one of the group Scrivener did not recognise. 'A cockroach infesting the kitchens.'

'Don't be hard on him,' said another. 'His sort make good servants.'

'Not this one,' said the viscount. 'He shirks his duties and takes refuge in the library.'

'A shirker, eh?' said the first. 'He needs to suffer.'

'Throw him in the river?' suggested another.

'Debag him first,' said the viscount.

'Black his balls,' said the first stranger.

'What with?' said the second.

'It just so happens...' said Copperthwaite-Smirke, feeling in his pocket and producing a lump of black heelball, 'that I carry a piece of this with me in case an opportunity arises to put fear into the lower orders. Always be prepared, I say.'

He bent down and wetted the heelball in the river. 'There, that will leave a good blacking on his miserable scrotum,' he said.

'Now let's scrag him,' roared the viscount, and five pairs of strong, well-nourished hands seized Scrivener and pulled his breeches off with such force that his belt burst open.

Then he heard Copperthwaite-Smirke's cruel laughter and felt the excruciating pain of the heelball pressing into the vulnerable flesh. Just when he thought he would faint, the pressure stopped. 'In with him,' someone shouted, and he felt the shock of freezing water – and terror – as his head went under the surface.

But the river was shallow and he struggled to his feet. Shivering and drenched, he clambered onto the bank to pick up his breeches. He was beaten to it. Viscount Bonewood got there first and held them out of reach, laughing mockingly.

'It seems to me that you are not properly dressed,' said Copperthwaite-Smirke. 'Should not items in your attire be consistent with each other?'

He took the breeches from Bonewood, trailed them through the water and then draped them, together with his undergraduate gown, over a bush. 'There, that should be sufficient,' he said. 'We'll leave you now.'

They walked on towards Cambridge. He heard their laughter die away.

So, though his clothes were drenched, he had to put them on and get back to college as best he could. He pulled up his breeches and threw the ruined belt in the river, even though he had to use one hand to stop the breeches falling down.

His teeth chattered, his limbs shook, he felt as if he would never move again. The worst misery that ever he had experienced enveloped him. Inverted contempt from below in the morning, cynical rejection from above now. Why did he even exist?

And then, at this, the lowest point of his life, he heard a voice say, 'You poor man. Let me help you.'

Chapter 8

The Stranger

As high as we have mounted in delight
In our dejection do we sink as low
    —'Resolution and Independence', William Wordsworth

This voice is a phantasm of the mind, Scrivener told himself.

The words came again. 'Let me help you to your feet.'

The voice was not English. He thanked a merciful God. He had learnt to be afraid of English voices – or at least those of his tormentors. Perhaps a man from a foreign land would understand his sense of exile.

When he tried to move, the cold struck again. His very entrails were chilled. He staggered and fell. But strong arms looped underneath his shoulders. He was pulled upright and then gently held in position as he recovered his balance and the feeling in his feet.

Then he looked at his rescuer. A man, a youth, about his own age, though nearly a head taller. His hair was black and his face had a slightly olive complexion as if he had lived under a warm sun.

'Who are you?' he managed to say through chattering teeth.

'I am a visitor to England, I come from Monreale, near Palermo in Sicily,' was the reply, in an accent Scrivener recognised as Italian. 'And you?'

'My name is Scrivener. George Scrivener. I come from a town called Hertford and I'm an undergraduate of the university.'

'I see,' said the stranger. 'At which college?'

'Jesus,' Scrivener replied.

'Strange,' murmured the stranger. 'Very strange.'

'You mean it is strange that someone looking as foolish as I do could possibly be a member of a Cambridge college?' Scrivener felt a gust of indignation.

'Not at all,' the stranger said. 'You are not foolish. You are brave. You have been assaulted by cowards. The unworthy rabble passed me, still laughing. I see men like them in Sicily. We must hold firm against such people.'

'Then why is it so strange that I am at Jesus?' Scrivener said, almost belligerently.

'I seek someone who was once at Jesus College. Perhaps you know of him.'

'I doubt it,' Scrivener replied. 'Who is he?'

'An English poet. Samuel Taylor Coleridge.'

Scrivener gulped in surprise.

'Do you know where I can find him?'

'No,' said Scrivener.

'Do you know his work?'

'Yes,' said Scrivener dazedly.

'You must come into the warm and dry your clothes in front of a good fire.'

'But I can't enter the college like this,' Scrivener cried. He did not add that the clammy garments were all he possessed.

'I have a warm room and clothes enough to lend,' said the stranger. 'They will be too big but you will look respectable. I am lodging at the Pickerel. We will go there.'

It was important that his new friend should hear of his discovery. 'I have something strange here that's to do with Mr Coleridge. I only found it yesterday.'

He felt in his sodden pockets for the paper on which he had

scrawled his precious sentence. It would be unreadable. But no matter. He could recite the sentence in his sleep.

He fished the paper out of his pocket. The stranger looked at the grey wash on the disintegrating sheet and said, 'Why do you show me this?'

'Because I remember what was written on it.'

Suddenly, wiping the words away became Copperthwaite-Smirke and friends' worst crime.

'What was it?'

'"The writer of the above had much better have kept his sleeping thoughts to himself, for they are, if possible, worse than his waking ones." It's about Mr Coleridge.'

'Where did you find it?'

'In a copy of "Kubla Khan" in the college library.'

'And who wrote it?'

'Nobody knows.'

'What does it mean?'

'It means the poem is just that. A sleeping thought.'

'And why should it be?'

'Because of the opium.'

The stranger was silent again.

Scrivener noticed. 'What is the matter?' he said. 'You look sad.'

'It's nothing,' the stranger replied. 'Let's go to the Pickerel. There's a fire in my room, and I'll find a change of clothes while you warm yourself.'

They walked on and Samuel Taylor Coleridge was not mentioned again.

*

The fire was warm, his own clothes were drying and the new clothes, though they hung loose off his scrawny body, were comfortable and of much higher quality than his own.

'You must be hungry,' said the stranger. 'We'll have a meal downstairs.'

Scrivener was alarmed. 'But the college says that I should eat in Hall every night.'

'Leave it with me,' said the stranger. 'I'll keep you from trouble.'

He led Scrivener downstairs into the snug behind the public bar, where the few other paying guests sat waiting for their dinners.

'Let's choose our food in honour of the hostelry,' said the stranger. 'A pickerel is a young pike. Let's have some.'

'But I've never eaten pike,' said Scrivener.

'Until last night, neither had I. But it is' – the stranger hesitated – 'interesting. Besides, it was swimming in the Cam this morning so it will be fresh.'

Scrivener thought it tasted of mud. But it filled him and warmed him and that was all that mattered.

They ate in silence. When they had finished, the stranger folded his napkin and said, 'Now I shall come back with you to Jesus because I want to see it for myself.' He settled the bill, and they stepped into the cold, dark evening. Scrivener's clothes were more or less dry and his companion found a bag to carry them in. They crossed the river, turned left into Jesus Lane and came to the Chimney, the cobbled path between brick walls which led to the gatehouse.

The porter was waiting. 'Mr Scrivener,' he said. 'You did not attend dinner in Hall. I must report this to your tutor.'

'Let me explain,' said the stranger. 'I saw five students set on this gentleman, assault him and throw him in the river. I rescued him, took him to my lodging, dried his clothes, lent him some of mine and escorted him back here.'

'And who are you, sir?

'A visitor from Sicily. I have business in Cambridge. I merely did what I believe any decent person would have done.'

Although the stranger could be no more than nineteen, Scrivener thought he saw the poise and confidence of someone older.

The porter looked at them shrewdly, as if he knew what had happened and who was responsible.

'Very well,' he said at length. 'Mr Scrivener, you'll hear no more of this. I bid you goodnight, sirs.' He disappeared back into the gatehouse.

'Thank you,' said Scrivener.

'Not at all,' replied the stranger. 'I think most people are fair and reasonable and with him, I guessed right.'

They reached Scrivener's rooms. He opened the door. 'Shall I make tea?' he asked.

'Thank you, no,' the stranger replied. 'I must prepare for my night's journey. I wanted to see you safely home first.'

Scrivener went into the bedroom, hung up his drying clothes, took off the Sicilian's, put them in the bag and donned his nightshirt. Then he asked the crucial question. 'You know a lot about Coleridge. Why are you so interested?'

The stranger was silent for a moment. Then he said, 'I am his son.'

'What?' said Scrivener.

Again, a silence. Then, 'I am his son. He is my father.' A pause. Then, 'My name is Samuele.'

Scrivener was dizzy with shock. He hardly registered the man's final words. It seemed as if Coleridge himself was speaking and he was thinking, *I know your name already. Why are you telling me again?*

When he recovered his senses, the stranger had gone and Scrivener wondered whether the whole day had been a fantastic dream. What a shattering coincidence! This was proof that he was marked out, his ambitions were real *and he knew he would fulfil them.*

He found the perfect words from his new hero. He got out of bed, opened the window and shouted defiance at his tormentors.

'And all should cry, Beware! Beware!
His flashing eyes, his floating hair!
Weave a circle round him thrice,
And close your eyes with holy dread
For he on honey-dew hath fed,
And drunk the milk of Paradise.'

He climbed into bed and felt dizzy again. And something else. He felt feverish. His head ached, he shivered uncontrollably and was almost delirious. But eventually he slept. A sleep of utter exhaustion.

PART II

Chapter 9

Sudden Death

Sicily, March 1824

...his countenance told in a strange and terrible language of agonies that had been, and were, and were still to continue to be.
—'The Wanderings of Cain', Samuel Taylor Coleridge

The corncrake concealed in the wheat shot up with sudden shockingness and a loud *chirruk!*

The grey horse reared. The rider lost hold of the reins and dropped silently, as if incredulous that his horse Benito would do this. His head smashed against one of the stones littering the fields on this plain in Sicily, near Floridia, eight miles west of Siracusa. His skull split and blood stained the stones crimson. Bernardo Gambino was snuffed out in the twinkling of an eye. Samuele, his only son, halted his black horse Giuseppe and tried to climb down. But he was in shock and could not move. Alfredo, the bailiff, jumped off his brown pony and bent to his master's body. As if penitent, Benito nuzzled his master's bloody face until his nostrils were red. Alfredo's weather-beaten, sunburnt face was streaked with tears. 'Your father is dead,' he said bleakly. 'You are the master now.'

Samuele found his voice. 'I didn't do it. You saw I didn't. Benito did.'

'It was the bird in the corn,' said Alfredo. 'He should be in Africa now with the rest. I'll hunt him and shoot him. Benito is innocent.' Then, solicitously, 'Why should anyone think you did it, young master?'

Samuele thought: *But I might have done.*

'Let me help you off your horse,' said Alfredo.

Samuele looked at Alfredo as if at a stranger. 'Yes,' he said, 'Off my horse. Of course.' He swung himself down and Alfredo caught him.

'It was an accident,' the bailiff said. 'Benito shied suddenly. He threw your father off.'

'Benito wouldn't do that. My father loved him,' said Samuele. He could not quell the thought: *That horse was the only thing you did love, and even he turned against you in the end.*

'Stay here and watch over him,' said Alfredo. 'I'll ride to Floridia for the priest and the undertaker. The rites must be performed and the body taken home. Bernardo's death will grieve his tenants here as much as his family in Monreale.'

Samuele nearly said, 'Only that much?' but bit it down. The bailiff regarded him solicitously. 'I am sorry to leave you alone, young master. I'll be as quick as I can. Be strong.'

He kicked the pony's flanks and galloped off towards Floridia.

Alone, Samuele had disturbing thoughts. *I should be grief-stricken. I should scream, 'My beloved father, don't leave us.'*

'I know,' he said aloud. 'But I won't. I can't.'

At last, tears started, not out of grief for his father but for himself, because he felt cheated of his birthright – that of loving his parents equally.

*

He waited for over three hours before Alfredo returned with the undertaker and priest. He cried freely when he knew his tears were only for his mother and himself. He had lived without love from this man for eighteen years. He had heard his mother crying as his father shouted, 'Left to you, that boy would be nothing. He's my heir, God help me, and I'll make him carry on the honour of the Gambinos if I have to maim him in the process. Why else should I bring him into the world?'

That last question lay like a cancer. Even so, crying done, he stood proud and guiltless. Lonely? Of course. He wanted to be.

Alfredo returned on a cart pulled by a bony chestnut horse and driven by a tall man in black. The undertaker. A wizened little priest sat with them. Alfredo and the undertaker lifted the body onto the cart as the three horses grazed, patient and uninterested. The undertaker closed Bernardo's mouth and eyes and placed his hands across his chest. The priest anointed his forehead, muttered prayers and made the sign of the cross several times. Samuele could not bring himself to say the responses. Only Alfredo and the undertaker spoke.

'My man is making a coffin,' said the undertaker. 'Tomorrow, I will ride with Signor Gambino's body and his grieving son back to Monreale.' He turned to Samuele. 'You and your mother must arrange the funeral. I've no doubt you have a family plot – perhaps a vault?'

Grieving son. He almost laughed aloud.

Alfredo took them back to his house. The coffin, rough and cheap, was already waiting. Such a coffin would do for peasants. Bernardo Gambino, once home, would be transferred into something ornate, made of finest oak.

*

Today had been the third and last in Bernardo Gambino's annual tour of his estates and for the first time he had brought Samuele with him.

The July sun burned as Samuele, Bernardo and Alfredo made their inspection. The horses picked their way delicately across the stony fields and peasants looked up from their hoeing and bowed obsequiously. The soil was not the best here. 'Good reason,'

Bernardo often said, 'for them to work hard if they want to eat at the end of the day.'

Something curled in Samuele's stomach. One day he would collect rents and profits, pay dues to the King of the Two Sicilies, give enough for bare existence to the peasants and then go home to live in luxury. It sickened him. But whenever he tried to say so, his tongue froze. Bernardo would have replied contemptuously, 'Then it's time you understood your station in life.'

Samuele cursed his cowardice.

On their tour, they passed through a cornfield. The crop was six weeks away from harvest. Bernardo bent down from his saddle, picked off an ear and rolled the grain between his finger. 'Yes,' he said. 'It comes on well. We'll have a good wheat harvest. Samuele, pick some yourself and learn what good grain feels like.'

Samuele dutifully bent down and rolled the ripening grain between thumb and forefinger and said, 'Of course, Father.'

Then he asked a question. 'Why if the grain is so good, are so few fields set aside for wheat?'

He expected the rough edge of Bernardo's tongue. But his father smiled and said, 'I'm glad you asked. It's time for you to know.' He turned Benito and trotted out of the field into a waste of grey dotted with clumps of bright red, white and salmon pink, which stretched away almost to the horizon. 'The poppy,' he said. 'Don't you know what the poppy is?'

Wild blooms on bad land going to ruin, Samuele thought.

'A few bushels of wheat could never pay for our villa nor keep us in servants and fine food. Now I'll show you what *does* pay for them. Get off your horse.'

Samuele slid off Giuseppe's back. Bernardo jumped down from Benito. 'Now your true education begins,' he said. He bent down and picked off a poppy head. 'Look,' he said. 'Only half grown. But now is the time, I believe.' He tore at the poppy head. Samuele watched the petals fall and felt obscurely sad. But Bernardo took a knife from his pocket and cut into the pod. With thumb and forefinger he brought out grains, twelve of them, and said, 'It will be a good crop.'

Samuele said nothing.

'This is the harvest that really matters,' said Bernardo. 'What's wheat? Enough to make pasta and bread and satisfy basic wants. And the tenants' wants as well, if they behave.' Bernardo always referred to the peasants who slaved for him as tenants. 'But this...' He examined the grains with a sort of rapt adoration. 'If I take all the grains from all the pods in this one poppy head, then I have what the English would pay one of their guineas for. My poppies spread their magic all over Europe. The English are the best customers. Theirs is a strange land. But it's a good market and makes us rich. Surely you know what the poppy seed gives? Opium, my boy. Opium, which takes away pain. And, if you are a little more indulgent, as the English especially seem to be, it brings wonderful dreams and ecstasies that men crave and pay well for.'

'Doesn't it also bring misery and death?' he asked.

'Yes. But that's no concern of mine,' Bernardo answered. 'Or yours. Your concern is to increase it so that your mother wants for nothing. Our fortune will find you a wife from a fine family. Rank and money united. That's my dream for you.'

Samuele said nothing. His intentions did not involve aristocratic girls.

'I'll order Alfredo to get the wheat harvest in on his own,' said Bernardo. 'The poppy harvest will follow and we must be here to make sure it's brought in properly.'

When the land is mine, I'll stop this even if it ruins us, Samuele thought to himself.

A few minutes later, Bernardo was dead.

*

Samuele and the undertaker left early. The undertaker was a man of few words: This suited Samuele. As they passed, men ceased working, bared their heads and crossed themselves. Samuele was strangely touched.

They came that night to what proved to be a good taverna. As they entered, the undertaker whispered to Samuele, 'Your mother should know before we arrive. To see her husband in a coffin would be a terrible shock. She should have time to compose herself.'

'What shall we do?' said Samuele.

'We must ask for someone ride to Monreale with the news. You must pay well for his trouble.'

'Of course,' said Samuele. 'If I had any money.'

'We'll use your father's.'

'But he never took much on journeys for fear of bandits,' said Samuele.

'Then your mother will settle up with him. I'll speak to the landlord.'

When he came back, the undertaker said, 'He has the ideal person for such a gallop. I'll pay him on account now. You must write your mother a message for him to take, saying what's happened and that she must pay him. He deserves well and we must not begrudge him.'

'Of course,' said Samuele. He called for pen, ink and paper and wrote a long, difficult note.

'Good,' said the undertaker. 'Now you'll be spared the experience of seeing a woman's first dreadful shock.'

*

By noon on the third day they were in the hills overlooking Palermo. By afternoon they had entered the city. Crowds fell silent as they passed. Soon they were climbing the slopes above the city. The air was pure and, as they essayed the last exhausting slope of Monte Caputo, spacious white villas peeped out through orange and olive trees.

They were home as the light began to fade. Oranges peeped through the trees like little lanterns lighting their way in. Samuele could see Giulia, his mother's maid, on a ladder resting on a branch, her skirts pushed up round her thighs, which appeared to glow in tune with the oranges she picked. It seemed she extinguished the lights one by one until only those thighs were left to see in the dusk. Samuele felt a stirring which he had often experienced before. Sometimes, when nobody was looking, he had snatched a few minutes with her, speaking in the old language of Sicily, which all the servants spoke and which he had taught himself, and he knew she returned his regard for her. Now his father was not watching, he could approach her and their feelings would deepen. Giulia might be a mere working girl from a poor family, but he thought she was beautiful. Now he could forget the girls of fine family lined up for him to choose from.

The undertaker led the cart and coffin past servants lining the sweeping drive. Samuele's mother waited, motionless and dry-eyed. *Has she finished her grief before we arrived?* Samuele wondered.

'We have brought your husband home, signora,' said the undertaker.

'So I see,' Samuele's mother replied. Her voice was finely controlled. 'Thank you. I have made the funeral arrangements already. Please bring the body into the house. Then take your horse to the stables. You may eat with the servants and a bed will be made up for you.'

'Thank you, signora,' said the undertaker and bowed.

Samuele followed his mother into the house. Her first words were, 'You must be hungry, Samuele. There's food ready.'

'Thank you,' he replied. Cold meats and fruit were laid out in the echoing dining room. He ate and then drank some wine. His mother watched him silently.

'I'm going to bed,' she said when he had finished. Giulia bustled in and cleared away. Her beautiful young face was framed by her black hair. She was too young yet for servanthood to roughen her hands, and her movements were lithe and supple. Samuele was seized again with longing.

Chapter 10

A Father's Funeral

Monreale, March 1824

But think, though still your joys remain
Think of that hour of bitterest pain
When mourning friends such sorrow know
They almost 'long themselves to go'
　　　　　　　—'Consolation in Trouble', Sara Coleridge

The mourners had filed outside the church of San Martino delle Scale. Samuele supported his black-veiled mother by the graveside. A press of people almost pushed them in, intent on seeing the last trace of Bernardo Gambino. The priest cast farewell grains of dry soil on the oak coffin, then handed some to Samuele's mother to throw on it. The earth rattled gently on the wood as if tapping out a final message. Finally, the priest passed a handful of loose dirt to Samuele. He shook his head. He would not join any show of grief.

Then, Samuele stooped, hooked his fingers and gouged out a lump of dirt, squeezed it in his palm into a hard ball hurled it downwards hard and true. It hit the coffin lid with an echoing thud. If only, he wished vindictively, it was a solid, sharp-sided rock which would split the lid, burst through and spoil the features of the man lying inside.

'There's no grief round this grave from anyone, especially me,' he cried.

There was a horrified gasp. The priest glared at him. His mother looked shocked. Why? Surely she couldn't have any love for her husband. Samuele took her arm and led her away. He walked proudly, head high, as if today were not an end but a beginning. And he hoped it would be the same for her.

*

Winds blew refreshingly round the villa. Marble floors were cool to their feet: high ceilings let people walk tall. When at last mother and son were alone, servants rushed in. Samuele shook them away and guided his mother to her room.

He thought she might want to be alone. Instead, she reached out and folded her arms round him. 'My poor boy,' she murmured. 'My poor shattered boy. What will you do now with no father to guide you?'

Samuele thought: *Didn't you see what I did at the graveside?* He hardened his heart and spoke out.

'Mother,' he said. 'I'm not a child. Father had nothing to teach me that I want to know.' He drew a deep breath and said the impossible words. 'He hated me and I hated him.'

'You're wrong,' she said. 'He wanted the best for you. Never forget. He's given you a respected place in the world. You're a rich man. How could anyone have done more?'

'So I'll inherit the profits from a rotten trade and push the peasants into slavery. He never cared who he ruined. I was born for something better than this. I thought you agreed with me.'

'I could see that sometimes you were discontented. I thought it was normal for sons. I can't bear to hear you say this. It's very wrong of you to think that just because you believe something, everyone else will.'

This stung Samuele. 'Mother, he did bad things to you.'

'Such as?'

'He made you stop singing. You were the prima donna. It was your life.'

'It was his right,' his mother replied.

'I don't believe that.'

'Believe what you like.'

'Did you know what he grew in Floridia?'

'Wheat, of course.'

'No. The poppy. Which gives us opium. The source of all our riches.'

'That, too, was his right,' she said. 'The good wife does not pry into her husband's business.'

'Well, it seems my course in life is set out for me already. But I think I was born for something better.

She looked at him searchingly. 'What do you think it is?' she said.

'I don't know. Something different. Something like…' He had no words to say what. He had never been to school. All he knew was what Signor Avellado, the dried-up tutor, had taught him. But he tried. 'Something great. Something with beauty and significance.' He searched for an example. 'Something like the operas you sang in years ago which my father made you give up. Something like the paintings and statues in the city galleries, not the gimcrack stuff he got for this place. Shelves of books saying great things. Something – anything – beyond weighing up profit and loss. Something so that I can say, "I did that and nobody else could."'

'How can you be born for such things?' his mother enquired mildly.

'I see them from afar. I've never been to the opera. Nobody told me why the paintings and statues in the galleries are great. Nobody let me look inside the books. If I was *forbidden* to, I want to know *why*.' The worst cut of all. 'Mother, I have never heard you sing.'

'You have,' his mother replied. 'I sang you lullabies. Night after night. Until you were six years old.'

'Mother,' Samuele cried. 'Why did you stop?'

'Bernardo ordered me to,' she said.

'Why was it so important to him to keep me away from anything but his own business? He was single-minded, but why should I be? It's as if—' He broke off suddenly. He'd had an extraordinary thought, something which he often muttered in private anger as a glorious wish but never believed.

He beat the thought down and continued. 'You gave me life and everything that I value. My father gave me misery, anger and contempt. You saw me hurl that clod at his coffin. That was just a gesture. I could have done worse. Mother, I hated him. Sometimes I've thought – *He can't be my father. I can't be his son.* If he were my father I'd want to follow in his footsteps because that's all I know. I deserve more.'

He stopped, breathless and sweating. He knew his mother's name was Cecilia, née Bertozzi. He knew she had been prima donna in the opera house at Siracusa years ago. Every night she sang the works of great composers and brought them to glorious life. But his father had made her leave. Why? Was his father exacting some sort of revenge on his wife? Revenge for what?

She looked away as if wrestling with something intractable. The silence lengthened. *Speak to me*, he pleaded in his head. *Say something, even if it's to turn me out of the house.*

The clock on the mantelpiece ticked slowly. Samuele watched its hands. The ticking continued but they seemed hardly to move.

At last Cecilia spoke. He almost thought she had said, 'Samuele, you're right.' But no faithful wife would say such a thing. What about family honour? Wives had been murdered on suspicion of violating the code. 'Bernardo Gambino has a bastard in his house because he can't control his wife and he's not man enough to have his own sons.' Even a whisper could have terrible consequences.

But that was what she said. And more. 'Samuele, I have a secret I thought never to tell. Now you must know.'

'Go on, Mother,' he said gently.

'I shall tell you a story,' she replied.

'I don't want a story. I want the secret.'

She shouted, sudden as a musket shot. 'Samuele! This is hard. I must do it my way.'

Shamed, he waited for her to begin.

'It was many years ago now. September 1804. Samuele, you know that I was an opera singer because of my voice and my looks. I started singing in Rome as a young girl, then I came to Palermo, just twenty-one and on my own. Cecilia Bertozzi, opera singer in principal roles. I liked the sound of that. But 1804 was a terrible year. Europe was racked with war. French armies were overrunning Europe. Napoleon was the emperor—'

Samuele broke in. 'Everybody knows this. Get on with the story.'

'Of course you know it. You have to bear with me.'

Shamed again, Samuele let her continue.

'You know this because the war ended in 1815, when you were ten. We feared that the French would pour down through Tuscany, Lombardy and Rome to Naples and then they would land in Sicily and we would be a vassal of France. A great war was raging at sea between the British and French. If the British lost the way was clear for Napoleon to reach India. If we didn't understand the dangers we'd go mad: we couldn't afford to anger the British, we dared not anger Napoleon. So we had to be nice to both. Sometimes that was hard. So, while I was happy singing in the opera, I was frightened, like everyone else.'

'This is not the story,' said Samuele.

'Have patience with me,' said Cecilia.

She paused again as if every word had to be thought out first.

'I met Bernardo soon after I came to Palermo. He was Italian, from Naples, though his family was originally from Sicily. He could buy land cheaply in Sicily, as many Italians did. He was older than me and perhaps rough in his manners, but he was rich and proud of it.'

Samuele's face twisted with dislike and she cried, 'Samuele! Why shouldn't he be proud? He hadn't been left a fortune like an aristocrat.'

'It doesn't stop him living like one, by peddling misery and starving his labourers.'

Cecilia was stung into defending her husband. 'That's not fair,' she protested. 'He'd made his money by his wits. That's admirable in a man, whether you like it or not. Why shouldn't he live in style? Now his legacy will all come to you.'

'I don't want it.'

'Remember this, my son. I was born in Rome. Bernardo comes from Naples. So you are Italian, too. You are not a Sicilian. I think you sometimes forget that. And as for not wanting your inheritance, we'll see if that's how you feel later. You've been born to privilege and wealth. You are one of the most fortunate young men in Sicily. As an Italian, you will have a better life than most Sicilians, who have to toil to stay alive. Don't forget who has left you in this enviable place. Your father. Renounce your inheritance and you'll suffer for your whole life. Perhaps there are things that even a boy of nineteen can't understand.'

Samuele winced and Cecilia retreated into dreamy reminiscence. 'Fabrizio introduced me to Bernardo in the green room after a performance,' she said. 'My first sight of him. He was tall, with a strong face which said "no one gets the better of me".'

How true, Samuele thought.

Cecilia continued. '"Be nice to him," Fabrizio whispered. "He especially asked to meet you. He's rich and he could do us a lot of good. Don't let me down." So I tried to be nice to him.'

Samuele was shocked. Being nice to a man because she was told to was surely what whores did.

'Bernardo was polite and formal. He said little, but afterwards he started coming round to the stage door after performances. And I did what Fabrizio told me. Perhaps I was too nice.'

Samuele caught his breath. Now the story was really starting.

'One night, Bernardo said, "Cecilia, I live in a new villa on the hills overlooking Monreale, far from Palermo's stink and filth. But the house lacks a mistress and I lack a wife. I see now it was built for you and only you can complete it."

'I knew what was coming. And now, Samuele, I must tell you what my first thoughts were. *Don't ask me to be your wife. I won't be anybody's wife. I want to be a prima donna and the greatest soprano in Europe.* And when he went down on one knee and took my hand and said, "Anna-Cecilia, will you be my wife?" I couldn't do it. I burst into tears like a little girl. "Bernardo, please don't ask. I can't be," I shouted, and ran out of the room and all the way to my lodgings. I locked myself in and hid in case he tried to force his way through. But nothing happened until there was a knock on the door early next morning. I didn't move. But a voice called out, "Cecilia, I must speak to you." I opened the door and there stood Fabrizio, very angry.

'"How dare you infuriate one of the richest men in the city?" he shouted.

'"I won't marry him," I answered. "Don't try to make me." Perhaps it occurred to Fabrizio that for me to marry might take a good singer away. He said, "All right, Cecilia, if you're sure then I won't let him near you again. Here's what we will do. Every year, the opera house sends a company out to Siracusa. How would you like to go with them? Perhaps he'll forget you. You'll go as prima donna." Prima donna – the first lady. The best, with a voice to soar over chorus, orchestra, audience, up to heaven. And me not twenty-one.

'I loved Siracusa. I loved the sea, the harbour, the people, the little boys who swarmed the streets of Ortigia, called my name and sang my songs back to me. I loved the ruins of ancient times which said this place had been strong for thousands of years and seen great events. Now the great event was this terrible war. But then this war threw up a great event for me.'

She stopped again. Samuele chafed with impatience. Every time his mother came to something important she stopped and made him wait. It annoyed him. But perhaps she did it on purpose. Perhaps this was how stories were best told and how operas were made.

'The opera season started in September. It was the end of a beautiful summer. I went on stage for my first role as prima donna. I remember well what the opera was. *La Clemenza di Tito*. And I shall never forget my great aria.'

To Samuele's inexpressible delight, his mother sang at last. Although she hadn't sung for so long, he could tell the beauty of her voice, its trueness of pitch, its depth of feeling.

I love you alone;
You alone I have loved;
You were the first,
And you will be
The last one
I shall ever adore.
When love is innocent
It grows so strong
That it lives within you
Until death –
That first love
You ever felt.

'As I sang and looked out over the orchestra through the smoky lights to the audience, listening to every note, I wished that there was one, one alone, among them for whom those words were meant. But, I thought, there wasn't. So I just sang as well as I could and when I'd finished, the roaring and cheering and cries of

"*Bravissima*" made me so happy. But how I wished for that one special person to know the words were meant for him, someone who wouldn't want to marry me without love.

'After the show, I went to the green room with the rest of the cast. The leading citizens of Siracusa – the mayor, the bishop – were waiting. They congratulated me, flattering things were said and then the mayor introduced three people I didn't know, a middle-aged man, a tall and beautiful woman and a much younger man with dark hair and dark eyes that seemed to glitter. "Signorina Bertozzi," the mayor said. "May I introduce our three English guests? Signor and Signora Leckie, the British Residents in Siracusa, and their guest, Signor Coleridge, who comes from England. And back in England he is, I have been told, a great poet whose works are admired by all Englishmen. I myself cannot read them. But I am assured by all who can that this is so. For him to be with us in Siracusa is a great honour."'

Cecilia paused again and Samuele's heart beat fast because he knew the story was nearing its climax.

'So I looked up and I had my first sight of Samuel Taylor Coleridge, the great poet from England.'

'Mother, why are you telling me this?' said Samuele.

'Ask no questions, my son,' Cecilia replied. 'Just listen.' So he listened, and with every word his heart swelled with a peculiar joy.

'I saw a man older than I was but still young. His dark hair was thick down over his shoulders, his brows were also dark and thick, but they didn't meet over the bridge of his nose and that to me meant he was to be trusted. His nose was straight, the nose of a Roman emperor. His lips were full and when he spoke they moved expressively, so that even though I had no idea what he was saying, not at first anyway, I knew that his words were full of meaning. He wore a flowing white necktie, a black coat and breeches and buckled shoes. But it was those eyes which drew me. They shone with feeling, character, and – Samuele, they shone with *genius*.'

Samuele stole a look in a mirror over the fireplace, as if he hoped to see this same face looking back at him.

'How could I tell all that from one look, you may ask, Samuele?'

Samuele was not asking.

'Well, I could. I knew it. I had eyes only for Signor Coleridge and I could see he had eyes only for me. Signor and Signora Leckie smiled and moved off to meet other people, but Samuel, my dear Samuel as I soon knew him, stayed with me. He spoke some Italian after working in Malta but I had not a syllable of English, yet we understood each other in a way which seemed miraculous.

'All that evening we talked. He told me how much he liked my singing, especially "Amo te solo", and I thought of how I had longed to be singing for just one person in the audience. Perhaps I had been and didn't know.'

Samuele's heart was beating fast. 'Perhaps he was thinking the same,' he replied.

'Perhaps,' she replied. 'He told me so much and I always seemed to know exactly what he meant. The evening went so quickly, then it was time for him to leave. I couldn't sleep that night. One day you'll know how it is when you meet someone who turns your life upside down. How would I see him again? I couldn't go to the Leckies' house; it was not my place to send him a note. He would go back to Malta, to England, out of my life.

'But he was at the opera the next evening, on his own now. And the next night, and the next. And every night, Samuel was there in the green room afterwards, waiting for me. After a few nights we took to walking outside, down the lane from the opera house in the night air, alone, then on to the shore, listening to the breakers on the sand, with Samuel reciting poetry in his own language, which I didn't understand except that it was wild and wonderful and he had written it.

'And then we moved away from the shore and into the town again and to my own lodgings. And then, at last – Samuele, I tell you this trembling, because I don't want you to think badly of me – I brought him into my bedroom.'

'Why?' Samuele asked, though he knew it was a silly question.

'There, I knew you would disapprove,' she cried.

'No, Mother, of course I don't. I just want to know.'

'It was the natural place to bring him.'

'And then what?' Samuele's heart was beating even faster.

'I can't tell you. That was the end of his visits. Soon he left Siracusa for Malta. I never saw him again.'

'You mean you've heard nothing since?' said Samuele, surprised.

'Oh yes, I heard. All of Siracusa heard. A week later there was a crisis. A British man-o'-war brought a French privateer into harbour and there was a – what do they call them? – diplomatic incident. Siracusa wanted neither ship near the place, because there could have been shooting, and if there was, the French and the British soldiers might have come here. But who should come down to the quayside to sort it all out but my Samuel, sent by Signor Leckie. He calmed everybody down, made them put their guns away and told the mayor of Siracusa to be quiet. The danger was over. My Samuel was a hero. And then, after that great triumph, he left. He was never seen in Siracusa again.'

'So that was all you ever knew of him,' said Samuele, disappointed. 'He's gone for ever. Why did you tell me this story?'

'But I haven't finished it yet,' said Cecilia.

In his own mind, Samuele finished it for her. He'd often wondered about his name. There was no Samuele that he knew of in the family. Names were passed down through the generations.

Cecilia hesitated. The slow tick of the clock seemed deafeningly loud. Eventually she spoke. 'The god in my life,' she said. Then she closed her eyes, put her head back and cried out as if suddenly given the gift of tongues, in English of a different order from the language which Signor Avellado had taught him:

'I would build that dome in air,
That sunny dome! those caves of ice!
And all who heard should see them there,
And all should cry, Beware! Beware!
His flashing eyes, his floating hair!
Weave a circle round him thrice,
And close your eyes with holy dread
For he on honey-dew hath fed,
And drunk the milk of Paradise.'

'Mother,' cried Samuele. 'You *can* speak English.'

'I wish I could,' she said. 'Yet I remember his poems as he spoke them and wrote them down as if he were here in this room with us now.' She seized him by his shoulders and repeated '...*and drunk the milk of Paradise*. So should I have, Samuele, so should I have.'

He struggled free. 'So should you what, Mother?' he whispered. 'What milk? What Paradise?'

Her shoulders slumped. 'Don't ask me,' she said.

Samuele thought of a question he dared not ask. But he made himself. 'Mother, you said you took him into your bedroom but you can't say what happened there. Is that because you don't know or because you don't want to tell me?'

She didn't answer.

'I'm sorry,' he said. 'I shouldn't have asked. It's not my place.'

But Cecilia gripped him by his coat lapels and insisted, 'It *is* your place. You asked if I don't know or don't want to say. The answer is both. I really don't know what happened that night and anything I say will sound stupid.'

'Never,' said Samuele.

'I didn't know that would be the last time I'd see him. I don't think he did either. I was sure he would be there waiting when the opera was over. I knew I would take him to my bedroom: after the show he was waiting, just as I thought he would be, and we walked from the opera house, to my lodgings and then quietly upstairs to my room.'

'And then what?' Samuele's heart was pounding.

'I knew what I wanted to happen. But I don't know if it did. Remember, I was young. I knew little about the world. All I wanted was to sing. Until I met Samuel. Did he think I was a dangerous woman used to ensnaring men? I didn't want to tempt him, I wanted to love him. I lay waiting, in an ecstasy I'd never known before or since. I seemed to know everything and yet nothing. Except...'

She paused.

'Yes?' said Samuele.

In English, so softly that he could hardly hear, she said, 'For I on honey-dew have fed, and drunk the milk of Paradise.'

Silence again.

Then Samuele said, 'What do you mean, Mother?'

She did not answer. Instead, she carried on with her story. 'I heard a great cry. I opened my eyes and saw him put back his disarranged clothing, then he was gone. His footsteps pounded down the stairs as if a wild beast chased him. I still hear them. The door slammed. That was the last I knew of him. Except when he was the talk of Siracusa after the ships came into the harbour.'

'But, Mother, if that was the last time you saw him and you don't know what happened, what are you trying to tell me?'

She didn't give the straight answer he longed for. 'For days I was racked with guilt. I kept thinking of that last visit. Sometimes I thought I knew what had happened and that a seed was planted in me. Sometimes I thought nothing had happened except wishing. When I heard that Samuel had gone back to Malta I felt desolated. I had been close to a god and then lost him. Nobody waited for me now and I trudged home alone. Until...' She seemed to fall into a different dream.

'Until what?' Samuele prompted.

'A week afterwards, Bernardo Gambino arrived. He was visiting his estates and was told I was in Siracusa. He still wanted to marry me. But what if I were pregnant? The child had to have a father and who could it be but Bernardo? So I said yes, I would marry him. Bernardo said he already had the bishop's special dispensation to marry at once. He took me back to Palermo, so, hardly ten days after Samuel went out of my life, I was a married woman with a rich husband, mistress of a great house and pregnant. Bernardo, of course, assumed the child was his and that I would be a dutiful wife. And so, Samuele, you were born, I insisted on your name and I loved you with fierceness. You were my Samuele and my secret.'

'But you can't say for sure whether this poet is my father.'

'I can, I can,' Cecilia cried in sudden anguish. 'Every time I look at you I see him.'

'Bernardo knew,' said Samuele.

'He couldn't have.'

'Think, Mother, think,' Samuele replied. 'You say he came to Siracusa. He will have had friends there. You and Coleridge were the talk of the town. He must have wondered. And then you insisted on calling me Samuele. That would have proved it. So he took his revenge. He made me as different from a poet as he could. Look what he did to you. He stopped you singing. He even forbade lullabies. Why else should he stamp out every trace of your old life?'

She looked at him as if this had never occurred to her before. Tears started in her eyes. In another second she might crumple into sobbing at the thought that her husband might have guessed her secret. He had to stop it.

'So that's why my name is Samuele,' he said. Cecilia nodded, unable to speak, looking at him with a love he could wrap round himself like a coat.

But this man had deserted her. A new thought entered his mind.

'Mother, was he married? Did he leave a wife in England?' Cecilia did not answer.

So he might be the son of a poet, a genius. Then he thought – *What use is just knowing? Who can I tell? What good can it do me?*

He bit his lip in frustration. If anyone outside this room ever found this out it would bring shame on her. He stared through the window at Monreale in its hot valley and Palermo beyond. This place was his lot, for all his life.

But his mother was saying extraordinary things. 'Oh, if only I had taken my chance, followed him to England and told him I was carrying his child. We might be living in England now. I should have taken my chance. But I didn't have the money.'

'Mother,' said Samuele gently. 'What if he didn't believe you? What would you have done?'

'Come home, with my lesson learnt.' She spoke calmly.

'What if you had found he was married?'

'He never said anything about that.'

'I see,' said Samuele.

Then something extraordinary flashed into his mind. *My mother couldn't follow him to England. But I could. So why shouldn't I?* And then: *I will.* A great project. He felt inspired. 'Mother, I want to go to England. I want to find Samuel Taylor Coleridge. I want him to know he's my father.'

She looked up, her eyes sparkling. 'I knew that you'd want to once you heard me,' she replied. Suddenly they were clinging to each other, laughing and tearful, and Cecilia was crying, 'Oh my son, my wonderful son, go to England and find him. But don't forget your other father. Bernardo doesn't deserve that.'

Chapter 11

Giulia

O how, love, must I fill
This weary, weary blank?
How do your eyes no ill
Yet fully use my frank—?

By putting there a token
Of what you call a bliss
When tender words were spoken
And you asked me for a kiss.

—'Oh how, love, must I fill', Sara Coleridge

It was decided there and then. The problem was, how and when? Should Cecilia go with him? '*No!*' she exclaimed when he asked, with a force which made him step back. 'I can't try again.' That was the end of the matter. But she was right and he was pleased. He must do this on his own.

'I'll be all right in England,' he said. 'I can speak some English. Signor Avellado taught me quite a lot, so he did something useful after all.'

'Be sure nobody there will speak Italian,' she replied. 'Once I might have helped you. But all I can do now is to show you the poems he wrote out for me and read them to you as best I can.'

She placed a finger on her lips as if enjoining him to silence. Then, almost guiltily, as if Bernardo might still be watching, she tiptoed upstairs. Samuele followed. She opened the door of her bedroom. Her son stayed outside. 'No,' she said. 'Come in. You must see me bring his poems out into the light after so very long.'

She opened a drawer in her writing desk, reached inside and brought out a tiny key, which she turned in the keyhole of another drawer, very small, below the others. From this hiding place she took a sheaf of paper, yellow with age.

'Look at these, Samuele,' she said.

He saw English, written in a flowing hand. 'His poems,' she whispered. 'We'll go downstairs again and I'll try my best to read them to you.'

So, with Bernardo in his grave for hardly half a day, Cecilia was reading to Samuele in the language of her husband's rival, from pages which he had written out himself, and neither felt the slightest twinge of guilt. But Cecilia had not spoken or read English for nearly twenty years and had not dared to look at those pages since her marriage. Poem after poem she started reading, then stopped, then started again, stumbling through a few more lines. She was close to weeping with frustration. Only the one passage, which she had recited to him, came freely. '...*and drunk the Milk of Paradise.*'

'Oh, Samuele,' she said. 'I'm so sorry. I thought it would all come back to me. I thought I would teach you some real English.'

'It doesn't matter,' said Samuele, much moved. 'May I see them?'

'But it does,' she answered. 'You can't go to England only knowing what Signor Avellado taught you.'

But Samuele was reading the poem on the top sheet. 'Kubla Khan'. This was a revelation. A thing of beauty, mystery, in an English which was nothing like Signor Avellado's version. He finished it and found that every word seemed lodged in his mind for ever.

'We must find someone to teach you more English, about English poetry, about how English people live, because it seems so different from Sicily,' said his mother.

Samuele heard a faint sound. 'Listen,' he said. There it was again. A quiet tap on the door.

'Come in!' Cecilia shouted, rather too loudly. The door was opened and there stood Giulia.

'I did not send for you,' said Cecilia, almost roughly. 'What do you want?'

Giulia was trembling. Whenever she spoke, Samuele couldn't help but notice her strong *palermitano* dialect, rough in these surroundings. He knew that the servants still spoke the old Sicilian language and Italian didn't come easily to them except to understand orders. He could speak Sicilian himself, a fact that he kept from Bernardo, who would have regarded it as traitorous. He believed that speaking Italian kept all people in their God-given ranks.

Cecilia came from Rome and knew nothing else. That was why Giulia now spoke in slightly hesitant Italian. 'I beg your pardon, signora,' she said. 'I came to ask if you wanted coffee yet. But I heard you say that Signor Samuele needed someone to teach him English and I think I can help.'

'Go ahead, Giulia,' Samuele said quickly before Cecilia could object.

'Signora,' the young woman said, innocently as if unaware she was confessing her eavesdropping. 'My cousin Peregrina is maid to an Englishman who lives in the city. He is a learned man: He has shelves of books all in English. He gives lessons in English. I will ask her if he can take any more pupils.'

'How much have you heard of what we said?' Cecilia demanded.

'Nothing, signora, nothing, I swear it,' Giulia replied. 'Except that Signor Samuele wants someone to teach him English. Is he going away from us?'

'That's none of your business,' snapped Cecilia.

'Giulia, what is this man's name?' Samuele asked gently.

'Signor Calvert,' Giulia answered. 'He lives on his own off the Via Toledo and behind the Collegio dei Gesuiti. Peregrina says he is a very nice man.'

'I'll go there first thing tomorrow,' Samuele replied. 'Thank you, Giulia. You have done us a great service.' He looked at her and remembered when she was picking oranges, her skirts up and her thighs golden in the dusk. What he thought then he remembered now, even though he was trying to fight it down. He thought more of her than this. He owed it to her to be straightforward. 'Giulia,' he said. 'Do you know why I need to see Signor Calvert?'

'Oh no, sir,' she said quickly.

That means she does, thought Samuele. 'Well, if ever you think you might know, you must tell nobody. If you do, you won't work here again. Or anywhere else.' He was silent for a moment. Then he spoke again. 'You know the rules of this house. They still apply.' His voice was quiet, his heart heavy, but the threat was clear.

'I promise, sir,' said Giulia. Her face crumpled as if she was about to burst into tears.

'You may go,' Samuele said, very unhappy. 'Thank you.'

She left. He had given hurt to someone he cared about. 'Don't be angry with her, Mother,' he said. 'She does not deserve that.'

'Beware of girls like Giulia. They are dangerous for rich young men.'

If that was a warning, it fell on deaf ears. Instead, he thought of a damsel with a dulcimer singing of Mount Abora.

*

Samuele could not sleep that night. His mother's story beat through his mind like a pulse. His head ached with the endless repetition, yet he never wanted it to stop. His real father was a famous man, a poet to charm, to mystify, to send his hearers into trances in a language he only half understood.

'...*that dome in air,*

That sunny dome! those caves of ice!'

Over and over again he said those words until he was in a waking trance himself. He was blinded by sunshine through the dome's crystal roof, chilled by frozen, deep caves, one moment high-ceilinged so his voice and footsteps echoed, the next, claustrophobically low so that he could not stand up, their walls sometimes blue, sometimes black, ribbed like starving men's chests, split with cracks and crevasses, solid with the weight of unimaginable time.

And then he was in the middle of a crowd of awed listeners, hushed until his father appeared in front of them and the cry went up:

'*Beware! Beware!*'

And there stood his father, poem in his hand and his voice ringing out. A great cry of joy came from deep inside Samuele. He had come from this man's loins; his father's genius must be in him and now he was sure of the path ahead. He, too, would be a poet.

On came those deathless words yet again.

'*His flashing eyes, his floating hair!*

Weave a circle round him thrice,

And close your eyes with holy dread

For he on honey-dew hath fed,

And drunk the milk of Paradise.'

And he, too, the true son of his father, would feed on honey-dew and he, too, would drink the milk of Paradise.

The clock on the landing and the clock downstairs chimed together, the first with a high peal, the other with a sonorous boom. Together they chimed, then together struck three chords in perfect harmony. Bernardo had bought them because they were expensive and would impress people. The harmony was a freakish accident. His real father would have meant it thus and would have scoured shops for these clocks, because his poet's soul would not bear discord. Everything would be perfect.

Three o'clock. Sleep must come now. And it did, deeply and refreshingly, until he woke next morning to the bright day on which he would meet Signor Calvert, holder of all knowledge, so that one day he, too, would drink the milk of Paradise.

And then a niggling little voice said, *Beware, Samuele. You do not know what the milk of Paradise is.*

Chapter 12

Departure

Palermo and Monreale, March 1824

Oh dear, dear England! How my longing eye
Turned westward, shaping in the steady clouds
Thy sand and high white cliffs
　　　—'Lines written in the album at Elbingerode in the Harz
　　　　　　　　Mountains', Samuel Taylor Coleridge

Next morning, Samuele walked the five miles into Palermo. He could
have ordered Salvatore to drive him in the trap or ridden his own
horse, but he chose to enter the city unobtrusively on his own feet. He
walked down Monte Caputo, came to the edge of Palermo, through
the Porta Nuova and into the Via Toledo. He remembered Giulia's
directions and passed the Archbishop's Palace and the mighty
Duomo. The Jesuit College was up one of the next turnings. He
passed the first turning after the Duomo and tried the second. The
street was narrow and crowded and he had to push his way through
close-packed, sweaty, shouting people. Then he saw a gloomy, austere
building, close up to the street yet separate from it, like an army
barracks but with an indefinably religious look. It seemed to say,
'Behind here is a different world. You know nothing of it and never
will.' It had to be the Jesuit College. Yet it was jumbled in between
ordinary tenements, where the common people draped washing from
balconies and shouted to their friends passing underneath.

Now he was stuck. Did Signor Calvert live in one of these tenements? It seemed unlikely. He tried to ask someone: 'Do you know where...?' But he had to shout and even so the man did not seem to hear. Neither did the second. But next he asked a young, black-haired woman carrying a basket of fruit, who looked up at him with big brown eyes and said, 'Follow me, sir.'

So he did, though it was often hard to keep up with her as she pushed expertly through the crowd and into the square in front of the Church of Sant'Agostino. It was quieter here. She led him to a block of high houses, austere, with no hanging washing and no tenants calling out to each other. Priests rather than their flocks would live in houses like these.

'Signor Calvert has rooms in there, sir,' she said. 'I will take you to them.'

'How lucky I am to find someone who knows where he lives,' said Samuele.

'Not lucky, Signor Gambino,' said the girl. 'I know who you are. My cousin Giulia told me you were coming. My name is Peregrina.'

'You must be Signor Calvert's maid,' said Samuele.

'Yes, sir,' Peregrina answered. 'He sent me out to buy food.' She led him up a gloomy staircase to a large, heavy oak door, knocked on it and listened. There was no answer. She opened the door and went inside. He followed. 'Wait here,' she said. 'Signor Calvert will soon come.' Then she left, shutting the door behind her.

He was in a large, high-ceilinged room in a cool gloom. A little sunshine and noise filtered in through the large, shuttered windows. The walls were lined with bookshelves. He looked at them almost greedily. Many were Italian: he recognised names he had heard of: Dante, Petrarch, Boccaccio, Torquato Tasso. But even more were English: names which thanks to Signor Avellado he could read – Chaucer, Dryden, Pope – and one which everybody could read even if they hadn't been taught by Signor Avellado – Shakespeare. He looked further, his eyes becoming keener.

And then he saw it. *The name*, on a slim book squeezed in at the end of a shelf. Daringly, as if handling fragile skin, he took it from the shelf. *Lyrical Ballads*, W. Wordsworth.

He was disappointed. It was such a small book. And why was Coleridge's name not on it? He opened it. He looked at the first verse of the first poem and tried to read it aloud. It was hard. The language and some of the spelling seemed strange.

'*It is an ancient Mariner,*
And he stoppeth one of three.
"By thy long grey beard and glittering eye,
Now wherefore stopp'st thou me?"'

When he had finished, a voice behind him said, 'Bravo.' He turned. The door had opened silently. There stood a tall man in his fifties, with a face wrinkled from years of sunshine. 'I see you're a keen student of English poetry. I am a little disappointed that you chose a radical work by two men who preached the very revolution that we fought a long war to stop.'

Samuele almost dropped the book in his confusion. An English phrase that Signor Avellado had used when he questioned him about life in England came to his rescue. 'I know nothing of that, Signor Calvert,' he said.

'I should hope not,' his host replied drily.

'I want you to teach me English,' said Samuele.

'Why? You do tolerably well already,' said Signor Calvert.

'I don't know real English. I only know enough to be of use to my father' (he shuddered slightly) 'in his business.'

'I see. Well, here's your first English lesson. I am not *Signor* Calvert. "Signor" is for Italian gentlemen. I am English. I am *Mr* Calvert.'

'*Meestare* Calvert,' Samuele replied experimentally.

'Very good,' said Mr Calvert. 'Now, what is this "real" English you're so keen to master? Most of my pupils seem content with less than you know already.'

'I want to learn how to read English books, English poetry. I want to know about England. What is it like to live there? Is London as big as Palermo?' Mr Calvert smiled. 'I want to speak English so I can go to England and not be ignorant.'

He was still holding *Lyrical Ballads* open at the 'The Ancient Mariner' so he hurriedly tried to put the book back on the shelf. Mr Calvert gently took it from him. 'Allow me,' he said. As he put the book in its place he said, 'You made a good attempt, Signor Gambino. Nevertheless, I wish your first efforts at English verse had been from a more worthy source.'

'What do you mean?' Samuele asked guardedly.

'I say nothing of Wordsworth. But *Coleridge*.' He almost spat the name. 'A wastrel, a wretch, an untrustworthy, irresponsible, opium-sodden, gross lump of a man.'

'How can you say that?' cried Samuele.

'A rare talent, I grant you,' Mr Calvert continued. 'But thrown away, dissipated, sunk into the sands of his own turpitude. We will never refer to him again. Now, sit by me at my desk. I have the necessary grammar books always ready to help my pupils speak English in a most polite, refined and genteel manner. Not that they often succeed.'

So Samuele sat as Mr Calvert told him to, anxious to arm himself for the quest ahead but miserable as well. He wanted to say, 'No, Coleridge was strong and decisive.' But he could see that henceforth Coleridge was a forbidden subject.

*

Samuele called on Mr Calvert every day except Sunday for the next two months. The Englishman was a good teacher. The grammar books were soon put away. Instead, they spoke together, long conversations about many things, English life, towns, people and customs. In all that time, Mr Calvert never enquired into Samuele's reasons for wanting all this and Samuele never told him how soon he would be in England. He was intensely curious as to why a dry Englishman from a land the priests told him was a nation of heretics should be living in Palermo, a city of bishops, priests and monks. *Still*, he thought, *if Mr Calvert doesn't ask me my business, I won't ask him his.*

In a short time, English became a living thing, something which said more things than Signor Avellado's syllabus had even hinted at. He read, wrote, conversed with Mr Calvert, until, at the beginning of September, he said, 'Mr Calvert, I shall soon stop coming to you. I have a journey which I must start before winter comes. To England.'

'May I ask why?' Mr Calvert asked, with no hint of surprise.

'I have an errand, a quest,' Samuele replied.

'Bravo,' said Mr Calvert. 'You are a fine pupil. You speak almost with the ease of an Englishman. You may scoff at Signor Avellado, but he gave you a good grounding. You'll get on well in England.'

'I have you to thank,' said Samuele.

And not only for the lessons. Often, Mr Calvert let him stay and browse through the books in English on his shelves. There were more poems by his father Coleridge, poems by all those writers whose names had meant nothing to him on his first visit, poems by the Mr Wordsworth who seemed to have so much to do with his real father. Poems by Lord Byron, Percy Bysshe Shelley, John Keats, Alexander Pope, John Dryden. And, of course, William Shakespeare. Their words and rhythms beat into his mind until they were part of it. And then Mr Calvert would talk to him about them. But never again about Coleridge.

Sometimes Mr Calvert talked about England itself and Samuele began to realise why he had left it. 'England is swarming with new ideas: democracy, a persistent sedition, questioning the fabric of Church and State. There is even talk of a Reform Bill which will throw parliament open to people whose low birth gives them no right to be there. I could not stay in a country like that.'

Samuele saw his eyes were sad: Mr Calvert was a self-willed exile.

'There are other reasons,' he went on. 'There are men there who tamper with nature: they think they have tamed powers of nature which are only God's to give. They have made steam engines to pump water out of mines, even to take ships across the sea instead of God's blessed gift of the wind. They even talk of great iron roads on which their manufactured beasts breathing fire and smoke will waft every fool from one end of the land to another so that the degrees into which God saw fit to place his people will be quite obliterated and our lovely land will be defiled for ever. It is a devil's prospect, and I gladly escaped here to a more peaceful and simple land where God is not mocked.'

At the end of the last lesson, Mr Calvert took a bottle and two glasses from a cupboard. 'Have a glass of Marsala with me, Signor Gambino,' he said. 'In England, you may have to put up with beer.'

When he had poured the rich red wine, they clinked their glasses together and Mr Calvert said, 'Samuele, if I may so address you, I have enjoyed teaching you. I wish you could have been here for longer. You will get on well in England, no matter to what depths it has sunk, and whatever your quest, as you so eloquently call it, is, I wish it every success.'

They drank. Mr Calvert poured second glasses and then said, 'By the way, take no notice of what I said about Mr Coleridge the first time you came. He may be a fool to himself, but he is a fine writer. What justification for existence can be greater?' He drank, then winked, and Samuele wondered what he might have guessed at.

*

He walked home with troubled thoughts.

What had Mr Calvert said about the man who might be his father?

'A wastrel, a wretch, an untrustworthy, irresponsible, opium-sodden, gross lump of a man.' And then: 'A rare talent, I grant you. But thrown away, dissipated, sunk into the sands of his own turpitude.'

How could this be? *Opium-sodden?* Barely two months before, Samuele had discovered the true source of the family wealth. Opium. Could Coleridge have bought opium from the Gambino estates? What a satisfying revenge it would have been for Bernardo Gambino on his rival.

He would keep this to himself. His quest now was to clear his new father's name, prove Mr Calvert wrong and make sure his mother never need face the destruction of her dreams.

*

Preparations for the journey were going well. At first, Samuele had wanted to sail to England, past Gibraltar and up the Bay of Biscay. Cecilia protested. 'Your ship could founder in a Biscay storm,' she said. 'Better go overland. I'll send to my cousin Antonio in Naples: he owns stagecoaches which travel up to Rome. He'll tell us how to plan your journey.'

So that was settled. Next, the question of money. 'I will see our bankers,' she said. 'Bernardo had much business in England.'

'The opium?' said Samuele.

'It doesn't matter. You'll need money over there. The bank here will give you letters of credit for the banks in London which Bernardo did business with. I'll give you enough for your journey and a money belt so that thieves won't find it, as long as you wear it, even in bed,' she said.

Her eyes sparkled: she was making it all possible, so he sat back and let her.

'I'll pack a trunk,' she said. 'You mustn't live like a pauper in a strange country.'

But when his departure day arrived and Salvatore was loading up the trap to take him to the harbour and the ship for Naples, Samuele felt afraid for his mother. This burst of activity had carried her along, but now she faced months of loneliness and worry. He must write home regularly.

The wooden chest was packed tight. His mother had been too insistent, too zealous. 'You'll be glad in the end,' she said.

'Yes, Signor Samuele,' cried Salvatore. 'Listen to your mother. You'll thank God for what she's made you do.'

The trap was loaded. Salvatore climbed up to the driver's seat and held the reins ready.

'Why not come to the harbour, Mother?' said Samuele. 'Come to Naples and stay with your cousin Antonio.'

She pressed his hand. Her eyes were cloudy with tears. 'You'll have me all the way to England with you next,' she said.

'Why not?'

'I could have followed him when he left. I still sometimes wish I had. But I had my chance and now it has gone.' She stopped. When she spoke again, it was quietly, so Salvatore wouldn't hear. 'But you will take something of mine. I never wanted to part with it, but now you must have it. When you meet your father, show it to him and he'll know you are who you say you are. Wait a moment. I shall be very quick,' and she disappeared into the house.

She came back with a much-crumpled piece of paper. 'Here,' she exclaimed triumphantly. 'He will recognise this. Samuele, you know English well enough now. Read it out loud, so all the world can hear.'

Samuele unfolded it. He had not understood these words when Cecilia read them after the funeral, but he did now and suddenly he was declaiming aloud, because the secret of his father's whole being was wrapped up in them:

'I would build that dome in air,
That sunny dome! those caves of ice!

And all who heard should see them there,
And all should cry, Beware! Beware!
His flashing eyes, his floating hair!
Weave a circle round him thrice,
And close your eyes with holy dread,
For he on honey-dew hath fed,
And drunk the milk of Paradise.'

The words would stay in his mind for ever, like the chorus in an opera, always about to burst into song. Salvatore couldn't understand any of it, yet even he seemed dazed and subdued at the sound and rhythm which had passed over his head.

'Bravo, my brave son,' Cecilia cried. She reached up to him, and they kissed, the last time now, Samuele thought, for many months. He wondered if he might come home with a companion. He imagined a dark magical figure, eyes flashing with a surging power, black hair floating in a wind of unearthly origin: he knew what holy dread would be like. In his mouth came the heavenly, unknowable taste of the milk of Paradise and he contentedly whispered to himself, 'That is my father.' Then he wondered whether he would have to tell his mother, 'The man is not fit to know. Be thankful that he's out of your life.'

All the servants came out to see him off. 'Goodbye, Master Samuele,' they chorused. 'Safe journey. Come back soon.' Among them was Giulia. She was not calling out with the rest. She was crying and Samuele grieved that he had not been able to say a special goodbye to her. As Salvatore flicked the reins and they moved off, he felt a shaft of remorse. But there must be no looking back, no memories, no guilt. He must be single-minded now.

Even as he made the resolution, he knew he would never carry it out.

'Goodbye, goodbye, my dear son.' Cecilia's voice faded as the trap rumbled out to the road down the hillside – 'Safe journey and happy return' – and Samuele was left to ponder on what her years with Bernardo had really meant to her. What did the notion of private happiness and public misery, or the other way round, mean to her? There must be a balance, but he could not understand it, because she seemed to hold such a high regard for Bernardo at the same time as she remembered her forbidden secret love with such ecstasy.

*

Two hours later, Samuele was climbing the gangplank up to the ship for Naples. The Greco still blew steadily from the north-east, though soon it would give way to the west winds of autumn and winter. Naples was nearly two hundred miles to the north. By constantly tacking against a steady wind over easy seas by day and running before the fresh night breeze, they should arrive some time on the morning after next.

As the crew poled the ship out of the harbour towards open sea and the sails were hoisted, catching the wind, spreading out and filling like great white wings, he imagined his father in England, known, loved and respected, pouring out verses of such beauty, such power. He imagined his life. A beautiful childhood, a wonderful education, learning his craft, perfecting his art, rising to high influence. Why, if his mother knew him when he was a powerful man in government, who knew to what heights he had risen since? He hugged himself to think he was such a man's son and was coming to claim kinship at last.

That night, swaying in his narrow bunk, he had different thoughts. He would find a faithless, opium-drenched wreck of a man who had squandered his gifts.

He was suddenly afraid of his English adventure.

Chapter 13

The Sickbay

Cambridge, April 1824

...O 'tis well
Since I am faltering, sinking on my way,
The sight of nature, ever young and gay,
Might teach my tutored spirit to rebel

—'Sickness', Sara Coleridge

As Scrivener slept, his body worked surely and fast. A chilled fever had taken him and when he woke he could hardly move or breathe. He was in the college sickbay, half conscious, with no memory of how he had got there. The nurse and the college doctor looked at him solicitously. The doctor felt Scrivener's pulse, listened to his chest and felt his forehead and said, 'Pulse regular but too fast. Lungs seem congested. He is running a temperature.' He stepped back and was silent.

'A severe chill,' he said eventually. 'I hope to God it's not something worse.'

'Poor young fellow,' said the nurse. 'Yesterday he was fished out of the river.'

'Drunk, I suppose, like them all,' the doctor replied. He looked at Scrivener's prone body. 'I shall give him laudanum,' he said. 'It will dull pain and help him sleep. I shall return tomorrow morning.'

*

The thick liquid slipped down easily and spread warming comfort. He was soon deeply asleep.

When he woke it was four in the morning and still dark. He tried hard to recall the experience he had just lived through. He knew it was a dream but 'lived' was the right word. A dreamland, staggeringly real, utterly beautiful. Now he felt frustrated, because he had no memory of what wonders this dreamland contained, who the beautiful people were with whom he had had gentle and profound conversations, or the alluring mythical creatures with whom he had communicated in ways beyond language and received their deep, ageless wisdom. All he knew was that they had vanished, shrivelled away, and he wept at their loss.

*

He slept again, a disturbed, restless, shallow doze. When he woke, he started shivering uncontrollably. The nurse arrived with a bowl of thin gruel. He rejected it with a shudder. He remembered again his wonderful, obliterated dream. Tears pricked in his eyes at the loss.

The nurse felt his forehead. 'You're shivering now, but you have a high temperature,' she said.

He asked to void his bowels but when he strained on the chamber pot, he was constipated. He felt weak and was developing a nasty headache.

The nurse helped him back into bed. The headache worsened. He knew about migraines and had once seen somebody suffering one. A dreadful sight.

He lay rigidly still. Now he was hot and sweating profusely. A bowl of soup was offered. He rejected it, hoping that the nurse had not noticed his involuntary retching.

She tried to spoonfeed him like a baby. At first he refused. But the soup was thin and he held it down because he had a raging thirst. He took a sip – and wanted more. He let the nurse feed him with half the bowl. That was enough; his thirst was slaked and he felt more comfortable.

'The doctor will see you this evening,' said the nurse. 'Call me if you want more water. You must keep drinking.'

He lay back. His head still ached. He feared his mind would burst if he revisited recent events, whether being thrown into the river or anything concerning Coleridge or the mysterious inscription.

There was one exception. The man who had appeared from nowhere, claimed to be Coleridge's son and then disappeared as strangely as he had come. Was he a hallucination? He hoped not, for he wanted to see him again.

*

The doctor arrived as dusk fell. He listened to Scrivener's chest and felt his forehead and back. His hands were cold as rocks on the mountainside against the raging hotness of Scrivener's sweating skin.

'More laudanum, nurse,' he said. 'In time it will clear the fever. You may not give it him while I am away. It is not your place to do so.'

Scrivener sipped the blissful laudanum and then slept. And dreamt. This time he knew he would remember the dream, because there were three presences in it. One he had met but did not know, one he knew but had not met. The third was neither. All three filled him with dread mixed with longing. It alarmed him that all his reactions were ambiguous.

But at least, when the first two rose up out of the mist, he recognised them. The Sicilian stranger and Samuel Taylor Coleridge himself, harbingers of what was to come.

The third was a shadow, incorporeal, threatening but alluring, wondrous but alien. The shadow had a woman's shape. Women were, for him, uninterpretable creatures. A stern, restrictive guardian, a boys-only school and a fiercely male college had seen to that. He observed the *droit de seigneur* of the gentleman commoners with shock: a world he would never enter. This dream left him with a disturbing sense of foreboding, which did not stop him falling asleep again.

*

He woke mid-morning. The nurse had brought him another steaming bowl of thin gruel.

'You must get this down you,' she said, handing him a spoon.

He waved it away.

'Then I must feed you like a baby again,' she said.

No baby could withstand the force with which she pushed the spoon between his tight-shut lips and prised his teeth open so he had to swallow the gruel or choke. But the hot, sweetish semi-liquid coursed down his throat very pleasantly and suddenly he wanted more. She fed him the rest as though he was three years old again.

When she had gone, he felt weak, fatigued even after sleeping well, empty of sense and feeling. He lay staring at the ceiling with a mind completely blank.

As dusk gathered, the nurse tempted him with bread and butter and a glass of hot milk. He chewed on the bread, swallowed half of it and drank the milk with something approaching pleasure.

Slowly he was coming alive again.

*

He woke sensing something was different.

He felt better: perhaps the worst might be over. The gruel seemed more like porridge and he ate most of it. Then he tried to sit up. The nurse made a bank of pillows to be comfortable on.

He needed to read. But there were no books in the sickbay. He remembered he was due to translate a passage from Virgil's *Aeneid*. He'd avoided it for nearly a week. But it had to be done.

He called the nurse over. 'Could you do me a favour, please?' he asked.

She did not answer but he read her expression. *Say what it is and I'll decide for myself.*

'I must get on with some work. Could someone find Mr Raggett, who has rooms in Pump Court? I'll give him a list of what I need.'

To his surprise, the nurse replied, 'I don't see why not. I'll fetch paper and pencil.'

She was gone and Scrivener considered what he needed. He had a grim suspicion about his translation. He saw what a brilliant, powerful, infinitely various work the *Aeneid* was and he feared what a miserable response his version would be.

No, he didn't want to translate Virgil. He wanted to read more Coleridge. But what other Coleridge was there, which he could find easily, except that one poem in *Lyrical Ballads*? 'The Ancient Mariner'. He knew it from school and remembered loving it. But all that was left was like a great wave breaking over him and leaving him gasping.

The nurse returned. 'Here we are,' she said. 'Elsie in the kitchens will take it for you.'

'Thank you,' he said. 'And thank Elsie for me, too.'

He rested the paper on a little table the nurse brought over for him and sat with pencil poised over it before he wrote. The materials he wanted would bring sheer drudgery. A text, a Latin grammar, and a concordance with all the notes. He asked Raggett to lend him his: Scrivener didn't want him rooting round his own rooms.

He finished and looked frowningly over what he had written. Then he added: *Could you find a copy of that book by Wordsworth and Coleridge,* Lyrical Ballads, *please? Don't worry if you can't.*

Then he handed it over to the nurse.

*

He didn't expect a quick answer. Raggett was not a friend – unsurprising because nobody was – he was merely in the same tutorial group with Dr Vavasour. Scrivener felt sleepy and dozed off until he woke to a familiar voice saying, 'Wake up. I've brought what you want.'

He opened his eyes to see Raggett standing by his bed.

'How did you get in here?' he asked.

'Natural charm,' said Raggett. 'I've got all you want here, plus some decent paper, a pen and a pot of ink.'

He handed over three bulky books and a bundle of paper. The pen and the ink he put carefully on the table. 'I couldn't find *Lyrical Ballads*,' he said. 'I'll ask around tomorrow and see if anyone can lend it to me. What do you want it for?'

'I want to read "The Ancient Mariner".'

'"The Ancient Mariner", eh? I know the poem. I know his family, too.'

'What do you mean, you know his family?'

'I mean what I say. The ancient mariner was real. He came from Woodstock, where I live. His name was Simon Hatley. Everybody in Woodstock knows the Hatleys. They still live in a house in the High Street.'

'But he's a character in a poem. He's not real.'

'Oh yes he is. He was a real sailor. And he shot an albatross.'

'How do you know this?'

'It's in a book by Captain Shelvocke about all his voyages round the world. I've read it. It's in the library in my old school.'

'Why did he shoot the albatross?'

'I forget. You'll have to read it for yourself.'

'What happened to this Hatley man afterwards?'

'Nobody knows. Last anyone heard he was in prison in South America.'

'How can I get hold of this book?'

'You'll have to come to Woodstock. I can get the school to let you in the library so you can read it.'

Scrivener was surprised at Raggett's show of friendship and even enthusiasm. He made up his mind. 'Good. I'll go,' he said.

'Term ends next week,' said Raggett. 'We'll go together if they've let you out.'

'We'll walk,' said Scrivener. His mind was racing ahead now. 'An epic journey. It may have great consequences.'

'Hold hard,' said Raggett. 'You're still getting over a nasty fever. Will you be strong enough? This could kill you.'

'Walking will make me strong again,' Scrivener replied.

'Woodstock's seventy miles away,' said Raggett.

'We'll give ourselves three days. That's hardly twenty miles a day. We'll eat and sleep each night at an inn.'

'But we can get the mail coach to Oxford and hire a cab to get to Woodstock. Two days at most.'

'We'll walk,' Scrivener repeated stubbornly. 'I'm used to walking.'

'Very well,' he said. 'But I don't like it.'

Scrivener noticed Raggett's strange smile as he spoke. But he couldn't understand other people's sense of humour, perhaps because he had none of his own, so he forgot about it. This was the start of his plan to be a poet. And Coleridge would help him. But not in the way that either he or Coleridge would expect. He would not reread 'The Ancient Mariner'. He would go to Woodstock, read Captain Shelvocke's book, find out about the joys and privations of the seaman's life, discover what made Hatley so vicious as to kill God's magnificent creature who did him no harm and put them together to make his own poem which nobody could say was an imitation because it was so long ago that he read the original. But when he had finished and then at last read Coleridge's poem closely, he could compare the two, take what he needed and reject the rest. And if ever Coleridge read his poem, he might even learn something from him.

The master as mentor, the mentor as master.

Besides, it would keep him away from Bengeo and his hateful uncle.

*

Scrivener woke to the fifth day in the sickbay feeling better. The doctor had not given him laudanum. He ate all his porridge and asked for bread and butter. Then he thought rationally of the previous day.

Why was he calling this a quest? It wasn't like finding the Holy Grail. He'd merely read a few poems he liked. He wanted to be a poet and thought he could learn from them. No more than that. Nothing noble at all.

But something stubborn in him wouldn't go away. *Why should I forget my yearning for greatness? The last week tells me nothing is impossible.* A Greek word he often heard, especially in Aristotle on Greek tragedy, was *hubris*. Was he being hubristic? 'Pride comes before a fall', a maxim his uncle was fond of reminding him.

Why should it? he thought.

He turned to the *Aeneid* and for an hour he struggled to start the translation. He gave up and dozed.

*

He was woken by a voice saying, 'I've brought you something.'

He looked up. Raggett stood there. 'You look better,' he said.

'I feel it,' Scrivener replied.

'Anyway, you asked for this and I got it.' He handed over a book with the unexpected title *Sybilline Leaves.*

'This isn't it. I wanted *Lyrical Ballads.*'

'I asked around. I was told that if you wanted "The Ancient Mariner", *Lyrical Ballads* is no use to you. But these are all Coleridge's poems, with his latest attempt to finish the "Mariner".'

'Well, thank you,' said Scrivener doubtfully.

'You'll be surprised at who gave it to me,' said Raggett.

'Who?'

'Copperthwaite-Smirke. He says you can keep it for as long as you like. No, that's not quite true. As long as *I* like.'

'I'm amazed,' said Scrivener. 'But I won't be thanking him.'

He placed the book on the table, wondering how he would resist the temptation to open it. Raggett was holding another book. 'What's that?' he asked.

'You'll thank me for this,' said Raggett. 'It's to cheer you up while you're in here. It's mine, so you don't have to thank our rich friend. It'll freeze your blood and turn your hair white.'

He placed he book next to the others. *The Monk* by Matthew Lewis.

'About walking to Woodstock,' he said. 'Have you changed your mind?'

'No,' said Scrivener firmly. 'I need to see more of the country I live in. The villages, the towns, different places, new people.'

Last week such an ambition was unthinkable. Villages, towns and especially new people were items he kept away from.

'I've seen all I need of those,' said Raggett. 'A coach takes two days. We'll be walking for nearer five. Don't expect me to sympathise when it all goes wrong.'

When Scrivener replied there was steel in his voice. 'We shall walk fast. Don't worry about me. I feel fitter than I've ever been.'

'Very well,' said Raggett. 'Term ends on Thursday. We'll leave early on Friday. I wrote to the headmaster last night, so you're expected at the school.'

'Thank you,' Scrivener replied.

Before Raggett reached the door he turned and said, 'I think you're mad. If anything goes wrong I'll never forgive you.'

When Raggett had gone, Scrivener was tempted to open *Sybilline Leaves*. But he had to find some willpower. He called the nurse. She took his request for string with bad grace but brought a length a few minutes later.

He tied it over the book as if it were a parcel, pulled it tight and knotted it so securely that it would need a knife to cut it. When he was satisfied he put it on the table, picked up his translation again and stared at it until dusk fell. Then he plumped up his pillows and tried to sleep. But he couldn't, so he lit his candle and started reading *The Monk*. An hour later he was too frightened to continue but frantic to see what happened next. With a huge effort of will he closed the book, blew the candle out and slept at once.

A line from the *Aeneid* came into his mind. *I do not trust the Greeks, even when they bring gifts.* Why should he suddenly think of that?

*

When he woke he felt strong and well. He had porridge, toast and, daringly, a boiled egg. The doctor arrived, took his pulse, listened to his chest and felt his forehead. Then he said, 'You've shaken off your fever already. You must have strong recuperative powers. I'll release you tomorrow.'

Strong recuperative powers? Who'd have thought it? He really could walk to Woodstock. Raggett was wrong. This great adventure must never be forgotten. He would write an account of it for all to see.

Then he opened *The Monk* again.

After half an hour of enjoyable terror, Scrivener heard the nurse talking. 'Mr Scrivener, you have a visitor. A foreign gentleman. Do you want to see him?'

Scrivener replied, 'Well, yes, I suppose so.'

She turned and beckoned. And in walked the stranger whose name he had not caught.

Chapter 14

Cecilia and Giulia

Monreale, April 1824

Nectar, nectar everywhere, but not a drop to drink
Of pure and purifying streams that in the spirit sink –
Beams and flashes everywhere but ne'er a little blink
Of Reason's strong and sturdy light, which leads the heart
  to think.

—'On the Same', Sara Coleridge

April was nearly over. The oranges were picked and Giulia had put her ladder away until summer. Evening came and a weak sun made everything, Cecilia thought, somehow sad, elegiac. She stood at a drawing-room window looking out over the orange orchard and beyond Monte Caputo to Monreale. The still-visible towers of the cathedral made her think of lighthouses and the sea over which Samuele, never absent from her mind, had set sail for Naples just over a month ago. She imagined she saw Salvatore driving the trap up the hill, with Samuele secretly smiling about the wonderful tidings he brought. Sometimes she even imagined he had a companion, a dark silhouette with an outline still familiar.

But the illusion vanished. She turned from the window and, as always, felt alienated by the high ceilings and cold marble floors and the meretricious artworks with which Bernardo had filled the villa. As did the presence of Bernardo himself, joyless, deadening but persistent.

She had become aware of the secret noises of an empty house. Wooden joists creaking, the patter of birds' feet and soft mewings of fledglings in nests under the eaves, sounds drowned out when rain drummed on the roofs. And sometimes she imagined footfalls on the landing and covered her head under the bedsheets lest Bernardo, unwilling to stay in his grave, was back to claim his marital rights.

The servants obeyed her orders sullenly, even when she mellowed them into requests, as if Bernardo would appear and berate them for imagined misdemeanours. Her mildness and courtesy confused them.

For twenty years Cecilia, whatever she had told Samuele, had chafed under Bernardo's mastery. Now she should be revelling in her freedom, not a released prisoner but a gazelle let out of its cage. But, alone in bed, night thoughts entered her soul. Though dead, Bernardo still tried to make her think as he had thought.

She tried to read but failed. She tried to write down her memories about those precious meetings with her lost English genius. But now they seemed wrapped in swirling fog and she could not find words for them. What she had told Samuele was fresh, sharply relived experience. Now it all seemed elusive, undefined, the words slippery.

If only Samuele would write. How long would a letter take to arrive? What if his letters never arrived because the mail ship foundered in a storm? But which was worse, a lost letter telling of wonders, or a received letter full of disappointment?

*

A small, shy voice with the familiar *palermitano* accent interrupted her thoughts.

'Signora?'

She turned. Giulia. 'What do you want?' she said brusquely. 'I did not send for you.'

'Forgive me, signora. But since Samuele left us, we have seen you become sad, as if the person we knew had left us.'

Cecilia was angry. 'So your colleagues deputed you to find out things I would never tell anyone. I advise you all to mind your own business.'

'No, signora,' said Giulia. 'We want to help you.'

'You can do that best by doing what I pay you to do.'

'Signora, we want to do more than that.'

Cecilia felt Bernardo's presence very close now. It made her heart harden. She found herself saying what Bernardo would have said.

'You are transparent, girl. I don't believe that you speak for the servants. You have come here of your own accord to ingratiate yourself with me. It's obvious that you've set your cap at my son. You hope to ensnare the heir of my late husband's estates by marrying him and stealing our wealth for yourself. Well, you won't succeed because I am dismissing you. You'll neither see nor hear of my son again. I won't let you entrap him. Your rough working hands and ugly, uneducated voice will never contaminate him.'

She knew she was harsh. Well, why not? She was mistress of the house and everything was hers now.

'Go,' she said.

Giulia turned and ran out of the room. Cecilia heard her sobs as she passed down the corridor.

For a moment she was pleased and felt Bernardo's approval. Then he seemed to fade away and she thought, with sudden clarity. *What were you but a working girl?*

'I was the prima donna of an opera company,' she replied aloud. 'A person of consequence.'

Yes, but before that?

Yes, what was she before that? A working girl from a low-born family living in a slum tenement in Rome. Her singing voice alone distinguished her from the masses. Without it, where would she be now? Who was she to lecture Giulia?

And had she never tried to entrap a man? Not a question she would answer, even to herself.

Bernardo had gone. Now she could speak with her own voice. She made up her mind.

She opened the door, left the drawing room and followed Giulia's steps, crying as she went, 'Giulia, Giulia! Come back. I am sorry.'

*

That night, Cecilia slept deeply and dreamlessly. She was content. She had found Giulia in the servant's quarters, still sobbing. She had called her out, taken her aside and told her that she was distraught by what she'd said. She had remembered her past and found she had no right to say those words.

She looked closely at Giulia almost for the first time and saw a frank, open face with clear eyes despite the tear stains, and realised she was beautiful. As mistress of the house it was her duty to Giulia to remind her she was a servant because that was the purpose God had prescribed for her. So a servant she would remain. But was that really true? Was Bernardo's influence waning? Yes.

The bed was suddenly not so cold. The wooden joists creaked and the footfalls on the landing were less.

Bernardo's ghost was beginning to understand that there might be no place here for him.

PART III

Chapter 15

Dream

...my own loud scream
Had waked me from the fiendish dream,
O'ercome with sufferings strange and wild,
I wept as I had been a child.

—'The Pains of Sleep', Samuel Taylor Coleridge

Afterwards, Coleridge remembered nothing of his tear-blinded progress back to Moreton House following the disappearance of Hartley. But outside the house he was aware of someone standing close to him.

'Hartley?' he breathed. 'My dear boy, you have returned.'

But it was not Hartley. It was the revenant.

He angrily took his door key from his pocket. 'Avaunt, evil spirit! What do you want with me?' he cried and shook the key at him threateningly. The revenant's lips curled into an enigmatic smile. Coleridge unlocked the door. Before opening it he turned back. The spectre was gone.

'Yes, what *does* he want with me?' A shiver spread a cold tremor as he closed the door behind him.

Mrs Gillman saw him. 'Oh, you poor man,' she cried. 'What has happened?'

For answer, Coleridge wept. 'Hartley' was all he could say. Mrs Gillman divined what had happened at once. 'I knew he would,' she said. 'Look, you're in no state to stay with Derwent tonight. John and I will take your watch and you must rest in your room alone. I can't bear to think of you watching over one son who may die on the same day as another has deserted you.'

She thought, though did not say, *And if you have any laudanum then you must take it if it brings you peace. We won't blame you.*

'Thank you,' said Coleridge. 'You are a good friend.'

He allowed her to guide him up the stairs to his room and opened the door. He saw his well-made bed waiting for him and felt again the strength of the protection John and Ann Gillman had given him.

'Can I get you anything?' Ann Gillman asked.

'Thank you, no,' Coleridge replied. 'You have been so good to me. But now I just need to rest quietly.'

He waited until her footsteps died away downstairs, then opened a drawer and took out the bottle of laudanum he had bought at Dunn's the day before. He opened it, lay on his bed and let his mind empty. He breathed deeply. The silence in his brain was like kneeling in a cathedral.

It was broken by more thoughts about the Gillmans. He owed them so much. They were weaning him off opium, giving him space to find peace which might ease him into freedom and lose the self-regarding pleasure of breaking rules and not being found out. Only yesterday he had been on the lookout for spies. He knew there were none, but he enjoyed the slight *frisson* of danger.

Now, he realised, things were changing. First, came a night which recreated crises that were his own fault. And now a day which made his worst fears real. Henceforth opium must be an occasional remedy, not an uncontrollable obsession. He blessed the good doctor and his dear wife.

He opened the bottle and counted out eight drops. For him, a small amount. He took them and waited. The familiar feeling of calm and profound peace. Then the brown cloud descended and the dream began.

He had been here before.

*

His dream mind expects an inspirational vision. Perhaps the next stage of 'Kubla', lost so long ago. But another vision appears, horribly familiar. A dark figure, which clarifies itself into the shape of a woman. Shadows hide her face but nothing hides her malevolence. She leans forward and stares hypnotically into his eyes. He is abjectly terrified. Yet though she radiates horror she is extremely beautiful. But such beauty chills the soul. A line he once wrote echoes in his mind.

Desire with loathing strangely mixed.

The deathly form reaches out a hand. He knows what will happen. It has happened before.

The fingers are hooked. The nails are long. They move inexorably towards his right eye. She intends to gouge it out. He screams; a great howl of terror.

*

The cry woke Dr and Mrs Gillman. They looked at each other, until Dr Gillman said, 'He is tranced. Leave him. Waking will do more harm than good.'

*

Mercifully, the vision vanishes. He is calm. Until, inevitably, another vision takes its place.

He becomes his Old Navigator, the damned man staring at the spectral ship.

Is that a DEATH, and are there two?

Is DEATH that woman's mate?

Her lips were red, *her* looks were free,

Her locks were yellow as gold:

Her skin was as white as leprosy.

The Night-mare LIFE-IN-DEATH was she,

Who thicks man's blood with cold.

But a new howl freezes on his lips as the second vision fades.
Now he remembers his Geraldine.

I guess, 'twas frightful there to see

A lady so richly clad as she—

Beautiful exceedingly!

But in Christabel's room her gown drops to the floor.

Behold! her bosom and half her side—

A sight to dream of, not to tell!

Oh shield her! shield sweet Christabel!

'A sight to dream of'. *Is it a dream of inexpressible loveliness?*
He has wilfully blanked out the reality, ever since Byron insisted
'Christabel' should be published. But now he remembers when he
knew that it was not Christabel in danger but he himself. And straight
away, the revenant comes abruptly and strangely into his mind.

Why should he call him 'the revenant'? Revenant – the one
who returns. But from what?

There is something of himself in the revenant's face. And
more. He sees another face, which enters his mind with sharp and
dreadful guilt.

Then he wakes, trembling.

*

It took time to collect himself and think. These were images which
haunted him, struck at his soul, and constantly returned to torture him.

He remembered his encounters in brothels in his youth. He
recalled a terrifying dream at university, in which he was pursued through the streets of Cambridge by a half-dressed harlot
in white. He told himself he found pleasure in whorehouses. And

sometimes he did. But more often he endured failure, humiliation and ridicule, and was filled with that familiar guilt. *Desire with loathing strangely mixed.* And then he remembered another line in the poem:

Life-stifling fear, soul-shifting shame.

Yes, that was it. Fear of these images, of being unmanned, emasculated, fears of the scourge of the Vampire, of the Life-in-Death consuming the soul. Yet with them was the shame of the cruel inadequacy of how he had treated the women in his life: Sarah, his wife, estranged, ignored, excluded, deserted. He had even made her drop the 'h' at the end of her name because he thought 'Sara' sounded more literary. His children: Hartley gone, Derwent perhaps dying, Sara, his daughter, beautiful, loved, who he had not seen for nearly twenty years until a visit the previous year let him see a mind which he could have moulded, because everything she said, everything she did, showed that she had wanted him to.

Why was the revenant here? What was he saying? Why should Cecilia Bertozzi be part of his dream, when had had told nobody about what happened in Siracusa? He had hoped it was forgotten, of no consequence.

But now he remembered what he had written about Cecilia, for his eyes only. In 1808, four years after the event, she had suddenly entered his mind from nowhere and he had written in his notebooks more about the affair than he had ever thought before.

It was long past midnight. He got out of bed, lit a candle and shuffled to his bookshelves. The notebooks were placed in order on the bottom shelf. He looked for the year. Ah, here it was. He drew the book out of the stack, sat down and riffled through it.

Yes, here it was. His eye lit on the one word he wanted. *Siren.*

...the too fascinating Siren, against whose witcheries Ulysses' Wax would have proved but a Half-protection, poor Cecilia

Bertozzi. Yet neither her Beauty with all her power of employing it, neither heavenly Song, were as dangerous as her sincere vehemence of attachment to me, vehemence, for I trust it was not Depth of attachment – *for it was not mere* Passion, *& yet Heaven forbid! that I should call it* Love.

Ulysses' Wax. For just a moment he lost himself in the *Odyssey.* Ulysses and his men, adrift on the Mediterranean, approach an island. On it live the sirens, beautiful women with the wings of birds. (*Angels of Death*, Coleridge said to himself). They sing beautiful music, which enslaves sailors so their ships founder on the rocks. The sirens are surrounded by the bones and mouldering bodies of their victims.

*

For a moment, Coleridge becomes Ulysses. His mind works fast. He is on the ocean, sees the rocks, hears the breakers, knows the inevitable outcome. 'Take beeswax,' he cries to his crew. 'Stuff it in your ears so you can't hear their fatal song.' Though the men grumble, they obey. But Ulysses has not finished. 'I shall have no wax in my ears. Strap me to the mast so I cannot break free.'

Unquestioningly they obey their leader. He hears the sirens' song. It is truly irresistible. He must go to them even though he dies. But he forces himself to give the order. 'Steer away while you are still free,' he calls. So they do and soon the songs can be heard no more, Ulysses is free, the men remove the wax and the ship, with a following wind, sails on.

*

Yet, he remembered with piercing clarity, Cecilia's beauty would melt any amount of wax in his ears and there was no escape for him – except one. And he had just written it, immediately before he even mentioned sirens.

...gracious Heaven! when I call to mind that heavenly Vision of her Face, which came to me as the guardian Angel of my Innocence and Peace of mind, at Syracuse, at the bedside of the too fascinating Siren, against whose witcheries...

Yes, on the very point of surrender, the face of Asra, Sara Hutchinson, the woman for whom he had a hopeless love, already rejected, appeared. The unattainable woman to whom he was enslaved said 'No' and he had escaped the siren.

As he thought on this, twenty years after he had last seen Cecilia Bertozzi and sixteen after he wrote about her, he doubted his memory of the vision of Asra's face warning him off a sin which would offend her moralistic soul. He could not now reconstruct her face in his vision, though he remembered it in real life. This intervention seemed so convenient. Was the human frame even capable of such a wrench between desire and duty?

But if Cecilia was the siren, then she was also the Vampire, the Life-in-Death, the consumer of men's souls. And that seemed so very hard. Such a delightful creature to be the arch-enemy. She should be a blessing.

The horror of the dream and the comparisons he drew from it were still vivid. He had to empty his mind and fill it with good memories, while John and Ann kept watch over his stricken son.

Chapter 16

Lamb

London, April 1824

Complaint, be gone! and, ominous thoughts, away
Take up, my Song, take up a merrier strain;
For yet again, and lo! from Avon's vales,
Another Minstrel cometh. Youth endear'd
God and good Angels guide thee on thy road
And gentler fortunes wait the friends I love!
—'Lines addressed, from London, to Sara and STC at Bristol,
1796', Charles Lamb

Samuele was in England, and in a mental fog. Now he was here, what would he actually do?

During his wearisome journey he had thought it would unfold itself when he stepped ashore. But it refused to. A month of jolting coaches, squalid inns, bad food, flea-ridden beds and useless longing for Giulia had jumbled his brain.

When the ship from Calais had reached Dover, he'd caught a London-bound coach, intending to find the bank which handled Bernardo's English transactions and present his letters of credit.

Where now? He was lost in a vast and frightening city and felt like a cobblestone that feet trod on and wheels rolled over. But somewhere out of the depths of his mind came a solution. His mother had told him a lot of inconsequent scraps about Coleridge and one of them was that he went to school in London wearing a blue coat and yellow stockings.

The coach driver took the passengers' luggage off the coach and dumped it on the ground. His worst struggle was with Samuele's trunk. He finally freed it, but it fell to the ground with a massive thud, and Samuele in dismay saw a big split in the wood. The coach driver mouthed a curse.

The other passengers had dispersed. There were no obliging porters. Samuele would have to fend for himself.

A man walked past. Daringly, Samuele spoke to him. 'Excuse me, sir,' he said. 'Do you know a school where pupils wear blue coats?'

The man didn't even pause. 'The Bluecoat school.'

'How do I get there?' he said.

'Hail a cab,' the man said.

Good advice. Samuele saw a little cart with a driver, one horse and two empty seats and presumed it was a hackney carriage. He stepped into the filthy road and held out his arm.

The driver stopped. 'Where to, mate?' he said.

'Where is the Bluecoat school?' Samuele asked.

'Newgate Street.'

'Thank you. Take me to an inn nearby where I can get a bed for the night.'

'I know the very place,' the driver said.

Twenty minutes later they drew up at The Salutation and Cat.

*

The tavern was noisy with the tipsy voices of men in rough working clothes and women sitting in corners drinking gin, except for one, standing behind the bar and giving as good as she got from the men clamouring for more drink.

Samuele pushed his way through to the front. The woman saw him, ignored the shouting drinkers and said, 'What do you want, young man?'

'Can I have a room for the night?' Samuele said.

'Of course you can,' she said. 'Clean, quiet and a tanner a night.' She saw his mystified face and added, 'That's sixpence to you.'

'Thank you,' said Samuele. He still had enough money. But tomorrow he must find the bank. 'I have a trunk,' he said. 'The driver left it at the entrance.'

'That's all right,' said the woman. In a loud voice which made him jump, she shouted, 'Billy!'

'Yes, Mrs Elkins,' came a voice from the other end of the bar.

'Get yourself here and take the gentleman's trunk upstairs to room two.'

'Yes, Mrs Elkins.'

A weedy youth about Samuele's age appeared. Samuele felt guilty about an under-nourished boy doing something he could do himself. He nearly said, 'No, I'll do it,' when Billy picked up the trunk as though it were a sack of feathers and disappeared up the stairs.

'Get rid of that clumsy thing,' said Mrs Elkins. 'Look at the crack in it. Buy yourself a proper leather case with a handle so you can carry it on a journey. Now, what would you like to drink?'

Not beer, thought Samuele. It smelt horrible.

'You look worn out,' said the landlady. 'Rum and ginger ale. That'll perk you up.'

Samuele had never drunk rum. But he had come here for new experiences so he would risk it.

'It's on the 'ouse,' said Mrs Elkins. 'What about something to eat?'

'Please,' said Samuele.

'Billy!' she shouted again. 'Fetch the gentleman bread and cheese and a cut o' cold lamb.'

'Yes, Mrs Elkins.' Billy was gone again.

'Eat in the snug where it's quieter,' said the landlady.

The snug was a haven of peace. Mrs Elkins brought him food and a huge tot of rum in a balloon-shaped glass. Samuele took a sip and felt a sudden rush of alcohol. Compared to this, Marsala was like mother's milk. He spluttered, wiped his lips and took another sip. Yes, this one slipped down easily and he felt revived already.

Mrs Elkins stood over him proprietorially. 'May I make so bold as to ask where you have come from, sir?' she asked.

'Sicily,' said Samuele.

'Well, I've never been north of Barnet nor south of Southwark myself and I don't want to. London's enough for me. But I remember Mr Elkins, God rest his soul, talking about Sicily. He was in the navy in the war and his ship fetched up in a port there once. What was its name? Ah, I remember. It was Siracusa.'

Suddenly, Samuele was all attention.

'Yes, they'd chased a Frenchy boat across the Mediterranean. The Frenchies made for Siracusa and Mr Elkins's ship followed 'em. They cornered the buggers in the harbour to sink 'em. But they couldn't. Something about the law of the sea. The mayor came down to see what was going on but he was bloody useless. So then they found some English poet to sort it all out, which he did, so everyone was happy. A *poet*! Well, I ask you! Mr Elkins said it was the rummest do he'd ever known.'

After his surprise faded, Samuele had a wonderful feeling of contentment. It was a sign. All would be well.

The bread, cheese and cold lamb were like a banquet. The rum and ginger made him pleasantly light-headed. He nearly asked for another. But he mustn't fall down the stairs before he got into bed.

*

The room was not of the cleanest, but he had slept in worse. At least it was comfortable. He slept long and well and was only woken by the sound of horses' hooves, rumbling wheels and men shouting outside.

What should he do today? First, find the bank. And then? Ask Mrs Elkins. She'd told him one extraordinary thing and maybe she might tell him more.

He dressed and went downstairs. The landlady was waiting. 'I've got porridge in the pot,' she said. 'Have a bowl if you like. And I'll bring a mug of tea.'

'I'd like that very much, Mrs Elkins,' he replied.

The porridge and very strong tea arrived. As he ate and drank, he asked, 'How far away is the Bluecoat school?'

'You mean Christ's Hospital,' she said. 'You can't miss it. We see a lot of them, the masters out for a quick break and the old pupils when they stay in London. They all come to the Sally Cat.'

Greatly daring, he asked, 'Do you remember a Mr Coleridge coming here?'

To his surprise, she burst out laughing. 'What, Sam? He used to come 'ere when I was your age. After he left school he was often in London and stayed here in the room you've just slept in. His best friend was Charles Lamb and they had great nights drinking and getting tipsy. He's not been here for many a year, but once seen, never forgotten. A lot of people came to see them here. They was all poets and writers and I didn't understand a word they said, but it was lovely listening to 'em. We still see Mr Lamb here sometimes. Why do you ask?'

Her question pleased him. Explaining why he was here would be a good rehearsal for when he told people a lot more suspicious than Mrs Elkins.

'It's because of my father. When Mr Coleridge was in Sicily they became friends and my father admired his poetry. Now he's getting old he wants to write a book about him so that people in Italy can know more about him, so he'll be as famous as Lord

Byron. He's too old to travel so he's sent me to find out all I can about him. What you've just told me will be very useful.'

'Pleased to be of help.'

'I'd like to see Mr Lamb. Where can I find him?'

'He used to live near here. But he moved to Covent Garden with his sister. I've heard they've moved again. I don't know where but be sure it's in London. He can't abide the country. He's a real townie, like me. They'll know where he is at the school.'

'I'll go there and ask,' said Samuele. 'May I have the room again tonight?'

'Course you can,' said Mrs Elkins.

*

Samuele sat on his bed and considered. Today he would find the bank. Then he would go to Christ's Hospital. He had better write a note saying who he was and why he was there. Then he must find more about Mr Lamb. If they spent nights getting drunk in the Sally Cat he might be a mine of information.

He opened his trunk and took out the letter of credit. The bank was in Gracechurch Street.

He went downstairs and asked Mrs Elkins for pen and paper. Then he wrote a note saying what he wanted, folded the paper, addressed it and she sealed it for him with wax. He asked her where Gracechurch Street was.

'It's a nice little walk from here, she said. 'Go down Newgate Street, then straight on past Cheapside, Poultry and Cornhill and you're be there. Easy.'

Yes, it was. The letter of credit was accepted and he arranged to come for money whenever he was in London. He took enough to last a fortnight, walked back to Newgate Street and looked for Christ's Hospital.

He couldn't miss it. He found the porters' lodge and gave the letter to the man there.

'I'll make sure the headmaster gets it,' he said. 'Come back in four days.'

Four days. Today was Monday. What to do now to keep the quest going? Obvious. Go to Cambridge. Coleridge would be remembered there.

He found a shop selling leather goods and bought a large carrying case with a proper handle and a leather satchel for travelling light.

Outside the shop he hailed a cab back to the Salutation and Cat. 'Where do coaches for Cambridge go from?' he asked the driver.

'La Belle Sauvage on Ludgate Hill,' was the answer. 'When are you going?'

'Tomorrow.'

'I can take you to there in time to catch the midday coach.'

'Thank you.'

'I'll meet you outside the Sally at ten tomorrow.'

'Thank you again.'

'No need. I don't miss guaranteed fares.'

Samuele couldn't believe how well everything seemed to be going.

Chapter 17

Cambridge

Lo! Through the dusky silence of the groves,
Through vales irriguous, and thro' green retreats,
With languid murmur creeps the placid stream
And works its secret way.
— 'A Wish: Written in Jesus Wood, 10th February, 1792',
Samuel Taylor Coleridge

Samuele paid Mrs Elkins in advance for the room again on Friday night. On Tuesday morning the cab driver was waiting and drove him to Ludgate Hill through London's filthy streets and cacophonous noise. The coach left La Belle Sauvage at midday and he had an inside seat. Rain sheeted down all afternoon and he was cold and miserable. But near Cambridge, the rain stopped, the darkening sky was clear and as they passed through Grantchester his spirits rose.

It was already evening when the coach pulled up outside an inn called the Blue Boar. Samuele reserved a place on a return coach on Thursday night, giving him two full days in Cambridge. The Blue Boar was full so he slung his satchel over his shoulder and stepped out into Trinity Street.

Where to go now?

He walked on northwards and crossed the river. And then, on his left, opposite yet another college, he saw an intriguing inn sign. *The Pickerel.*

He entered it and asked the man behind the bar if there was a room free. There was, so he paid for two nights. Then he asked, 'What is a pickerel?

'A young pike. Eels and pickerels, that's what they like round here. Straight out of the river.'

'Can I have dinner here?'

'Of course. I recommend the pickerel. Anything to drink?'

It had been a tiring day. He remembered Mrs Elkins's choice. 'Yes. A rum and ginger ale, please.'

*

The pickerel, he thought, was tasteless. But the rum and ginger was like nectar. *And drunk the milk of Paradise*. That summed it up. The room was airy, the bed was comfortable. He slept at once.

When morning came, he wondered what to do next. He'd had a vague idea that people would flock to him with reminiscences of Coleridge. He asked the man serving breakfast how to get to Jesus and the man, smiling as if this wasn't the first time he'd been asked, fetched him a map.

Breakfast finished, he stepped out into the street. He now knew the building opposite was Magdalene College. Map open, he walked down Magdalene Street, then Bridge Street over the Cam. He saw that after crossing the river he would pass the end of Jesus Lane. Jesus College was further down. He took a few steps, then stopped. He was not ready for this.

He passed St John's College on the right, and went on into Sidney Street, past little Sidney Sussex College, Christ's College and on and on until he reached Emmanuel. He was taking pleasure in passing beautiful buildings but they offered him nothing in return.

He turned back the way he came. By Christ's College, he turned right into Christ's Lane. *Anything to postpone Jesus*, a voice in his mind said. 'Nonsense,' he replied aloud, but he knew it was true.

Before him lay a wide expanse of green. Christ's Pieces. He sat on a bench to consider.

Today was Wednesday. The reply from the Bluecoat school was due on Friday. Two full days to find so much. But so far, nothing, and he feared this was how it would be tomorrow as well. He wished now he had not booked the Thursday night coach to London. Should he go back this afternoon?

No, said the voice. *Stay here. You never know.*

He was hungry. He stood up and set off back into Sidney Street. He saw Market Street opposite and, sensing food, crossed the road, found a stall selling pies, chose a chicken pie and wondered where to eat it.

He left the market, walked down Trinity Lane, past Gonville & Caius College and Trinity Hall and out into Garret Hostel Lane and the river. To his left were the famous Backs. He sat down on a bench by the river, took a huge and delicious bite and realised this beautiful place was beginning to weave a spell on him.

Now he was prepared to go to Jesus College.

*

In Jesus Lane, the atmosphere changed, as if he had crossed an invisible portal into the countryside. Trees and grassy acres with a stream running through, and then, in lonely isolation, Jesus College. He hastened on. He came to iron gates standing open and looked down at what was marked on his map as the Chimney, the stone path between brick walls leading to the college. At the end was the gatehouse, brick, imposing, forbidding, with a crenellated tower, which, for all Samuele knew, hid bowmen poised to rain arrows down on him. Beyond the gatehouse, he had a tantalising glimpse of green and a hint of another brick building. He would never see further, he was sure.

The busy town centre and its crowded jumble of colleges, chapels and shops seemed far away. He felt that here was a college keeping its distance, self-sufficient, with no need for anyone else. The silence was profound, almost uncanny.

He took three steps down the stone path. Then he stopped. He had no idea what lay behind that forbidding building but he feared it might not be friendly.

Besides, what would he say? He might be ejected at once. He would go back to the Pickerel and think again.

*

Next morning dawned. The image of the lonely fortress in the fields haunted him. He did not sleep until the many clocks all over the town struck three. Even then, his slumber was fitful and disturbed. It was already light when deep and dreamless sleep took him and he slept until ten o'clock.

The day was half gone already and he had done nothing. He would sit downstairs in the snug reading more Coleridge until it was time for the coach.

At last he roused himself, dressed and went downstairs. The snug was empty. He sat down in an armchair and dozed off again.

He was woken by voices. Men laughing and shouting. They seemed to be playing some sort of game.

Then he heard another voice. A young man's. There seemed to be a transaction going on between the owner of the voice and the man behind the bar. Then there was quiet. He stood up and stepped into the bar. He was just in time to see the departing figure of the young man, a nearly full tankard of beer left on the table and the barman lifting it up and swallowing the contents in two gulps.

An odd little scene but nothing to do with him. He returned to the snug.

Half an hour later, he needed fresh air. He had enjoyed the river yesterday. Why not see what it was like out of town towards the east and the flat lands? Besides, he would be on his own and able to think clearly.

*

The fresh breeze was invigorating. He stepped out eagerly and felt as if he could carry on walking to the end of the world.

Then he stopped. An extraordinary sight. Five big men assaulting one small man. He watched them tear off his breeches and heard them laughing as they tipped him into the river. One of them trailed the man's breeches in the water and draped them over a bush. As the victim struggled back on the bank the five attackers walked on, still laughing.

Samuele was appalled. The guilty five walked straight past him. The victim was struggling to put on his sodden trousers. He was crying.

Samuele hurried to him. 'You poor man,' he said. 'Let me help you.'

Chapter 18

Return

I have been laughing, I have been carousing,
Drinking late, sitting late, with my bosom cronies,
All, all are gone, the old familiar faces.
 —'The Old Familiar Faces', Charles Lamb

Samuele walked quickly from Jesus College and was well in time for the London coach. He slept little. As the coach jolted its way through the night, his thoughts turned to Mr Scrivener. This had been an extraordinary and perhaps significant meeting. To first see the one person in all Cambridge who might help him after almost drowning made the coincidence of Mr Elkins and Siracusa trivial. But Scrivener needed warmth, silence and sleep, so he had told him his name and then left. When his business in London was finished, he would come back to Cambridge and they would talk.

One thing pleased him. Jesus College was not a lonely fortress. It was a welcoming place. He had met a sympathetic, sensible man. He looked forward to visiting the college again.

The coach reached the Belle Sauvage at nine on a cool morning with high cloud and sunshine. He was quickly on the street and hailing a cab to the Sally Cat.

Mrs Elkins again gave him porridge and tea, which revived him enough to face the Bluecoat school.

At the porter's lodge, he was told he was expected and welcome, that he would see the headmaster first and be shown round the school, see essays and Greek and Latin verse in Coleridge's flowing handwriting, and be introduced to masters who knew the poet personally, including some who had been pupils with him. And some might want to continue the conversation in the Sally Cat in the evening.

So began a bewildering day. First, a tour of this extraordinary school. Samuele was bemused by the pupils in their belted blue coats, blue knee-breeches and yellow stockings. At first he felt cowed by the severe-looking masters in their black gowns like giant bats. But as the day wore on he began to enjoy himself. Information about Coleridge's schooldays came out, including one story he would never forget: the swim over the New River which gave Coleridge a chill, rheumatic fever and an introduction to opium. When someone mentioned Charles Lamb, the masters became talkative and happy.

'Oh yes, Samuele, you must meet Charles,' said Mr Prothero. Samuele had identified him as a mathematician. 'He and Sam were thick as thieves.'

'Indeed,' said Mr Blenkinsop, who taught Classics. 'Their friendship still rings down the ages. It was certainly a significant association.'

'What Charles can't tell you about Sam isn't worth knowing,' said Mr Jenkins, teacher of music.

'Tell you what,' said a gnarled old man whose name and subject Samuele had not registered. 'Let's meet up in the old Sally this evening, have a few potions and then go up to Islington to beard Charles in his den.'

'I disagree,' said another, who, Samuele had gathered, taught science, didn't believe that Joseph Priestley discovered oxygen and still taught the phlogiston theory, something he was proud of.

'Let's go to Colebrook Row, fetch him out and bring him back to the Sally. He likes a drop of stingo.'

'He's getting old. It's a mile to Islington. He'd never make it,' said someone.

'A few pints inside him and he'd certainly never make it back,' said another.

'His sister would be furious,' said a third. 'We can't have that.'

'We'll put him in a cab,' said Mr Prothero.

'Samuele can keep him company, and introduce himself,' said Mr Jenkins.

So it was decided. Except for those masters on duty that night, anyone could join the party. Six had no duties and decided to meet outside the Sally at eight – outside, because they did not want to go to Charles's house tipsy already.

*

After eating toasted cheese, which Mrs Elkins said was Mr Coleridge's favourite, Samuele went outside at eight. They were all waiting. He followed them to the end of Newgate Street, into Aldersgate, then up Goswell Road, across the City Road and into Colebrook Row, Islington.

Samuele was surprised. Mrs Elkins said that Lamb could only be happy in London. But in the gathering dusk Colebrook Row seemed quite countrified, with trees and fields. And it was so quiet.

They stopped outside a detached white cottage. Mr Prothero hammered on the front door and shouted, 'Come on out, Charles. We've come to take you away.'

A small man opened the door. He wore a dark, tight suit and his thin legs ended in gaiters and straps. His head was topped with dark hair, now greying but still thick and curly. There was something noble but melancholy about his face and his eyes were watchful and penetrating. All this Samuele saw and understood, and he knew that this would be a significant meeting.

*

They explained to Lamb what they proposed. He was pleased, especially because Samuele was going with him in the cab. 'Thank God,' he said. 'At last, some decent company.'

The masters took this in good part. Indeed, Samuele thought they would be disappointed with anything else.

They flagged a cab down and Lamb and Samuele climbed in. Lamb said, 'Now, tell me who you are and why my friends are so insistent that I see you.'

Samuele once again rehearsed his reasons. When he had finished, Lamb said, 'A book about my dearest friend to add to his fame in Italy? A project in which I would be delighted to take part.'

Samuele felt a twinge of guilt and shame that his first request to this remarkable man was a lie. He hadn't thought of that before. Now it seemed obvious. He was in England under false pretences. Should he not be truthful about why he was here?

He knew he could not. He had his duty to his mother.

'Let me think how best I can help,' said Mr Lamb.

*

The session in the Sally Cat lasted an hour and a half. Much beer was consumed, though little of it by Samuele. He resisted the temptation to have a rum and ginger ale. The laughs were many. Charles Lamb was in his element, happy and talkative, and the strains of 'For he's a jolly good fellow' rang out several times, twice for Samuele. But the masters had been looking doubtfully at each other for half an hour already before Mr Prothero said, 'Gentlemen, we must leave. We must not enrage the headmaster.'

Outside, another hackney was hailed and Lamb and Samuele climbed on. There was silence for a moment, then Lamb said, 'Sam is my best and oldest friend. We've had periods of estrangement, but his generosity of spirit ensures that anger doesn't last for ever. We confide in each other, we can say what we like, because we know that what one says the other will understand. That's my experience. But many don't see things this way. They are the people you must see.'

Lamb paused. Then he said, 'I'll prepare an itinerary for you. It will mean long journeys. You'll be following in Sam's footsteps. You'll know England pretty well when you have finished.'

'Thank you,' said Samuele.

'When do you leave London?'

'There is someone I have to see in Cambridge the day after tomorrow,' said Samuele.

'Come to Colebrook Row tomorrow morning at eight o'clock,' said Lamb. 'I'm having a rare day free of that cursed counting house. I won't detain you more than two hours. By then, I will know who to see and the best order to see them in – and perhaps give you an idea of what to expect. Then you go to Cambridge.'

They had reached Colebrook Row. Lamb shook Samuele's hand heartily. 'Goodnight, Samuele. Till tomorrow, then.'

'Thank you,' said Samuele. 'I am very grateful to you, Mr Lamb.'

'Samuele, by the time we've completed our business, we'll be on familiar terms,' said Lamb. 'I think this will entitle you to call me Charles. Starting from tomorrow.'

And then he was gone. The front door opened and for an instant Samuele saw a woman in the doorway. Then the door closed and Samuele asked the driver to take him back to the Sally.

*

Next morning, he was up early, ate his porridge and set off to Colebrook Row. The air was fresh and he saw even more clearly how surroundings changed as he crossed City Road into Islington, quiet in a rural world. Perhaps Mr Lamb knew youth was gone and life must be slower.

He knocked on the door of the white cottage. A woman, the figure he had seen fleetingly last night, opened it. Lamb's sister

Mary. He knew her story. Mrs Elkins had told him last night as he drank his rum and ginger.

'Oh, 'tis a sad tale,' she said. 'Mr Lamb's sister has always been a bit funny in the head and she killed her own mother in a fit of rage thirty years ago now. She was sent to Bedlam and Mr Lamb only got her out after promising to look after her for the rest of their lives. And that's what he's done, because he's a good man and you can trust him. He's given up his life for his sister. He could have got married several times, but no, he put Mary first. I think he's a saint. But he likes his drink and a laugh. It was wonderful to see him here. It brought back old times.'

And now here she was, a small dark-haired, grey-eyed woman who welcomed him with a smile and took him to the dining room. Surely not a murderess. Samuele noticed the odd-looking marbled wallpaper, piles of books and small windows looking out at a mean back yard. Mr Lamb sat on a shabby horsehair chair. He rose as Samuele entered and motioned him towards a similar chair opposite.

'Good morning, Mr Lamb,' said Samuele.

'What did I tell you last night? I am Charles, you are Samuele. We are engaged on a project, a joint endeavour, and so we are on Christian name terms.'

'Yes, Mr... er... Charles.'

'That's better. Now it seems to me that you'll learn most of what you need to know by visiting three people. STC has lived in many places. Until he found Dr Gillman he was just a wanderer. Sometimes imposing himself on people's generosity. Sometimes accepting money because he has so little of his own. Sometimes half-crazed by opium, sometimes at his brilliant best. But he is always running away from his responsibilities to those who love him the most but whom he treats the worst.'

Samuele was silent.

'You think I've described a monster,' said Charles. 'That's the paradox. He's no monster. His secrets lie in the houses of three people. Thomas Poole in Nether Stowey, William Wordsworth at Rydal Mount and Robert Southey at Greta Hall. Poole lives alone. I think he feels forsaken. But in the other houses there are more people besides the master of the household who need to be heard. They may speak to you; those who won't may tell you more by their silence. At Rydal Mount you'll see Dorothy Wordsworth and Sara Hutchinson. At Greta Hall you'll meet Sarah, STC's wife, to whom he has done his greatest wrong, and Sara, his daughter. Estrangement and desertion. You'll hear conflicting opinions. You must make up your own mind. You will be lucky if any of the three Saras will speak to you. But if one does, listen well.' Charles smiled. 'That's a lot to take in. But you'll have plenty of time to think because there's much travelling ahead. The Quantocks to the west, and the Lakes to the north. A coach to Minehead takes five times as long as one to Cambridge. The journey to the Lakes is almost interminable.'

Samuele smiled. 'Charles,' he said. 'I'm sure I shall enjoy every hour.'

'And when you return, we'll talk over what you've seen. Till then, farewell and good luck.' Then he said as an afterthought, 'I'll write three introductory letters, one each to Poole, Wordsworth and Southey. They will say who you are and that you have my full confidence. My imprimatur should ensure a hearing, but then it's up to you.' He wrote for some minutes, blotted and folded each letter, then sealed them and imprinted the still hot wax with his signet ring.

'Here you are,' he said. 'Your passports.'

*

Samuele's path lay clear now. He packed his satchel, told Mrs Elkins that he wouldn't need his room that night but would for the next and that he would be away for some time but would be back eventually. Then a cab to Ludgate Hill and the Belle Sauvage, now almost a routine.

He secured a seat on the afternoon coach to Cambridge and asked at the office where to find a coach to Minehead, and also one to the Lakes.

Chapter 19

Samuele and Scrivener

Goodness is never perfect in one mind,
But widely o'er the earth in parcels spread:
As gold, in fragments to the streams consigned,
Was ne'er discovered in its mountain bed

—'To My Son', Sara Coleridge

The Cambridge coach left at one o'clock. They arrived at the Blue Boar at eight and Samuele set out to the Pickerel. His room was vacant. He ate pickerel again and slept well.

Next morning he was up early to Jesus Lane and down the Chimney to the oddly aloof college. He called at the porter's lodge and was answered by the helpful man he saw last time.

'Ah, good morning, sir. Very nice to see you back again so soon.'

Surprised and pleased, he said, 'I never had a chance to thank you for what you did for Mr Scrivener. I'm very grateful, and I've no doubt he is, too.'

'I wouldn't know, sir, I'm afraid. Mr Scrivener is ill and in the sickbay.'

'Oh dear. Can I see him?'

'I wouldn't like to say. But I'll send a colleague with you to see what the doctor thinks.'

'Thank you,' said Samuele. Ten minutes later he was standing by Mr Scrivener's bed.

*

So the stranger was not a hallucination. 'I know your name,' said the man by Scrivener's bed. 'And I told you mine but I'm not sure you heard me. You were exhausted and needed rest and I had a coach to catch. Now I've come back and I find you ill.'

'Is Mr Coleridge really your father?' asked Scrivener.

The stranger drew up a chair and began his story.

'My name is Samuele Gambino.' Then he recounted all that had happened from the day the corncrake frightened Benito until he came to England to search for the truth about a seemingly flawed person.

'I came to Cambridge hoping it would be full of people who remembered him. But it wasn't. Meeting you seemed too good to be true. I needed to speak to you.'

'Go on,' said Scrivener.

'I went to the Bluecoat school in London. I told the masters about my father's book. They said I should meet Charles Lamb, his best friend. Then they told me about things he did at school. And there's a strange coincidence between him and how we met.'

'Another coincidence?' said Scrivener. 'There are too many already.'

Samuele smiled. 'Like you, he was in the sickbay with a fever which he caught after he fell into a river. This developed into rheumatic fever. Yours, I'm told, was just a nasty chill. But they gave him laudanum and that's how he started on the opium.'

Scrivener said nothing about his own laudanum.

'When I say "fell into", that is not quite true,' Samuele continued. 'Some friends dared him to swim to the other side of the New River which flows past the school. So he jumped in fully clothed and got there. He was ill after that.'

'Friends?' said Scrivener disbelievingly.

'They were good friends. There was Bob Allen, Val le Grice, Tom Evans and especially Charles Lamb.'

Scrivener listened. The weight of coincidence. Did being Coleridge's disciple mean he had to relive his life in a minor, humdrum, way? Once again, he felt the disturbing guiding hand on his shoulder. But guiding him to what? A cold, sunless sea far away from land?

Samuele had not finished. 'And I wondered if you would be my companion on this search.'

Scrivener already had a search to make. Now he was being offered another. For a moment he envied this traveller, obviously rich, free to go where he wanted and meet new people. But why go with him? Samuele would find his father and what happened afterwards would be between them alone. He had no part in the great denouement. He would merely be an observer.

The only travel for him was a walk from here to Woodstock to look at a book, though he must make sure first that there wasn't a copy in the college library. His was a journey into how a poet thought, felt and wrote and whether he himself could understand these magical processes. And perhaps reach them himself. No. There was no comparison between the two searches.

'I'm sorry,' he said. 'But I have a duty to your father as well and I must see it through.'

'I'm sorry, too,' replied Samuele. 'What do you mean, your own duty?'

'I can't come with you because, except for vacations, I can't leave Cambridge. And my duty is to understand how your father wrote and what he can teach me. He'll be – though he'll never know it – my mentor.'

Samuele was silent for a moment. Then he said, 'George. May I call you George?'

'Of course, Samuele.'

'What you say is wonderful. We're both on pilgrimages. When they're finished we must meet and discuss what we've found.'

'I would like that,' Scrivener replied. Then something else occurred to him. 'Samuele,' he said. 'You told the schoolmasters that your father was writing a book. Yet you told me your father was dead. Why tell me the real reason for being here, but tell them something which isn't true?'

Samuele answered:

'The moment that his face I see,

I know the man who must hear me:

To him my tale I teach.'

'That's from "The Ancient Mariner",' said Scrivener.

'Of course,' said Samuele. 'It says what I think. But now I must go, to get ready for tomorrow's journey.'

'Where to?' asked Scrivener.

'Back to London. I met Charles Lamb yesterday and next I'll go to Somerset to see his friend Tom Poole and then to the Lakes to see Wordsworth and Southey.'

So Samuele would meet poets Scrivener could only dream of.

'We'll keep in touch,' said Samuele. 'Goodbye, my friend.'

Then he was gone and Scrivener was left with a troubled mind. Suddenly, he was afraid of 'The Ancient Mariner'.

Another thought troubled him. That day in the library. He hadn't found the book with 'Kubla' in it. The book had found him.

He shivered.

Chapter 20

Cecilia Waiting

Monreale, May 1824

Though I be young – ah well-a-day!
I cannot love these opening flowers
For they have each a kindly spray
To shelter them from suns and showers,
But I may pine, oppressed with grief,
Robbed of my dear protecting leaf

—'Phantasmion', Sara Coleridge

No letter arrived from England. Sometimes at night, as joists and floorboards still creaked, dreadful fantasies filled Cecilia's mind. Samuele killed by bandits on lonely roads. The ship crossing the English Channel foundering and Samuele drowned. A footpad on London's streets striking at him with a knife.

Or worse. Perhaps an English girl would sweep him off his feet. She should have warned him about foreign girls on the lookout for innocent men. What if he stayed in England? That would be the cruellest betrayal of all.

No, she thought. *I know my son. He could never do that.*

A doubt welled up in her mind. Betrayal. Had she never betrayed anyone? Yes, perhaps she had. She had betrayed Bernardo into marrying her to avoid making the child she was sure she was carrying a bastard. She had been shocked when Samuele said Bernardo must have known. That made it worse.

She had seen the profound effect on Samuele of the breathless account of her encounter with Coleridge. She was reliving being twenty-one, swept off her feet by a force of nature. Old feelings were new again as if they happened yesterday. But she was a mature woman and only now, when her son was away, could she look dispassionately at those years and wonder not only about Coleridge and his failure but of herself: what she had done and why.

A voice broke into her reverie. 'Signora?' said Giulia.

Her son's future wife and lover? She still balked at accepting this. Was it a step too far for her, the mistress of the house, responsible for upholding the family honour?

Of course, they might be lovers already for all she knew. When Giulia was just a servant girl and orange picker Samuele would hardly boast about it. Even if he had, she would have dismissed it as *droit de seigneur.* That would be Bernardo's attitude and it was still hers.

Yet she couldn't deny that Giulia had become almost a friend, which would give her as much right to marry a rich man as she, a working girl, had to marry Bernardo. More so, because Giulia loved Samuele for himself.

So she must bite down these fears. Samuele betraying Giulia was as unlikely as it was horrible.

'Signora, I'm sorry to interrupt. I could see you were deep in thought.'

'My thoughts are my business, not yours.'

'I know, madam,' said Giulia. 'Only I have a question.'

'What is it?'

'Since Samuele went away you've been very good to me. The other servants are happy to share my work between them because they want the best for you. I'm happier than I can tell you.'

'Thank you, Giulia.'

'But soon the first oranges will appear. My grandfather Clario used to look after the orchard but the job became too much for him so I took over. I don't think you were even aware of it.'

Giulia was right, she wasn't. But to take on such responsibility without the permission of the master of the house was dangerous. If Bernardo had found out he would have stopped Clario's wages.

'I'm telling you this because I want to carry on with it,' Giulia continued. 'I love the shape of the year that the orange trees live through. They hibernate in winter, they come to life in spring, we tend them as if they are our children. Then we gather the fruit and quietly leave the trees to sleep soundly again. If only we could all live like the oranges.'

'I see what it means to you,' said Cecilia.

'I've done it for three years. But if I carry on with it, I will have less time to be with you.'

Cecilia was perplexed. What answer could she give? She decided she would be mistress of the house again. She was Italian, Giulia was Sicilian. That still mattered. 'There is a house rule. Any servants who cease doing their jobs are denied future wages. I cannot break that rule.'

She saw the tears starting in Giulia's eyes and partly relented. 'Except that Clario may keep his wages. In future, though, the rule still applies.'

Now Giulia was really crying. 'But that would make the other servants hate us,' she sobbed.

Cecilia knew that as mistress of the house, she should now say, 'That is no concern of mine.'

But though she tried, the words stuck in her throat. She had come to her inevitable crisis and there was only one way through it that she could see. 'Giulia,' she said. 'Forget I said that. From now, the only reasons for wages being stopped are for leaving the house or death.'

There, it was done. Abrogation of her own rights. And with it came a feeling as of chains falling off her body, leaving her to take the next inevitable step. Taking a deep breath, she said, 'Of course you must continue your work in the orchard.' Another inevitable consequence came into her mind and she knew she must say it. 'And I will be with you. We'll work together and you will teach me.'

She was suddenly so happy. They would be a little commonwealth. All her sad thoughts vanished. No more standing at the window looking out for Salvatore bringing Samuele to his home. He would come when he was ready.

Intermezzo I

Siracusa, October 1804

...the too fascinating Siren, against whose witcheries Ulysses'
Wax would have proved but a Half-protection, poor Cecilia
Bertozzi. Yet neither her Beauty with all her power of
employing it, neither heavenly Song, were as dangerous as
her sincere vehemence of attachment to me, vehemence, for
I trust it was not Depth of attachment – *for it was not mere*
Passion, & yet Heaven forbid! that I should call it Love.
—From the Notebooks of Samuel Taylor Coleridge

Coleridge is early in the opera house. He sits alone in the Leckies'
private box, watches and listens.

The auditorium fills up with the best of Syracusan society: silks
rustle, murmured words of Sicilian gallantry combine to make a
humming which underscores the chattering and whistles from the
gallery where noisier Syracusans, not society's best, have come to
shout and cheer and, if they don't like what they hear, catcall and
throw rotting fruit.

The orchestra assembles. Coleridge sees the tops of their heads.
He hears the delicious sound of tuning up and his stomach twists
with anticipation and a sort of fear. He sees the world etched
more sharply than most do. He will not forget this night. He is
approaching another moment, another epiphany to add to the

many which have teased his life. This one may have consequences which will not easily leave him. He tries to prise open the future as if it were the proscenium curtain and see the secrets of the stage set. He wonders what these consequences would be, revulsion or ecstasy, strength or weakness, bravery and boldness or cowardice and retreat. He has so often set out on course for triumphs which have plunged him into misery. Will this be different? He surveys every imaginable possibility the night may offer and sees good and evil in all of them.

The maestro stands on his rostrum. The orchestra is ready. There is a sharp smell of burning lime from the stage lights. The orchestra strikes up the overture. La Clemenza di Tito. *Cecilia will sing again the aria which reached so deep into his soul.* 'Amo te solo.'

To hear it the first time left him breathless: to hear it again tonight, only for him – surely he will die in ecstasy. That first time it was his fancy. Now he knows it is true.

He tries to lose himself in the sounds of the orchestra, to let the chasing notes, harmonies and rhythms, different timbres, violins and cellos, flutes, horns and trumpets, quieten his furious anticipation. But the music does not work. The chatter and shouting of the audience carries on: they have no ears for the overture. They are here for the singers, the arias and, despite the orchestra's fineness, so is he.

The curtain rises: the brightness almost hurts his eyes; the colours of the chorus's costumes dazzle him. He hears their voices: bass, tenor, counter-tenor, mezzo-soprano, soprano, a harmony which seems to rise to heaven. The principal singers emerge, acting out a story of emperors, warriors, princesses. Their voices wind through the air like clouds of butterflies, bright-plumaged birds in bewildering formations, delighting his ear, calming his mind.

And now here is Cecilia. She stands radiant at the centre of the stage. Her expressive eyes seem to seek him out. She sings again:

'Amo te solo
te solo amai,
tu fosti il primo,
tu pur sarai...'

The liquid notes drop into his heart like honey-dew, the very milk of Paradise, another vision which haunts him. He watches and hears and with every note he knows he is lost, lost, lost...

'Yes, I am lost,' he says aloud and people in the audience turn to look at him. He does not care. Now the opera, the music, means nothing. They are merely hindrances. Clear them out of the way, don't let them take up his time. He wants to be out of the theatre, into the night air, walking through the streets with Cecilia, heart bursting out of his body, every sense alive, nearer and nearer to where she lives, that door to open, that room to enter, that...

And now he closes his eyes, grips the arms of his seat, shivers, hears the thud of his heart drown the music and knows how deeply he is mired and that if the waters close over him there is no coming back.

*

La Clemenza di Tito *is over. The audience is shouting, cheering, ecstatic. The principals stand at the front of the stage, so near to the footlights that their faces are unreal, even nightmarish, chalk-white skin and hard-edged shadow. Cecilia is at the centre, dominating the cast for all her smallness, as if she is buoyed up, lifted off her feet, by the others. Bouquets of extravagantly hued flowers are thrown onto the stage and pressed on her. She curtsies time and again: the audience cheers even more wildly. Coleridge does not cry 'Encore!' with the rest, nor clap until his hands are sore. He stands silently, oblivious to all sound, eyes focussed on the small figure as if the adoring mayhem simply is not there.*

It is nearly twenty minutes before the audience begins to disperse. He remains in the Leckies' box, his thoughts awhirl.

He must rouse himself from this paralysed trance. It is easy and pleasurable to share in the adulation. However, conclusions, summations, must be reached.

*

People crowd round the stage door. He wonders if this is a deliberate barrier between him and her: 'Go away, Englishman. She is one of us. Only Sicilians may adore her.' But he is wrong. When he tries to make his way through they part as miraculously as the Red Sea on another fated journey. The stage door seems to open for him. He walks an unimpeded pathway with a strange sensation that it leads downward to a destination he suspects he might fear. He remembers the old choice, between the broad highway and the narrow path, desire and duty. He expects the crowd to burst in, filling the room so there is no air, no way to breathe. But the door closes behind him. He hears an ominous click as it shuts. He is alone except for the bouquets thrown on the stage for Cecilia. Their colours hurt his eyes, their scent is overpowering.

Cecilia appears. She smiles and takes his hand. 'Samuel,' she says.

Only then do people burst in. They push up against Coleridge, separating him from Cecilia, bearing her away. Her hand is torn away from his. He despairs of seeing her again. The cacophony of loud voices beyond his understanding, drowns thought itself. Bedlam swirls round him.

As suddenly they are gone. He and Cecilia are alone in that public room, she flanked by flowers, he awkward and English.

'I brought you no bouquet,' he says at last.

'I do not need another bouquet.' She holds out her hand to him again. 'Come, Samuel,' she says.

*

They walk together along streets cool in the night air. From everywhere, behind lighted open windows, through open doorways of tavernas, from people aimlessly wandering arm in arm, comes singing, high and lovely voices, deep, out-of-tune voices, drunken voices. 'Amo te solo'. The pair move untroubled and unrecognised. Neither speak. They come to a tall house in a terrace, with wooden shutters, balconies at high windows, red terracotta pantiles on the roof. Cecilia opens the door.

'Come in, Samuel,' she says.

He follows, his mind aflame with the struggle between passion and doubt.

PART IV

Chapter 21

The Journey

Cambridge–Bedford, May 1824

...'tis a sweet country that we see before us.
—From the Notebooks of Samuel Taylor Coleridge

hen Scrivener was released from the sickbay he made straight for his rooms with his *Aeneid*, *Sybilline Leaves* and Raggett's *The Monk*. He put the *Aeneid* back on his desk. There would be no translating today.

The bedmaker had been and his rooms looked unnaturally tidy. He sharpened a pencil, took a sizeable sheaf of paper, clutched it and *Sybilline Leaves* to his chest, left his rooms and locked the door.

He did not sport his oak: drawing attention to his absence with a firmly shut outer door was folly, though nobody would think there might be a woman, in his of all rooms. The worst offence in the university.

Why should I worry? he thought. *I'm only going to the library.*
Yes, but he should be going to a lecture.
They won't notice I'm not there.
He crossed First Court to the library, found a catalogue and worked his way through it. Then he made a tour of the bookstacks. No sign of any book by Captain Shelvocke. The walk to Woodstock would happen. His return to Hertford thankfully was postponed.

He took *Christabel* down from the shelf, opened it at 'Kubla Khan' and started copying it. He felt like a medieval scribe and half wanted to make an illumination as well. An odd fancy, which soon disappeared.

But he could write quickly and clearly. 'Kubla Khan', a mere fifty-six lines, was soon finished. He read the preface and found it interesting. He was especially taken by the idea of the 'person from Porlock' who interrupted Coleridge so that he forgot the ending. Then he thought he saw an anomaly in the story. Ash Farm, Nether Stowey, Lynton and Porlock. He needed a map of Somerset to check his suspicions.

Then he looked through 'Christabel'. Nearly seven hundred lines, so five and a half thousand words. This required a clear copperplate hand. It wouldn't do to find he couldn't read his own writing. 'Christabel' also had a preface. He would leave it out but make notes.

'The Pains of Sleep', with no preface, was the same length as 'Kubla Khan'. So his timetable was set. Today, 'Kubla' and 'The Pains of Sleep.' They should take up the morning. This afternoon, reading and studying 'Christabel'. Tomorrow he would write it out. And then he'd be ready for the walk to Woodstock.

By midday he had finished his copying of both poems and made his notes. Then he left the library and went to Hall to find what short commons were left.

He ate alone, inconspicuous enough not to have people asking why he wasn't at lectures.

Back in the library, he read the preface to 'Christabel' carefully. Why did Coleridge blame his own indolence for never finishing it? There must have been a better reason. Why did Coleridge fear he might have copied from other poets? But he would think about these things later. He had to read the poem first.

*

Yes, it was indeed a wild and romantic tale. But there was something more here. Christabel and Geraldine. And Geraldine frightened him. There were things going on here which he did not understand. And the further he read, the more his uneasiness grew. He even had doubts about Coleridge being a suitable guide.

But if Coleridge was writing about things he didn't understand, that was the poet's problem, not his. He only need admire the way he wrote them. The images were unforgettable.

He finished reading. He was puzzled. Where was the third part Coleridge promised? Though the book was only published six years ago, the poem was written nearly twenty years before. *That cannot be just indolence.* Besides, the conclusion to the second part had nothing to do with the story. It was all about his son Hartley.

A mystery, beyond him to solve.

Time to eat. He arranged his papers ready for the following day, left the library and walked to Hall, where this time he ate a proper meal.

*

Next day was taken up with copying out 'Christabel'. When he had finished, he cut a tiny hole in the top left-hand corner of each page with his penknife and tied the leaves together with string, gathered everything up, left the library and crossed First Court to his rooms. This evening was for preparing for the great walk to Woodstock and they had to be away early.

But before he left, he looked for a map of Somerset and found Bacon's survey map of Somerset, Dorset and parts of Wiltshire. He carefully noted the positions of Porlock, Culbone and Nether Stowey, where he knew Coleridge had lived when he wrote 'Christabel' and 'Kubla Khan'. He committed the map to memory, to think about what it told him later.

Once in bed, he wondered if anyone had noticed he'd attended no lectures or classes since he had left the sickbay. Might there be repercussions next term?

A little doubt which was to grow all through the Easter vacation.

*

Scrivener and Raggett were on their way. They were now beyond the purlieus of Cambridge. It was a fine morning. There had been no rain for days, the roads were hard and mud-free and the land was flat, so with the sun on their backs they were making good progress. Scrivener felt he could walk all day and through the night.

At midday, they reached the village of Orwell. 'At this rate we'll be in Bedford by this evening,' said Scrivener. 'We'll stop in Potton for something to eat.'

But Raggett was breathing heavily and beginning to slouch.

'Potton's miles away,' he said. 'I'll never get there.'

'Of course you will,' said Scrivener. 'You'll get your second wind.'

Raggett answered with an explosive splutter.

'We've hardly walked ten miles,' said Scrivener. 'Coleridge could walk forty miles in a day.'

'Well, I'm not bloody Coleridge,' Raggett replied. 'Go with him next time.'

Scrivener sensed that this might be the first sight of trouble ahead.

They reached Potton nearly two hours later and bought bread and cheese. They sat under a tree eating but not speaking. Then Raggett said, 'There are plenty of alehouses here. I'll go in the first I see and have a long, strong drink.'

'I'll come with you,' said Scrivener.

'Suit yourself,' Raggett replied.

His voice had changed. He was no longer the well-spoken Cambridge undergraduate. Scrivener noticed he sounded coarser and rougher than before, with a countryside accent that started to sound like a farmer's. Which was his real voice?

'I'll have a quart of your best and strongest beer,' Raggett shouted as they walked into the nearest inn.

'Are you sure?' said the landlord. 'It's a potent brew.'

'Just what I need,' Raggett replied.

The landlord poured two pints of a dark and sinister-looking liquid into a stone jug, which he handed to Raggett together with a pint pewter tankard. Raggett gave him coins which the man examined suspiciously.

He turned to Scrivener. 'And for you, sir?'

'Nothing for me, thanks. I'll just watch. Can we have beds for the night?'

'This is an alehouse, not an inn,' the landlord answered. 'If you're not drinking any more then bugger off.'

That sounded reasonable. Scrivener left and sat on a bench opposite, near enough to go back in if he needed. He was not feeling so well after all. But he must carry on. Captain Shelvocke's book was a shining chalice from which he must sip.

He whiled away the time by reading *The Monk* and was soon lost in Lewis's mad world. But after four chapters, he stopped. Raggett should surely be out by now. He crossed the street and unobtrusively looked into the alehouse. Raggett had obviously finished his first quart of beer and the landlord was bringing him another. Scrivener quietly left and returned to *The Monk*.

He was interrupted by angry shouting from the alehouse. Reluctantly, he crossed the street again.

The landlord shouted, 'Hey, you!' Scrivener had been seen. 'Get this idiot out of here or I'll do it myself and someone will get hurt.'

Scrivener went up to the table, grabbed one of Raggett's arms and tried to pull him up. The young man was asleep, open-mouthed and snoring noisily. He tried to hook his hands under his shoulders to pull him upwards, but Raggett remained a snoring, inert lump.

'Out of the way,' said the landlord. 'Let me do it.'

He seized the end of the bench and marched forward with it until it was nearly vertical. Raggett slid off in an ungainly heap. He picked himself up without a sign of a stagger, faced the landlord and said, with no trace of a slur, 'What in God's name do you think you're doing, you worthless fool? Who do you think you are?' in the educated language he normally used.

'I'm the king of this alehouse and I can do what I like.'

Raggett squared up to him like a bare-fist boxer.

The landlord laughed. 'Lay a finger on me and I'll likely kill you. And if not me then any of these gentlemen will.'

For the first time Scrivener was frightened. A moment later, he was fearful for his life when Raggett spoke in his best Cambridge voice.

'Have a care, fellow, I can have you thrown out of here and you and yours made destitute.'

This was extraordinary. The landlord snorted. 'Who do you think you are? Lord of the bloody manor?' He turned to Scrivener. 'You don't see eye to eye with him. But I reckon you can see through him. So what do you think?'

'We're on a journey,' Scrivener replied. 'Cambridge to Woodstock. We were walking. But we can't carry on now.'

'You should choose your friends better. I want to see the back of him, but I'm sorry for you.' He turned and faced the crowd of drinkers. 'Caleb,' he called.

A large, strong man stepped forward.

'Can you take these two home with you to Bedford and stick them in someone's barn for the night?' said the landlord, 'One of them's all right but the drunk's a stuck-up snob.'

'How much is it worth?' said Caleb.

'A pound. I'll pay you now and you can punch the lights out of the drunk if he doesn't give you his own pound.'

'A pleasure,' said Caleb. 'If he doesn't hand it over, I'll make sure he'll wish he was dead.'

He means it, thought Scrivener.

'Follow me,' said Caleb. He led Scrivener out into the yard. Raggett followed, now visibly frightened.

They clambered onto the dog-cart. Driver in front, two seats at the rear facing backwards. Scrivener and Raggett sat awkwardly side by side. Underneath was a cage for a large dog, luckily empty. Caleb flicked the reins and they set off.

Raggett spoke. 'Hah! You thought I would demean myself by making a journey with a bloody sizar. What do you know?'

Scrivener did not answer.

Raggett went on. 'I've got a rich uncle who pays for everything. I've heard about the uncle you've got. No more than you deserve. You don't fit in with the rest of us. You may as well get out of Cambridge now.'

Not another word was spoken for ten miles.

*

It was dusk when Caleb turned off the road again, just before they entered Bedford. Another farm. They stopped outside an old tumbledown barn.

'This is good enough for you,' said Caleb. He lit a candle lantern, which made eerie shadows, and shone it inside. Scattered straw and darkness beyond. 'You'll have to feel your way round in the dark. But it's all old straw in there so you shouldn't trip over and break a leg. You've got nothing to eat or drink but I can't help that. And be out of here before sun-up or Farmer Syrett will find you and you'll be in court for trespass. Now give me the pound you owe me.'

'You'll get nothing from me,' said Raggett.

'I said I'd punch the lights out of you if I don't get it. And I'm starting now.'

He put the lantern down and squared up. Scrivener could just make out fists as big as hams. Raggett produced a pound note at once. Caleb examined it suspiciously. Then he climbed back onto the cart and disappeared into the dark without a word.

Scrivener was satisfied. Raggett had suffered a humiliation nearly as devastating as his own at the hands of Copperthwaite-Smirke and friends.

Then he had a strange notion, that the two might be connected in some way.

*

Raggett disappeared into the barn. Scrivener followed. Then he stopped. An alarming thought.

He's angry. He'll want revenge. He'll take it out on me. What shall I do?

He walked up the track towards lights in the farmhouse. Then he turned off the track and into the undergrowth. His eyes had grown used to the dark. As he pushed through long grass the ground suddenly sloped slightly and he realised he had found a little declivity, almost a nest, with a mattress of long grass and a natural pillow at the far end. He lay down to test it. Yes, perfect. He opened his knapsack and took out his topcoat for a blanket. And then – oh, joy! – he found some bread and cheese left over from their stop in Potton. Did he have an unconscious premonition? He ate it thankfully and hoped Raggett had not saved any.

Comfortable and safe.

He thought he would be reviewing today's events before he slept. But instead he found himself thinking about his problem with 'Kubla Khan' and the irritating person from Porlock. What did Coleridge mean by saying he had 'retired to a lonely farmhouse' with a 'slight indisposition'? Did he mean he lived there? Or was he walking along the clifftop path to Lynton when it started raining and he didn't feel well, so called at the farmhouse for a rest? If the second, how had the person from Porlock known he was there? The evidence of the map in the college library was damning. Surely that person would have had to go to Nether Stowey, nearly thirty miles away, to be sure of meeting him. Surely the person would not have said, 'I need to see Coleridge on business so I'll go to a lonely farmhouse, wherever it is, just in case he's been out walking, fallen ill and asked for shelter there.'

It didn't make sense. There was more – or perhaps less – to this person than met the eye.

He curled up on the grass in unexpected contentment. He had sent Coleridge an unheard message. 'Explain yourself.'

And now the bad things of the day fell away. He saw through Raggett's ridiculous posturing, from agricultural drunk to local magnate threatening to pauperise the landlord. He remembered Raggett mocking him for being a sizar. That didn't hurt him. He now knew what Raggett was. His petty concerns and trivial anger did not concern him. His search for poetry overrode everything and the workaday world would not impinge on it. Tomorrow would be a good day.

But a voice deep inside him said, 'Don't believe it until you see it. There are bad things ahead. Today has been a warning of what they might be.'

*

He slept soundly and woke, as Caleb recommended, at sun-up. He rose almost reluctantly from his comfortable nest, not hungry but badly needing something to drink. Then he was aware of a tinkling sound nearby, as if from a small spring. He looked and found there was indeed a spring of bubbling clear water only a few yards away. Cupping his hands, he drank until his thirst was slaked, and marvelled at this blessed spot which provided him with all he needed. Even nature seemed on his side.

He picked up his knapsack and walked back to the barn. Raggett was shambling out. His face was grey with sleeplessness, hunger and thirst.

'Where were you?' he grunted.

'None of your business,' Scrivener replied.

'Keeping out of my way, were you? Frit, were you? You had good cause.'

'We have to be on the road,' Scrivener said quickly, fearing a beating up.

'We won't be walking and I'm not demeaning myself on a carrier's cart again. I shall walk on to Bedford and hire a decent equipage.'

'Why do you say "I"?' said Scrivener.

'Because I'm paying. So why should I share it with a sizar who only wanted to walk because he can't afford anything else? No, you wait for the carrier. More suitable for people of your class.'

Scrivener had expected. this. 'That suits me,' he said imperturbably. 'See you in Woodstock.'

Did this sting Raggett? 'Very well, come with me. Think of it as charity.'

'I accept your offer in the spirit in which it was given. Thank you.'

He would not have dared to speak like this yesterday. But now he had inflicted another humiliation, thin though it was, on his tormentor.

He did not consider what revenge Raggett might take.

*

On the outskirts of the town they saw a sign: FOR HIRE. They went through the gate into a courtyard of stables. Various coaches, traps and carts stood unattended. Horses watched mournfully from their stable doors. But no people.

Except one. A man was polishing the lanterns of what looked like a post-chaise. It was old but well-kept and Scrivener deduced it had once carried mail but had been sold on for private hire.

Raggett saw it, too. 'Fellow, we wish to go to Woodstock.' His best Cambridge voice.

'Not with me, you're not,' the man replied.

'Have a care, my man. I will not be spoken to like that.'

'I won't take you to Woodstock because it's too far and I want to be home tonight. I picked up a fare in Buckingham to this place yesterday, stayed here, spent the night in a stinking hovel and vowed I'd be back in my own bed tonight.'

'Buckingham will suffice.'

'I don't live in Buckingham.'

'Where do you live?'

'Winslow. And not a step further.'

'I have never heard of Winslow.'

'Then you need educating.'

He's seen through you as well, Scrivener thought.

'You'll be better off,' the man went on. 'It's just a few miles through the villages to Bicester and from there it's but a short hop to Woodstock. And you can have a good night's sleep at the Bell. Better all ways.'

'How much? said Raggett.

'Two passengers. That's ten shillings.'

Scrivener said quickly, 'It's an act of charity for which I thank you.'

Raggett handed over the money with bad grace and once again they were sitting side by side.

'We stop in Fenny Stratford for something to eat,' said the driver. 'Food is not included in the fare.'

Once again, they had to sit side by side. But the seats were more comfortable than the dog-cart's and faced forward. Also, there was a hood to put up if it rained.

Comfort. He could think about Coleridge and Kubla uninterrupted.

Chapter 22

STC and 'Kubla'

Highgate, April 1824

If there is any man in the history of literature who deserves to be hanged, drawn and quartered, it is the man on business from Porlock.
—*The Road to Xanadu*, John Livingstone Lowes

For Coleridge, the nightmare had come first and then a day of quiet grief as the tragedy of Hartley's desertion the day before sank in.

Sons. One gone, the other might still die. Tonight he would watch over Derwent. He owed it to Ann Gillman.

He climbed the stairs to Derwent's attic to relieve the nurse. Derwent slept soundly and even calmly. Had he reached the turning point?

Without meaning to, Coleridge found himself dreaming of a bright, safe future when he and Derwent could rekindle a relationship to make up for the loss of Hartley.

No, he must not wish for such things because they never arrived. Instead, his mind wandered to another time when hope was not fulfilled.

*

The year was 1797. Coleridge, Sarah and Hartley were living in Nether Stowey. Wordsworth and Dorothy were installed in Alfoxden.

They walked. Mile after mile, day after day. Charles Lamb came to visit. One day, Lamb, the Wordsworths, Coleridge and Sarah – who was soon to be excluded from all their expeditions – were to go on a long walk through the Quantocks:

Friends, whom I never more may meet again,
On springy heath, along the hill-top edge,
Wander in gladness, and wind down, perchance,
To that still roaring dell, of which I told:
The roaring dell, o'erwooded, narrow, deep,
And only speckled by the midday sun.

Coleridge would be there again. But not that day.

Before they left, Sarah accidentally dropped a skillet of boiling milk on his foot. As a result, he could not walk for days. So he retired to a seat under the lime trees in Thomas Poole's garden next door and wrote a poem directly from his heart: 'This Lime-Tree Bower My Prison'. A poem for them all, except Sarah. But mainly for 'gentle-hearted Charles', who objected to the description, saying 'dunderheaded' or 'drunk' would be more suitable.

But the walk set the stage for many, many more walks. Wordsworth, Dorothy and Coleridge, but no Sarah.

*

Months passed. Coleridge needed money. There was nothing in the house and Sarah, tight-lipped and stony-faced, would hardly speak to him as she did her best to feed and look after Hartley.

Still, one morning the sun shone, the Quantocks looked beautiful and Coleridge knew the sea would be calm. There was a change of clothes in his knapsack and paper and a pencil because he must always be ready to write. He slammed the front door of the cottage behind him and made for the hills.

The clifftop path between Lynton and Porlock always gave him calm and solace, especially when he was alone. At first, the sun still shone. But clouds were rushing in: a cold wind blew when he had walked eight miles and was close to Watchet. He shivered but carried on. Eight miles more and he was near Porlock. He began to feel ill and the first drops of rain spattered his coat. He looked for shelter.

He was now at Culbone, with its tiny church set in the middle of a wooded combe and a brook bubbling through towards the sea and shaded by trees.

Where to go? There was a house near the church. Upstream was Parsonage Farm. But would the parson let him in? Next upstream was Ash Farm, half a mile away.

He had called there before. The farmer and his wife gave him a roof, kindness and sometimes food. A void in his stomach made him fancy he was hungry again; a spasm in his stomach said he must move his bowels urgently. He hurried towards the farm, calling 'Halloa there!' in case anybody was outside. There was no answer. By now the rain was drenching him, seeping through to his skin. He panted up to the door and hammered on it. 'Halloa there!'

The door opened and there – welcome sight – was the homely face of the farmer's wife. 'Why, you poor man. You're quite soaked through. There's a good fire going in the kitchen. Come you in and stand beside it.'

Not only was there broth but also bread and cheese and cider. But his first words were, 'May I use your privy?'

Of course he could. He emerged refreshed but aware he might need it again soon. At the farmer's wife invitation, he sat by the fire and drank broth and ate bread, yet did not feel refreshed. His stomach was churning. He stood in front of the window facing the sea and looked down the path disappearing into the woods lining the sides of the combe. A path and a stream vanishing into mysterious regions sent him into fantasies of secret gardens, shining domes, deep, silent caves, old travel stories of mystic places far away.

But behind his fantasies was an ominous shivering. He remembered his swim across the New River, months of illness in Christ's Hospital and a putrid fever. Above all, he realised he needed to move his bowels again. Inevitably, the memories brought a craving so strong that he was faint with it. He called out, 'Do you have laudanum?' and heard the answer: 'Why yes, sir, a little in case anyone is sick, though the Lord knows that's seldom enough out here.'

Since the rheumatic fever, he had of course taken laudanum medicinally but had not developed a habit, though every time this alcoholic, peculiarly bitter liquid touched his tongue he knew how close he was to a craving. And this time he needed what he most feared.

The farmer's wife bustled in with a small bottle. 'Here you are,' she said. 'You can keep this. We have another. But be careful. 'Tis quite strong. I have a room where you can be alone.'

She showed him to a tiny room containing a bed. 'No one will disturb you here,' she said and left, closing the door softly behind her.

*

He sits on the bed and opens the half-full bottle. He takes a first sip. It is indeed quite strong. He takes a little more and waits. First, a glow, light-headedness, such heightened senses. Fantasies of domes, caves, secret gardens erupt into shining, vivid life. He is unimaginable miles and years away from Ash Farm. He feels air on his face, excruciating cold in the dark of caves, sees strange wonderful beings and knows he is one of them: he lives a life in that short trance which beats deep into his soul and he says aloud, 'I will stay here for ever and it will be my home.'

And then it is gone and he is awake, filled with regret and longing for the glories which were. Already they are fading.

*

He takes pencil and paper from his knapsack and writes feverishly.
In Xanadu did Kubla Khan...

He writes for as long as his first impulse takes him. Then he stops.

For he on honey-dew hath fed,

And drunk the milk of Paradise.

He waits for the next lines. Nothing comes. His mind is a fire grate full of cold ash. He looks at what he has written. Yes, it is well worth reclaiming, to turn it into the semblance of a poem. He knows where Kubla Khan and the Pleasure Dome come from. Samuel Purchas's two-hundred-year-old book of travellers' tales.

And he has just walked through the deep romantic chasm of the combe. How can the brook become Alph, the sacred river? Who was the waiting woman and who her demon-lover? Whose were the ominous ancestral voices? Why is the earth in sudden turmoil? Why an Abyssinian maid with a dulcimer? What are the songs about Mount Abora she sang? Who is the dangerous poet – for poet he is – filled with honey-dew and the milk of Paradise? He asks – but does not want answers because he knows them already and the knowledge is disturbing. The poet is himself. He knows the honey-dew on which he feeds. It is opium, and opium is a curse which could kill him.

He looks again at the pages, sees a confused mess which he does not want to work on: there is more to come from this dream. He is ashamed of where the words sprang from. And yet he was sure there was more. This is not a poem. He has written a fragment.

Now begins a disputatious conversation with himself.

First voice: 'I shall never publish this. So I will not work on it.'

Second voice. 'Of course I must. It would be self-harm not to.'

First voice. 'Why waste time? I should be writing works to earn sorely needed money.'

Second voice. 'Such as bad plays? There are things worth keeping here. And besides…'

He sees himself at Alfoxden, reading the finished work to William and Dorothy, drinking in their praise. What might Thomas Poole think of it, or even Robert Southey?

*

The farmer and his wife invited him to stay the night. He gladly accepted.

Next morning, the sun was shining again and his clothes were, if not dry, at least bearable and he felt a lot better, so he left Ash Farm and swung onwards along the path, the sheet with the first stirrings of 'Kubla Khan' and the remains of the bottle of laudanum safe in his knapsack. He was unsure of what he had done.

Chapter 23

Onwards

May 1824

O'er rough and smooth with even step he passed,
And knows not whether he be first or last.
—'Time, Real and Imaginary', Samuel Taylor Coleridge

Scrivener and Raggett set off into Bedford and beyond. The two horses maintained a high-stepping trot which Caleb's ungainly beast could never have aspired to. Fenny Stratford was twenty miles away. At this rate they would be there in two hours.

Scrivener glanced at Raggett, who had the air of one who always travelled like this. He vowed he would not look again. Instead, he gazed ahead at a wide panorama, full of people he had never noticed before. They were always there and he knew about them, but he was so wrapped up in his tiny world that he had never noticed them. Whole families, husband, wives, thin ragged children, searching for work which would be at the whim of a farmer. It would be hard, involving their children as well, and earning barely enough to survive. He saw unremitting work in the fields, men walking alone carrying their tools to hiring fairs. Poverty, destitution. The rural poor. He had never seen the urban poor. Perhaps that was even worse.

Suddenly he was filled with anger about Raggett's threat of destitution to the landlord yesterday and the personal contempt which lay behind it. This anger and the sights that provoked it wiped 'Kubla Khan' out of his mind, which was still swirling when they entered Fenny Stratford.

*

The post-chaise drew up in the courtyard of an inn. The driver led them into the bar and said, 'You'll get good food here.' He ordered roast beef and so did Raggett. Scrivener counted his money and reckoned he could just afford scrag end and potatoes.

Then Raggett said, 'I need to go to the privy.'

'In the stables outside,' said the driver.

'Thank you,' said Raggett and left them. He returned ten minutes later looking happier.

Scrivener enjoyed his scrag end and did not envy the other two.

*

They were on their way again. Once more, the poor and destitute filled Scrivener's vision. He looked over at Raggett, who returned his gaze with, he thought, a mocking smile. One thing was sure. He did not register the poor. They didn't exist so they weren't there. He saw the back of the driver's head. He was looking straight ahead.

The same seemed to apply to him.

How could this be? Yesterday he had thought he didn't see them because he was wrapped up in his own tiny world. Now he knew he was wrong. People were very jealous of their rank in life, so the middle rank would not make contact with the gentry and conversely would not be aware of the lower orders. The upper rank, the gentry and even higher, would not acknowledge the middle rank. The poor, to those people, were invisible. Everyone knew they existed; nobody actually saw them.

Scrivener, if he thought about it at all, presumed he was in the lower segment of the middle rank. So he hadn't left a tiny private world. He had burst the bonds of what he had been taught to believe was the place God had chosen for him and his sympathy and understanding had increased.

And Raggett was trying to burst the bonds as well. But his ambitions to join the gentry were doomed to failure. Scrivener would not tell him that.

*

They entered Winslow, turned left into Sheep Street and up the shallow hill to the Bell, a four-square, two-storey building, an image of permanence. It faced the Market Square, the heart of the town, as if warning it to keep order and trade fairly.

Men's voices, shouting, laughing, reached them even before they entered. The driver went straight through the throng to the bar, dragging Scrivener and Raggett behind him. In this good-humoured crowd, nobody shouted or started a fight. A large, hearty-looking man behind the bar was pulling beer and keeping up a running conversation with his customers. His face was redolent with good beer, good food, warm sun, sharp rain and searching winds. His customers were similarly weather-beaten. Scrivener had a feeling of timelessness and permanence. As coins clinked and paper money rustled over the counter, he thought over sights that he had seen that day and realised that they, too, were timeless. Farm labourers toiling in fields, trudging in search of employment, signs of malnutrition, beaten people.

He wondered how many of these prosperous-looking farmers – with ready money in their pockets which they were not going to give away – were responsible for them.

At last, the driver was noticed. 'Mr Neal,' he called. The man pulling the pints turned round.

'Ah, Josiah,' he said. 'Here for your evening tipple, I suppose.'

'Not this evening. I'm tired and I want to get home.'

Scrivener was ashamed that he did not know the driver's name. Obviously Raggett saw him as a servant who didn't warrant one.

'I've two lads here who are on their way from Cambridge to Woodstock. They've got here from Cambridge in two days.'

'And what do they do in Cambridge?' said Mr Neal.

'They're students at the university.'

For the first time the landlord looked at them.

'Them?' he almost snorted. 'University men? I thought they were all gentlemen. These look like tramps.'

'I resent that,' said Raggett. 'I am a gentleman.'

Mr Neal looked searchingly at both in turn. When he seemed satisfied he said, 'All right, here's the best I can do. We're full tonight with farmers here for tomorrow's market. So one of you can doss down in an attic with a bed in it. The other sleeps in the stables with the horses. The attic will cost you, the stables are free.'

'I'll take the attic,' said Raggett quickly.

'Not much love lost here, I see,' said Mr Neal. He beckoned to another man serving beer. 'Joe, show this young *gentleman*, as he calls himself, up to the attic so he can decide whether it meets his gentlemanly requirements. Meanwhile, I'll take my friend here to the stables to find a sweet-smelling place with dry straw well away from the horses.'

'Right-ho,' said Joe.

'Come with me,' said Mr Neal and led Scrivener outside again, with a lantern already lit.

They entered the stables. The sounds of resting horses, the quiet shifting of hooves and occasional quiet, bubbling whinnies were like gentle music. The lantern light cast moving shadows over the walls and raftered ceilings. The smells of straw and horse dung were strong.

Scrivener followed him to the far end and the final stable. Mr Neal opened a small window and fresh air poured in. The horses were far behind. There was no smell or sound. The straw was clean and sweet-smelling.

'I'll tell you this,' said Mr Neal. 'You'll get a deeper sleep here than you would in that old attic. I call it the punishment room. I knew he'd get in first.'

So he had set Raggett a trap.

'When you're a landlord you have to be observant,' Mr Neal continued. 'This place gets filled with hard-working, hard-drinking men. A brawl can start any time. The landlord's job is to stop it. But he must be careful. Too strict and he'll lose his custom. He's got to spot the troublemakers early. So he must read his customers like books. And that's what I've done with you two.'

'What do you mean?' said Scrivener.

'You started a journey yesterday. Cambridge is a long way off and you're bound for somewhere a lot further west than little old Winslow. Oxford?'

'No, Woodstock,' said Scrivener.

'I know it well,' said Mr Neal. 'Now, this is how I see it. You started out together. If you were friends before you started, you're not friends now. One of you hates the other. I don't think you hate anything. I reckon you're living in your own little world.'

'Well, I did till yesterday.'

'So now you're in the real world. And it's not a very nice place.'

'I'll find my way round it.'

'Here's what I think,' said Mr Neal. 'Neither of you are true gentlemen, like what you usually see from Oxford and Cambridge. You can spot them a mile off and keep out of their way. Not hard, because they keep out of yours. Your friend would like to be one but he's not. I don't think you want to be a gentleman – I reckon you're one of those the university takes on because they're clever, give them some money to live on and make them work for it.'

Scrivener said nothing.

'Your companion isn't. Perhaps he has rich relations. How will you get to Woodstock?'

'I don't know.'

'Where will you stay?'

'I don't know.'

'Why are you going?'

'There's something I have to see there.' It sounded a slim reason but he was too tired to explain.

'How much money have you got?'

Scrivener felt in his pockets and brought out a few miserable coins.

'That won't buy you bread and cheese. Mr Raggett might pay to travel in style and leave you to walk.'

Scrivener thought this was very possible.

'How long will you take to see what you're looking for?' said Mr Neal.

'A day, Mr Neal.'

'No. I'm John to you. And you are...?'

'George.'

'So, George, you don't know how you're going to travel or where you're staying and you've no money. Where do you go after Woodstock?'

'Back home to Hertford.'

'I see. Well, it's about time I took a couple of days off. So here's what I'll do. I'll take a ride out to Woodstock in the chaise and take you both. We'll get there by evening with a stop for food. Then the other one can go wherever he wants and I'll stay the night at the Bear. You'll stay there, too. Next morning I'll drive back to Winslow and you can see what you've come for. You'll stay another night in the Bear and next morning there'll be a pony and trap to take you into Oxford.

Scrivener gulped. How was this possible?

'Everything will be paid for until you get to Oxford. After that you'll need money. So I'm giving you this.'

He produced a pocket-book, took out a folded sheet of paper and handed it to Scrivener. A five-pound note. The first he had ever seen.

He gulped. 'But Mr Neal...' he began.

'John,' he said. 'Don't ask questions or I might change my mind. I believe a horrible trick is being played on you. This money means little to me but a lot to you. It's worth every penny to see justice done.'

Scrivener's heart welled with gratitude. 'Thank you, John.'

'On second thoughts, I've changed my mind,' said John. 'Give me back the note.'

Scrivener's face fell.

'Don't look so sad! You can't go waving a note around and expect people to give you change. I'll count out five pounds in coins. That way they'll welcome you.'

He produced a huge purse full of coins and emptied them out on a handkerchief. He counted out five pounds and put them in a separate pile. Then he scooped up the rest back into his purse and wrapped Scrivener's share in the handkerchief. 'Don't worry,' he said. 'It's fresh washed.'

He tied the corners so it made a little bag. 'That will do for now,' he said. 'Buy a good stout money belt as soon as you're in Oxford. We'll meet at breakfast. When I say I'll drive you both to Woodstock you must look as surprised as he does. I don't think you'll have much to say to each other. I'll be looking straight ahead, so it will be a quiet journey. I hope these arrangements suit you.'

'Oh yes,' said Scrivener. 'Thank you, John.'

'For Christ's sake don't call me John tomorrow.'

*

Next morning, Scrivener and Raggett were eating breakfast in the snug. Raggett's eyes were red-rimmed with sleeplessness. Scrivener was relaxed and refreshed. He had slept like a log. *John Neal is a crafty old bugger*, he thought.

The publican entered the snug. 'Good morning, lads,' he said. 'Good news. I'm doing to do you a good turn. I need a few days off so I'll take you in the chaise straight to Woodstock by this evening. Nothing to pay, it's out of the goodness of my heart.'

'Thank you, Mr Neal,' said Scrivener.

Raggett said nothing.

'So get yourselves ready and be out in the courtyard in fifteen minutes.'

Scrivener returned to the stable, picked up his knapsack, put his bag of coins in it and returned to the courtyard. John Neal was already in the driver's seat. The ostler hitched the piebald horse between the shafts. Raggett appeared and sullenly took his seat. Scrivener sensed his hostility at once.

'All right, lads?' said John Neal. 'Then let's be on our way.'

*

After leaving the Bell they turned left and trotted down Horn Street and out on the open road through the Claydons, Marsh Gibbon and Launton.

At midday John Neal said, 'Bicester soon,' His first words since they left the Bell. 'We'll stop there for victuals.'

Scrivener had forgotten Raggett's malevolent presence.

As he was thinking, so he was observing. The same slavery in the fields, the miserable hovels, the half-starved farmworkers, poverty and destitution. He thought of the prosperous farmers in the Bell and wondered what manner of world he lived in.

*

They reached Bicester. 'We'll eat in the King's Arms,' said John. 'We each pay for our own.'

No more scrag end, but food for thought for Raggett.

They all had roasts. If Raggett noticed anything, he stayed quiet. He had so far not said a word all day.

Afterwards, the landlord approached them. 'Why, John,' he said. 'I didn't know you were here. Where are you bound for?'

John told him. He answered, 'Woodstock? A mere step away. You'll have time for a bottle of port in the snug before you go, I don't doubt.'

Scrivener was doubtful. Port was swilled regularly at Jesus by Fellows and the richer undergraduates, but it would be a new experience for him.

To his surprise, he liked it very much.

*

So they came to Woodstock. John Neal drove the chaise into the courtyard of the Bear and spoke to Raggett.

'Mr Raggett, get off now and go wherever you like.'

Raggett picked up his knapsack, jumped off the cart and glared at them malevolently.

'You're well rid of him,' said John.

If only I was, thought Scrivener.

*

The evening was a good one. John was of course a friend of the landlord, who found them two rooms. Then all three sat down to more roast beef and a mountain of vegetables. Scrivener was dizzy with too much food topped off with more port.

The room was small but the bed was comfortable. He emptied his knapsack – to find disaster.

Sybilline Leaves was missing, together with *Lyrical Ballads* and the three poems he had laboriously copied out in the library. And the unkindest cut – *The Monk* had gone, too.

How could this be? Then he remembered. He had left his knapsack in the post-chaise at Fenny. And Raggett had gone to the privy.

Raggett had triumphed after all.

Chapter 24

Shelvocke

'God save thee, ancient Mariner!
From the fiends, that plague thee thus—
Why look'st thou so?'—With my cross-bow
I shot the ALBATROSS.

—'The Rime of the Ancient Mariner',
Samuel Taylor Coleridge

When Scrivener came down to breakfast, John was already there.

'Don't forget. Buy yourself a good strong money belt as soon as you can and keep it safe round you. There's many a ne'er-do-well who would love to get his hands on it. That money could keep you going for a long time. And another thing.'

'What's that?'

'Keep your wits about you. There are strange goings-on here.'

*

After breakfast and when John had settled the bill, they went outside. The chaise was ready and the horse waited patiently. John paid and thanked the ostler, who touched his forelock, said, 'Thank'ee, sir,' and returned to the stables.

John shook hands with Scrivener. 'Goodbye, George. It's been good to meet you. You'll always be welcome at the Bell.' He climbed into the driver's seat, flicked the reins and the horse set off.

Dennis Hamley

As he passed under the archway he looked back and said, 'Keep your eyes peeled. You never know what you'll see.'

Then he was gone and Scrivener's extraordinary journey from Cambridge was over.

*

Scrivener had to get to the school first. Raggett mustn't beat him there. He asked in the Bear where it was and scurried into the street with paper, ink and pen, ready for the day.

Woodstock Grammar School was for parents or guardians rich enough to pay the fees. Scrivener had been lucky. Before he died, his father had set up a trust which his uncle could not touch to pay for him to go to the grammar school in Hertford.

Yes, they were expecting him. He was led to the little library, which was empty, though he heard boys' voices from other rooms. *A Voyage Round the World by Way of the Great South Sea* by George Shelvocke waited for him on a desk, with a bookmark at the page he wanted. Raggett must have been detailed in his instructions. Why had he done that?

He found Captain Shelvocke's story of how Simon Hatley shot the albatross. He took out pen, paper and ink and copied it.

We had continued squalls of sleet, snow and rain, and the heavens were perpetually hid from us by gloomy, dismal clouds. One would think it impossible that anything could live in so rigid a climate, and indeed, we all observed, we had not sight of one fish since we were come to the southward of Strait le Maire, nor one sea bird except a disconsolate black albatross, who accompanied us for several days, hovering about as if he had lost himself, till Simon Hatley, my second captain, observing, in one of his melancholy fits, that this bird was always hovering near us, imagined from his colour, that it might be some ill omen, and being encouraged in his superstition by the continued series of contrary tempestuous winds, that had oppressed us ever since we had got into the sea, he, after some fruitless attempts, at last shot the albatross, perhaps not doubting that we should have a fair wind after it. I must own that this navigation was truly melancholy and was the more so for us who were by ourselves without a companion and, as it were, separated from the rest of mankind to struggle with the dangers of a stormy climate.

He could imagine the squalls, like repeated attacks by invisible enemies, first disguised as snow, then as sleet, then as rain. He could make a lot of the dismal clouds, the perpetual dark, the cold which defied life, the absence of living things and, the albatross, harbinger of doom, stalking them across this hellish sea.

But did the albatross signify doom? Perhaps the bird merely sought company. He needed to understand Hatley's 'melancholy fit' and question any remorse he might feel later.

There were the makings of a serviceable poem here. No wonder it caught Coleridge's imagination. He only hoped it would catch his. He wouldn't start the poem now but wait until he was in Hertford. It would light up the wastes of barren time in his uncle's house.

Copying the passage and thinking about it took an hour. That was enough for now. But it was nowhere near time to eat. Still, here was a book that Coleridge must have read so he must, too. Soon he was so absorbed that he read all day without pause until the bell rang, the boys dashed out shouting and laughing and then all was silent.

Should he go too? The door opened and a man entered. The headmaster. 'I can see you're still reading that amazing book,' he said. 'Here is a set of keys, which I will trust you with. When you're ready, lock up and take them to the caretaker, in the cottage next door.'

'Thank you,' said Scrivener.

'Goodnight, Mr Scrivener,' said the headmaster and closed the door behind him.

Alone again, Scrivener remembered John Neal at breakfast.

Keep your wits about you. There are strange goings-on here.

What if this were a plot? What if Raggett had been to the school after all and he and the headmaster planned to make a fool of him?

The thought was disturbing and he stopped reading.

But he could not live like this. He read until the light faded and his stomach reminded him that John Neal had paid for his dinner at the Bear.

So he regretfully closed the book, wrote out a letter of thanks, put his papers back in his knapsack, took the keys to the caretaker and returned to the inn and a good dinner.

*

That night he lay awake for a long time. Tomorrow he would travel relatively comfortably to the only home he had. And there he had enough to do to keep him out of his uncle's way.

He was ending the journey a different person from the one who started. He had seen poverty and destitution in fields and on roads as he had not imagined. He had been with memorable even if unlikeable characters and had an urge to write about them. But he dismissed it. He aspired to greater things.

He was tired and had a headache. He remembered the laudanum in the sickbay and the wonderful forgotten dream. He wanted the headache to go so he could sleep. And laudanum to take him to new states of being.

He had enough money now. Tomorrow in Oxford, he must buy a bottle of laudanum. And a money belt. But he wished Raggett hadn't removed *The Monk*. Some delicious horrors would have cheered him up.

At last, he slept.

*

Next morning, the trap to take him to Oxford was waiting. Half an hour later he was at the Angel in Cornmarket. He secured a seat on the next London coach and went shopping. He found a chemist who sold him laudanum with no questions and bought a money belt in Boswells in Broad Street. He saw that, as Raggett had said of Cambridge, Oxford overflowed with bookshops. He entered the first he saw, scanned the shelves and found a copy of *Sybilline Leaves*. He looked further and found *Lyrical Ballads*. He bought it because he wanted to have both versions of the 'Mariner'. He noticed that Wordsworth's was the only name on the cover. He also bought *Christabel*, with 'Kubla Khan' in it as well, so the task in the library was not wasted. Then he saw *The Monk* and knew he had to get it because he was still desperate to see how it ended. Thus he repaired Raggett's carnage.

The uneventful journey to London ended in the evening. He found a bed for the night there and next morning took the Hertford coach. After the coach drew into the Salisbury Arms, he started the walk up the long drag of Port Hill to the dark house in Bengeo and repressive misery.

Another chapter was over. He wondered how Samuele's parallel search was faring.

Chapter 25

Poole

Nether Stowey, May 1824

*May God preserve me for your friendship and make me
worthy of it!*
—Letter to Thomas Poole from Coleridge, 26 October 1798

Samuele's coach reached Minehead at last. For nearly two hundred miles he had felt every rut and pothole in the road. Through the tiny window he saw hills, fields, sheep and an occasional drover with cattle bound for the slaughterhouse.

Like the other passengers, Samuele bought a meal in the coaching inn, and asked a waiter if he knew Mr Thomas Poole.

'Tom Poole?' the waiter answered. 'Everyone does round here. He owns the tannery in Stowey. A good man to those who work for him, unlike many I could mention.'

A man at the next table overheard. He turned round, banged a fist on the table and shouted, 'The man's a filthy democrat. Old England will be ruined if his sort get their way. He has unsavoury friends. All those poetical fellows. Don't trust 'em. Young lad like you should steer clear of such people.'

Samuele thought this was a recommendation. 'How do I get to Stowey?' he asked the waiter.

'Why, I'd go to the market and find a cart loaded with hides. It will be bound for Mr Poole's tannery. The driver will let you on if you pay him.'

The driver did indeed. With Samuele perched on top of a cart-load of rough cowhides, the old horse plodded ponderously on through gentle green hills. After four hours Samuele smelt an acrid stink. 'That's the tannery,' said the driver. 'Stowey's not far now.'

They passed down a tree-lined road with a church on their left. The clock struck five. 'We're there,' said the driver.

Cottages on both sides of the road. The tannery smell was almost overpowering. The driver turned the cart off the road and Samuele saw a hive of activity in front of him.

'I'll unload if you'll be so kind as to step down,' the driver said. He handed the hides down from the cart to waiting men who stacked them up on barrows and wheeled them away. Two men stood watching. They each took a hide and rubbed it between thumb and forefinger.

'What do you think, Barnes?' said one, dressed well in jacket and breeches. He was tall, burly, with a high forehead, balding, the remains of his hair swept back from his temples.

'Fine quality, Mr Poole,' said the other. 'Fetch a good price, these will.'

'I agree,' said Thomas Poole and Samuele knew he had found his quarry.

'I have an introduction here from Charles Lamb,' he said and handed him the letter.

Mr Poole gave him a wary look, scrutinised the seal, then read the letter and said, 'Charles is a good friend without an ounce of deceit in him. Welcome to Stowey, Signor Gambino.'

*

They sat drinking cider in a bower of lime trees in the garden of Poole's large, rambling house. 'Samuel and I often sat drinking cider just as we are now,' he said. 'In happier days, Sarah would join us. Samuel would read from his poems. I can still hear that melodious voice. When he had finished he would talk, fascinating ideas never thought before, let alone with words to express them. To interrupt would be like interrupting a god.'

'Sarah?' said Samuele.

'His wife. He wrote a poem sitting where you sit now,' Poole said. 'I'll not easily forget that day. Wordsworth, his sister Dorothy and dear Charles Lamb. We were to go for a long tramp over the hills to the sea and STC was to be our guide. I still hear his shriek and the cursing when Sarah dropped a skillet of hot milk on his foot. The rest of us went on our own and I had to be guide instead. When we were gone he took paper, pen and portable inkstand, limped up his own garden through the little gate in the hedge and into mine, sat in this very bower and wrote a wonderful poem. Sarah did well to injure him that day.' He paused, then added sadly, 'He injured her enough later to make up for it.'

'What do you mean?' said Samuele.

'I'm not a poet,' said Poole at last. 'I didn't go to Cambridge. Everything I know I taught myself and everything I have I worked for. I run my tannery well. I look after my workers. I run a benefit fund for them. I care about their health and help in their sickness. I care about what they go home to each day after work. Some say that makes me a filthy democrat, a Jacobin, not to be trusted. Well, be it so.'

'Coleridge is like that as well, isn't he?' said Samuele.

'He was back then. If he had employed men himself he would have treated them fairly. But his business would be ruined in a week. He was a democrat in those days and we met at a like-minded group in Bristol. He burst on us like a comet, amazed us with his ideas, people flocked to hear him. Why, at his and Robert Southey's bidding we were to escape to America and make a new ideal world. But Samuel and Southey are poets, you see, and when poets speak, you listen. It was then he met Sarah. Ill-starred union.'

'You didn't go to America,' said Samuele, a statement, not a question.

'We did not,' Poole replied. 'And Samuel now had a wife when the only reason for marrying was destroyed. He fell out with Southey; he had no money. Only Cottle and I kept him stable. I tried to save him from himself and while I have breath I will go on doing it.'

'Cottle?' asked Samuele.

'His publisher. I brought STC and Sarah here to Stowey. I found them a cottage and kept an eye on them.'

'Where did he live?'

'Come with me. I'll show you.'

They stood up. Poole led him through the garden and an orchard where rotting apples lay on the ground. At the far end was a hedge. Samuele followed Poole to a gap, filled in with a secure wooden fence.

'The gate Samuel opened was here,' said Poole. 'We built it so he and Sarah could come through any time they wanted. It's been boarded up long since.'

Samuele saw a long, unkempt garden on the other side. A few cabbages and turnips grew on a neglected vegetable plot. A pig grunted and snuffled in a pen. Chickens strutted and clucked. At one end was the back of a small, untidy cottage, raggedly thatched. Washing hung on a line. He heard children shouting and crying and a woman's voice rising above them, angry, at the end of her tether.

'Yes, that is where they lived,' said Poole. 'A man like him.'

'Who lives there now?' Samuele asked.

'A farmworker and his family. I try to help them but I can't do everything. There's much wrong in this England of ours.'

Yes, Samuele thought. *Thomas Poole is a good man. I would want him as a friend.*

*

In the gathering dusk, Poole led him to his spacious, comfortable house. A maid served them a meal, fish fresh from the sea, warm bread, butter and cheese from the farm, apples from the orchard.

'I knew I had lost him when Wordsworth came,' said Poole. 'They were destined to meet. They had great work to do. Sarah and I were not part of it. It was hard to bear.'

'How do you mean, lost him?' said Samuele.

'STC is a selfish man. I can't close my eyes to it and nor could Sarah. He had always to be with the Wordsworths. Sarah was left behind. Hartley hardly saw his father.'

'Is he a weak man?' asked Samuele.

Poole thought. 'No,' he said at length. 'He's a strong man with a weak will. There is a difference.'

Greatly daring, Samuele asked, 'Were you jealous?'

'Who of?'

'Mr Wordsworth.'

'Yes, I was. I still am.' He looked hard at Samuele. Then he said, 'God help me, I was jealous of STC as well. He didn't value Sarah as a man should. A bachelor may spend his time away from home. A husband may not. But he ran away to Racedown until the Wordsworths were slung out and then to Alfoxden where they lived afterwards and then to Germany. And he left Sarah with a newborn, poor little Berkeley. I did my best to help her through the horrors she endured. She was alone when Berkeley died. Can you imagine what that was like? Not even Berkeley's death would bring him home.'

Samuele said, 'He's a bad man, then,' tentatively, trying the words out before absorbing the thought.

'*No!*' cried Poole with a passion that seemed to rock the room. 'No, that's *not* what he is.' He was silent again. 'He is a law unto himself. Somehow, normal rules don't apply. They should, but they don't. People close to him are offended. He hurts them, he makes them unhappy. Yet by some strange chemistry they forgive him. That may be bad, but it's true.'

A lot to take in.

'I lost him again when he upped sticks and took his family off to the Lakes and the Wordsworths.'

'He went to Sicily,' said Samuele.

'He did indeed. And Gibraltar and Malta and then Italy. I'm glad he went. He was in a bad way with the opium. He had to be far away in a warmer clime. We could breathe again, though we were concerned about his progress. Yet he came back in a worse state than ever. We should have known.'

'A worse state?' cried Samuele, distressed.

'Yes,' said Poole firmly. 'I rarely see him now and when I do I have to travel. He writes long, warm letters and I reply. I send him money when he needs it, which is often. So do others. We set up funds for him and his children. The Wedgwoods still give him an annuity. I try to help him shake off the opium but it's a hopeless task. I watch his wanderings. Some well-disposed people give him a home, until he outstays his welcome and they ask him to go. It's as if the whole world tries to keep him afloat so he can work the magic that's in him.'

He paused again.

'He has had misfortunes he does not deserve,' he continued. 'And he is handing them down to the next generation. Hartley grows too much like him. Brilliant but hopeless. Hartley will have the same end, though it's drink and not opium with him.'

'Before I leave for Sicily I hope to meet Mr Coleridge at Dr Gillman's,' said Samuele. 'I need to speak to him face to face.'

'Oh,' said Poole distractedly. 'I wish you wouldn't. You admire him and that's as it should be. But if things are going badly you might not admire him any more. That would be unfair, both to him and you.'

'You're wrong. I would still admire him,' cried Samuele.

'You say so now. I respect him too much to give you the chance not to. And I respect you, too.'

'I will take the risk,' said Samuele stubbornly.

'It's late,' said Poole. 'You'll sleep here tonight. When tomorrow dawns you may find that I'm right.'

*

It was wonderful to sleep soundly in a soft bed in a sweet-smelling room. He woke to a clear day. After breakfast Poole said, 'I'm not going to the tannery this morning. We'll take a walk and I'll show you something.'

As they walked down a lane to Holford they passed a large house surrounded by trees. 'Alfoxden,' said Poole. 'Where Wordsworth lived. See how close it is to Stowey, not three miles.'

They went on, up the wooded Quantock Hills to Watchet, Dunster with its castle, Minehead and the sea. Now they were on a cliffside path. The Bristol Channel stretched wide and blue to their right and worried at the shore beneath. They had walked twenty miles and Samuele was tired.

'Keep going,' said Poole. 'Samuel thought nothing of a walk like this. There's more miles yet to Lynton.'

'How many?' Samuele gasped.

'Don't worry. We're bound for somewhere nearer.'

Already the sun had reached its zenith and they had passed Porlock. 'Nearly there,' said Poole.

But they still walked another four miles until they came to a farm. 'Ash Farm,' said Poole. 'STC often called in on his walks.'

A labourer straightened up from his work as they passed. 'Fine morning, Mr Poole,' he called. 'You off to Lynton, sir?'

'No, George. I want my young friend here to see the combe and Culbone church.'

'Well, you be careful. That Culbone's a strange place. It don't do to go there by night, though the sun's shining bright enough now to keep the bad things away.'

'Why shouldn't we go there at night?' Samuele asked when they had passed.

'It's a chapel built on a plague site. People's ancestors in their scores lie there. A place sacred and cursed at the same time.'

Samuele saw that Poole believed it as much as any credulous local.

'Ash Farm is at the head of the combe,' said Poole. Samuele looked down. The narrow valley, thickly wooded on each side, ran to the sea. 'There's a hidden stream underneath the church.' Samuele could see it, tiny, a little toy chapel. 'The river flows into the sea. This is where STC wrote "Kubla Khan".'

Samuele took in the scene and fixed it in his mind. Then he said:

'Where Alph, the sacred river, ran
Through caverns measureless to man
Down to a sunless sea.'

Today, though, the sea beyond the combe was bright and sparkling. Then Poole said:

'But oh! that deep romantic chasm which slanted
Down the green hill athwart a cedarn cover!
A savage place! as holy and enchanted
As e'er beneath a waning moon was haunted
By woman wailing for her demon-lover!'

'I wouldn't come here by night,' said Samuele.

'Like you, I know the poem by heart,' said Poole.

*

As they walked back to Stowey Samuele asked if he knew anything of Coleridge's time in the Mediterranean.

'Not much,' was the answer. 'He had his chance of redemption, happiness and stability to live a new life, and he threw it away. He might even have sent for Sarah and the children to join him in the sun. That would have been salvation indeed.'

A new life. Redemption. Samuele asked another question, tentatively, almost shyly. 'Did he speak of anyone he met there?'

'But few. Admiral Ball, the Governor of Malta. Samuel often talked about him. He admired him just short of idolatry. A great leader of men, he said. Did you know Samuel was his secretary? He almost governed Malta himself and did it well. A talent nobody knew of. He might still be there, a powerful, influential man.'

'Why did he come back?'

'Because he was English and a poet. He needed a public, other poets to rival and argue with. He needed Wordsworth. Maltese life would be heaven to most people. In the end, though, not to him.'

'Did he speak of anyone else? No one in Sicily?'

'I remember an American artist, who painted his portrait during that dreadful time when he was trapped in Rome. He never mentioned Sicily.'

'No woman?' Samuele could hardly say the words.

'I don't think so. He would be too guilty about Sarah. Besides there was that one in the Lakes who he thought he loved. She's distorted his life, though I don't think she meant to. Samuel shows too much ill-judged ardour. One of his curses.'

'Could you tell me about her?' Samuele asked.

'I can't. I'm not privy to his feelings.'

'I see,' said Samuele miserably.

*

They reached the house in the late evening. The maid served dinner, shoulder of lamb. They ate silently, until Poole said, 'I shall drive you in the chaise to Minehead tomorrow in time for you to pick up the coach.'

Samuele slept dreamlessly. After breakfast the chaise was brought out, the horse harnessed and they set off at a smart trot through the village and out onto the Minehead road. As he drove, Poole spoke. 'I've enjoyed your visit,' he said. 'I hope it's been useful.'

Samuele said it had. 'But...' he began.

'I know,' said Poole. 'You wish I knew more about his time in Sicily. When you go home you must ask your father. There may be things he has never told you, just as Samuel never told us. Perhaps your father did not want to betray a friend's secrets.'

The horse was feeling its way through the carts and people thronging Minehead High Street until they reached the inn. Poole helped Samuele down. 'Where shall you go now?' he asked.

'Back to London,' said Samuele. 'I shall ask there.'

'You won't find answers there, except from Charles. Only ask those who have a right to tell you, if they think fit.'

'Charles gave me introductions to Mr Wordsworth and Mr Southey as well.'

'Then you're in safe hands. When you get back to London, find a place on the coach for Kendal. Mr Wordsworth's the man to ask first, if he will deign to speak to you.'

*

Samuele was still tired as the coach jolted him back to London. Nagging questions teased him. Who was 'that one in the Lakes'? Was his father thinking of her even while he knew Cecilia? Why had he not stayed in Sicily, or even Malta? When worn out with speculation, he slept fitfully, sometimes dreaming of Culbone Combe at night. He saw his mother there, kneeling, bright against the dark chapel, hosts of trees hanging, grasping down threateningly, as she cried piteously for her demon-lover. He imagined himself as a demon-lover with Giulia wailing but was not convinced. Even so, in his dream he found himself moving quietly, falsely, towards her. Why falsely? He loved her. She had come to mean everything to him. He loved her for the way she heroically spoke Italian even though her real language was the old true Sicilian. It spoke of wider horizons, a new life of freedom and release when he returned home, everlasting fulfilment. *So why falsely?* Because he was Italian and this decreed they should keep their distance. If Bernardo had ever found out he would call Samuele a traitor. His mind was troubled.

London was here. A day to rest, then the long haul to the Lakes. It was a long way to go to find anything out, but find out he would.

He felt he was making progress. He wondered if Scrivener was.

Chapter 26

My Old Navigator

Highgate, May 1824

The very deep did rot: O Christ!
That ever this should be!

He prayeth best, who loveth best,
All things both great and small

—'The Rime of the Ancient Mariner', Samuel Taylor Coleridge

Derwent's fever was in its fourth week and most nights Coleridge still watched over him through the dead, vast middle of the night. Tonight he slept normally. No anguished cries or waking up in distress and begging for water but unable to swallow. Dr Gillman thought he might be on the turn, as did Coleridge, desperately. Sometimes he felt he could die in his stead if that was what it took. He longed for Hartley to return and sometimes thought he saw him. But no, it was the revenant with that disturbingly enigmatic expression.

'Who are you? What do you want?' He was beginning to say the words aloud, and people in the street would stop and stare at him. The revenant would nod and then be not there. He did not vanish spectacularly: Coleridge was never able to interpret what he saw. It was as if the revenant was swallowed up into his brain, to wait for the time to reappear, together with that nonsensical phrase, 'He looks like a son.'

He hardly ever took opium on these vigils. The Gillmans' magic was slowly working. But he still became lost in memories like dreams, though he did not sleep. He had to stay awake because if he slept, good times would turn into horror. There were many things he wanted to fix in his mind, because not all of them were bitter.

The year at Stowey was always close to him: the flawed times when the ideas, discussions, fusions of thought and feeling burgeoned between him and his friends. And, more and more he was thinking of the most magical time of all. The 'Mariner'.

*

It was 1798. He was walking the Quantocks with William and Dorothy, silhouettes on a sharp horizon in deepening dusk. The sun set over Longstone Hill; the sea darkened. Soon the moon would rise. Sea and land would change from the colours of sunlight to the silver of moonlight.

This was the start of a long tour through Somerset, from village to village, inn to inn, the first of many. Sarah, pregnant, stayed at home with the demanding Hartley, resigned but discontented. Coleridge was unconcerned.

He watched the dance of foam as the waves took the tide out and listened to their unceasing roar and suck. Images, memories, filled his mind. The homely Bristol Channel became a wide, unknown ocean. He dimly recalled old ballads sung to him in the cradle, stories heard and read of voyages across hostile oceans, thirst swelling the throat and drying the tongue, hunger shrinking the stomach and darkening the sky as the eyes dimmed. He imagined himself adrift on a wide sea and felt hunger's pinch and thirst's agony with physical exactness. He remembered words of deprivation and a sort of salvation, though he could not place them.

They lay down crying and weeping,
No crumb was left for eating.

There came a dove from heavens high
It sat down on the sailing tree.

'I am no bird to be shot for food,
I am from heaven an angel good.'

The lines left faint impressions of a quiet voice and a childish understanding. Dorothy said, 'The sun goes and I can see the moon already. One falls, the other rises. They are dancing.'

Wordsworth spoke. 'Look,' he said. 'The last light on the ribbed sand shows like bones in a thin body. A tall, grim man burnt brown by sun and wind. An old sailor, perhaps.'

Coleridge half listened. Thoughts of thirst at sea horrified him. How could he have borne it? How could anyone? But sailors did, because they had to, when they were surrounded by salt sea and not a mouthful of fresh water near them.

He mused on this and shuddered. Then he asked, 'What was that you said, Wordsworth?'

'Have you ever read a book by Thomas Shelvocke?'

Coleridge recalled the myriad books he had read. The name was not familiar.

'Shelvocke tells of a voyage into the southern oceans, where ice floes close in on ships and men can freeze to death. It seems an albatross followed the ship for days until the second captain, Hatley by name, thought it boded ill and shot it. The result was that the crew were even more lonely and accursed than before.'

'Why should you tell me that now?' said Coleridge.

'No reason. It came into my mind as I looked out at this placid sea. We live sheltered lives, you and I.'

The story dropped into Coleridge's mind with a great chime and now he could think of nothing else.

*

In succeeding days, Coleridge told Wordsworth more about the poem forming in his mind. 'I see a ballad with a rhythm to hypnotise the reader, like the ballads of old,' he said. 'It must deal with ice and cold, storm and calm, stifling heat, a great wrong leading to a greater misery. A mariner struggles to shake it off. That mariner must shoot an albatross, like poor Hatley.' He paused. 'And the story must be supernatural.'

'Perhaps,' said Wordsworth, 'shooting the albatross might awaken avenging spirits of the ocean.'

'Perhaps,' Coleridge replied. His mind whirred with thoughts too deep and frightening to give words to yet.

*

Whenever he came back to the cottage, great thoughts still chiming like complex music in his head, he felt a depressed flatness. Arguments, short and bitter, flared up. Today, his mind full of a wreathing mist forming the ghost of a poem, he was especially intolerant. Sarah was in the scullery peeling potatoes and keeping one eye on Hartley.

'This house gets more squalid by the day,' he said.

'You've no right to say that,' Sarah replied heatedly. 'I've no doubt Alfoxden is paradise by comparison.'

'There was a sheen of love over this cottage when we moved in and it made it worth coming back to. I gloried in it, almost as I did when we were in Clevedon. Where's that sheen now, eh?'

'Nobody wiped it off but you,' Sarah replied.

He looked at her with loathing. 'How differently we live now. There's no "oh Esteesee" any more, is there?'

Except for these sudden squalls they hardly ever spoke. There was silence for a moment, then Coleridge, worrying at the comparison like a loose tooth, said: 'William and Dorothy. They strike sparks off each other, they think alike, they guide each other. They are two aspects of the same person. I need a wife who will be the same for me. Once I thought I had such a one.'

'You were obviously wrong,' said Sarah sarcastically.

'I need a guide, a confidante, a sounding board.'

'As I'm not that person, get out of my sight and run back to your friends.' She turned her back on him.

'I shall,' he said and began to push past her. Hartley howled. Coleridge looked down. The little boy's eyes were wide with fear. Impulsively he cried out, 'My son! No, I can't go.' He picked him up and felt his body stiffen, then relax. 'My love is for Hartley now. He's a fitter object for it than his mother.'

Not answering, Sarah willed him to look at her. He saw a haggard, harassed, careworn face and was suddenly full of compassion and guilt. He recalled a letter to Southey – *to be perhaps not displeased with her absence* – and his stomach twisted with the hopelessness of a foolish action that could never be repaired. *Without Hartley, and therefore without Sarah, my life would be empty, but without William and Dorothy it would be ashes*, he thought. *I am locked in a cell which I made myself.*

Only opium kept him going now and tonight he would take it.

*

SARAH

I sit alone in the cold scullery in the mean little cottage in Nether Stowey. Now Wordsworth and Dorothy are here I have lost him completely. I am not allowed to go with them on their long walks because Dorothy and William have decided that I have no creativity, no talent, and could contribute nothing. And of course, Esteesee at once agreed. Had he forgotten our lives in Clevedon when we shared everything? I had read Mary Wollstonecraft's A Vindication of the Rights of Women, *in which she said that a wife should be her husband's friend, and for those blessed months in Clevedon this is how we lived. We talked and thought and argued about things which mattered. He wrote poems for me and I wrote poems for him. I remember them all, especially 'The Silver Thimble' which he thought wonderful. Does he still? Or has he wiped it out of his mind?*

You much perplexed me by the various set:
They were indeed an elegant quartette!
My mind went to and fro, and waver'd long;
At length I've chosen (Samuel thinks me wrong)
That, around whose azure rim
Silver figures seem to swim
Like fleece-white clouds that on the skiey Blue,
Waked by no breeze, the self-same shapes retain;
Or ocean-Nymphs, with limbs of snowy hue
Slow-floating o'er the calm cerulean plain.

William and Dorothy arrive, decide I have no talent and nothing to offer. Esteesee agrees and now I spend my days either exchanging harsh words with him or alone in silence in this mean little cottage with Hartley. Do I deserve such misery?

They are out walking. They have been away for two days. But now I hear excited voices outside. I can tell they have been talking about some great project, about which I shall be the last to know. They come in.

At least it wasn't raining. If it had, I know what would have happened now. It has happened before and will happen again.

Dorothy would say, 'Don't mind me, Sarah' and rush upstairs. A few minutes later she would come down again clutching her wet clothes and wearing dry ones of mine.

When I complained to Esteesee about this he replied, 'But, my love, that is what true friendship is, that we are willing to share what we have with those dear to us who are in need.'

He meant no malice. He really could not understand what I meant. Would he let William borrow his? No, because they would be too small.

'When I consider how my light is spent...' Words written by a poet greater than either of them.

*

Over the last weeks, Coleridge's beautiful dreams had been less frequent: tonight was worse than ever. He tried to sleep. But his eyeballs were dry: his lids drooped and lifted over them like sandpaper. He realised a terrible truth. *I can no longer control my dreams.*

He lay sleepless and shivering, feeling the familiar agonies of 'desire with loathing strangely mixed'. Even after he drifted into sleep they continued seamlessly. He teetered on a precipice, balancing, horror-struck, staring at the drop down to an obscure hell. When he woke he tried to sit up. But he was paralysed with guilt and desolation. No power on earth could make him stop taking the easeful draught, in ever greater doses. A life of inescapable slavery stretched before him.

Somehow, his misery caught up with his new poem. He would write of the supernatural, the fantastic, and plumb depths of human experience no one had dared to think of since Shakespeare. The resolve gave him a strange joy.

A shadowy ghost, a figure who frightened him yet drew him close, because he saw himself in it, walked his mind. The figure was tall and gaunt, ribbed like the sea sand, wiser than a human should be, sinking lower than any human should, yet who still might find a sort of salvation. But once done, nothing could take the sin away. He would suffer thirst, hunger, despair on a ship becalmed and the sea heaving with the sailors' filth and the blessed, cooling wind would never come. But something else would, and the thought of it obsessed him because it was an image for himself.

*

He sat at a table in Alfoxden, blank sheets of paper in front of him. Earlier that day, he and Wordsworth had sat opposite one another at the same table. They talked of a great joint venture – a collection of poems, some by one, some by the other. It would seal their friendship, their partnership. But now such talk was over. Coleridge was alone with his mariner.

The presentiment that the mariner was himself became stronger, not as he was then but as he would inevitably be. As he imagined this man, he became him, saw through his eyes, knew what he felt, experienced where he had been although he had never set foot in a ship but depended entirely on old stories remembered.

It is an ancient Mariner,
And he stoppeth one of three.
'By thy long grey beard and glittering eye,
Now wherefore stopp'st thou me?

Guilt. It was all guilt which now kept the mariner wandering the world, searching for listeners. And such guilt. In the cold depths of the ice floes the Albatross found them and followed.

And every day, for food or play
Came to the Mariner's hollo!
But:
'God save thee, ancient Mariner!
From the fiends, that plague thee thus!—
Why look'st thou so?'—With my cross-bow
I shot the ALBATROSS.

His own fears become the mariner's travails – but part of him stayed detached, looking at them coolly. He wrote on because this was his curse as well as the mariner's. And as he wrote, he found for the mariner something which was like salvation, an impulse towards good which let him reach a sort of forgiveness. He came through the mariner's despair, felt it, suffered it, because it was his own as opium took him over completely, though he could not guarantee the salvation for himself.

But he knew there was a fitness in his work. He had written something wonderful. An impulse to self-delight rose in him: he could not wait to stand triumphantly with this first draft in front of William and Dorothy, say, 'Listen to this,' and see Dorothy's face light up with admiration and William's brow furrow with concentration, ready for comment which would cut to the poem's heart.

What glory! What achievement! What a wonderful opening his 'Old Navigator' would provide for *Lyrical Ballads*. He hugged himself with delight and anticipation when he thought of their shared revolutionary book.

*

Yet when it is finally published, 'The Ancient Mariner' is his only poem in it. And Wordsworth's is the only name on the cover.

The great friendship will soon be no more. But it is not Coleridge's wish.

Chapter 27

Scrivener Composing

Hertford, May 1824

Now, granting for a moment that whatever is interesting in these objects may be as vividly described in prose, why am I to be condemned if to such description I have endeavoured to superadd the charm which by the consent of all nations is acknowledged to exist in metrical language?
—Preface to *Lyrical Ballads*, William Wordsworth

The poet, described in ideal perfection, brings the whole soul of man into activity.
—*Biographia Literaria*, Samuel Taylor Coleridge

Scrivener had been at home for four days. The atmosphere had not changed. Perhaps he should be spending time on the work he was given – or, rather, had found in his pigeonhole – from Dr Vavasour, together with a note regretting his recent illness, presuming that he had not been to supervisions or tutorials because he was convalescing and ending by hoping that he would soon recover.

The daily pattern was soon established. After a silent breakfast, under his uncle's baleful gaze, Scrivener knew he could not stay in the house. Today was fine. He would take pencil, notebook and the extract from Shelvocke's book and wander around the Hertfordshire countryside thinking and making notes until it was time to return and eat whatever meagre fare the maid would have found for an evening meal.

Breakfast over, his uncle disappeared to wherever he spent his mornings. Scrivener cut four slices of bread, spread them with rancid butter, cut a lump of cheese, wrapped them and put them in his knapsack. Then on an impulse he put in a tinderbox, two candleholders and six candles. The maid would not miss them. He'd had an idea. He would go to Scott's Grotto and walk the tunnels until he reached the cave deepest inside the hill. Shelvocke's account was in the darkness of storm. Writing his poem by candlelight in pitch darkness might spur inspiration.

So he slipped his knapsack over his shoulders, took his key (his uncle had at least given him a key when he left the grammar school, an unexpected concession) and set off from Bengeo down to King's Meads and the River Lea.

He continued along the riverbank until he came to Ware, a town he had always loved. Especially for one place. He crossed the river by the bridge and set off to Scott's Grotto. He could have been there quicker, but he loved to walk over the meads and along the river and forget his frustrations. Most people were not allowed into the grotto, but he was and his leanings towards literature, especially the classics, were known there. This, he thought, was a privilege which nearly matched getting into Cambridge. Just as well: he had few enough others.

'What are you doing this morning, Mr Scrivener?' called a gardener as he entered the grounds.

'Writing a poem,' he answered.

Soon he was outside the stone gatehouse leading into the little wooded hill.

He took the tinderbox, a candle and a candle-holder and soon had the candle lit. Then he entered into the first passages, with sea shells mortared into walls which, by candlelight, gave eerie reflections.

He knew his way. He tiptoed along the tunnels, because it was sacrilege to disturb the silence, until he emerged into the furthest and deepest cave.

He sat down on a stone block which made a convenient seat, placed the lighted candle by his right foot, lit another to put by his left and by their flickering light opened his notebook and read the extract from Shelvocke's book again.

Sitting here in this strange, romantic place with the atmosphere of a Gothic novel, he felt an affinity with Coleridge as he imagined him reading the same passage and letting his imagination carry him wherever it may.

He lit upon the words '*the heavens were perpetually hid from us by gloomy, dismal clouds*'. Yes. Perfect. The little light was lost in the Stygian blackness of the opposite wall of the cave. Even the shells could not send out reflections and the entries to other tunnels were blind eyes of darkness casting illimitable nothingness into the committee room.

He had his first image. He was not sure where he would put it, but he would know when the time came. He wrote busily in his notebook, sure that Coleridge would nod approvingly.

He read on, noting the absence of life in this '*rigid climate*'. No fish, no seabirds. Except one trace of a living creature. The lost albatross, black as the clouds and black as the walls of the grotto.

What had Coleridge made of this image? Scrivener did not know. It was many years since he had read the poem and his recollections were sketchy. He had trapped the 'Mariner' in Copperthwaite-Smirke's missing copy inside his roped-off cage. He had not even opened his new copy. So, there was no chance of new words being influenced by memories of the old. His poem would stand alone.

Hatley's melancholy and obsession with the albatross as an ill omen could engender some fine writing and the notion of 'contrary winds' might reflect his state of mind. Most of all, Scrivener was fascinated by Hatley's 'fruitless attempts' at shooting the bird. What an opportunity! One thing he remembered about Coleridge's poem was that he was content merely to write:

'...*With my cross-bow*
I shot the ALBATROSS'

He would make more of it than that.

Did Hatley feel remorse after killing the albatross? Shelvocke did not try to look inside Hatley's mind: Scrivener must do that himself.

Now he came up against something disturbing. When Samuele visited him in the sickbay he had asked him why he was telling others about his father writing a book but had told him that he was Coleridge's son. And Samuele replied:

'"*That moment that his face I see,*
I know the man that must hear me;
To him my tale I teach."'

The sudden impulse, with its hint of fate, recognition and surely supernatural insight was something he could not emulate. He needed the idea of choice but how would he attain it? Leave it till later. He'd find it in the end.

But first he must find a method, almost a philosophy, of poetry. Strangely, the first person he thought of was Dr Vavasour. Scrivener had not forgotten what he said in the library: *As to poetry, Mr Scrivener, you would do well to confine yourself to Ovid and Horace.* The first time Dr Vavasour had met all the students in Scrivener's group he had given a talk on poetry.

'You will be reading much poetry in the classical languages. And you must remember that poetry obeys its own rules and methods common to all languages.' He cleared his throat and said, almost reluctantly, 'Even in English.'

He waited for the ripple of nervous laughter, the reward which he expected every year. It duly came, so he continued. 'The best account of writing poetry comes from a poet whom I believe to be the finest poet in English since Shakespeare. I refer of course to Mr John Dryden, of whom Dr Johnson said, "he found it brick and left it marble", which allows him to be ranked alongside the poets of the classical age.'

Scrivener could see the gaunt figure of the old scholar gesturing genteelly as he spoke. 'First, the poet's imagination in the finding of the thought...' (*I've found it*, Scrivener inwardly exulted) '...fancy, the moulding of the thought...' (*that's what I'm doing now!*) '...and elocution, adorning the thought in apt, significant and sounding words.'

Then he had a doubt. Wordsworth and Coleridge, everyone said, were writing poetry in a new way. The previous evening, in his lonely bedroom in the silent house, he had read Wordsworth's preface to *Lyrical Ballads*.

The preface was heavy going. Wordsworth said more about fancy and imagination, but Scrivener had no time to work out the differences. But then he came to *elocution*, which was, according to Dryden, *adorning the thought in apt, significant and sounding words* and found how Wordsworth saw it. One word, later repeated, stood out: *superadd*. Something here jarred. Would Coleridge agree? Coleridge was surely not the sort to add charm by conscious thought to anything. There was so much about Coleridge that he did not know. Perhaps he would find an answer in *Biographia Literaria* when he had time to read it. Meanwhile, he would have to make do with Dryden and Wordsworth.

Now, here in the grotto, he felt a real tremor of fear. The moment had come to start writing. He sat in darkness, illuminated only by two weak candles. A slight cold wind blew through the passageways into this cave. Yes, this is what it must have been like. The lonely ship butting its way in rough seas through the dark night, a hundred years ago and three thousand miles away. And he was there on board.

So, haltingly, almost fearfully, he wrote his first tentative words.

Through this wide world in all its moods,

Harsh or forgiving, storm or calm,

I pass alone, by sea, by land,

A ghost with tales of shock and harm.

He put his pen down and looked at it critically. He felt he had reproduced the metrical pattern accurately. But it plodded clumsily and said little. Everything he recalled about Coleridge's poem was fleet-footed.

Could he ever hope to emulate that? He felt he had failed already. Then he brightened. For God's sake, he'd only written four lines. He must carry on, learning as he went. He would get there.

He stopped. He was realising how hard being simple was.

Keep on going.

He left this unsatisfactory opening, which was going nowhere, and considered the first image he took from Shelvocke.

Suddenly, he felt happier. Shelvocke had given him the thought. Now came the verse form which Wordsworth said must be 'superadded'. He started writing.

We southward drove midst sleet and rain,

A dismal show of mantling cloud.

A Stygian blackness chilled the nerves

Of fearful men who cried aloud.

One candle flickered. Soon it would sputter and die. But he could use this flickering. He'd heard of strange lights at sea.

No Jack o' lanterns dance and trick

With their bright, deceiving lights

No harbingers of better things,

No ways to ease these endless nights.

Yes, this was better. He now knew in advance what he was writing about. This was truly *superadding*. Wordsworth would be pleased. Now the albatross enters and he must shift the point of view. Except for the opening verses, which now seemed part of an awkwardly different poem, he had been writing Shelvocke's narrative as the spokesman for the entire crew. But the albatross was solitary. Its only connection with the ship was Hatley. So this would be Hatley's narrative. Would a simple change of personal pronoun from 'We' to 'I' suffice to make it seamless? Was this important?

To know, he had to write it first.

He composed three stanzas as the black albatross showed itself under the black sky, and Hatley realised how deep was their connection.

Day after day, night after night,
While others slept or worked the sails,
I kept a vigil on this bird.
Sometimes he pierced the dark cloud's veils,

And disappeared. I groaned aloud
For grief that he, my only friend
On all that ship, deserted me
And brought my vigil to its end.

He put his pen down. He had reached the end of an episode. It was not perfect: it needed some grease in its joints. He would look at this in the next draft. Hatley, by being alone on deck, has become the crew's representative and, for the moment, speaks for them.

He remembered Wordsworth again, how poetry begins with 'the spontaneous overflow of powerful feeling' but that it is written as 'emotion recollected in tranquillity'. Well, that was what he was doing and his next draft would be really tranquil.

But wait! My friend appears again,
His pinions spread protectively
Above my head. And I am safe.
The albatross is guarding me.

And all my shipmates. Soon the gale
Will ease, the clouds disperse,
The sun will shine, the ship will sail
O'er the seas as calm as verse.

But then came the fatal change.

The nights and days progress and still
The storm does not abate. The bird
Flies on impassively. No sign
He gives, no friendly word.

He is no saviour but a scourge
Sent by the fiend who stalks the deep
To lure the innocent sailors on
And thus its human harvest reap.

I loved the albatross before
But now I hate it. 'Evil Sprite,
Devil's messenger sent from Hell
With doom. Misery and eternal night,'

I cried, and instantly
The crew were on the deck, their eyes
Were wide and fearful, faces pale,
And muttering in wild surmise.

'Wait here. Move not,' I shouted then
And ran below deck to the place
Wherein I slept and quickly seized
My crossbow, as the means of grace

To free us of this scourge. When I
Returned the crew stood still
And silent, cowed and mystified.
Did my wild cries bode good or ill?

'It bodeth ill. The albatross
Is baleful agent of the night.
His plumage shows he presages
Our deaths and chuckles at our plight.'

''Tis true,' say some. 'Not so,' say more.
'We must agree, we band of brothers,'
I plead. 'The bird must die,' say some.
'No. Let him live in peace,' say others.

Yes, there are clumsy phrases here. Perhaps the diction is too packed. Again, all to be returned to. Hasten on, for now come the beginnings of the poem's climax.

I heard the doubts but cared no whit.
I locked the string and fired the bolt.
But were my hands too wet with rain?
For when I fired I felt a jolt,

The crossbow slipped, the bolt flew wide,
The bird flew on. Some sailors said,
'It is God's wish the bird flies free.
His would-be murderer should be dead.'

While others said, 'Not so, not so.
Some evil spirit turned the shot
Away and let the bird escape.
But it must drown and sink and rot.'

I locked the string and fired again,
But now we felt the ocean swell.
I staggered and the bolt dropped short.
The doubters' laughs rang like a bell

In my sick mind. 'The elements
Rebel against this killer damned
For ever more.' While others said,
'This bird means death. We understand

How bad our plight is. Let him go?
You'll see our travail turn much worse.
The bird must die, the bird must die
To free us from this evil curse.'

He was quite pleased about how he had expanded Shelvocke's hint, *After some fruitless attempts, (he) at last shot the albatross.* The debate about the albatross's fate pleased him.

But now I brace myself, my feet
Four-square upon the deck, my eyes
New-sharpened and my hands
Rock hard. I'll gain my prize

With thrice-time shot. The bird flies low.
I take cool aim. The bolt flies free.
It does not miss. The albatross
Turns his head and looks at me,

His message clear. 'I trusted you.
You never will feel peace again
Your treachery will rouse the heavens.
Your sentence is eternal pain.'

I laughed aloud. 'Deluded bird,'
I cried. 'The sun breaks through,
The clouds will clear, the sea will calm,
Life will return, our spirits too.'

The albatross, in throes of death,
Shuddered, dropped and fell like lead
Into the angry blood-dark sea
To join the ruined deep sea dead.

He paused again. He had reached the poem's crisis. But now he faced the last part, the consequence, the fates of ship, crew and mariner. He had to get this right.

He remembered old tales about ghost ships cursed to sail for ever and never find port. He knew of lost souls, Cain and Ahasuerus, fated to wander the world for eternity, paying for transgressions against the moral order. And often the innocent suffered because of the guilty. He knew how to start this ending. Could he finish it?

He wrote ten more stanzas and reached an end of sorts. He read them through. Then, firmly and at last confidently, he crossed them out.

The last candles began to sputter. He had to pack away and be off before he was in the dark. He felt sick with failure. However, as he began the walk out of the grotto into the blessed open air, his spirits lifted. He would read Coleridge's poem afresh and see where he had gone wrong.

*

After a silent meal, Scrivener went upstairs to his room and shut the door. This was a moment of truth. He unfolded his poem and then opened *Sybilline Leaves* at the new 'Ancient Mariner'.

First he noticed Coleridge's annotations, as if he were a scholar editing a historical document. Then he read through the whole poem, at first quickly and then, as if he could not believe the evidence before his eyes, more slowly. First, he looked for Coleridge echoing the descriptions in Shelvocke's book and did not find any. Second, after reading it more carefully, he realised there was no reference whatever. After a third reading, he was sure Coleridge had never even read it. So the whole day had been a waste of time.

Coleridge had let his imagination roam where it would. He, though, had borrowed Hatley's imagination, so he was describing, not possessing. Coleridge's was an expression of himself but his was simply an account of someone else.

So any poet could have written this poem, but only Coleridge could have written his own. This meant that not just today but the journey to Woodstock was a waste of time.

Except that he knew that it hadn't been.

Then he found an interesting corollary. If Coleridge had written a poem which nobody else could, it wasn't very likely that when he'd sorted his ideas out he would then work out how he was going to turn it into poetry. He also noticed that when he read the poem, the rhythm was like a natural drum-beat which drove the story along.

So Coleridge's poem was not just words but a living being and rhythm and rhyme were as much parts of it as the heart is to a human body.

Oh, now his brain was aching with mental effort. But he had found out quite a lot about Coleridge – and, he was sure, himself as well. He wasn't afraid of 'The Ancient Mariner' now. He was lost in admiration.

Though exhausted, he didn't want to sleep yet. He craved easier reading. A pleasantly scary Gothic novel perhaps, with ruined castle, ghosts, mad monks and bleeding nuns.

What else was there to read? *The Monk*? Well, no. He felt too lazy to get up and look for it. So he might as well try to go to sleep.

Then he remembered that he had copied out 'Christabel' in the college library. It was a wild tale full of ghosts, castles, mysterious woodlands and not one but two damsels in distress. Just like *The Monk*.

He took his copy of 'Christabel' and opened it.

Ah yes, this was what he wanted.

'Tis the middle of night by the castle clock,
And the owls have awakened the crowing cock;

As owls hoot, the clock strikes midnight. A mastiff bitch howls in her sleep sixteen times. *Some say she sees my lady's shroud.* Supernatural and foreboding. Coleridge should write Gothic novels. He would make a fortune.

Christabel walks through the wood, dreaming of her lost lover. She finds the lovely lady Geraldine, victim of a foul kidnapping and left in the forest. Christabel is so trusting and kind that she takes Geraldine to Sir Leoline's castle. Strange things happen. Geraldine has to be helped past the iron gate. Why does she not like iron? And the mastiff moans in her sleep as the ladies pass.

Yes, this gave him the frisson of excitement he got from *The Monk*. He read on. Then he noticed something strange and troubling.

So half-way from the bed she rose
And on her elbow did recline
To look at the lady Geraldine

Beneath the lamp the lady bowed
And slowly rolled her eyes around;
Then, drawing in her breath aloud
Like one that shuddered, she unbound
The cincture from beneath her breast:
Her silken robe and inner vest
Dropt to her feet, and full in view,
Behold! her bosom and half her side—
A sight to dream of, not to tell!
O shield her! shield sweet Christabel!

All very ambiguous. Two women going to bed together, something he had heard of, but which nobody openly talked about. He was more concerned with something else. After a day spent worrying about rhythm and rhyme he was more sensitive, especially to his own anomalies. But here was one by Coleridge, so obvious that he surely must have noticed it. Why hadn't he corrected it?

The lines:

Her silken robe and inner vest
Dropt to her feet, and full in view,

were the first two lines of a quatrain. The passage consisted of what should be consecutive quatrains and a rhyming couplet to end, like a Shakespearian sonnet. So where was the line finishing this quatrain which should rhyme with 'view'? It should come after *Behold her bosom and half her side* and describe the *sight to dream of, not to tell.* But the reader can't dream of it or tell it because it isn't there. Scrivener's first thought was the dreaming would be so wonderful that the dreamer couldn't find words to describe its beauty. But that was impossible – Coleridge must have written and then crossed out a whole line. Why?

Scrivener read on. He finished the first part. The force of the story led him on to the second. He met Bracy the Bard, the poet who dreamt of the dove and the snake. The dove was Christabel and the snake Geraldine. When Geraldine hears Bracy's story she looks *askance* at Christabel and her eyes have become snake's eyes. And Christabel faints with *a hissing sound*. Geraldine has passed the snake on to her. What did this mean?

His mind would worry about this new problem and put him beyond sleep. Then he remembered that he had bought opium in Oxford. He found the bottle, took four drops and resealed it.

Perhaps he would repeat the wonderful forgotten dream in the sickbay and this time remember it.

His last thought before he drifted away was the mysterious inscription in 'Kubla' – *The writer of the above had much better have kept his sleeping thoughts to himself, for they are, if possible, worse than his waking ones.*

Well, yes, he would keep his sleeping thoughts to himself. Unless he dreamt a new 'Kubla Khan' tonight.

Chapter 28

Return to Cambridge

...for soon the evening clouds descend,
Slackening our hands, that fain their work would mend
And lo, there cometh Night, which all our work must end.
—'Toil not for burnished gold that poorly shines',
Sara Coleridge

No, Scrivener did not dream of Kubla. He spent a restless night. Even though it was broad daylight when he woke and the sun was shining, he lay in bed for several hours. Why should he get up? Yesterday he had risen with hope in his heart. But back in daylight, he recognised reality. 'Christabel' had given him nightmares and questions to answer, not only about Coleridge but also himself. The horrors of fear and inferiority, never far away, especially at Cambridge, had dealt a devastating blow. His brush with Coleridge's poetry was over.

*

The books he needed for the vacation work stood undisturbed and there they would stay.

He spent his days walking. He avoided his few friends from school and never went near the school itself. He felt liminal, poised between two lives. He never speculated on what might succeed them. He ventured out every day; expeditions started early each morning and ended each evening. He walked to Braughing and back, to Buntingford, Welwyn, Wheathampstead. One day he went as far as Berkhamsted, found an inn and stayed there for four nights. From here, he made forays to Tring, and across the Buckinghamshire border to Great Missenden, Wendover and Aylesbury. He considered making for Winslow and seeing John Neal again but thought it was too far. On all sides he saw the same poverty, misery and destitution that had shamed him on the journey to Woodstock.

One morning, he picked up the sheet of paper bearing the cursed inscription in 'Kubla Khan' which he held responsible for his plight. He remembered the first sheet, which he tried to give to Samuele, even though the Cam had washed away every word. This copy would have the same fate. When he reached the River Lea, he tore the paper into pieces and threw them into the water. The current took them away to fetch up who knew where and he walked on to Wadesmill feeling as if he had shed a heavy load.

So the vacation continued. Easter passed unnoticed. Apart from brief monosyllabic grunts to his uncle he had spoken to nobody.

Now it was time to return to Cambridge. He nearly didn't. But that would be a positive decision beyond him to make.

*

Unnoticed and without farewell, he dragged his trunk out of the house and made his way to the Salisbury Arms. He secured a seat on the coach and his journey started.

He reached the Blue Boar eight hours later and trudged to Jesus Lane and down the Chimney. A porter nodded to him as he passed through the gatehouse. His return had been recorded but the porter did not help him carry the trunk.

He entered his rooms and dragged his trunk up close to his bed. He did not open it. Instead, he lay on his bed, his mind empty.

Then just one positive thought occurred to him. He would not leave his room to eat. But he would, now the college still seemed deserted, go to the buttery to buy food to last him for a few days.

Twenty minutes later he was back, with bread, butter, cheese, apples, tea and milk. That would suffice.

*

He stayed in his room for two days. When he woke on the third, he was thinking again, tentatively at first, then more clearly. He remembered the puzzle about whether Coleridge would agree with Wordsworth on the subject of 'superadding'. So he left his room and sidled unobtrusively to the library to find out.

It seemed empty. He found Coleridge's *Biographia Literaria*, skimmed through it and lit on chapters thirteen and fourteen. And there he found what he wanted. Imagination and fancy. A difference, not in degree as most thought, but in kind. Imagination was the true creative principle. It brought everything together in unity. Poetry called out 'the whole soul' of man. It found unity in division, the reconciling of opposites, was an esemplastic power which brought forth poems whole and entire: a perfect form which would be unique. Coleridge's friend, the scientist Humphry Davy, would say that the result was like a compound, old objects fused into a unique new substance. But fancy merely saw objects which 'are fixed and dead' and put them in a different order with no imagination. The elements would remain separate and the metrical form worked up from whatever whims the poet brought to the task.

He remembered his difficulties with rhyme and rhythm. He remembered the story he had cobbled together from Shelvocke's book. And now he realised that what he did was exactly what Coleridge described as fancy. But imagination was beyond him to contemplate.

Here were the roots of his failure. They exposed his efforts as the inferior objects that they were.

He closed the book, replaced it on the shelf and crept quietly out of the not quite empty library, hoping that nobody had noticed him.

But someone had.

*

He remained hidden away for the next day, still crushed with the feeling of failure. At midday on the following day an envelope was pushed underneath his door. He looked at it as if it was a strange object risen from the seabed, then roused himself enough to cross the room.

He opened it. Inside was a sheet of college-crested note paper. He read it with a choking sense of inevitability.

Mr Scrivener
  Please be so good as to present yourself in my rooms on L staircase at five o'clock this evening.
  H.D.C. Vavasour (D.Litt.)

He stared at it almost unseeing for some minutes, then realised with a dull feeling around his heart that this might be the greatest crisis yet.

Chapter 29

Piccadilly Terrace

London, April 1816

Thy victims ere they yet expire
Shall know the demon for their sire,
As cursing thee, thou cursing them,
Thy flowers are withered on the stem.

—'The Giaour', George Gordon, Lord Byron

The house in Piccadilly Terrace, the temporary home of George Gordon, Lord Byron before he left England for ever, is an impressive, high-ceilinged residence and Coleridge does not feel at home in it. He is here to discuss the forthcoming publication of his three opium poems, 'Christabel', 'Kubla Khan' and 'The Pains of Sleep', which Byron has persuaded his own publisher, John Murray, to take on. Before this, the poems have been circulated in manuscript copies to a select few. And now he is about to meet Byron himself for the first – and only – time.

As he waits, he reflects on Byron's hair-raising reputation. The celebrated poet has overstepped the mark at last. He has had too many mistresses not to escape public outrage. Most shocking is an incestuous affair with his half-sister. There are rumours of sodomy, homosexuality. Nothing human which moves seems safe from him.

He is living in Piccadilly Terrace because it is the home of his wife. But this is a loveless marriage. He thought his wife was rich. But she is not rich enough, so the marriage will soon end.

Byron is known to be interested in vampirism and some even say he must be a vampire himself. Coleridge thinks there might well be something in this.

The door opens and Byron enters. Coleridge is dazzled by the figure standing before him. Soon, he will write effusively about the noble face, the handsome features, the magnetism that flows from him.

'My dear Coleridge,' he says, taking his hand in a firm grip and shaking it. 'My much-respected fellow poet and, I trust, soon my friend. Welcome.'

His voice is caressing and seductive. Coleridge can well understand why women have no defence against it.

His corrected copy of the whole volume, which he made for John Murray, lies on the desk. Other pages are placed next to it. He recognises them as poems he had copied out to be read by a fortunate few but is too far away to identify which.

'Coleridge,' says Byron. 'Before we start our discussion, would you oblige me by reading "Kubla Khan" aloud? I am told by many that to hear you read is an experience indeed.'

'Of course,' Coleridge replies. He extracts the poem from the pile. Byron sits in a large armchair and closes his eyes in blissful anticipation. Coleridge begins.

'*In Xanadu did Kubla Khan...*'

He continues, lost in his own imagination. As he reads he recreates his vision anew. This is not a reading any more but an offering to the one man who can fully appreciate it.

He ends. '*And drunk the milk of Paradise.*'

He draws breath and puts the page down.

There is a long silence Then Byron opens his eyes. 'Magical,' he breathes.

Another silence. Then Byron says, 'Coleridge, why has this sublime work not been published?'

'It's a fragment,' Coleridge replies firmly. 'An opium dream. I recalled what I could and was continuing well when I was interrupted.'

'Yes, I know. I've read your note. The mysterious person from Porlock. Well, I'll tell you here and now. There was no man from Porlock because there was no more poem to write. This is not a fragment. It is a perfect structure.'

'How you can say that?' Coleridge replies.

'It describes the course of the sacred river. From the dreamy realm of Kubla through the great chasm lined by trees straight from the sides of Culbone Combe, the wild romantic scene where the woman wails for her lover who is also a demon and then the world erupts into chaos. *Your* chaos. It dies, to be succeeded by five miles of meandering. *Your* wandering, Coleridge, which finishes in the icy darkness of the measureless caves echoing with grim prophecies from the past.

'But enough of this, you say. Wonderful visions ensue. Grim warnings soften into sweet music as the damsel with the dulcimer sings her haunting melody. Yet even this is in the past. You cannot bring her melody back but if you could, you would create Kubla's dome as something airy, incorporeal, an act of imagination. And then the final vision. Kubla Khan is gone and the poet takes over. The *poet*, Coleridge. That poet is *you*. The prophet who sees deeper into the life of things, who is beyond the understanding of ordinary mortals and strikes fear into them. And the fuel which energises you is the milk of Paradise. And what is that? The opium, which sustains you and ruins you at the same time.

'Coleridge, this marvellous poem is a journey deep into yourself and reaches its only conclusion. Sustenance or ruin. Life or death? The unresolvable clash of opposites. It is the perfect ending.'

After another silence, Byron smiles. 'I know how you feel. It takes one to know one.'

Coleridge still cannot speak.

'Take a few moments and then we'll come to the real business of the meeting,' says Byron.

Coleridge still sits silent, wondering what Byron means. Byron is now holding the complete volume and the poem in manuscript which Coleridge had not recognised. But he recognises it now. 'Christabel'.

'Coleridge,' says Byron. 'Please find the line *A sight to dream of, not to tell.*'

He does so.

'What does it mean?' Byron asks.

'It is a dream you can never forget but never share.'

'That only makes sense if you know what the sight is. Is it beautiful and too precious to share, or repulsive, which no one would wish to share? Or does it not matter and readers are free to make their own minds up?'

While Coleridge thinks of an answer, Byron asks another question. 'Where is the word to rhyme with "view"?'

Coleridge's heart sinks. He knows what is coming.

Byron is remorseless. 'This is in your handwriting. Leigh Hunt gave it to me. And here is what it says.

'*Behold! her bosom and half her side—*

'*Wizened, old and foul of hue.*

'Not very nice, is it. *Wizened, old and foul of hue.* I wouldn't want to tell anyone that. But it's the truth. Why did you strike it out?'

'I didn't think it was fitting,' Coleridge mumbles.

'Then why not write a new line, which is?'

'Such as?'

'Well, let me see. Ah, I have it. *Sweet lily paps, in number, two.*'

'Lily paps? That's Spenser.'

'Yes, *The Faerie Queen*. Sir Guyon in the Bower of Bliss. My sort of poem.'

'That would be a travesty.'

'Then write the truth. Geraldine is not human. She is a shape-shifter. She is a vampire. She aims to take the soul of Christabel. You know this. *Oh shield her! shield sweet Christabel!* And if she can take Christabel's soul, she can take yours. You know this, too, and so you must restore that line.' He suddenly grasps Coleridge's shoulders and cries urgently, even despairingly. 'Promise me you will put that line back. I beg you, for your own sake.' He pauses. Then he says, 'And mine.'

They part soon afterwards. Coleridge wishes Byron well on his travels and Byron hopes their friendship will continue. Then Coleridge leaves and Byron sits by an empty fireplace waiting for the end of his empty marriage.

*

Coleridge does what Byron said. Next day he finds there is enough space on his copy to insert the missing line. Then he carefully goes through the whole book one last time. The day after that he takes it to John Murray, who thanks him and tells him that terms are being arranged and agreed before printing and publishing can take place.

*

Three days later, Coleridge moves in with Dr Gillman and his wife Ann. Byron sails away from England for ever.

A letter arrives a few weeks later. Coleridge opens it and this is what he reads.

The Villa Diodati
Lake Geneva
Switzerland

My dear Coleridge
I am writing to let you know of a most intriguing event which I think you will find interesting, if not alarming. I am

here with my friend Percy Bysshe Shelley and his wife Mary (a convenient fiction to disguise the true nature of their partnership) and my personal physician John Polidori, together with Claire Clairmont, an old acquaintance.

The night was dark and riven by flashes of lightning, which put us into supernatural mood. We read and told ghost stories and then I read them parts of 'Christabel' from the manuscript copy which includes the line you erased and which I said you must restore. 'Behold her bosom and half her side, withered, old and foul of hue.'

The line had an extraordinary effect on Mr Shelley. He rose screaming from his seat, placed his hands over his ears and ran out of the room still screaming. Most singular.

Afterwards, when he had composed himself, he told us that when he heard the line he looked at Mary and saw instead a bare-breasted woman with eyes where nipples should be. The sight had terrified him.

I at once thought of Bracy the Bard's dream of a green snake coiled round a dove. I thought of Geraldine's eyes narrowing into the eyes of a snake and her hissing sound. And then Christabel's own hissing sound when the snake is passed from Geraldine to her and we know she is lost.

Shelley knew the woman he saw was the serpent-woman, the Lamia, the Vampire, who embodies men's deepest fears and claims them for her own. Vagina dentata. And she was also Geraldine, whose old and withered breasts, the sight to dream of, showed she was a shapeshifter, because they are restored to youth next morning. But she is not with Christabel. This is your deepest fear. She is with you.

I think you must agree that your own fears are justified and I applaud your decision to restore the line. It proves the honesty and clarity of thought which I associate with you.

Coleridge reads no more. The letter has enraged him. How dare Byron use someone else's reaction to assert his own opinions? Why should he accept this?

He savagely tears the letter up into little pieces, scatters them over the fire and watches them shrivel away. He feels he is scoured clean. It has been an exorcism.

Then he remembers that there is still work to do.

*

Next morning he rises early, packs an inkpot and pen into his knapsack and hails a cab to John Murray's printshop. He dashes in and pants, 'Is my book printed yet?'

'The type will be set today, sir,' says the foreman.

'Thank God,' cries Coleridge. 'May I have my manuscript for a moment?'

He finds the line, opens the inkpot and strikes the line out. And again. And again, until nothing is left but a layer of impenetrable black. Then he puts ink and pen back in his knapsack and strides out happily back to Highgate.

But soon his mind is working again and before he gets home he knows he has to accept that Byron is right and that he is doomed.

Chapter 30

Ordeal

Cambridge, June 1824

*If a student is sent down from their university or college, they
are made to leave because they have behaved very badly.*
—Dictionary definition, *Collins Cobuild Dictionary*

At five o'clock, Scrivener knocked on Dr Vavasour's door. A voice inside
said, 'Enter,' and Scrivener hesitantly obeyed. He had been here before,
in happier circumstances. This time he felt the chill of foreboding.

The walls panelled in dark wood, the loaded bookcases and
desk piled high with papers bespoke a comforting air of academic
chaos. But there was nothing comforting about Dr Vavasour,
sitting at his desk, his gaunt face looming over the documents in
front of him.

'Good evening, Mr Scrivener,' he said icily. 'I will come straight
to the point. Why have you not handed in the work you were given
for the vacation?'

Scrivener looked back at him dumbly.

'Answer me.'

'I have not done it.' What else could he say?

'And why not, pray?'

No answer.

'Mr Scrivener, I am sorry you were ill at the end of last term.
And I am sorry also about what I have gathered was its cause. I

understand why I did not see you when you were in the sickbay. But, apart from occasional sightings in the library, you have not been seen since the day you were released. Except once. I shall come to that in a moment.'

Scrivener felt an ominous twinge of alarm.

'First, however, in regard to work you have not done, may I remind you of your status in this college? For someone from your class in society, being admitted to this university is a privilege not given lightly. It is dependent on a delicate bargain between undergraduate and college. Slacking in your work, indulging in habits that those from the ranks of gentlemen are, if not entitled, at least permitted to indulge in, are options which are not open to you. You are here to repay the debt by taking full advantage of your fortune in being allowed to study here and thus enter a profession, very likely with the Church established, and a status in life to which you would otherwise not aspire. If you are not prepared to follow these precepts, there is no place for you here. Do you understand that, Mr Scrivener?'

'Yes, sir,' Scrivener answered miserably.

'Up till now I have trusted you to do as I require. I previously had a high opinion of you and because of that I would like to be lenient.'

Sudden relief.

'However, a more serious accusation has come to my attention. Two days ago I was not present in the library. I was performing teaching duties at which your presence was required. However, I am reliably informed that you were in the library that morning. Is that true?'

'Yes, sir.'

'And what were you doing there?'

'Reading, sir.'

'And what were you reading?'

'*Biographia Literaria* by Coleridge.'

'And what, pray, caught your attention?'

'I was interested in what he had to say about fancy and imagination.'

'I see. So are accounts of poetic composition of the sort that I have given you not to your liking?'

'I wanted to see what Coleridge thought.'

'Interesting. Your sudden interest in that scoundrel has already come to my attention. But I will come to that later. I have a more urgent matter to discuss. Did you notice that someone had, carelessly and unknowingly, left two one-shilling coins on the table at which you were sitting? Or, perhaps they may have been carelessly left there by you. Think carefully before you answer.'

'I neither saw, nor did I place, any money on the table,' said Scrivener.

'But I have it from what I regard as an unimpeachable source that the coins were on the table when you entered and that you were seen picking them up and putting them in your pocket.

'That is not true, sir,' said Scrivener.

'Turn out your pockets.'

'Yes sir.'

He searched his pockets and found three pennies and two ha'pennies.

'Are you sure that is all?'

'Yes, sir.'

'Look again.'

Scrivener had a sudden fear that his money belt would be found. Explaining away over four pounds in coin was beyond contemplation. 'I have no more money,' he said.

'So what else is in your pocket?'

How do I explain a bottle of laudanum? he wondered, horrified. 'Nothing, sir,' he said lamely.

'You are lying. There is guilt written all over your face. Produce whatever it is or I will call a porter.'

Scrivener took the little bottle out of his pocket and placed it on the table. Dr Vavasour recognised it at once.

'Ah, laudanum,' he said. 'And owned by that man who reads Coleridge with pleasure and approval and, for all I know, wrote the mysterious inscription on "Kubla Khan" himself. You are treading a dangerous path, Mr Scrivener.'

Scrivener sensed imminent doom. He was caught in a net which came from he knew not where.

'There is one matter still outstanding,' said Dr Vavasour.

Scrivener stayed mute.

'It concerns Mr Copperthwaite-Smirke's copy of Mr Coleridge's *Sybilline Leaves*. An unexpected interest for someone such as he, but nevertheless the book is his property. It is missing and the finger of suspicion has been pointed at you, especially in view of your new professed interest in its author.'

'May I ask who by, sir?' said Scrivener daringly. He was beginning to understand who had cast this mysterious net.

'You may not, for obvious reasons. Nevertheless, porters have been despatched to search your rooms, with a view to bring it here if it is found.' He rose to his feet. 'I believe I hear them outside.'

He walked to the door and opened it. 'Ah, good evening, Mr Turner,' he said.

Scrivener felt a sliver of hope. *Sybilline Leaves* would be found, but it would be a new copy with his name in it.

The head porter entered. 'I believe this is what you have been looking for, sir,' he said and placed a copy of *Sybilline Leaves* on the table.

Scrivener gasped. This was not a new copy. It had string tightly bound round the front cover, so that the 'Ancient Mariner' could not be read.

'Mr Turner, please remove the string,' said Dr Vavasour.

As Mr Turner carefully took it off, Dr Vavasour said, 'I find it ironic that a library clerk who complains about the defacement of one book should himself be responsible for damaging another,' he said.

Scrivener was mortified.

'Hand me the book, if you please, Mr Turner.'

The head porter did so and Dr Vavasour opened it at the flyleaf. He handed the open book to Scrivener and said, 'Please read what is on it.'

Scrivener miserably read aloud what he saw. '*EX LIBRIS R.S.F.J. Copperthwaite-Smirke.*'

'Explain this, if you please,' said Dr Vavasour.

Scrivener could not speak. Raggett's treason struck him dumb with anger. He had done this. Why?

Then he remembered something. The Bell, John Neal and his warnings.

Yes, they were the key. He was the victim of a vicious plan. The fellow commoners wanted more sport with hm and Raggett saw a way to please them. But if Raggett believed this would elevate him to the rank of gentleman in their eyes he was likely to be very disappointed.

Even though his whole world was collapsing round him, the thought gave Scrivener some unworthy pleasure.

But Dr Vavasour was speaking again. 'Mr Scrivener, I had high hopes of you. But you have let me, yourself and the college down. Any one of these offences might have been enough to have you sent down. But three at the same time is insupportable. With Mr Turner as witness and with the full authority of the Master and Fellows, I hereby send you down from Jesus College and from Cambridge University. You will now return to your rooms and you will not emerge until eight o'clock tomorrow morning, when you will be roused by a porter who will guide you out of the college. Mr Turner, please be so good as to escort Mr Scrivener back to his rooms. Please also ask one of your colleagues to make sure Mr Scrivener is fully prepared to leave so that no trace of his presence remains.'

'Very well, Dr Vavasour,' said Mr Turner.

Scrivener had thought that there was no humiliation worse than when Copperthwaite-Smirke and his friends threw him in the river.

But that was nothing compared with what he was feeling now.

Chapter 31

End

My genial spirits fail;
And what can these avail
To lift the smothering Weight from off my Breast?
                    —'Dejection', Samuel Taylor Coleridge

Mr Turner was a benevolent guide as they crossed First Court to Scrivener's rooms.

'I'm sorry to see you like this,' he said. 'I reckon there's some devilry here. We remember what happened to you last term and we've a pretty good idea of who it was. Don't be resentful towards Dr Vavasour. He was doing his job on the evidence he was given. He's not a detective. He has to carry out the rules of the college.'

Scrivener said nothing.

'I will send Mr Trott to fetch you out tomorrow morning. He helped you and the Italian gentleman. He is well disposed to you.'

'Thank you,' said Scrivener, on the verge of tears.

They had reached his rooms. Mr Turner unlocked the door and followed Scrivener in.

'I'm afraid I will have to relieve you of your keys now,' he said. 'You cannot leave these rooms until Mr Trott arrives tomorrow. Make sure you are ready.'

Scrivener handed him the keys.

'Thank you,' said Mr Turner. 'I'll say goodbye now. He held out his hand and Scrivener shook it. 'May I wish you all the luck that's going. I repeat, I think you've been badly done to.'

He turned and walked back to the lodge, his top hat shining slightly in the evening sun. Scrivener watched him through the window until he disappeared into the lodge. Then he threw himself onto the bed and cried until he was exhausted and his stock of tears was used up.

*

When he was calmer he considered the immediate future. He knew this would be a long night and sleep would be simply exhaustion.

He opened his clumsy travelling case and packed his meagre supply of clean clothing. Then he put his own few books in his knapsack. He found his own copy of *Sybilline Leaves* among them. At least Raggett hadn't removed that. His copy of *The Monk* was where he had left it and that went in the knapsack as well. He checked the books which were the college's property. He looked then at the papers on the table. Not as untidy as Dr Vavasour's desk but still a mess. He must sort them through and put the dross in the waste paper basket.

Most of the papers were expendable and he had to push down hard on them to make them fit. But then he came across something he had completely forgotten.

'Lines Written on Jesus Green'
As through the dusky silence of the groves,
Through tiny valleys and past green retreats,
With easeful ripple flows the shining stream
Along its hidden course,
So flows my Life, unnoticed in the throng
Of chattering seekers-out of worldly fame,
Always the observer, never the observed,
And thus...

He read it through carefully. Lame. Self-pitying. But now he saw it afresh after two months of bitter experience.

He read it again, looking at the language, the rhythms, the rhyme scheme. Odd. When he wrote it and even when he read it afterwards, he had hardly noticed the complete absence of rhyme. The calm and regular rhythm was enough. And what was more encouraging was that he had managed to find in the stream an effective metaphor for life, admittedly a commonplace one, but fit for his purpose, which meant whether the metaphor had been overused did not matter. And besides, the smooth, lulling rhythm *was* the stream.

Everything fitted. He compared it with the strained, unwieldy efforts towards 'superadding' metrical form to Simon Hatley's adventures. And now came another revelation. He remembered the moment of writing 'Lines'. Not for the first time he had been in a low state.

He thought of Wordsworth and 'emotion recollected in tranquillity'. Then he thought of the Coleridge he had just been reading, of the difference between fancy and imagination. Perhaps imagination was not beyond him after all. He took a new sheet of paper and wrote out a fair copy. Then at last he dropped his despised first attempt into the waste paper basket with all his other memories.

This had been a good experience. Perhaps there was something ahead for him as a writer after all. For the first time in almost a month, he felt a little spark of hope.

*

In the end, he slept quite well. He woke at seven, swilled his face in the washstand, dressed and checked that everything was as it should be. When he was satisfied he sat down to wait for Mr Trott.

Precisely at eight o'clock a voice outside called, 'Mr Scrivener, are you ready?'

'I am indeed, Mr Trott,' he replied.

The door was unlocked and there stood the young porter who had taken no action when Samuele had argued his case for him.

'Good morning, Mr Scrivener,' he said. 'Let me take your bag.'

Scrivener handed him the travelling case but kept the knapsack round his shoulders. Halfway along the stone path to the porter's lodge, Scrivener stopped. 'Mr Trott,' he said. 'May I stand here alone for a few moments?'

'Of course you may,' said Mr Trott. 'Come to the lodge when you are ready.'

He took Scrivener's travelling case and walked on. Scrivener turned towards the west and the open side of the court.

Now he was alone, the silence hit him almost like a blow in the face. Nobody was stirring yet. Beyond the railings sealing the college from the world he saw pastureland and trees. He could hear the bustle of the town centre and the colleges filling it as their day started. But this spot, solitary in its separateness, seemed compressed, like an invisible capsule in which he was the only living thing.

The sun shone, the grass was emerald green, the brick walls of the handsome buildings round him glowed richly mellow in the sunshine.

As he stood there, he felt as though others were standing with him. But they were not leaving the college for ever. Though dead, they would always be here.

He saw Thomas Cranmer, the first protestant Archbishop of Canterbury. He saw David Hartley, philosopher and physician, who described a theory of how the human mind and body worked and who also gave his name to Coleridge's first son. With them stood Thomas Malthus, the economist who was the first to work out a relationship between food and the growth of the world's population. He thought of Laurence Sterne, the cleric who had written the mad, eccentric but beautiful *Tristram*

Shandy. And there was Coleridge himself, whether the college liked it or not!

But they had all made a mark which would not fade. The brightest sons of the college.

And was not this insular college itself rather eccentric? Other colleges had been founded by kings, queens, noblemen, great families, mighty prelates. Jesus College had replaced the nunnery of Saint Radegund, when John Alcock, Bishop of Ely, closed it down and dispersed the nuns because it was the local brothel. What to do with the redundant buildings? To put a new college in them was as reasonable as anything else. Even the college crest was a pun on the old bishop's name.

As he looked westward he imagined John Milton, Christopher Marlowe and Sir Isaac Newton also standing in the courts of their colleges and he felt the weight of the history of the whole university.

And then the sense of exclusion, rejection and finality engulfed him and he stood still and lonely, with tears streaming down his face.

He turned and trudged his way to the porters' lodge. Then he had a wonderful saving thought. Coleridge hadn't been asked to leave without taking a degree. It was his decision. He was setting out on a new life. Scrivener's sending down was a cheat. He was leaving of his own free will, also to set out on a new life.

As he walked down Jesus Lane towards the Blue Boar, his heart lightened.

Chapter 32

Bengeo

The only justice is to follow the sincere intuition of the soul, angry or gentle. Anger is just, and pity is just, but judgement is never just.

—D.H. Lawrence

Scrivener found a seat on the London coach. This did not go through Hertford, but Wadesmill, a tiny hamlet three miles away with a coaching inn, The Feathers, where he would have a good meal before the three-mile walk to Bengeo and the house where he would have to forage for food.

He drifted off into a doze, emotionally exhausted. There must be a stubborn streak of optimism in him which he had not suspected before.

Well, perhaps. He felt in his pocket for his fair copy of 'Lines written on Jesus Green'. After last night's euphoria when he reread it, he wondered if he would still have the same reaction. He read it carefully three times. The lack of rhyme seemed natural and unforced. There was no superadding, no adorning. This was the pure thought, which emerged without any striving after effect. It was itself and no other. Coleridge was right.

He understood the difference now between fancy and imagination. His poem was not an act of the imagination. There was nothing original about thought or feeling. What mattered was its fitness for its purpose. And that lay in the words, the form, not the originality. Imagination meant seeing and making real what nobody had seen before. And now he knew he must find it out for himself. Nobody could teach him.

He was not angry with Coleridge now. He had a quality which no one else could attain and, unless a miracle (never impossible) happened, certainly not him.

He found his thoughts turning to Raggett. His anger was turning into pity.

It was not hard to know who had accused him of theft or who had hidden his own copy of *Sybilline Leaves* and substituted Copperthwaite-Smirke's.

But Raggett's plan had succeeded too well. The outcome was its victim being sent down. So Copperthwaite-Smirke, Viscount Bonewood and the rest were deprived of their sport. Raggett would supply it himself and not be accepted as a gentleman. He would be an object of ridicule and contempt. And serve him right.

No, don't be triumphal, show pity. Much more satisfying.

Besides, he had much to thank Raggett for. Thanks to him, he had been jerked out of his little private world. After that embarrassing episode in Potton, suddenly he could see the world as it really was. He was learning to cope. He realised that there were matters outside himself to take seriously. And he was beginning to see better his place in the world.

He was glad now that he had felt rejection and exile as he stood in First Court with tears streaming down his face. Sent down, banished, no longer a part. Then, Coleridge came to his rescue again. Coleridge would stay part of the tradition, not because he led a chaotic life ruined by opium, but because of what he had achieved.

Yes, that was Coleridge's true legacy.

*

The coach reached Wadesmill at one o'clock. The coachman handed down his bags and, with the other passengers, he had the expected filling meal. He thought of using his cache of money to hire a horse and trap for the rest of the way, but he felt refreshed and so decided to walk after all. Besides, he had a feeling that he was going to need every penny.

The long journey was nearly over. Now back to the dark house and taciturn, unwilling, hostile uncle and the difficult search as to what to do next.

*

The squat house with windows like blind eyes stood before him. Unable to locate his key, he knocked three times on the front door until he heard movement.

The door opened. There stood his uncle, dark and squat as his house.

'Oh,' he said. 'I thought I was rid of you. Come in if you must.'

Without answering, Scrivener took knapsack and bags upstairs to his room.

His uncle followed. 'You've only just gone. Why are you back?'

'I've left Cambridge,' said Scrivener.

'You mean you've been thrown out.'

'If you say so. Anyway, I won't be going back.'

His uncle smiled. 'I knew no good would come of this. People like you should not go to those places. You've been found out. What did you do wrong?'

'I didn't do the work I was set.'

'Why not?'

'I didn't see fit to.'

Silence again. Then, with hatred in his voice like shifting gravel, his uncle said, 'I never wanted to take you on. It was a favour to my sister as she lay dying. I should have sent you to an orphanage.'

'Even an orphanage would be better than living with you,' Scrivener replied hotly. 'Am I expected to thank you?'

'I tried my best for you. I would have got you out of school, working and earning money. Good enough for most boys round here. But your worthless father had left money to send you to that grammar school. It's what your mother wanted, too. I wouldn't break a promise. I shouldn't have been so squeamish. When that headmaster said you could go to Oxford or Cambridge I said I'd forbid it. But he said your mother and father would want you to have a chance, so I said so be it. More fool me. I should have thrown you out of the house there and then.'

This speech increased in noise and rage and his face was red and sweating. Scrivener did not answer. His uncle's face contorted even more with fury.

'Go on, get out!' he screamed. 'I never want to see you again, you worthless scoundrel.'

Now Scrivener spoke. 'Everything in my life that is worthwhile I've done by myself, without help except from the masters at school. I owe you nothing but my scorn.'

He turned on his heel, marched downstairs, opened the front door, which his uncle had not bothered to lock, found his own keys in his pocket, threw them on the floor because he would not need them again, slammed the door behind him and strode away.

He walked east again, towards King's Meads. He stopped outside St Leonard's church, with its view over the meads to the River Lea. He surveyed it for some time in silence. He might never see it again. Then he remembered that if he was leaving for ever, he had better take his baggage with him.

A thought struck him. *What a fool. He'll have locked the door. And I've thrown my keys away.*

He broke into a run. Yes, there was the house, as blank as ever. But rising into the air from behind it was a cloud of blue smoke.

The door was locked. The garden was surrounded by a high brick wall made of the same blueish-grey brick of the house. It was as if his uncle had designed the house as a brick-and-mortar version of himself. And it meant that the front door was the only way in.

Scrivener ran round the house to the walls. He heard a crackle of flame. Perhaps there was after a gate in the wall that he had never noticed, maybe hidden by a shrub.

There wasn't. He walked round again. Now he could smell the burning. He looked desperately for cracks in the pointing which might give a fingertip hold. He thought he saw one quite high up. He ran at it and jumped. He only grazed his fingers on the brick. He looked for something to stand on. Nothing. So he looked lower, hoping to find a foothold.

Yes, this might just do. He placed his toe in the tiny crack and somehow managed to grasp the fingerhold. Too desperate to be tentative, he swung his other arm up to grip the top of the wall. He had a sudden horror that broken glass might be stuck into the mortar. When he hoisted himself up, he saw that there was, all the way along, but miraculously, his fingers had avoided it.

He now had a good purchase on the wall. He raised himself up, then, avoiding the glass, dropped down into the garden, to see his clothes, his books, all his possessions, burning in front of his eyes. *Sybilline Leaves* was almost completely consumed. He saw its cover crumple. *Lyrical Ballads* was already a little pile of ash. *The Monk* suddenly burst into a separate flame before it shrivelled like the rest. The few other books he possessed were charred ruins. His papers and notebooks were black flakes climbing into the air and blowing away free. All his spare clothes were alight.

His uncle was stoking the flames like an automaton with a long stick, soulless, vicious. A blind urge was impelling Scrivener to bundle him into the flames. He started to lunge at him, not involuntarily but grimly purposed.

Then, as suddenly, he stopped and cursed his cowardice in not taking this final revenge. It would do him no good to be arrested and put on trial for his life. He had much to do yet and this creature was not worth hanging for.

So he thought rationally. There was a pile of logs next to the house. With it was an axe. He strode over to the pile and picked up the axe. He looked back at the blaze. His uncle still stoked it.

He entered the house, walked to the front door and attacked it with the axe, blow after blow, until splinters lay all around him and there was a gap big enough to get through. Then he saw his keys still on the floor and picked them up. As he stood up, he noticed his uncle's keys hanging on a hook on the wall. So he seized those as well. Still carrying the axe, he walked through the shattered door towards St Leonard's, across the meads to the Lea and dropped axe and keys into the water. That would have to do as a revenge.

What to do now? He had no home, no possessions and no clothes except what he stood up in. But he still had his money belt.

He would survive. The image of John Neal and the sound of his voice when, unknowingly, he had saved Scrivener's life, were clear in his mind, generous as an uncle should have been. The image stayed as he ran back along the river towards Hertford, down Fore Street and up Gallows Hill. Here he stopped and looked back at the town he was leaving.

First Cambridge, then Hertford. The centres of his life so far, both left for ever on the same day.

For the very last time he surveyed the town where he had grown up. Dusk was approaching. He turned away and walked south. He would keep going through the night until he dropped with exhaustion. Then he would sleep under a tree and make himself ready for his entry into London, for he was already thinking of a future there.

A thought crept into his mind like a blue break in a grey sky. Why not visit Coleridge himself and tell him his story? And would Samuele visit him as well and find the truth?

PART V

Chapter 33

Rydal Mount

The Lake District, June 1824

'Mr Wordsworth is not to be interrupted.'
—Mrs Wordsworth to John Keats when he
attempted to ask her husband a question

After two nights in the Sally Cat, Samuele set off again. The coach to Kendal was well patronised and he could only find an outside seat. As they rumbled northwards the weather worsened. For half the second day and all the third he was drenched by rain and chilled by wind. He endured flea-ridden beds and inedible meals of mutton burnt to a cinder or bloody and nearly raw. Thankfully, he reached Kendal on the afternoon of the fourth day and found a place on a carrier's cart, pulled by a phlegmatic ox which kept up an irritatingly slow walk along rough tracks. Samuele perched unsteadily on boxes, barrels and bales of hay. High fells flanked the road on each side. The sky was dull grey, a cold wind blew and he was spattered by odd flecks of rain. He dreamt of Giulia, of taking her in his arms and letting the warmth of her body flood through him. But each time, he woke from his shallow doze and felt the bitter cold again.

At last they came down through trees to the shore of a large lake. 'Windermere,' the carrier grunted.

The rain eased. He looked through a veil of drizzle and wet mist at dull, metallic water. The wind wrinkled its surface like an old man's face. Samuele asked the carrier, 'Do you know of a Mr William Wordsworth? I'm told he lives at Rydal Mount.'

'Aye, he does that,' said the carrier. 'Big house near t'lake.'

'What, this lake?'

'Nay. Rydal Water. Near Ambleside. Nobbut three mile away, along t'road by Windermere. Ask about t'house there.'

As the miles progressed the drizzle ceased, and clouds lifted and move fleetingly across a pale blue sky. Samuele saw mighty crags and fells, brown, green and grey. Their colour changed from dark to light and back to dark as clouds obscured the sun and as suddenly exposed it again. Eventually he reached Ambleside. The little village was deserted, except for a man standing on a wooden jetty about to clamber into a rowing boat.

'Excuse me,' Samuele said politely. 'Can you tell me where Rydal Mount is?' The man looked at him testily. 'Where Mr Wordsworth lives,' Samuele added.

'I know it well,' the man replied. 'So do they all, round here and from far away as well.' He jerked his thumb towards the road north. 'That leads to Grasmere. You'll pass Rydal Water. Look up at the fell. There's a lane. You'll see it. If you don't, you're daft.' He turned away to his boat without acknowledging Samuele's thanks.

More walking. He came to tiny Rydal Water and looked up the fell as the man had said. Yes, there was the narrow lane. He fancied he saw a large house surrounded by trees at the top. Happy not to deserve the 'daft' epithet, he left the road and began the climb.

The last leg was the worst. The lane was a rough trackway. The evening was darkening by the time he walked up a path to a large garden with tiny rockpools set out on terraces carved out of the fellside. The year was waning and so the garden was lank, wet and dying, but it still hinted at bright summer colour to come. At last he reached Rydal

Mount, solid, stone-built and ivy-covered. It had slate roofs and three high chimneys, a far cry from his putative father's hovel in Stowey.

He pulled his shoulders back, marched up the steps to the front door, found a bell-pull and tugged at it. After a few moments the door was opened by a tall woman who looked in her sixties, though something about the way she stood and moved hinted she was younger. Her weather-beaten face was brown with wind and sun, and Samuele thought she had a wild, almost animal look. The candlelight made her almost witchlike. 'Yes?' she said.

The curt monosyllable unsettled Samuele. Before he could answer, the woman said, 'Are you yet another disciple who wants to gawp at my brother? He's too busy. He has many responsibilities.'

Samuele feared this ominous gatekeeper. He must risk everything. 'I'm sorry to burst in on you unannounced but time is short for me. I have come here from Sicily. My father, whose name is Bernardo Gambino, admires your friend Mr Coleridge and is writing a book about him for Italian readers. He is too ill to travel, so he has sent me to find out more about him from people who know him well. Mr Lamb told me that you were the most important to visit. I have an introduction from him.'

The woman stepped back and regarded him searchingly. Then she said, 'Stay there,' turned away from him, walked to a staircase, climbed four steps, stopped and shouted, 'A gentleman from Sicily wants to know about Coleridge.' Her voice would carry from the tops of mountains.

'Tell him go away,' a man's voice, equally strong, answered from far above.

'He tells me he has come here especially from Sicily. He has brought an introduction from Charles Lamb.'

A short silence. Then, 'Bring him up here.'

By now, Samuele had deduced that the woman was Wordsworth's sister Dorothy.

She escorted him up the darkening staircase to an attic room lined with books. A fire burned in the grate. The maidservant tending it straightened up when Samuele entered. A dark, severe-looking man sat at a desk lit by three candles in a candelabra made of black iron. He had been writing: a pen stood in the inkwell and sheets of paper were spread out on the desk's surface. At a curt, 'You may leave,' the maidservant gave a quick bob and scurried out of the room.

Another woman sat on the other side. She had been copying the sheets as they were produced. Some sort of secretary?

'Here is my brother,' said the woman who had brought him upstairs, 'and here is Mary Hutchinson, his wife. She is copying his poems as he writes them because he needs many scripts.'

The tension between the women seemed to crackle through the room.

Samuele handed the letter over. Wordsworth took it, picked up a candle and with its light peered closely at the seal. When he was satisfied, he spoke.

'Well, sir? To what do I owe this entirely unexpected and, I may say, not altogether welcome visit?' Mr Wordsworth's voice was harsh, the accent remarkably like that of the carrier and the man at Ambleside, although his words were clearer, measured and precise. The candles cast flickering shadows over the desk and his face. His eyes were sunk in shadow, yet the pupils gleamed brightly and intensely.

'I have come from Sicily, from Palermo,' Samuele answered. The familiar story came easily. He ended with, 'I, too, admire Mr Coleridge. I hope that before I go home I might meet him.'

'And you think I will tell you the details of our once intimate friendship?' The tone was disapproving.

'I know it is a great impertinence...' Samuele started.

'Yes,' said Mr Wordsworth. 'Yes, it is.'

'Mr Lamb told me that you were the most important person to meet.'

'I am impressed that Charles has written an introductory letter. Have you spoken to him?'

'Yes.'

'Where?'

'In his house in Colebrook Row.' Samuele realised he was being interrogated.

'Was anyone else there?'

'His sister Mary.'

'Was she well?'

'Yes. But I'm told that she's not always so. She has a great guilt to carry.'

'Who else did Charles recommend?'

'Mr Poole. I have already spoken to him.'

'And how was he?'

'He was well. We walked through the Quantocks from Nether Stowey, along the clifftop path to Lynton and then back to Watchet. We broke our journey at Culbone, saw the church and the combe and stood outside Ash Farm and thought about "Kubla Khan".'

Wordsworth looked almost wistful. 'Ah, those names. Such memories. *Bliss was it in that dawn to be alive, but to be young was very heaven.*'

'William,' said Mary reprovingly. 'That is not an apposite quotation.'

'For a few blessed months it was. We have fond memories of our once close companion and colleague. But I have to tell you those days have long gone.' He looked up at his sister. 'Have they not, Dorothy?'

'I fear so,' said Dorothy. 'He was our dear, dear friend. We shall for ever miss his company.'

Samuele felt tears starting in his eyes. 'If he deigns to speak to you,' Thomas Poole had said and it seemed he was right. He had come so far for news from the man he knew was once Coleridge's greatest friend and a door seemed slammed in his face, so hard that he nearly forgot the visit which promised the most news. 'And Mr Southey, too,' he said.

'Ah, yes. Like the world, he is too much with us.'

Mr Wordsworth, stern, tall, seemed to detect Samuele's unhappiness and relented slightly. 'But you've come a long way. We cannot let you leave us empty-handed. So here is what I can tell you. The last I heard which is not mere rumour was that he was lodging with a doctor and his wife in Highgate.'

Samuele did not say that he knew this already.

'The name is Gillman, I believe. As to Mr Coleridge's status there, I have no information: it seems shrouded in mystery and rumour. But I have no doubt that it is quite respectable.'

'I see,' said Samuele. 'Mr Lamb told me that he's there as a patient. Dr Gillman will wean him off his opium habit.'

'I wish him well with that,' said Wordsworth. 'Even so, I will not speak about a one-time friend to a complete stranger. I'm sorry.'

'Then I will take my leave of you, sir,' said Samuele. 'Thank you.'

But Mary said, 'William, you cannot let the poor boy go like that. He deserves more and he's shivering with cold.'

'What more can I give him?'

'You heard what he said. He thought you and Coleridge were friends. He can't go away with a mere "we are friends no longer".'

'There are things I will not divulge to a stranger.'

'William, it is a matter of record. All England knows about how your ways parted. This gentleman has travelled across Europe. He deserves to know the truth, I implore you. We have a guest here. We have a duty.'

'Very well,' said William unwillingly. He cleared his throat, collected his thoughts, then began. 'You'll know that when we were young, we were closer than brothers. In Somerset and here in the Lakes we laughed, thought, talked and wrote together.

I believe we did many remarkable things. There could be no finer companion than Mr Coleridge. He was… he was…' – he lowered his head and blinked, almost as if he, too, had tears starting – 'he was a *wonderful* man. Together we were a little commonwealth. But the years and human weakness combined to take a terrible toll.'

Dorothy spoke, her eyes dreamy with reminiscence. 'I remember, I always will remember, that blessed day so long ago when we first saw him. It was at Racedown. He vaulted over a stile and ran through the big field down to us: a race down indeed.'

'And now he is as good as destroyed,' said William.

'It was the opium,' said Dorothy. 'And a wife who did not understand him. And the constant need to make money. And also there was—'

'He had to go to the Mediterranean,' William interrupted, as if Dorothy was straying onto forbidden ground. 'If he'd stayed here he would have died.'

'And yet he came back in a worse state than when he left,' said Mary.

'Opium again,' said William. 'It was hardly his fault that he was trapped in Rome for a whole year before a friendly ship could bring him home.'

'He met an American artist there who painted his portrait,' said Samuele.

'How do you know that?' said William sharply.

'Mr Poole told me.'

'Poole is a decent man. He's short in imagination but his good nature makes up for it. He's been as good a friend as any of us to our dear colleague.'

'I know,' said Samuele.

'Poole was mightily disapproving when Mr Coleridge broke with his wife and children,' said William.

'The marriage should never have happened,' said Dorothy. 'She cramped his style, she had no understanding of his needs, no fellow-feeling. She was the worst of all wives for him.'

'That does not mean he had the right to cast her aside, Dorothy,' said William.

Cast her aside. If he could cast one woman aside, might he not cast another?

'The upshot was that he was rootless, homeless,' said William. 'He could not live in Greta Hall with his wife, especially as her own sister and her husband lived there as well. Southey had supplanted him as the man of the house, even as far as being a father to his children. So he came to live with us. But our little home in Dove Cottage was too small. We moved to Allan Bank. Dreadful, smoky house. Mr Coleridge wrote *The Friend* there.'

'*The Friend*?' asked Samuele.

'His own journal. He'd tried to do one already: *The Watchman*. It failed, of course,' said William.

'This one worked better,' said Dorothy. 'A little more temperate and philosophical. Yet it failed as well.'

'Not before it had caused pain,' said William.

'It was the burden he placed on poor dear Sara,' said Mary.

'Sara? You mean his wife?' said Samuele. Ominously, it did not sound as if she did.

'No, not his wife. My sister-in-law,' said William. 'Sister to my wife. She lives here with us.'

Samuele remembered Thomas Poole. *That one in the Lakes.*

'My brother has three adoring women to see to his every need,' said Dorothy. 'Poor Esteesee has none.'

'A name once used affectionately by the other Sarah, his wife,' said William. 'No more, I fear.'

'But, since we are talking of old times, we shall use Sarah's Esteesee again tonight,' said Dorothy.

So many Saras and Sarahs. Samuele's head was reeling. 'About *The Friend*,' he said in attempt to get back to the narrative.

'Yes,' said William. 'Well, Sara Hutchinson is our dear friend. Mr Coleridge called her Asra so he would not mix up the Saras. She was responsible for any success that journal may have had. She it was who copied every illegibly scribbled article, every poem. She saw to the stamp duty on the paper, sent each complete issue to the press, kept the subscribers' address list intact. Without her, *The Friend* would have stayed what so many other projects of dear Esteesee have remained, mere speculations twisting round in that all-too-fertile mind. And why? Because she was sorry for him, because she knew he needed help, because...' He stopped short, the sentence incomplete.

Dorothy spoke. 'Because he loved her.'

'I wish you hadn't told our friend that,' said William.

So do I, thought Samuele miserably.

'But I have to,' said Dorothy. 'It was the root of all our troubles. Nothing will make sense if our young friend does not know it.'

'I suppose you are right,' said William reluctantly. 'It could not last. The toll it took on Asra was too great. She had to work for a man whose obvious feelings had become an embarrassment to her – and to us, I may say.'

'What happened?' Samuele asked miserably.

The two women looked at each other. Samuele saw William give a little nod. Dorothy saw it, too, and continued as if it gave her permission.

'I think that our Sara truly loved Esteesee at first and knew he loved her. But no woman can bear a selfish love, which thinks only of the lover's own feelings and nothing for those of the beloved. She was truly thankful when he went away to the Mediterranean. She told him before he left that she didn't want to hear from him any more.'

'But…' Samuele began, then stopped. What did that say about how the man he wanted so much to be his father regarded Cecilia?

'Besides, we had a great blow,' said Mary. 'Sara had intended to marry John.'

'John?' asked Samuele.

'Our dear brother. He was captain of an East Indiaman. His ship foundered off Portland Bill and he went down with it. He was Sara's one hope of escape from Esteesee. When Esteesee returned, he was in poor shape, worse than when he went.'

'I know,' said Samuele. 'Mr Poole told me.'

'His wife ejecting him from Greta Hall was painful,' Dorothy continued. 'It was inevitable that he would come to us—'

William broke in. 'I had to get to the root of this problem. I took a walking tour with him and Asra, just the three of us, along the River Duddon. I thought it might clear the air, or at least bring things to a head. It did neither. But I think that by the end even Esteesee knew that all Asra's love for him was dead. That's what made producing *The Friend* so weary a process for everybody and especially Asra, the sadness that he could not see what we knew perfectly well.'

'She even took to wearing a mob cap to hide the hair he loved so much,' said Dorothy. 'We had to rid ourselves of him.'

'He had become impossible,' said William. 'He was riddled with opium. His judgement had gone. He had been back to Greta Hall, where no great happiness ensued for anybody. I was determined he would not come to us again.'

There was a sudden silence. Samuele detected tension in the air. Something might be said now from which there would be no going back.

'Our final parting of the ways,' said Dorothy eventually.

Another silence. She looked at her brother as if asking whether she should say any more. William's fierce expression said clearly enough, 'I forbid you to.'

Samuele waited. The silence became oppressive. One of them had to say something. Should it be he, taking his leave of them because there was indeed nothing more to say?

It was William who spoke, heavily and reluctantly. 'I had no alternative. Our good friend Basil Montagu visited the Lakes while Esteesee was at Greta Hall. Montagu was perhaps dazzled at meeting so great a man, as he thought. He invited Esteesee to stay with him in London for the whole winter—'

'That was good,' Samuele daringly interrupted. Wordsworth lifted a hand. The gesture said clearly enough that he should not interrupt again.

'As I said, Montagu is a good friend. I would not risk that friendship or make him regret a foolish action which would inevitably give him pain when I could prevent it. I told him in no uncertain terms about his opium, ill-health, selfishness, inability to bend himself to his proper work unless in a frenzy brought about by opium, the demands he would make on the household. I had to say what was true, that the man's personal habits had deteriorated so far that he was no longer fit to live with. I make no bones about it. That was what I said and I meant it. I still do.'

Samuele drew breath again, but once again the curt hand warned him.

'You wonder why I talk like this this to a stranger. I have no regrets. What I did is no secret. Montagu is a powerful man: he made sure others knew. Now everybody in the land knows it, because a rift between two such men as we were, thought of by the public as almost one being, could hardly stay unknown. Because it was the final rift. I know that Esteesee was bitterly angry with me. His visit to Montagu was curtailed almost to nothing. He was humiliated. I should, I suppose, feel guilt, but I cannot. He has been a fool to himself and his misfortunes are entirely of his own making. We have not seen him since. I believe we never shall again, unless by chance.'

The speech swept over Samuele like a great wave. It made him think of something else, an odd reaction while his mind came to terms with this revelation. 'Mr Wordsworth,' he said. 'Do you ever go to Cambridge?'

'On occasion,' William said. 'It is my university. I am likely to visit it from time to time. Why do you ask?'

'I was in Cambridge recently. I went to Mr Coleridge's college.'

'Did you now?'

'I met a man, an undergraduate, who had a special interest in Coleridge. He had made a discovery in the Old Library. There is a copy of "Kubla Khan" along with "Christabel" and "The Pains of Sleep".'

'Yes. Published at last.'

'He found something had been written in it.'

'What do you mean, written in it?'

'Someone had written a note at the end of "Kubla Khan".'

'What did it say?'

Samuele knew it by heart. '*The writer of the above had much better have kept his sleeping thoughts to himself, for they are, if possible, worse than his waking ones.*'

William looked at him. 'And did you think that might have been me?' he said.

'Yes,' Samuele replied uncomfortably.

'Have you not listened to a word I said?' He was angry now. 'Such words as those are dreadful. I could never have such a thought. I split with him because he had become impossible. That he could hardly bring himself to his work emphatically does not mean that when he did the result was not sublime. Did I not say that he was a *wonderful* man? "Kubla" is inspired, visionary, perfect. Except of course that it is not finished.'

'I know it is a wonderful poem,' said Samuele quietly.

'Yes,' said Wordsworth. 'And written by a wonderful man.'

A wonderful man. The third time he had said that. Samuele was suddenly reminded of Mr Calvert. *He may be a fool to himself but he is a fine writer. What justification for existence can be greater?* It occurred to him that Wordsworth and Mr Calvert had a lot in common.

William's anger died. 'All we have told you must be hard for a questing admirer such as yourself to accept,' he said gently.

Samuele said, 'Is there no more you can tell me?'

'No,' said William. 'Thank you for not flaying me with impertinent questions. I should have been obliged to have you thrown out of the house.'

But there was a question, the last he had asked Thomas Poole. 'Mr Wordsworth, did Mr Coleridge ever mention anybody that he met when he was in the Mediterranean?' He added as an afterthought, 'Especially Sicily?'

'Why do you ask?'

'Our friend wants to know if you've heard of his father,' said Mary.

'I fear I have not, nor anybody else in the Mediterranean except for the few who are well documented. Certainly none from Sicily.'

It was as if Samuele's longed-for father had never met Cecilia. 'I must be on my way now,' he said. 'I know I have been unwelcome. I'm sorry.'

Wind moaned round the eaves of the house and through the window frames. The ivy on the outside walls rustled eerily. Mary looked out at a dark, hostile fellside. 'Where shall you go?' she said. 'It will be a rough night outside.'

'I'll walk back to Ambleside and find an inn,' said Samuele.

'You'll do no such thing,' said William. 'You'll stay the night with us and leave in the morning with warm dry clothes.'

A clock downstairs struck eight. 'It's time to eat,' said Mary. 'You must sup with us. William, will you eat up here?'

'No, I shall come downstairs this evening,' her husband answered.

Dorothy led the way down. Samuele followed.

Halfway down the staircase, William said, 'Poole was right. You need to see what they have to say at Greta Hall. You might find Mr Southey's version of events interesting. At least Esteesee's wife has male protection, the companionship of her sister and the company of her children. It would be a bad business otherwise.'

They ate oatcakes and turnips dug from the hillside garden, with warm, slightly sour-tasting milk to drink. A frugal supper for so famous a man, Samuele thought. Another woman ate with them. Asra was small, even dumpy, wearing a mob cap from which wisps of hair, still auburn, curled round her neck. She was livelier than Mary: she talked quickly and amusingly and Samuele warmed to her energy. The most obvious feature of her face was her square, determined jaw. He could see that she had never been a beauty but somehow it did not seem to matter.

She looked at him curiously. Mary told her who he was and why he had come. At the mention of the name Esteesee, Asra looked away and concentrated on her turnips. She never looked him straight in the eye. He felt embarrassed and wished he had not come. He had a strange feeling that she saw through his story.

Chapter 34

Greta Hall

I thought I was sad because my dress did not please
or because I could not be more than myself.
I thought I was sad because of wishes I could not read,
or understand, or know how to finish.

But I was sad for me because I knew life would be half-
truths, and lives half-lived and sometimes,
emptied of it all, bared of itself, no life at all.

—'Song of the Saras', Jane Spiro

Next day was better. The clouds had cleared, the drizzle gone. A bright sun pointed out the grandeur of this place. Samuele headed north towards Keswick. As he walked the changing views lifted his spirits. He pondered on what he had learnt last night. He should be cast down at how his father's life had been such a sad decline. Yet the sunshine and the fells, the hint of water from far-off lakes, the sunlit expanse of Rydal Water, the white sheep with black faces, sometimes in unlikely places, gave him a selfish, almost vindictive satisfaction. His father should have stayed in Sicily, married Cecilia, and become a great man throughout Italy. It would have been for the best.

It took four hours to walk to Keswick, at the northernmost tip of Derwentwater.

He entered the town from the south, walked up the bustling High Street and crossed the stone bridge over the River Greta. Before him, surrounded by trees, was the white frontage of Greta Hall. A house of substance, he thought, fitting for great men to live in. He climbed the steps to the front door and knocked. For a long time there was no answer, though he fancied he heard women's voices. Eventually a man's voice, loud, that of one who expects his own way, said, 'I shall go myself.'

The door opened. Samuele expected a servant. But here was no servant. This man was tall, his face lean, almost hawk-like. Robert Southey. 'Well, what do you want?' he said brusquely.

Samuele collected himself and said, 'Please excuse me, sir, but I was advised by Mr Wordsworth at Rydal Mount to see you. I am sorry that I was unable to ask at once for your permission. I have come directly from there. I also have here a letter of introduction from Mr Lamb.'

He handed the letter over and Southey, like the other two recipients, looked carefully at the seal. To his surprise, the ghost of a smile softened Southey's face. 'I would not dare to countermand any advice given by Mr Wordsworth or reject an introduction furnished by Mr Lamb,' he said. 'So please state your business so that I can decide whether this advice was worth your taking.'

Samuele prepared to start his well-rehearsed introduction. However, in spite of Southey's slightly relaxed manner, he felt he should couch his request in more formal language, which would test Mr Calvert's teaching skills to the limit. So he tried. 'I have come from Sicily,' he said, 'on behalf of my father, who is too weak to withstand the trials of such a journey.' A good start, he thought. And, after telling his story, he ended with a flourish. 'He has sold his estates to devote himself to the task. He asked me to come here to talk to those who know Mr Coleridge best. This will make his book a dependable source. I was directed to you as one of the most important witnesses.'

A girl stood in the hallway behind Southey. As he waited for an answer Samuele could see that she was small, dark-haired and, he thought, beautiful. She seemed about his age. His mind was suddenly filled with images of dryads, nymphs and nereids, magical feminine figures of myth. She had obviously heard every word Samuele had said. She looked at him as if Southey wasn't there and for the merest instant there seemed a fleeting recognition between them. Southey turned round. 'Go back in, Sara,' he said.

A door opened into the hall and an older woman appeared. Samuele saw what the girl would look like when she was that age. 'Come away, Sara,' she said. 'Let your uncle deal with it.'

'Yes, Mother,' said Sara and followed the woman back inside.

Of course. Coleridge's wife and daughter. So this young Sara might be his half-sister. And her mother – he was suddenly mystified as to how his father could prefer the Asra he had met at Rydal Mount to the woman he had just seen, let alone Cecilia when she was young.

'Mr Coleridge, you say?' said Southey.

'Yes, sir.' It was quite clear that he was not to be let in.

'Let me tell you this,' said Southey. 'I am not interested in giving anybody, least of all a stranger, any information about Mr Coleridge. If someone were to bring me news of him, even that he wished to return to Greta Hall, I would not listen. I will not have the calm of this household disturbed any further by mention of him. He has wilfully cut himself off from his wife and children and reneged on all his responsibilities. They have found peace without him. I will not see that peace shattered on his account. I hope I make myself clear.'

'You do, sir,' said Samuele.

'Then there is no more to say. I bid you good day, sir.' The door was slammed in Samuele's face.

He stood for a few moments, shocked and silent. At last he moved away from the porch. The morning was suddenly dull and his heart was heavy. He was finished with the Lake District. He wanted to be back in London to mull over all he had learnt. Wanted? No, he *needed* to speak to Charles again. He should at least explore Highgate alone, with no distractions. Perhaps a visit to his father was nearer than he thought. But he might not find what he hoped for when it came.

He took the first stride of his walk back to Keswick and the search to find a bed for the night.

And then he heard a woman's voice behind him.

'Please don't go.'

He turned. It was Sara, who might be his half-sister.

*

After a moment of shock, Samuele said, 'Why should I not? Mr Southey has made his views clear.'

'Uncle Southey's are not the only views in this house,' she said. 'I may not be loud but I want to be heard.'

Samuele said nothing. 'What do you mean?' would sound impertinent. In the silence he saw again her fragile, understated but perfect beauty. This image would stay with him as vividly as Giulia's thighs as she gathered oranges in the dusk.

'Let us walk to the lake and talk as we go,' said Sara.

They set off, silently at first but gradually with a companionship which made Samuele feel surprisingly elated. But surely Sara would start the conversation.

At last, she spoke. 'We're only here in Greta Hall because Uncle Southey and my father were the closest of friends,' she said. 'In fact, my father invited him and Aunt Edith to come to the Lakes in the first place, as well as Aunt Lovell, Aunt Edith's sister, who had nowhere to go after her husband died. They are my uncles and aunts, not just through blood but because of my father's desertion. Uncle Southey has been as good to me as any father. But that does not mean that I need obey him like a daughter.'

'What do you mean?' Samuele asked.

'Uncle Southey and my father were once the best of friends,' she said. 'Never forget that. I won't, ever. Uncle Southey used to talk about the first time they met. My uncle was at Oxford and my father walked from Cambridge to see him. They soon became like blood brothers. They had plans for making an ideal world far away in which everyone would be free but united in a common purpose. They would show the world what perfect happiness was. When I heard Uncle Southey speak of it I could see how he wished those days could return. But he soon saw how impossible this ideal society would be in real life. My real father never forgot. That's what I remember. But I was only little then and might have misunderstood. Even so, I've carried the thought ever since. It is one place among many from which love and admiration for my father comes.'

She paused and studied his face as if testing whether he was worthy of confidences. Samuele feared he might fail the test and felt regret of unexpected force.

It seemed, though, that she accepted him. 'I never went to school,' she said. 'Uncle Southey has a big library. I was set free in it, allowed to read whatever I liked and he guided me. He gave me my education, better than any school because he didn't treat me as a child. I can never thank him enough. I should have wanted to emulate him because he is a fine poet. But always I knew that the man I wanted to please most was the man who wasn't there when I was born and who I hadn't seen since I was a little girl. And if I wanted to please him I should show him I was a writer, too. The best way was to write a book.'

'A book?' said Samuele, surprised.

'Of course. It's what Coleridges do. My father, then Hartley and now me.'

'What sort of book?'

'It's a translation. It's about the Abipones, a tribe in Paraguay in South America. They were great horsemen. The writer was Austrian. He was a Jesuit monk and a missionary and his name was Dobrizhoffer. Uncle Southey was writing a book about South America and asked if I would translate Dobrizhoffer's book for him.'

Samuele could only stare in amazement. That this small, heart-stoppingly beautiful woman, the same age as him, could do such an extraordinary thing was difficult to accept.

'But I thought you would write poetry,' he said.

'I shall. One day. When I am ready.'

'Has your father read your book?'

'Oh yes. My mother and I travelled down to Highgate last year. We saw him and spent some days together. It must have been fifteen years since the last time I'd seen him.'

'What did he think of it?'

'He was delighted. He loves translations. He won university prizes for his translations from Greek. He was only eighteen then, the same age as I was when I was writing it. He was so pleased that I translated a whole book from Latin into English.'

'Latin?' said Samuele. 'I thought you meant in German.'

'Dobrizhoffer was a monk and wrote in Latin,' she said. 'But I know German as well and I sometimes wish it had been. But just learning it in an ordinary way, like telling the time or hailing a cab or buying meat in the butcher's shop, isn't knowing a language. You have to feel it as something that lives and breathes, can express all the things that are worthwhile, to capture its spirit.'

Samuele immediately thought of the difference between Signor Avellado and Mr Calvert. He felt sudden gratitude mixed with affection for his old teacher.

'So if you translate a book, you must use your language so that a reader in England will have the same experience as one in Germany. That means you understand the writer as well as you understand yourself. And that is how you learn to write.'

Samuele was for a moment lost for words. But eventually he said, 'Thank you. You've opened my eyes.'

They had reached the lake. 'I shall leave you now,' said Sara. 'Stay here until I come back. I shall try to persuade Uncle Southey to let you in.'

Samuele found a rock to sit on and then said, 'Till later then.'

'Yes. Till later,' she said.

Then she was gone, and Samuele was left with unsettling thoughts.

The lake gleamed in front of him. He felt he was seeing it through his putative father's eyes, Derwentwater, the mountains crouching round it. Like 'giants' tents', Coleridge once said, and Samuele saw what he meant. And then a thought entered his mind so strong that it made him shiver. *I hope he is not my father.* Where had that come from? It was faithless, traitorous, to his mother and to Giulia. And at its root was someone he had known for less than an hour.

Another disturbing thought. *Can it be possible that I would rather have a father whom I hated and despised for all of my conscious life?*

One thing was certain. What started as an adventure to prove what he treasured as glorious truth had, after less than an hour in the company of a truly magical creature who had cast a spell on him, turned into a crisis which could completely reorder his life. And if it didn't and he returned to Sicily and a future which had seemed laid out before him – peace of mind for his mother, marriage to Giulia – then he would be living a lie for the rest of his life, for he knew this unexpected memory would never die.

He sat alone with his thoughts for an hour before he reached the obvious conclusion.

Put this out of your mind. She is your half-sister. It is forbidden.

Then another thought. Perhaps he *would* rather have Bernardo Gambino as his true father.

There was a connection between these thoughts, but he did not dare explore what it might be.

A voice behind him spoke.

'Yes, please come back. Uncle Southey would like to speak to you after all. He has much to say.'

He turned: Sara again. Utter beauty, superb mind. No wonder he was trembling.

'Come with me,' she said.

*

He followed her to Greta Hall. Neither spoke. He fancied he saw someone at a front window watching them. Sara opened the front door – and, to Samuele's surprise, Southey stood there as if he'd never moved.

'Good afternoon,' he said. 'My niece has persuaded me to speak to you and I gladly acquiesce in any request she makes because I know it will be founded on good sense. That is one of the many differences between her and her father. So come with me into the drawing room and we will talk. Sara, you must come, too.'

Samuele followed him into a large room with an ornate fireplace. Southey sat in an armchair on one side of the hearth and motioned Samuele to the armchair opposite. Sara sat on the couch facing them.

'Well now,' said Southey. 'Tell me again who you are and why you are here.'

Samuele repeated his reasons.

'I see,' said Southey. 'And was this friendship so important that he named you after him?'

'Yes,' said Samuele quickly. Southey's shrewdness spelt danger.

'Remind me why are you here and not your father?'

'My father is unwell and such a journey as this would kill him.'

'I understand,' said Southey. 'And he must have confidence in you because your command of English is superb. I presume he taught you.'

Another surprising and uncomfortably shrewd question. He must choose his words carefully. 'Yes,' he said. 'And careful reading of Mr Coleridge's poetry.'

'Tell me how he and Mr Coleridge met?'

Samuele had an answer ready. He knew he was being interrogated and had better pass muster, so he spoke carefully. 'My father is a patron and benefactor of the Siracusa Opera. He, with other patrons, frequently visits backstage to meet the cast and director. So does Mr Leckie, the English Resident with whom Mr Coleridge was staying. He introduced Mr Coleridge to my father.'

Southey seemed satisfied by this, so Samuele continued. 'They struck up a deep friendship.'

'Not deep enough for my brother-in-law to mention it,' said Southey.

'Maybe so, sir,' said Samuele. 'But my father never forgot. He often said that Mr Coleridge could rouse admiration and even love, which he might forget but the admirer never would.'

He was pleased with his answer and so was Southey. He smiled and said, 'Your father is man of insight and generosity. I think I would like him.'

Samuele sighed with relief. Southey was won over.

'I've called you back because there's another side to my experiences with Esteesee, as Sarah, his wife, rather sadly continues to call him. I retract nothing I said before. He has behaved abominably to those he should love best and I will never forgive him. But our friendship was deep and rewarding and its ending was sad because there were mistakes and misunderstandings on both sides.'

He paused and a look almost of pain crossed his face. 'Sara has, she tells me, told you of the circumstances of our first meeting,' he continued. 'Who could ever forget it? Some friends in Bristol and I had conceived the idea of leaving England in its fog of ignorance and starting afresh, free of accusations of sedition. We knew where we wanted to go. America, Pennsylvania, the Susquehanna river. Esteesee, like us all, was then a true revolutionary. France's example had fired us. And he was the most fervid of us. 'By God, Coleridge, you really mean it,' I remember I said to him. And afterwards I realised that was the moment I began to doubt my own project. 'Pantisocracy' as we called it. The society which governs itself. Each member to be completely free and all decisions made cooperatively and harmoniously. Each man a king, both of nature and of himself.'

'And each woman a queen, both of nature and herself,' Sara murmured.

'Well, perhaps,' said Southey.

Samuele thought, *If Sara were there, that is how it would be.*

'But soon I felt sure it would never be. I suggested that surely our purpose would be just as effective on a farm in North Wales. And then I said we ought to take servants. It was then that our friendship began to decline. He believed humanity was perfectible. I believe that man is a fallen creature. Does he still feel as he did then? I don't know. But his conduct towards his wife makes me wonder if he ever did.'

Samuele listened with mixed feelings. To be told of this early ambition which others dismissed, by the man who was at its birth, struck deep.

At last, he thought. *Something of my presumed father which I can unreservedly admire, even though it came to nothing.*

Southey continued. 'It was his suggestion that we came to live here. He and Sarah were on the point of estrangement. He knew there was no place for him any more here. But who better to replace him – a quiet family group, three sisters, eight children and me as father and uncle? And so it has continued. But here's a conundrum. One day he might be in London writing for newspapers, the next back in the Lakes walking with Wordsworth and Dorothy and trying to resurrect his doomed affair with Asra. And yet he was an ill man. The opium was taking its toll. But he could still perform Herculean feats. He could walk forty miles a day. He climbed mountains. Skiddaw, Scafell. He nearly killed himself on Scafell. But he came through by his own extraordinary efforts. He is a creature of extremes which seem beyond human capacity. You may disapprove of him but you can never stop admiring him. That is his paradox – greatness mixed with degradation.'

Yes, thought Samuele. *I think I have found the pattern. Four men with different perspectives who agree. And two women bruised and cheated by his selfish waywardness to prove it.*

And today he had found a third woman, who loved him for what he did, not what he was, and would preserve his memory like no other.

How would he express all this to his mother?

Southey, suddenly genial, said, 'There, I have no more to say because if I start again I shall never stop. Thank you, Samuele, for listening so intently. If you have questions, I'll do my best. Mercifully, you weren't taking notes.'

'I had no need to,' Samuele replied. 'Every word spoken to me since I came here is etched on my mind. I must go now. I've taken too much of your time.'

'Nonsense,' said Southey. 'You have changed from threat to welcome guest. And you have my niece to thank for that. You must at least eat with us. Sara, find the others and tell them we have a guest. I believe a pie is being made which will satisfy us all.'

'Of course, Uncle,' said Sara, and was gone.

'What a girl,' Southey said. 'Such rare gifts. And, it would seem, rare fortune. She has a suitor who wants to be engaged to her.'

'And will she accept?' Samuele asked hesitantly.

'Who knows? Sara does not grant favours lightly. But he is a good man. Henry, another Coleridge. Her first cousin.'

Samuele tried hard to hide his resentment. *Why should first cousins be allowed to marry while half-sisters and half-brothers are not?* He knew at once what a futile thought that was. *I must stop such fantasies or I'll make a fool of myself.*

*

The steak and kidney pie was excellent. It compared well with the turnips and oatcakes at Rydal Mount. He accepted a glass of fine claret. Life was obviously lived at a higher level in Greta Hall.

The table was crowded. Besides Sara there were three other women, the Fricker sisters. Sara's mother he recognised at once. She did not look at him and he felt she was warning him off speaking to her. The others were introduced to him as Southey's wife Edith, and Mary, Aunt Lovell. None of them spoke a word. Was this out of suspicion of him or awe of Southey? Probably both. Wordsworth seemed just as much the head of the house but the atmosphere was different and he could not place exactly why. The five Southey children were being fed elsewhere and Samuele felt relieved about that.

Southey was still in genial mood and now anxious to give Samuele more information. 'I expect you know that Esteesee has found some stability in his life. He is writing again, his *Literaria* has been mainly well received and his *Sybilline Leaves* is a valuable collection. But I'm suspicious of the influence Dr Gillman and his wife have over him. I believe they are exploiting him because of his fame. They seek reflected glory by claiming the credit for his new-found stability. I saw no reason to alter my opinion when Sara and her mother visited them last year, fruitful though that visit was.'

Another piece in the jigsaw, thought Samuele, but said nothing.

The meal ended. Samuele was offered a glass of port, which he accepted.

'Where will you go now?' asked Southey.

'Back into Keswick,' said Samuele. 'To find a room for the night.'

'May I recommend the George in the High Street?' said Southey. 'It's a coaching inn and if there's no coach to take you to Kendal tomorrow you can hire a trap there.'

It was clear that he was not to be asked to stay the night.

*

It was a fine evening. He strode down the slope towards the bridge over the Greta. As he crossed it he heard, yet again, footsteps behind him and Sara's voice calling, 'Samuele, wait.'

He stopped and turned. Even in semi-darkness, her fragile beauty shone through. He felt a stirring which he had quietened in the house and he tried to beat it down again. But he knew that it would not die easily.

'Samuele,' she called. 'I can't let you go without talking to you again.'

He stood still, in wonderment.

'Don't be deceived by what you've seen,' she said. 'You must know the truth about Greta Hall.'

Once again, he said nothing.

'You think you've seen a united family, secure in my uncle's strength,' she said.

'That's how it seems,' he replied.

'Seems?' she said. 'I know not seems.'

Silence.

Then. 'I owe my uncle so much. He taught me, he let me loose in his library, he enabled me to write. How could I be ungrateful for that? What a fortunate girl to be taught all she knows by the Poet Laureate himself, chosen as the best poet in the land? And he did it through the goodness of his heart.'

Again, no answer.

'That's not sarcastic, Samuele. I mean it. But there's another side.'

He determined not to answer until he knew where this was leading. But the words *disloyal* and *ungrateful* seemed to sum her up and he was disappointed. That there might be another side was a shaft of light. But it came in an unexpected form.

'I was so angry when he was talking to you about the first time he and my father met,' she said. 'I saw how fascinated you were by all that he said about my father and Pantisocracy and the glories of youth and the longings for an ideal world and that *bliss was it in that dawn to be alive* feeling, which meant they could do anything they liked to wash away all the sins and filth of the past and make a new paradise on earth.'

'I thought it sounded wonderful,' Samuele said. 'I hadn't heard much about it. No one I've spoken to took it seriously.'

'It was wonderful. But for my uncle it wasn't true.'

'What do you mean?'

'Uncle Southey and his Bristol friends started their plan to escape to America. But the more I think and the more I hear, the surer I am they were just playing with an idea. Then my father enters and it's he who has the great vision. Pantisocracy. A society of equals. And it frightens them. But I do know that my father married my mother not out of love but the excitement of Pantisocracy. From that, all our troubles have come.'

Samuele followed all she said but still did not speak.

'Samuele, what do you think it's like to live in the same house as the Poet Laureate?'

'I don't know.'

'It's like living under a blanket. When you are officially the leading poet in the land you don't want to answer questions. I'm told that Mr Wordsworth, too, will not be interrupted. But he has better reason because he is the better poet.'

'Then why did they make Mr Southey the Poet Laureate?'

Sara ignored the question. 'I don't want to believe everything just because of who tells me. I want to know things properly, I want the qualities I have but don't know yet drawn out of me by someone who understands, has insight, whose work shows a great mind. And that is my father. I've read all his poetry and all his prose. And I've read all my uncle's poetry and all his prose, too. And I can't begin to tell you how superior my father's is. I would be my father's disciple as well as his daughter. Uncle Southey knew that.'

'How can you be sure? Did he tell you?'

'I told you about the book I wrote.'

'Yes. I thought it was marvellous.'

'But why should I care about the Abipones? I'm not interested in people riding horses in Paraguay.'

'I wondered about that, too.'

'I translated it because my uncle asked me to.'

'Well, wasn't that good of him?'

'In a sort of way. I was pleased with the result and thrilled about what my father said about it. But it wasn't really writing, not to me anyway. I told Uncle Southey I wanted to write poetry. He said I should "take care of over-excitement and endeavour to keep a quiet mind". I know he was warning me off my father. It's also what he expects from all the women in his house. I couldn't take my uncle's advice seriously. And this separation from my father is one of the two tragedies of my life.'

'And what is the other?' said Samuele.

'The tragedy I share with my dear, darling mother. Exiled from the man she still seems to love but knows she can't live with, banished to a little group of women living under the thumb of a man who is not a beast but who brooks no argument. I sometimes fear for Aunt Edith's reason. I see Aunt Lovell, widowed, with nothing to call her own, including her life, and dependent on my uncle's goodwill. The lot of too many women in this world.'

'I know,' said Samuele.

'I sometimes think that my father did find his Pantisocracy after all and lived it almost as he planned.'

'What do you mean?'

'When my mother and father lived in Nether Stowey and the Wordsworths were there, too, he, Wordsworth and Dorothy were free, like kings and queens of their own lives, making miracles in words in a single year. A miniature Pantisocracy. But, like all good things, it died. My mother was not part of it. She was rejected. The shape of her life to come.' She suddenly smiled mischievously. 'I sometimes wonder if dropping the skillet of hot milk on his foot so he couldn't go for a walk with his friends was entirely an accident.'

The smile disappeared. 'Take no notice of me. Of course it was an accident. Though I wish it wasn't. Then she could claim the credit for the writing of a great poem. How ironic that would be.'

Samuele said nothing because he couldn't.

'So there we are,' said Sara. 'My mother is everything to me. We've lived an intense and loving life together. Yet it's also been a half-life for us both because we are in a prison as deadly and hopeless as Aunt Lovell's. And now a good man has offered me a way out.'

Samuele knew a lot depended in his own mind on this next question. 'Will you take it?'

'Who knows? There may not be another chance.'

He knew the interview was over. 'I must get into Keswick and find the George before it's too late.'

'Goodbye, Samuele, and God speed you on your journey. I won't easily forget our talks. I hope you've enjoyed them, too.'

'I cannot thank you enough,' said Samuele.

She suddenly leant forward and for a blessed moment he thought she would kiss him.

But it was not to be. She took his hand and squeezed it slightly. Then she was gone, half running up the slope almost as if she feared a scolding for stopping out late.

As he set out for the town he was desolated that he would never see her again.

Chapter 35

Sara Considers

It is politic to tell our own story, for if we do not, it will surely be told for us, and always a degree more disadvantageously than the truth warrants.

—Sara Coleridge, letter to John Taylor Coleridge, February 1849

'Where have you been?' said her mother.

'I slipped out to say goodbye to Samuele.'

'But you said goodbye when he left.'

'He'd come a long way. I thought he deserved more.'

Sarah looked quizzically at her daughter. 'Why should he? He was a chance visitor. Nothing more.'

'It was not chance. He had a serious purpose.'

'I don't trust him. Be careful.'

'Mother, he's gone. We won't see him again. I know you want the best for me. But with Henry, I have it already.'

'I know, my love,' said Sarah and kissed her goodnight.

*

Sara didn't sleep for a long time.

She heard again her uncle's brusque rejection of Samuele. It upset her. A letter from Mr Lamb deserved a better reaction. And she heard Samuele's reasons for being in England. They were intriguing, but she wasn't sure she believed them. That was why she had run after him. She had important things to say. And also she had seen something in his face which disturbed her.

She needed to talk to him. He must not take these matters at face value. *I may not be loud but I want to be heard.* Yes, that summed up her life. And he must know everything. He had come a long way to find out.

He had told them why but to her it sounded made up. Uncle Southey had quizzed him and was satisfied. But he hadn't made the request which would clinch it. Why didn't he ask for a copy of the book when it was published? Did he, deep down, share her doubts? And for the same reason?

As she spoke to Samuele, she had studied his face. And the closer she looked the surer she was. His face reminded her of her father.

Nothing specific. But she was sure there were resemblances which surely could not be accidental.

Painful memories returned. When she was very young, hardly four, her father came to visit them at Greta Hall. He took her away from her mother to Allan Bank, where the Wordsworths now lived. He seemed so pleased with her. Every night he read her stories, folk tales, fairy stories, stories he made up specially for her. They often frightened her. Had he expected her to show delight, rapturous appreciation, as Hartley would have done? But this was how she was and couldn't change. So when she heard him complain about her 'want of affection' for him she was quietly devastated. She took to hiding away in misery.

Unwittingly, he had almost destroyed her. Why should he think she should show affection to him when she had hardly ever seen him? It must be some fault in herself. Even now, it stained her mind.

Her mother once told her that when her father conceived his hopeless love for Asra, he actually brought her to Greta Hall, saying that it was a condition of their marriage that she should love equally those who he loved. *How was that different from what he said to me? I hated him for that.*

Why hadn't she told this to Samuele? She had said that what he saw at Greta Hall was not what it seemed. But wasn't she part of the deception? She told him her love and admiration for Esteesee were complete. But no. She could never forget how he once treated her so cruelly, and her mother equally so. She had misled Samuele. Why?

Well, if her suspicion were true, the one thing he would not want to hear from her was criticism of her father. He must have heard enough already. And if he really was his son then she shouldn't needlessly add to it. The idea of her being his half-sister was hard to take, but she was beginning to think she had to.

So how old was he? Younger than her, she was sure. More than a year? So when would he have been born? It must be 1805. But in 1806 her father was coming home from the Mediterranean, in a worse state than when he went. So what had happened? What had Samuele said about his Sicilian father? That he was a patron of the Siracusa Opera and had met Esteesee there, which sounded very specific. But did it mean that Esteesee had met some woman there who had preyed on his weakness and loneliness to take advantage of him?

Something like that. But if so, she would never mention it to anyone. Perhaps her mother had seen the likeness as well so she didn't trust him. But she would never ask her dear long-suffering mother.

No, this secret would be closed to the world.

Then her thoughts turned to something quite alarming. She'd seen ominous signs.

How Samuele looked at her, with a deep longing shining through eyes which reminded her of her father's. How he hung on to every word she said, as if missing just one of them would be a tiny tragedy. How, at the very end, when she took his hand in farewell he obviously thought she was going to kiss him and how a brief light of joy glowed in those – yes, *familiar* eyes, disappearing like a snuffed-out candle when he realised that she wasn't.

This gave her no pleasure. She wanted no other attention than Henry's. He was her future and she was naturally faithful to those who deserved it.

Samuele was gone and had taken his illusions with him. She prayed that he would soon forget them. She would never see him again and that would be good for them both.

Chapter 36

Samuele's Madness

We are born weak, we need strength; helpless, we need aid;
foolish, we need reason.
—*Emile, or On Education*, Jean-Jacques Rousseau

Samuele walked back into Keswick, his mind aflame. Something important had happened. In two short conversations Sara had dug a crater in his brain.

And she was clear-eyed about her position in the family and the house. She and her mother were here on sufferance because her father had deserted them. If Southey were not a good man he might have thrown them out. But he made sure they knew their place. A close intense relationship between mother and daughter. But a half-life – and sometimes, no life at all.

Two tragedies. One, the fate of her dearly loved mother, the other the absence of her deeply admired father. What she said about his influence on her was oddly similar to George's hopes. He wondered where his friend was and how far had he progressed. He wished him well.

But that was a passing thought submerged by the fever in his mind. She was promised to another. A marriage of cousins. Once again, the feeling of unfairness came. If first cousins could marry, why could not half-sisters and brothers?

But this was a dangerous fantasy. He had been with her hardly an hour and he would never see her again. Who did he think he was? Dante seeing Beatrice once and loving her for ever?

Dante could do that. He wrote the most famous poem in the world and this entitled him. But he was no Dante. Perhaps he wasn't a Coleridge either. A new thought came: *Perhaps I don't want to be.*

Without meaning to, Sara had enslaved him.

Samuele wondered if this was what happened to his mother when she met his possible father. It would be grimly ironic if he had come to England to have his mother's experience in reverse.

He came to Southey's recommended inn. He found a room for the night and arranged for a trap to take him to Kendal next morning.

*

He lay awake, the same futile thoughts whirring round his brain. Sleep came at last. When he woke his mind had formed a plan without him noticing, a plan so desperate that he could not bring himself to think of it until they were halfway to Kendal. He tried to damp it down but it refused to die and there would be hours of mental strife before he reached London. The scheme that had evolved overnight repelled him with its treachery and betrayal of all he had held dear, but elated him as nothing else had, even the revelation of his parentage.

He knew that if he carried it out there could be no return. It might lead to a life of ecstasy. If not, he would lose everything, homeland, family and inheritance. The love of his mother and Giulia would turn into hatred. Giulia. How absence had made him long for her so much. But he should not dwell on it. The other memories which had come to comfort him and fill him with yearning when he was lonely, frustrated when matters did not take the course he wanted, the conviction that he would be destroying Cecilia's dreams. Then Giulia appeared in his mind consoling him, understanding him. He thought of her beauty, her love of the old language. Samuele could speak Sicilian and frequently did – Sicilian to Giulia and Italian to Cecilia, born in Rome.

The London coach had been on the road for three hours before the plan was complete. He reviewed it. No, it was beyond foolish: it would be disaster for him, for Cecilia, for Giulia and in the end, Sara, too. It would be the supreme betrayal. His mind still ached as he finally slept, despite the jolting on the rough road and the snores of his companions. He woke seven hours later. The sleep had not refreshed him. He was exhausted by the battle between reason and desire. And reason had been defeated.

This escapade was inevitable. Why else should he question whether he wanted to be Coleridge's son? Why should he hope that the man he hated was his father after all? Why so angry that half-siblings marrying was sinful incest while marriage between first cousins was encouraged?

Nobody except George know why he was here. It was common knowledge that Bernardo Gambino was his father. The law said so. If Coleridge was his father then Sara was his half-sister. But nobody else knew that Coleridge might be his father. If Bernardo was his father there would be no legal impediment.

So he would not go home. He would stay in England, and wrest her away from this too closely related suitor. Dante and Beatrice? Once seen, never forgotten? No, he was better than Dante, because he would do something about it.

Then he thought of a way to hide his tracks in England. He was intrigued and now inspired by Southey's talk of the ideal society by the Susquehanna and what Sara said about it afterwards. They would elope to America, find like-minded people by the Susquehanna and make Coleridge's dream come true. The true memorial to her father and his as well.

*

The coach drew into the Saracen's Head at midday. What now? First, claim a bed at the Sally Cat, hoping that Mrs Elkins was still well disposed to him. Second, go to Colebrook Row and report on his visits.

Mrs Elkins was her usual self. 'Welcome back, Mr Gambino. I've kept the room empty. I'll have a rum and ginger ale ready in a trice and there's boiled beef for later. I expect you'd like a lie-down after your journey.'

'No, I'm not tired, Mrs Elkins. I have things to do this afternoon, including seeing Mr Lamb. But I would be very glad of the rum and some bread and cheese would be welcome.'

'Right you are, Mr Gambino,' she said, and five minutes later, a platter lay in front of him. The bread and cheese filled his stomach and the rum and ginger was sublime as always.

When he had finished, Samuele said, 'I'll be back by eight,' and left for Colebrook Row.

*

The noisy walk up City Road and the peace of Islington was familiar now. He knocked on the door of the white cottage and Mary opened it almost at once.

'Why, Mr Gambino,' she cried. She turned away and shouted, 'Charles, Samuele is here and I think he brings many secrets.'

'Bring him in, my love,' replied Charles, and Mary ushered him into the study with its old horsehair chairs, piles of books everywhere and marbled wallpaper.

Charles shook his hand and waved him towards the opposite chair. Mary took one from next to the table and placed it between them so she could see both their faces and sat down. The same formation as at Greta Hall, Southey and he facing each other, Sara in the middle. Samuele wondered whether Mary's observations would be as shrewd as hers.

'Well, Samuele, was your trip worth the effort and expense?' said Charles.

'Many times over,' Samuele replied.

'I'm glad,' said Charles. 'So tell me, how is my good old friend, Tom Poole?'

'He's well.'

Samuele recounted all that Poole had told him, then of Rydal Mount and Wordsworth's early hostility ('mollified by your letter' he added), and that he had spoken to Dorothy and Mary but her sister Sara had said not a word.

'And probably never looked at you. Asra wouldn't. Too many bad memories.'

'That's right.'

'You had come looking for matters concerning STC. Asra wants to forget him so she would avert her eyes. Best not to interfere. How are matters at Greta Hall?'

'Interesting,' said Samuele and cursed himself for this inadequate word. 'Mr Southey told me their early friendship was so strong and immediate that I swear there were tears in his eyes – but he wept over the end of the friendship.'

'You may be right,' said Charles. 'I'm glad nobody approached me about going to America. They would have got a short answer. But I'm intrigued by what you say. I would have thought that it was Southey who broke the friendship.'

'But nobody had told me about Pantisocracy. I thought it was a marvellous idea.'

'It wouldn't work. Human nature wouldn't let it. Southey saw that. Even the word is ugly. Actually, I'm quite surprised he let you in at all.'

'At first he wouldn't. He refused to talk about Coleridge.'

'So why did he unburden himself to you?'

'I was walking back to Keswick. I heard someone running after me, telling me to stop.'

'Young Sara,' said Charles, without hesitation.

'She said something I can't forget. "I may not be loud but I want to be heard."'

'Exactly. I can hear her saying it. She is a marvellous girl. The best, most talented, most sensible of Sam's children. She has all the strengths of Sam and his wife with, as far as I can see, none of the weaknesses. So she prevailed over her uncle. Did you see her mother?'

'Yes, but she didn't speak to me.'

'That does not surprise me.'

'Sara said she loved her mother and admired her father. She said Southey opened his library to her and guided her reading, but her father was her great influence. She wrote for his approbation, not Southey's.'

'A pearl of great price,' said Charles. 'Happy the man who marries her.'

Samuele gulped but said nothing.

'I laid in some Marsala for the next time we met,' said Charles. 'The wine of Sicily. Let us share a bottle.'

Mary found some glasses and Charles fetched a bottle from a cupboard. He uncorked it, poured two generous glasses of the rich red wine and then said, 'Are you drinking with us, Mary?'

'One small glass,' she answered. 'You know me.'

Samuele took a tentative sip. The familiar taste suddenly caused a wave of longing for his own country. He remembered the last Marsala he had tasted, with Mr Calvert on their last meeting. But now he was ending his quest he was in a denser cloud of unknowing than he had been at the start.

Unless he could steel himself to meet his presumed father tomorrow and find answers to his new dilemma.

Chapter 37

Night Walk

Hertford–London, June 1824

Dearly I love the hours of night,
Where bashful stars have leave to shine;
For all my visions rise in light,
While sunlit spectacles decline;
And with those starts they fade away,
Or look as glow-worms look by day.

—'Phantasmion', Sara Coleridge

Scrivener started his journey southwards. The dusk darkened into night. He walked along footpaths, across fields, through woods, keeping away from highways, a lonely sprite flitting through a world lit by a gibbous moon and hearing the sounds of the night. Small nocturnal animals rustled in the undergrowth and short lives began, were lived and then ended. The heavier plod of larger animals, for these were the Broxbourne Woods, home of Brock the Badger. Once, he came to a clearing where the badgers, male and mate, stood outside their setts watching their cubs protectively as they played in the moonlight. He watched with them, hardly breathing, entranced and knowing he was privileged. When the male badger sniffed the air, detected danger and led his mate and cubs back into the sett, he felt bereft.

He heard the scritch of vixens and the soft voices of owls. Sometimes he saw their ghostly forms flying over him. He felt pleasure and supreme content. He remembered Wordsworth:

One impulse from a vernal wood
May teach you more of man,
Of moral evil and of good,
Than all the sages can.

Yes, this night walk was connecting him to his world more than anything he had ever experienced.

He had a feeling that his journey into the real world to the search for true understanding was reaching its end. He had been tested severely for over a month and now he was through it, he may be sadder but was certainly wiser.

He must have been walking for six hours before overwhelming tiredness took him. He lay down on soft, springy grass and slept soundly until the rising sun roused him.

*

He walked on and entered a town just waking up. Enfield. The northernmost tip of mighty London. He found a shop selling food, bought a pork pie and found a bench by the street next to a water pump. His thirst slaked, he ate the pie. It was excellent. Now he could face the new day with confidence.

Yes, he would see Coleridge, tell him of his quest, how it started with the inscription and had guided him through a process which brought new understanding, both of Coleridge and himself. He imagined the great man's delighted reaction.

Or would it be bored indifference? Just another insignificant disciple among many? He could only hope.

He remembered the address Samuele had given him. Moreton House, Highgate.

Where was Highgate? It could not be far away.

He asked a passer-by, who pointed vaguely southwards but

volunteered no other information.

He found a cab rank where drivers enjoyed a smoke as they waited for fares. He approached the driver of a hackney.

'Can you take me to Highgate?'

'Where in Highgate?'

'Moreton House.'

'Opposite the church?'

'Yes,' said Scrivener. So were a lot of houses and he might be right. 'How far away is it?'

'About four miles.'

'How much?'

He named a sum which Scrivener thought quite reasonable. 'I'll want half of it before I let you get on. You can't trust anyone these days.'

That, too, seemed reasonable. He felt in his money belt and selected a few coins. The driver looked at them, actually bit one, and put them in his little bag for fares.

'All right, hop on,' he said.

Scrivener sat back to enjoy the comforting sound of the horse trotting easily along. Horse and driver were not master and servant but good friends. The thought pleased him and filled him with hope for a good day.

After twenty minutes they skirted the edge of a wide expanse of land. 'Hampstead Heath,' said the driver. 'We're nearly there.'

They came to Highgate Hill and stopped outside Dunn's chemist's shop. Scrivener wondered if Coleridge was a customer. He paid the balance of the fare and a bit more beside. The driver pointed across the street. 'Moreton House is over that side. You can't miss it.'

'Thank you,' he said.

'Best of luck,' the driver replied.

Scrivener crossed the road and saw the house. He had an unsettling feeling that something extraordinary was about to happen.

The words of the inscription came back into his mind. *The writer of the above had much better have kept his sleeping thoughts to himself, for they are, if possible, worse than his waking ones.* Since seeing those enigmatic words he had travelled down a strange road. Every event was significant, coincidence had piled on coincidence and now came the most unexpected one of all. The wheel had come full circle.

A young man was walking towards him fast and purposefully. Samuele.

*

Samuele saw him at the same time. 'I cannot believe this,' he said.

'Nor I,' said Scrivener. 'And yet...'

Samuele finished the sentence for him. 'It seems we had to meet now. My quest is finished. Now I must decide what it means.'

'That's true for me, too,' said Scrivener.

'Let's find a coffee house where we can tell each other about our searches,' said Samuele.

Chapter 38

Revenant

Highgate, June 1824

O the mind, mind has mountains; cliffs of fall
Frightful, sheer, no-man-fathomed. Hold them cheap
May who ne'er hung there...

—'No Worst, There Is None', Gerard Manley Hopkins

Coleridge woke early. Derwent still slept. Coleridge listened for a change in his breathing. Lately, his son's fever had shown signs of abating. Dr Gillman was optimistic about his chances. After five weeks of strain and fear, relief spread through the household.

Coleridge reasoned his son could safely be left for a while. He had not been outside for a whole week. The sun shone. The day would be fine. He longed for fresh air. Derwent would sleep on.

He dressed, quietly opened the door and crept down the stairs.

Moreton House two doors away was showing signs of life. Should he call in and tell them what he was doing? No. He was too anxious to be walking and headed for the heath.

The air was invigorating. He walked easily and breathed deeply. He reached the heath and, eschewing the paths, set out straight across the middle.

He was conscious of a presence behind him. He looked back. Nobody. He walked on. The presence was still there. He thought of the Walk to Emmaus and wondered what revelation was to come.

Soon he knew. The presence now seemed to walk beside him. He looked to left and to right. Still nothing. Then it materialised, not in a sudden spectacular flash but slowly, easily, almost intimately.

It was the revenant.

Coleridge said, 'What do you want of me?'

The revenant turned his familiar face with its enigmatic smile and looked him straight in the eyes. The intense gaze made Coleridge flinch.

Until now the revenant had only given Coleridge vague intimations of something familiar about his features and resentment at his persistence.

Now, for the first time, he felt real fear. Why? He was used to hallucination, of not being able to distinguish between reality and dream. Was this revenant a real ghost or a phantasm of the mind?

The strange smile disappeared and was replaced by unmistakable threat. This revenant was preparing to bring his message, and Coleridge was terrified.

The heath was a dangerous place if it could raise such spirits. He must escape it. He turned back to start the walk to Moreton House. Stepping off the heath and into the road was like making landfall after a tempestuous voyage, like his ancient mariner. No, he was rather the wedding guest, sadder, though not yet wiser.

He struggled to find meaning. But his mind would decide for itself when it chose to reveal it.

*

He came back to the house of Derwent's isolation and climbed the stairs. The bedroom door was open. Dr Gillman was bending over his son's still sleeping form. 'Ah, Mr Coleridge,' he said. 'You deserted your post, I see.'

'I needed air and space to think,' Coleridge replied.

'Good heavens, man,' said the good doctor. 'I'm not angry. Derwent is safe to be left on his own now. You have borne the strain so well. Now he is on the mend and you can be your own man again.'

That, thought Coleridge, was the trouble. Too often now he wished he wasn't.

'Go back to the house and take breakfast with Ann. Then you can rest. You need it.'

'Thank you,' said Coleridge, and left. After breakfast with Ann Gillman he retired to his room.

At first, he thought he would continue with his *Aids to Reflection*, a little book of which he had high hopes.

But he soon tired of it. The shocks of the morning had befuddled his mind. He was suddenly so tired and his head was aching. *Shall I take opium?*

No. *Keep your mind clear. This is no time for fantastic dreams. Stay clear-headed. Just sleep.*

So he lay down on his bed fully clothed and closed his eyes. He slept at once, and entered into the worst dream of his life.

※

He is back in his first dream, the one he had the night after Hartley's defection, which had started under the brown cloak of opium. A desolate, formless void. And then the same terrifying vision. A dark figure before him which resolves itself into a woman's shape with a startling, disturbing, malevolent beauty. He sees again the long fingernails and remembers what they are for. He tries to shut his eyes. But his terror increases even more when he finds that he cannot close them: His eyelids are paralysed.

The woman's eyes, previously profoundly dark, hinting at sub-terranean depths where monsters lurk, change.

And the lady's eyes they shrunk in her head,

Each shrunk up to a serpent's eye.

And Coleridge, for he is half-aware of life outside the dream, remembers 'Christabel'. These are Geraldine's eyes. These are the eyes of Bard Bracy's dream that, according to Byron, made Shelley run screaming from the room when he seemed to see them on a woman's breasts. And he knows that something far worse than his eyes being torn out is going to happen.

His deepest fear. The Nightmare Life-in-Death *of his mariner, the half-clothed harlot of his dreams chasing him through the streets of Cambridge, fears beyond his own poems. 'The Lamia'. 'La Belle Dame sans Merci'. His own 'Ballad of the Dark Ladie'. Tales of vampires from the many romances and folk tales he has read since he was a boy. And all with the same end in view. To* thick man's blood with cold *and then suck his soul away and destroy him.*

Now he knows what his dream is about, he has to sit powerless and accept what is coming to him. He is full of hideous revulsion but must bear it because he is impotent.

Geraldine still hypnotises him with her snake's eyes. And slowly, almost imperceptibly, he is transported to another place, this time in the world outside, somewhere he has been but cannot remember. He is led up a staircase lit by a small chandelier. He is led into a bedroom by a woman whose face is shaded so that he cannot recognise her. She slowly divests herself of her clothing, comes close, kisses him and says, 'Dear heart, how like you this?' He has heard those words, that voice before, remembers the poem they come from.

They flee from me, that sometime did me seek

With naked foot, stalking in my chamber.

But the women in this dream are not going to flee from him. They want to destroy him.

It was no dream: I lay broad waking.

The woman leads him to the bed. Now he knows who she is and where they are. He seems to detect the aromatic scent of the poplar trees lining the green lane. And then he recognises the woman as Cecilia Bertozzi.

He knows he is taken over with lust. Desire with loathing strangely mixed. *He gives in to the desire, because he cannot loathe this beautiful woman.*

But then the face changes. It is not Cecilia's. It is Geraldine's. She may be a fantasy but he would know her anywhere. But now she has her snake's eyes set small, sinister and malevolent and boring into his mind. And it is too late.

'What have I done?' he cries out.

And then he wakes up, to hear a knocking at the door.

*

'Enter,' he called.

The door opened and the maid stood there. 'Mr Coleridge,' she said. 'Your son is here.'

Sudden joy. The dream had gone and now his dearest wish had come true.

But again, it was not Hartley. It was the revenant.

Coleridge looked at him, half mystified, half horror-struck.

'But you are a trick of the mind,' he said. 'You have no corporeal existence.'

'Not so.' The revenant had an Italian accent but his English was excellent. 'If it were, the maid could not have let me in, brought me upstairs and knocked on the door. She did not seem to think I was a ghost.'

'So what are you?'

'The maid told you. I am your son. You are my father.'

Coleridge remembered his dream and its ghastly finale. 'No,' he shrieked. 'You are no son of mine. You are devil's progeny.'

'I know,' said the revenant. 'And the devil is you.'

Coleridge felt dull, suffocating despair.

The revenant continued. 'Perhaps I'm not a hallucination. Perhaps I'm a ghost, a real ghost who can walk abroad. But who am I a ghost of? The young man living an untroubled life back in Sicily?

Or how that young man might have grown up had his mother not had a miscarriage? Or perhaps he was stillborn or died in infancy in his childhood, leaving a cheated and grieving mother. Perhaps I am the ghost of an orphan, because his father disappeared and his mother died in childbirth. All these may be consequences of what you did. And you will never know. Such doubt will make the guilt worse and sooner or later it will kill you.'

Coleridge held his head in his hands and sobbed.

'I shall go now. You must stand at the window and watch me as I leave. That will give you food for thought.'

And he was gone. Coleridge heard the front door slam shut. He wearily rose and went to the window. He saw the revenant emerge, stand by the gate, look up, wave ironically and then go. Not by walking back down the street but gone, vanished.

Just as any self-respecting ghost should.

Coleridge turned away in misery. But something made him turn back again. What he saw amazed him. *The revenant was returning.* The same black hair, same healthy Mediterranean face, same clothes. He was walking fast towards Moreton House and when he arrived at the front gate he reached out to lift the latch. Coleridge watched, his heart beating fast.

The revenant looked up and saw him in the window. Then he looked away again, took his hand off the latch and half ran the way he had come like a soldier deserting the battle.

There was one explanation. The revenant was returning to renew the torment. 'Sooner or later it will kill you.' Perhaps sooner. Now, in fact. But the revenant's nerve had failed him. Which must mean all he had said was untrue. He was going back to his own infernal region and Coleridge was free. He could absolve himself of guilt.

He sat back with a contented sigh. His demons were leaving one by one. Derwent was getting better. He had a daughter who had her own genius and who had enchanted him last year. He was in his final home with good people.

He was as near to content as he could remember.

Then he had a delightful thought. He remembered 'Kubla Khan' and the shadowy person from Porlock. Was the revenant the *second* person from Porlock?

Of course he was. And Coleridge was satisfied with the fitness of things.

Then another thought. Perhaps it was not the revenant but a real person coming to call on him. And who might that be? Instinctive knowledge flooded him. He lifted the window. 'Come back,' he shouted.

But the young man did not hear. He was gone for ever. And Coleridge felt an aching loss, because his instinct said he had just thrown away a part of himself which might have brought him happiness. It was too late now.

Chapter 39

A Proposal

Oh ye fair and pleasant place
Where the eye, delighted, ranges;
Oh ye dear and friendly faces,
Loved through all your mortal changes.
—'To a Fair Friend', Sara Coleridge

They followed the smell of roasting coffee beans down Highgate Hill until they found the coffee house. Coffee served, they talked. First, Samuele recounted the meetings with Charles Lamb and the visits to Nether Stowey and the Lakes.

'Have you spoken to Mr Coleridge?' asked Scrivener.

'No,' said Samuele.

Scrivener had expected him to say, 'Not yet.' Even so, he asked, 'Is he your father?'

'I don't know,' said Samuele. 'I have to think.'

There was an awkward silence. Then Scrivener asked a daring question.

'Do you still want him to be?'

'I don't know.'

'So you haven't found your father after all.'

But I've found things about myself which I don't like, Samuele thought. 'And what of you?' he said. 'How has your quest ended?'

'It hasn't ended yet. And I'm even less clear about what I'm looking for. But it has changed me. I'm not the shy, easily led little boy that I was the last time we met.'

'I can see that,' said Samuele. 'I'm glad for you.'

'But I've lost everything. Thrown out of my college, thrown out of my home. My books, papers, clothes except for what I stand up in, burnt in front of my eyes.'

'So you are destitute?' said Samuele. It was a statement as well as a question.

'Yes. As destitute as the poor wretches I see tramping the countryside. Except that I do have money because of a good and generous man. I can buy new clothes, new books. I can start again.'

Samuele looked at him enviously. 'You chose right not to come with me,' he said.

'Yes,' said Scrivener. 'In spite of everything, I think I did.'

'Why are you here? Were you going to call on Coleridge?'

'Yes.'

'Why?'

'At first, I wanted to tell him it was his fault and trying to learn from him had ruined my life. Then I remembered that he'd left Cambridge early, too, and now he's famous. I wrote a poem which didn't work. I only knew the old way to write poetry, but when I read him on how the imagination worked I saw what I was doing wrong. His poetry is of a different order from any other, utterly his own and beyond anyone to match. So I had something to thank him for.'

'Is that what you would have told him?'

'Yes.'

'It isn't his fault. He's never heard of you.'

'I know. I could walk away and forget him.' Scrivener paused. Then, 'No. I'll never forget him. Who could?'

'I wish my mother could,' Samuele replied.

'What do you mean?'

'I'll tell Coleridge nothing because I won't see him. If I did, I'd tell him that my mother remembers him and still loves him, but he would have betrayed her like every other woman he's ever met.'

'Isn't that worth telling him?'

'Why? He knows it already. Besides, I've been to Moreton House. I think I saw him looking out of his window as if he was waiting for me. I was frightened. So I ran away. I'd failed. And then I saw you.'

'If you failed then so have I,' said Scrivener. 'What will you do now?'

'Come with me to the Salutation and Cat and see if Mrs Elkins can find a bed for you. Then we'll go to Colebrook Row and see if Charles is in.'

'Charles?'

'Lamb. Charles Lamb, his best friend. I told you. I'd have got nowhere without him.'

'But you have got somewhere. You've found Coleridge isn't the man your mother thought. But surely you've found something good?'

'Poetry isn't everything. But there are two things I really admire him for. First, when he was young, he and some others had this plan to go to America and start a wonderful new society, where nobody would rule over anyone else, they would work together simply and frugally, share equally in the good things and in the failures as well.'

'I know about it,' said Scrivener. 'And the other?'

Samuele had to swallow hard before he answered. 'He has a wonderful daughter.'

'What's so wonderful about her?'

'She's beautiful and clever. She's hardly twenty, yet she's written a book already and it's been published. She'll write more – and poetry, too. Her name is Sara. I'd heard something about her and Pantisocracy, but it all came together when I went to Robert Southey's house. And I thought, wouldn't it be wonderful if I could make a new society like that and finally fulfil those dreams.'

'How?'

'I've inherited all my father's estates in Floridia, where they grow the poppy. Opium, my possible father's downfall. I thought that the best way to remember him would be to grub up the poppies and replant the estates with vines and turn it into one huge vineyard. We will make wines which will spread pleasure all over Sicily and the rest of Italy and in time all Europe. And all the people who live and work there, from lowliest labourer to chief vigneron, will be equal partners.'

Scrivener was thrilled. This, he thought, was wonderful.

But another plan was forming in Samuele's mind. Eloping with Sara to America still obsessed him. But now he realised there was another way to Pantisocracy which would remove the temptation. If he could tell his mother he was bringing a companion with him...

It wouldn't be Coleridge. But here was a new candidate.

'It's strange,' he said. 'I thought of the estates as a burden which I'd rather not have. But now I'm talking to you everything seems clear.'

'How?' said Scrivener.

'You've lost everything but it hasn't beaten you. Why not come to Sicily with me and share the project? A good life in a warm climate and making a new way of living to save the world.'

For a moment Scrivener couldn't speak. Then he said cautiously, 'I must think. It's a lot to take in.'

Samuele knew he would have to wait. But not for too long. There was another reason for his offer. If Scrivener suspected it he would refuse because it was what Samuele had damned Coleridge for. A betrayal. And now Samuele felt sick. He was using his friend to solve his own dilemma.

Though Scrivener offered, Samuele insisted on paying the bill. Then they went outside and Samuele hailed a hackney to take them to the Sally Cat.

*

The only bed Mrs Elkins could offer Scrivener for the night was a mattress on the floor of Samuele's room. Samuele went upstairs with his satchel: Scrivener waited downstairs with nothing.

When Samuele came down again, Mrs Elkins said, 'Rum and ginger ale, Mr Gambino?' and he, like a dying man offered a reprieve, said a heartfelt 'Please!'

'And for you, Mr Scrivener?'

Rum sounded dangerous. He would prefer water but this was a place of serious drinking. So made his usual request. 'A small tankard of mild, please.'

As Mrs Elkins poured the beer she said, 'You can have cold cut of beef and some potatoes in the snug.'

They took their drinks into the little room in which Lamb, Coleridge and friends once gathered to talk uproariously about books and slander their authors. The cold cuts came and they ate hungrily.

'You'd have a good life in Sicily,' said Samuele. 'A new beginning.'

Yes, thought Scrivener. It sounded wonderful. Coleridge would see this as a metaphor for his old radical zeal.

'We'll sell the villa at Monreale,' Samuele continued. 'We'll move to Floridia and rebuild the labourers' houses and make them fit for their new lives. Until Bernardo died they were hovels and the labourers were slaves. We'd build new houses for those joining us, no better and no worse than for the labourers. And we will work, work, work until we make wine to be proud of.'

So, Scrivener thought, the rural poor were in Sicily, too. Yes, this in itself was reason enough to go. But could he survive the change? A new country, new people, new language.

Cut off from his ambitions, his writing. It would be like living on the moon.

He said as much to Samuele.

'But we must explore new countries,' Samuele replied. 'Since I've been here, I've seen so much, met fascinating people, learnt more about life. I'll go back a different person.'

No more than I did on the walk to Woodstock, Scrivener thought. But there was a difference. 'You spoke English before you came.'

'And you can learn Italian the way that I did,' said Samuele. 'I have the perfect teacher for you. His name is Mr Calvert.'

Samuele remembered what Sara said about knowing a language... *You have to feel it as something that lives and breathes, which can express all the things that are worthwhile, to capture its spirit.*

Signor Avellado had given him the first way. Mr Calvert gave him second and he had talked on equal terms with people far above how he once saw himself.

'He is a wonderful teacher of English and his Italian is perfect. He'd introduce you to Italian poetry. You know about Coleridge and Wordsworth. You should know about Dante and Petrarch as well. George, you *must* come home with me.'

But for whose sake? Scrivener's or his? Now the word *betrayal* came into his mind again, with the vivid memory of Sara Coleridge in the dusk outside Greta Hall. Two ambitions, equally urgent. To go home, forget those visions of Sara – though he knew he never could – tell his mother everything, persuade her that he wanted to marry Giulia and set up his dream of the ideal society. The other was to stay here, wrest Sara away from her cousin and make the ideal society together in America.

George would be his insurance. If he wrote home saying he was bringing a companion he would be in honour bound to go. If he were free, he could not trust himself. This was beyond foolhardy. But he had to try.

He continued the persuasion. 'You'll meet my mother and know what a wonderful woman she is. You'll meet my lovely Giulia, who will be my wife. And she has a cousin who's lovely, too. Peregrina. You never know. You'll see how beautiful Monreale is, high in the hills and surrounded by orange groves, and when you see Floridia and the rolling fields we'll fill with vines and Siracusa and the sea close by you'll catch your breath in wonder.'

He finished almost breathless. Perhaps his treachery had damned him for ever.

Scrivener merely said, 'I see.'

They had finished the cold beef and potatoes. 'Let's walk to Islington and see Charles and Mary,' said Samuele.

*

The walk to Colebrook Row was so familiar to Samuele that he could do it in his sleep. For Scrivener it was a revelation. The crowds, horses and smell of dung along the City Road were like a bad dream. Far worse than Cambridge or Hertford. To enter the silence of Colebrook Way was balm to the soul.

Samuele knocked on the door of the white cottage. It was opened by a small, gentle-faced man. 'Samuele. Here again. And with a friend, too. I'm so glad. As will be Mary. It's always good to meet new people.'

Lamb ushered them into the chaotic sitting room. A small, mild-looking woman sat by the overloaded table. *This woman murdered her mother*, Scrivener thought. But he saw her contented, peaceful face and thought what a patient, faithful and good man Charles Lamb must be.

'Samuele, will you introduce me to your friend?' said Lamb.

'Charles, this is George. George Scrivener. We met in Cambridge. He was at Jesus College like Coleridge, and he, too, has left without a degree.'

Lamb laughed. 'Then he's in good company. There seem to be more men sent down from Oxford and Cambridge than stay there. And they all seem to make their mark. It's almost a rite of passage. So don't you worry, Mr... I can't go on saying Scrivener. Samuele and I are on first-name terms, so you should be, too. I'm Charles.'

'George,' said Scrivener.

'Good,' said Charles.

'George is a great admirer of Mr Coleridge,' said Samuele.

'I should think so, too. People might hate his life but they love his work. How good that you two should meet in Cambridge and find such a connection. God moves in a mysterious way, so I'm told.'

They talked for some time. Samuele said little about what he had found but was lyrical about his walk with Poole from Stowey to Culbone and thinking of the woman waiting for her demon-lover. Scrivener listened and envied them. All he could offer was the search for Simon Hatley. But he did talk about the poverty and destitution he had seen as he moved through the countryside, the terrible plight of the farm labourers ('Because of the accursed Corn Laws,' Charles said) and how deeply it had affected him.

'I am ashamed that I reached my twentieth year unaware of it,' he said.

'Don't blame yourself,' said Charles. 'When we are young we all live in our worlds of stories and magic.'

Scrivener nearly said, 'It was more than that,' but shut his mouth just in time.

'My friend William Hazlitt has introduced me to a remarkable man. William Cobbett. He is riding round the country and writing about what he sees. He does not mince words. Hazlitt has transcripts of some of his papers – they make dreadful reading. One day Cobbett will publish them as a book. And the whole nation will be angry. Except, of course, those who are the cause of it. Have you read William Blake's poetry? If not, you should.'

Scrivener made a mental note. Cobbett and Blake.

'This is why the ideal society is so important,' said Samuele. 'And that is what I am going home to make. A new commonwealth.'

Now Scrivener was really torn. Which did he want? Cobbett and Blake? Or a vineyard in Sicily in which poverty and destitution would be wiped out? He forecast a sleepless night ahead agonising over the choice.

'So Samuele,' said Charles. 'When do you think you will be going home?'

'Very soon,' Samuele replied. 'Tomorrow I'll find a shipping office and get a ship to the Mediterranean, close enough to Palermo for an easy return. I can't face another coach journey through Europe.'

'But at least you wouldn't perish in a Biscay storm.'

'I'll take the risk,' said Samuele.

'And you, George. What will you do?'

'I've not yet decided,' Scrivener replied.

'Take your time,' said Charles. 'I tell you what. Tomorrow morning I shall take a cab to the old Sally Cat and we'll have a walk round London, look round the bookshops, talk to the booksellers and even meet some writers. You'll get a feel for literary London.'

'Marvellous,' Scrivener replied.

Mary had listened avidly but not said a word, until, 'Samuele, would you like some Marsala?'

'Oh, wonderful!' replied Samuele.

'And you, George?'

Scrivener had no idea what Marsala was. He looked at Charles and Samuele's delighted faces and thought that he would probably come to no harm.

'Yes, please,' he said.

Mary produced a bottle and four glasses. She uncorked the bottle and poured the red liquid. 'Three large ones for the men and one small one for the lady.' They lifted their glasses, said 'Good health' and drank.

And when Scrivener swallowed the rich red wine he realised that if this was what Samuele intended to grow in the Pantisocracy, then he wanted to be there to taste it.

Chapter 40

Preparing to Depart

Signals, Drums, Guns, Bells and the sound of voices
weighing up and clearing anchors... no happiness without work.
—From the Notebooks of Samuel Taylor Coleridge

Scrivener did not spend the night fretting over his decision after all. After his night walk and this tumultuous day, he could not keep his eyes open. He slept long and deep and when he woke he had made up his mind.

Over Mrs Elkins's usual hot porridge he told Samuele.

'I've decided. I shall come with you.'

Thank God, thought Samuele. Of two great temptations he would choose the honourable, moral decision without treachery, over the wild, romantic, impossible dream. Head over heart, the universal choice.

He would live a life outwardly calm and happy, but there would be a permanent fissure in his mind filled with the image of Sara outside Greta Hall and desires to which he could never ever confess.

Nevertheless, he could still speak as though all was well. 'George, I'm so glad. You have a good day with Charles while I go down to the Thames and find berths on a fine ship.'

They finished their porridge. Samuele left to find a cab while Scrivener sat in the snug to await Charles.

✣

He did not have to wait for long. Charles bustled in and said a cheery hello to Mrs Elkins, who answered, 'He's in the snug.'

'Morning, George,' said Charles as he came in. 'Samuele is on his way to find a safe berth, I see. So let us be on our way. There's much to see. The hackney is waiting outside. First, we go to Finsbury Square.'

'What's there?' asked Scrivener.

'Ask no questions,' said Charles.

When they reached Finsbury Square, Charles asked the driver to stop outside an imposing building.

'Here we are,' he said. 'The first proper bookshop and still the biggest. The Temple of the Muses.'

Charles paid the cab driver, who touched his forelock and drove off. They entered the shop and Scrivener gasped. He had never seen so many books in one place. In the middle of the room was a round desk with queues of people in front of the cashiers. Scrivener wondered if they would ever queue to read his books. He noticed many not buying but browsing, picking up books, skimming through them, sometimes lighting on a passage which caught their eye, concentrating on it and then replacing it. Book after book after book. Pick up, look through, replace. He noticed also that most then walked out again without buying. But they departed with contented looks on their faces.

He had never entered a bookshop without knowing what he wanted to buy. He had always been frightened of a hand on his shoulder and a voice saying, 'If you're not buying it, put it back. This is a shop, not a library.'

He mentioned this to Charles.

'Browsing is encouraged here,' he replied. 'If people know they can come in just to have a look, they'll come again, knowing what they want. But no time to browse today. We have places to see.'

'But I do want to buy some books. I want *Sybilline Leaves*, *Lyrical Ballads* and *The Monk*. I watched them burn on my uncle's bonfire.'

'George,' said Charles. 'I'd rather you didn't.'

Scrivener felt almost indignant. 'Why not?'

'I'd rather you bought them somewhere else. We shouldn't be adding to the fortunes of the Lackington family. I'd rather you bought them at my good friend Mr Porson's shop, nearer the Sally Cat. He needs the money more. But first, it's Dr Johnson's house and the Cheshire Cheese.'

Charles hailed a cab to Fleet Street. Scrivener was pleased to see where the great doctor had lived and died, but was less pleased about not being able to go inside.

Charles said, 'Well, if he's not in it, I suppose it's only a house,' and took him down Fleet Street into the Cheshire Cheese. 'Ben Jonson drank here and if he did, then likely Shakespeare drank with him. Oliver Goldsmith was a regular, too.' Scrivener didn't answer.

'You don't seem very interested,' said Charles.

'Yes, I am,' said Scrivener.

But in truth, this was going over his head. He was preoccupied with his own thoughts.

'What will you have to drink?' asked Charles. 'I'll have a tankard of my favourite stingo.'

Scrivener wanted Marsala again. But he looked round and listened and decided that it wasn't even worth asking. So he fell back on his usual request.

'A small glass of mild.'

'Is that all?' said Charles.

'Yes,' said Scrivener firmly.

Charles bought bread and cheese and they ate and drank quietly. Charles looked disappointed. Scrivener felt poised between two worlds and detached from both.

He toyed with his mild while his companion had another stingo. When he had finished Charles said, 'Come on George, drink up. We'll go and see Mr Porson.'

Scrivener miserably followed him. He felt he had somehow let Charles down. This day had been planned for him and he should be revelling in it. He was ashamed and knew he should confess.

Another hackney took them back to Newgate Street and Charles told the driver to stop outside a small, unprepossessing little shop in a narrow three-storey building. A board over the door said *PORSON, BOOKSELLER.*

They entered. Again, shelves stuffed with books. A few people browsed the shelves and loaded tables. There was no cashier behind the counter. A small, rather plump man was perched unsteadily at the top of a ladder, putting books in order on an upper shelf. Scrivener thought he was about to fall off, so he darted across and held the ladder steady.

The man looked down. 'Thank you, sir,' he said. 'Uncommonly good of you.' He saw Charles standing close by. 'Hello, Mr Lamb,' he said. 'Is this kind gentleman by any chance with you?'

'He is indeed, James,' said Charles.

'Then not for the first time, I must congratulate you on your friends.'

He scrambled down the ladder and held out his hand to Scrivener. 'James Porson at your service,' he said. 'Bookseller to some in the aristocracy, but mainly to people like you and me.'

'George Scrivener.' They shook hands.

'Mr Scrivener has just been sent down from Cambridge,' said Charles.

'Good for him. We get a lot of his sort in here.'

'He is a great admirer of our friend Mr Coleridge and knows more than most about him. A rare understanding, I venture to think. And he has some purchases to make. Books to replace those burnt in a fit of rage by his uncle.'

'Splendid,' said Mr Porson. 'He really is a man after my own heart.' He turned to Scrivener. 'And which books will replace your piles of ash?

'*Sybilline Leaves*, *Lyrical Ballads* and *The Monk*.'

'An eclectic mix indeed.'

Scrivener had an afterthought. After all, his laborious copying-out in the Jesus library had perished as well. 'I'd like the book with "Kubla Khan", "Christabel" and "The Pains of Sleep" in it as well.'

'Better and better,' said Mr Porson and searched again – this time, mercifully, on shelves a lot lower.

Scrivener felt in his money belt. Five pounds in coins minus the price of cruelly destroyed books and the mercifully still intact money belt bought in Oxford. And two coach journeys. He had better be careful.

Mr Porson found the books. 'That will be two shillings,' he said. 'Sixpence a book.' He handed him the change.

Scrivener had an unworthy thought. When he was with Samuele he would not have to worry about money. Samuele seemed to have unlimited supplies.

They talked amicably for some time. A few customers came in. One came to Mr Porson and asked for advice about poetry.

Mr Porson paused in his talking to Charles, turned to Scrivener and said, 'George, see to the gentleman, if you please.'

Scrivener for a moment could not believe what he was hearing. Nevertheless, he said to the customer, 'What is it that you want to know?' and this started a long conversation, which he very much enjoyed and ended with the customer departing with four books under his arm.

Mr Porson smiled. 'Well done and thank you, George,' he said. 'I don't expect you'd be interested in taking rooms on my top floor and working for me?'

They left soon afterwards. Back in the Salutation and Cat, they found Samuele sitting in the snug.

'What a day I've had,' he said. 'I asked everyone I saw and nobody knew about ships for Italy. I thought we'd have to go by coach again and I was dreading it. Then I saw a man in a navy uniform and he told me to try Greenwich. So I got a ferryman to take me across the river and found a shipping office. There's a mail ship sailing the day after tomorrow for Gibraltar with supplies for the garrison on the Rock. The brig *Arethusa*. And there were two berths available so I bought them there and then. We can find a ship in Gibraltar for Sicily.'

'I'm glad for you,' said Charles. 'But why do you need two berths?'

'George is coming with me. A new life for him.'

'I see,' said Charles. He looked at Scrivener reproachfully. 'I wish you'd told me.'

Scrivener felt too ashamed to speak.

Charles stood up. 'I think I'll leave you now. You have much to do. Samuele, my sincere good wishes. It has been good to know you. And I'm glad to have been of some use to you.'

'Charles,' said Samuele. 'I could have done nothing without you. My debt to you is everlasting.'

'And give my best wishes to your father and tell him I expect a copy of his book when it is published. I shall have to ask Sara to translate it for me.'

'Thank you,' said Samuele. He could say no more. This would be the last sentence he would hear from his friend and it brought the ever-present memory of Sara outside Greta Hall clearly and painfully to his mind. It also reminded him that he had told everyone, except George, a lie about why he was here. He wished that he had never come in the first place. He was filled with relief that George was going with him. He could go home with an easy conscience, although he had cheated his friend. While he waited for them to return, he had written to his mother telling her he was not coming alone. Only now did he think of what the effect might be if she thought it was Coleridge. He had put the letter out with the rest of the mail for collection and could not take it back and alter it.

Charles then spoke to Scrivener. 'George,' he said. 'I'm sorry our acquaintanceship has been so short. But I wish you every success in your new life and that you'll always think kindly of old England despite the unpleasant tricks it has played you.'

He shook hands with them and left. They heard him say goodnight to Mrs Elkins and then he was gone.

'Tomorrow we must prepare for the journey,' said Samuele. 'You'll need a proper travelling case and new clothes.'

Scrivener agreed and worried whether he had enough to cover the cost. If not, he would depend on Samuele again. But perhaps he could earn money working among the vines in the new Pantisocracy.

Time would tell.

Intermezzo 2

Siracusa, October 1804

Of a quintette in the Syracuse opera and the pleasures in the voices... there is no Sweeter Image of wayward yet fond Lovers, of Seeking and Finding, of the love quarrel & the making up, of the losing and the yearning Regret, of the doubtlet then compleat Recognition and the total melting union...
—From the Notebooks of Samuel Taylor Coleridge

They enter a hallway lit by four candles in a small chandelier hanging from the ceiling. A staircase at the far end stretches upwards until it is lost in shadow. He follows Cecilia to the first step and hesitates. She takes his hand again, murmuring, 'Samuel, do not be afraid.' Her hand is small and warm. He can feel the pulse of her heart where her slim wrist begins: it is like picking a small bird up out of its nest.

She draws him upstairs. With every step his hesitation drains away. There are three doors at the top of the staircase. A sort of foreknowledge tells him which door is Cecilia's even before she is near enough to open it.

The light from a smaller chandelier hanging over this upstairs landing hardly penetrates through the door. Cecilia slips into the room's darkness, leaving him standing outside. He has a sudden memory of the first night of his and Sarah's marriage, when they had come home to the cottage in Clevedon and the aeolian harp, their laughter at finding it bare of even the simplest necessity, and knowing it did not matter. He had been happy beyond all belief then and part of him feels the same tonight. But Sarah and he together had brought misery on themselves: no joy could ever last. He thinks of the whores in London, the drunkenness, the guilt which drove him into the army and knows that, no matter what nightmares they might bring, no revulsion will last either. He does not know what this night holds for him: joy which will not last or revulsion which will not last either?

Cecilia lights more candles and a soft flickering light shines through. She reappears, takes his hand again and, with the slightest of pressures, pulls him inside. Her lips brush his in the faintest of kisses. 'Come in, dear Samuel,' she breathes. As always, her halting, accented English makes his heart swell with an acute joy. He knows she has made herself learn what she could of the language only for him. Her hesitations, her reaching for words that are beyond her but which he always gently supplies, her laughter when she knows she is wrong, fill him with a yearning, affectionate pity.

The room is cool. A delicate scent teases his nostrils. It is somehow like – though he knows it isn't – the aromatic scent of poplar trees, which teases him every time he walks up the green lane to the opera house. The window is open, but by now the street noise is faint, far off in another world. Cecilia closes the shutters. The room is dominated by a bed, white sheets cool and subtly inviting, the coverlet turned down.

Cecilia takes off the light top coat she had worn against the night air. She slips off her shoes and loosens her bodice. She shakes out her long, dark hair, then turns to him. She reaches up, puts her arms round his neck and kisses him again, more firmly than before but still light and gentle. 'Dear heart,' she says. 'How like you this?'

Her strange inversion of language makes his heart sing again. Then he frowns. He knows those words. They are part of a poem. She cannot possibly be quoting: the strange word-order must be pure accident. What is that poem? He knows it speaks of delighted, dangerous anticipation, an illicit joy. It fits the situation with painful accuracy. But now his heart is racing. Logical, rational thought is slipping away and particular poems, even poetry itself except for that of the immediate moment, have vanished from his mind.

Still with her arms round his neck, with naked foot she pads about the chamber, drawing him with her. They reach the side of the bed where the coverlet is drawn back. He is dreaming, he knows this is all a dream – yet it is no dream: he is broad waking. Still looking up at him, her deep, dark eyes intently on his, Cecilia begins to loosen his necktie. She repeats what she said on the stairs. 'Dear Samuel, do not be afraid.'

But he isn't afraid. Every sense is alert, every touch sends excited shocks through his body. His heart races: it hammers in his ears until it almost hurts. His loins ache, strain. Cecilia's face, small, perfect, a heady mixture of naivety and knowingness, fills his vision: his hands, now round her waist, feel a body so delicate that he could break it, yet it pulses with a strength he has no defence against. She eases his jacket off now, almost shyly begins to take off her own clothes, then clasps her hands round his neck again and gently pulls him down as she subsides onto the bed.

'This is the time, Samuel,' she says.

'I know,' he replies and prepares to give himself up to the moment. She lies beneath him, smiling. Her breasts are bare. Her nipples in their aureoles are taut. He is made speechless by their perfection, their beauty. The struggle which has ruled his last weeks in Siracusa since he first set foot in the opera house is over. This is his place, this is his time.

'I know, sweetest Cecilia,' he says again and gives himself up to the moment.

Then, without warning, everything changes. It is as if a door in his mind opens and a guest walks in, half unwelcome, half desired. He sees, as clearly as if it obscures Cecilia's face and breasts, another face, fringed with lustrous auburn hair, square where Cecilia's is oval, with a jaw which juts determinedly. He knows full well it is not a beautiful face, not like Cecilia's or even Sarah's once, yet it is beautiful to him. Its expression contains sadness, sternness: its eyes shine with an earnest innocence. 'Asra,' his mind says, though his voice does not. 'What do you want of me?'

'Samuel, what is the matter?' Cecilia murmurs. 'Do not be afraid, my love.'

He looks at Cecilia again. He knows he is lost, quite lost. He has known it since he started his lone walk along the green lane that night, he had even known it when he first saw her with the Leckies when they took him to the opera.

But here is Asra and she has come – as what? A deliberate spoiler of happiness or a guardian angel? He does not know and her expression is not telling him. But he must decide quickly, for his whole body is throbbing and he does care for Cecilia, he does, he does, and he would not willingly hurt her. Yet Asra is insistent.

What will the next few moments hold? Whatever they bring forth, he fears they will determine his peace of mind, such as it was, even his life, for years to come.

*

Cecilia is on the point of ecstasy. But suddenly she hears a great howl of frustration, the sound of clothes being hastily thrown on, his voice crying out. 'I'm sorry, I'm sorry.'

Then the door slams and running footsteps echo on the stairs and die away.

*

Has a seed been planted in her? If so, she would have a part of him for her own. His memory would live again every time she looked into the child's eyes.

But that child will be illegitimate. That will mean disaster for them both. The child needs a father.

Bernardo Gambino wants to marry her. He is rich. He has a special licence from the bishop so the marriage will be quick. Bernardo will never know that the child is not his. She will go on singing – but she will have a place in society and a wonderful life that a girl from the slums of Rome could never have dreamt of.

Yes, she will do it. She will tell Fabrizio tomorrow.

PART VI

Chapter 41

Scrivener's Choice

September 1827

[I] give you truth broken into prismatic hues, and fear the pure bright light, even if it is in me.

—Robert Browning

The opium-bearing poppies had been grubbed up and so had the spirit of Bernardo Gambino. The land where the source of misery once flourished was now covered in vines, the bringers of joy. Moscato grapes for white wines, Frappato for red. The vines were planted only three years ago in the chalky soil but had already produced good wine. In ten years, thought Scrivener, as he, Samuele and Alfredo inspected the vines under a bright sun in a cloudless sky, this would be among the best wineries in Sicily.

As they passed the spot where Benito had thrown Bernardo to his death, Scrivener marvelled at how perfectly their discussions in the Salutation and Cat about Coleridge's vision of building an ideal society by the Susquehanna had foreseen the future. For Coleridge, hope born to die. Not, it seemed, for Samuele.

But here it was, just as they had forecast. Bernardo's harsh rule was long gone. Now there was a little commonwealth of like-minded people. Alfredo remained, a wise and gentle guide respected by equal partners, once virtual slaves. They now took pride in their work and equal shares in the profits. Samuele had no extra privileges. He took his turn with them as he made himself an expert vigneron. Scrivener reflected that 'vigneron' was the ideal occupation for Samuele. The satisfaction of honest toil combined with the creativity of producing fine wine to delight thousands. More than poets could ever imagine for their work.

Bernardo had left the whole estate, including the villa in Monreale, to Samuele, and he had at once made the villa, its grounds and orchards over to his mother. After the villa's auction, which raised far more than they had dreamt of, Cecilia was an independently rich woman. But they had agreed that all this wealth should go towards making the estates the shared community they craved.

They refurbished and extended the house of Alfredo and his wife and turned the peasants' hovels into decent dwellings. They built new houses for servants from Monreale.

Another house had been built, larger but no more luxurious than the others. In it lived Cecilia – and also Samuele and Giulia, now married, with two children and another on the way.

And living in an annexe was another new arrival. Mr Calvert. Samuele had visited him on his return from England; they had long talks about Coleridge and, with their opinions modified by time, thought and experience, came to wide agreement. So when Samuele invited him to join them he left his lodgings in the grim building he shared with priests. Now he lived in Floridia with his books, a wise philosopher and fount of knowledge. He had never been so happy in his life. And he quickly showed that Marsala was not the only wine he enjoyed. Mr Calvert had found paradise.

Scrivener was so pleased by this. When Samuele had first told him about Mr Calvert, alone and absent from his native country, he thought that his roots might have shrivelled. But Mr Calvert had found new roots.

Mr Calvert and Samuele's mother had become very friendly. Samuele told Scrivener that he wished them well and hoped for a culmination to bring them the comfort and fulfilment they both so much deserved.

Scrivener saw all this, understood fully and rejoiced.

And then he woke up.

*

The dream was so clear, so real. He had felt the sun's heat and the welcome shade of the vines. He heard Samuele and Alfredo as if he were standing next to them. His thoughts gave him pleasure which he was sure would not recede. Samuele's world seemed all – and more – than he had even dreamt of when they discussed their plans in the Salutation and Cat three years earlier.

But Scrivener was in his lodgings over a London bookseller's off Newgate Street and thought of Charles Lamb. How lucky he was to be his friend. And how much better for him if he had found Charles first and not Coleridge, the errant star. Because in him Scrivener could envisage the sort of writer his talents might enable him to be and through Charles's advice and influence, he had achieved his first small successes.

Yes, he was at last content.

He would never forget the flash of insight as he and Samuele had been about to board the *Arethusa* for Gibraltar three years before. He thought of his euphoria about the marvellous prospects – a life in a warm climate, no more stench of failure, a new start free of his burdens, the leaving of a country with nothing left to give him, the honour of being a founder member of an ideal new society and, most intriguing of all, Samuele's faint but alluring hint about the mysterious Peregrina.

But then, like waves crashing through the timbers of a ship's hull, came the revelation. What would he be but a hanger-on, a parasite, almost a dependant of Samuele already? Scrivener did not want to be a charity boy again. A sizarship in Cambridge was not a glorious position.

No. Going to Sicily was simply an escape. Or was it cowardice? He was still his own master. His destiny was not in an unknown faraway land but in his own country, among the people he knew and whose language he spoke.

And what Samuele had told him about Mr Calvert had worried him deeply. Yes, he probably could have long conversations with him about poetry and literature and would have enjoyed them. But was that enough? Mr Calvert was a voluntary exile. Scrivener felt exiled enough already.

Failing to emulate Coleridge didn't mean he couldn't be a writer. To write in English he had to be in England. If he wanted to write he had to be with other writers and close to the booksellers and publishers, because they would be his gateway.

He remembered with painful clarity the moment when he had made up his mind. He and Samuele stood at the foot of the gangplank ready to go on board. He summoned all his strength to speak, nearly failed at the last second, then found the words coming out.

'Samuele. I'm sorry. But I can't come with you.'

Samuele had been facing away from him, looking downriver and thinking about the open sea beyond. He turned round slowly. 'What did you say?'

'I can't come with you.'

'But you must. I've written to my mother and told her that I have someone with me. She will wonder if it's Mr Coleridge.'

'Write to her again.'

'It's too late. We'll be home long before it arrived.'

'She'll be thankful you're on your own. To have Coleridge there would be disastrous, for both of you.'

'I know,' Samuele replied.

'This is the second time I have refused an offer from you and I am sorry. But I had a search, too, and you agreed that, for me, mine was more important.'

'I know,' said Samuele.

'But mine failed. So has yours.'

'That's no reason to refuse my offer.'

'But now I know I have a duty to myself.'

'Which is?'

'Since I found the inscription in "Kubla Khan", I thought I knew what I had to do. When I was too frightened to see Coleridge, I thought it was over. But it isn't.'

'Would you have thought that if you hadn't met me running away because I didn't dare face him either?'

'I can't say for sure. But what would he have thought if I'd said, "I can never do what you do because the way your mind works is beyond me to understand, but finding this out has had me sent down from your own college and thrown out of my house, and I demand restitution"?'

'But it wasn't Coleridge's fault.'

'I know that. I can't be a Coleridge, but I can be a writer. It must be here, though, with my own people. You introduced me to Charles Lamb and I thank you. He could be my guiding star. He's Coleridge's friend and I want *him* to be my mentor. Sicily would shrivel my roots. Your Mr Calvert might have been a good friend. But his roots are shrivelled already.'

He waited for angry recrimination. Samuele was deep in thought. At last he said, 'George, I understand what you say. I want to go home, you want to stay home. That's as it should be. You have been my good friend and you always will be.'

Scrivener was thankful. He had expected anger and resentment.

'We'll keep in touch and perhaps one day you'll visit us. And perhaps I'll bring Giulia and my mother here to see you.'

'And might you visit Samuel Taylor Coleridge?'

Samuele smiled enigmatically. 'We shall see,' he said. 'Will you? After all, he's your neighbour now.'

'We shall see,' Scrivener replied.

A sailor approached them. 'Might I take your luggage aboard for you, my good sirs?'

'Please,' said Samuele. 'This is mine.'

'Leave mine,' said Scrivener. 'I shall not be sailing.'

Samuele ran lightly up the gangplank. Once on deck, he leant over the gunwale and looked down. 'Goodbye, old friend,' he called.

'Goodbye,' Scrivener called back. 'God speed you.'

After the ship cast off and was poled slowly away from the quay, Samuele waved until Scrivener could see him no more. But he stayed where he was as the ship headed out past Wapping, and Tilbury, towards where the Thames ended and the sea stretched deep and untrustworthy.

When he could see the ship no longer, he picked up his meagre luggage and started the walk back to the Sally Cat. And all the way, the question was raging through his mind.

Have I made the right choice?

*

Mrs Elkins stood behind the bar as usual, and saw Scrivener push his way through, trying not to jostle the drinkers. 'Back already?' she said.

'I didn't go,' he replied. 'Can I have my room again, please?'

'You're in luck,' she replied. 'Just this once. No other takers tonight but I think there's one tomorrow. Sorry.'

The luggage seemed to weigh a ton as he humped it up the stairs. It was late afternoon. He slumped into a chair numb and exhausted. He could only think of Samuele on the ship, as the Thames widened and the smell of the sea grew stronger. For a moment, he felt the same breeze on his face and heard the cries of sailors, the creak of ropes on wood and the ruffling sound of wind in the sails. He found himself saying aloud:

'The ship was cheered, the harbour cleared,
Merrily did we drop

Below the kirk, below the hill,
Before the lighthouse top.'

Those words. What delighted anticipation they conveyed. How he would love to be on the *Arethusa* in a moment of freedom, release, closeness to the elements, a wonderful future and a fulfilled life. How monumentally stupid to pass up on such an opportunity.

However, the voyage in Coleridge's poem had led to terror, death, descent into innermost reaches of the human soul. He suddenly feared for Samuele.

But if he expected contentment in his own voyage, might he be disappointed? Yes, he meant what he had said about being a writer and about Charles Lamb being his new mentor. But Lamb didn't know this yet. He had said goodbye and given them his best wishes three nights before.

Scrivener rose from the chair and made a pot of tea. Then he thought about a strategy. After five minutes, his mind was blank.

He needed advice. Who from? Well, he wanted Charles Lamb to be his mentor so it was Charles Lamb he must ask.

When? Why not now? Did he dare burst in, unexpected and unannounced? Yes, he did.

*

He arrived at the white cottage in Colebrook Row and knocked on the door. He heard voices inside. Female and male. Mary and Charles. Which of them would answer his knocking? He was ashamed of hoping that it would not be Mary.

He heard footsteps. The door opened. It was Charles. 'Why, George,' he said. 'You're supposed to be at sea now.'

'I changed my mind. My life is here after all.'

'I see,' said Lamb. 'Please come in.'

He ushered him in to the small drawing room. 'I'm afraid Mary will not be with us this evening,' he said. 'This has not been one of her better days.'

He motioned Scrivener to the same shabby armchair and sat down opposite on its equally shabby twin. 'Now, what can I do for you?'

'I need your help,' said Scrivener.

'How so?' Lamb asked.

So George told him about the annotation in 'Kubla Khan', his strange feeling it was aimed at him with an ambiguous message, how he had thought he could fulfil his dreams of being a poet by seeing how Coleridge went about writing poetry, learn from it and therefore make him his mentor, even if they never met. But the attempt had cost him everything.

Lamb listened attentively. When Scrivener had finished, he said, 'George, I could see there was more to your interest in Coleridge than you were willing to say. I could understand your friend's interest: he had a clear purpose. Samuel Taylor Coleridge is my dearest friend and has been since we were at school. We have had our arguments and estrangements. He is flawed, like us all. He has behaved appallingly to many people and some will never forgive him. But with him, friendship somehow always wins through. I believe, though many do not, that he has genius higher than anyone else in this land – in fact, in the world. There seems no end to his knowledge, his understanding, his power to connect the unconnectable, to see correspondences between opposites, to bring everything together into a unity. His work will last for all time and may change how humanity thinks. That is why many make allowances and excuse him. But equally, many cannot. And that is why he can be mentor to nobody. We can listen, read and marvel. But, unless we are equal geniuses, we cannot emulate.'

Scrivener was silent.

'And that is why your search not only failed but brought you to the lowest point of your life.'

'But it's not over,' said Scrivener.

Lamb looked closely at him. Then he smiled. 'George,' he said. 'Those are wonderful words. Tell me more.'

'I'm not a genius. But I want to be a writer. I want to produce work which will please people, bring knowledge, share life's experiences so we know that what's true for one may be true for another in a shared world of thought and feeling, and that our insights and understanding come from the same place, though we won't know where they will lead us until we arrive. To know we are not alone.'

'Well spoken,' said Lamb.

'I have read some of your essays.'

'Ah, yes. Good old *Elia*. He serves me well and will for many years yet.'

'And what you do in them is what I have just said. And that is what I want to do as well. I'm not a genius. But I believe I have a certain talent and it's my right to use it.'

'It's everybody's right,' said Lamb. 'But why are you telling me?'

'Because I want you to be my mentor instead of Coleridge.'

Lamb smiled again, with the air of one who could see what was coming.

'Let me think about it,' he said. 'We'll meet tomorrow in the Sally Cat over tankards of stingo at eight of the clock. I'll be free by then of that wretched counting house where I drudge through each long day. We'll talk until Mrs Elkins throws us out.'

A woman's voice sounded from another room.

'Ah,' said Lamb. 'My sister calls. I must bid you goodnight.'

*

Scrivener walked with a lighter step. On an impulse, he turned down the street where Mr Porson's bookshop was. There was a light in the window. He saw the bookseller poring over a volume taken from his shelves. Mr Porson looked up expecting a late customer.

Discomfited, Scrivener blurted out, 'Mr Porson, I'm not going to Sicily after all. But I need somewhere to live. Could I take the upstairs rooms on a proper lease? I don't think I'll be leaving London now.'

'What brought this on?' asked Mr Porson. 'East, west, home's best, eh?'

'It just came on me. I couldn't bring myself to climb the gangplank.'

To his surprise, Mr Porson smiled. 'Of course you may have the rooms. I'm glad to welcome you. It will be good to have a real book lover upstairs. I saw how you dealt with the customer the other day. I was sorry to spring that on you but think of it as a test that you passed. The job's yours if you want it. I'll pay a fair wage and ask a fair rent, which I'll stop out of your wages so you don't have to find it each week. Where are you staying now?'

'The Salutation and Cat. But only for one night.'

'Then bring your luggage over here tomorrow, we'll get you settled and you can start work at once. I'll show you the ropes.'

Scrivener was too speechless even to thank him.

'Well, it's getting late and I think it's time to shut up shop.'

He held out his hand. His grip was strong and his handshake firm. 'Till tomorrow then, Mr Scrivener. A new start for us both.'

Scrivener had an afterthought. 'Mr Porson, may I buy a copy of *The Essays of Elia* by Charles Lamb?'

'No, you may not,' was the reply.

Scrivener looked crestfallen.

Mr Porson crossed to the shelves on the opposite wall and selected a book.

'Here you are,' he said. 'My welcoming gift.'

*

Scrivener returned to the Sally Cat in a state of semi-shock. The day's events were extraordinary yet all of a piece. An important encounter, permanent lodgings and a job, all in one evening, after a life-altering decision almost on the spur of the moment. He ate a pie in the snug and, because Lamb assumed he'd be partial to stingo, dared a half-pint of bitter beer. Then he read Lamb's essays until eleven o'clock. He had read some before but not with the close attention he gave them now. He felt the rhythms of the prose, the elegiac tone, the closeness of the observation, the sudden shafts of gentle humour, the fullness and satisfaction at the end of each essay. And he wondered at the range of unexpected subjects. Nothing seemed too odd or insignificant for Lamb's astute gaze. Scrivener lit on an essay called 'The Praise of Chimney-Sweepers'.

I like to meet a sweep – understand me – not a grown sweeper – old chimney-sweepers are by no means attractive – but one of those tender novices, blooming through their first nigritude, the maternal washings not quite effaced from the cheek – such as come forth with the dawn, or somewhat earlier, with their little professional notes sounding like the peep-peep *of a young sparrow; or liker to the matin lark should I pronounce them, in their aerial ascents not seldom anticipating the sunrise?*

I have a kindly yearning towards these dim specks – poor blots – innocent blacknesses...

Charles was saying new things about what we took for granted. One of life's dispossessed, of no account. Like the rural poor, whom nobody noticed. The message was clear: *Look at this boy. Think of what you expect from your fellow human beings and recognise your guilt.*

Charles was right. Coleridge was not a mentor for a task like this. But Charles Lamb was.

*

At eight o'clock sharp next evening, Scrivener entered the Salutation and Cat after a day with Mr Porson. Charles was already there, a tankard of stingo in front of him.

He stood up. 'Ah, George,' he said. 'Perfectly timed. Can I tempt you to a pint of this heavenly brew? Stingo could only have been produced by divine intervention.'

The very word 'stingo' chilled Scrivener's stomach. But he had to make a good impression, so he gamely replied, 'I certainly would. Thank you.'

The beer arrived. Another pewter tankard, brimming over with a dark, suspicious-looking liquid. He forced himself to take a tentative sip. Then another, less tentatively. Charles Lamb lifted his own tankard and leant across the table. Scrivener responded, they clinked tankards and Lamb said, 'Good health, George. And welcome.'

Scrivener took a deeper swallow and marvelled. Stingo was full-bodied and smooth, like velvet. The familiar words *and drunk the milk of Paradise* flowed effortlessly into his mind. He remembered the Pickerel before the fateful walk along the Cam. That seeming disaster, he now realised, was merely a marker of progress. From a sip of a foul liquid in the Pickerel as the ultimate outsider to the contented consumption of a stronger brew in the presence of a prince in the world of books and now his friend. A lifetime in two months.

'So what exactly do you want from me?' Lamb asked. 'Mentor is a slippery word. Can you define what you mean?'

'I mean a fine writer to guide me, advise me on what works and what doesn't, criticise my work and not shirk to tell me if it's not good enough and why, to help me find my own voice. In short, to help me mould any talent I may possess until we're both satisfied with it.'

'I see,' said Charles. 'You didn't say you wanted guidance round this weird, competitive world of writers and publishers. It's threatening but I can help you find your way in it. And you didn't say you wanted help to be published by introducing you to the right people.'

'No, I didn't,' said George. 'But if that's what you're offering, I'll gladly accept it.'

'Well said,' Charles replied, smiling. 'But first, I must decide whether you'll be worth my precious time. That may be a hard task.'

'I'd expect nothing less,' said Scrivener.

'First rate,' said Charles. 'Another stingo? You made short work of the first.'

*

Well, Scrivener thought now, as he woke from his dream of Sicily. The last three years had been sometimes frustrating, sometimes enlivening. He had worked hard. He had written poetry with none of the thought and care he'd brought to his doomed 'Ancient Mariner' effort. Even so, it had a small but faithful following. His first poem, published in an obscure, little-read journal after Charles introduced him to the editor, was harmless to its readers but made him wonder if he was a lying hypocrite. It had been a satisfying triumph at the time: now he squirmed with embarrassment and tried to forget it. But it was done, so he couldn't.

'Thoughts from Long Ago'

This doubtful world of ours is often merciless.
Cold winds, sharp words can hurt the weary mind.
But memory will wake the aching heart
To friendly ghosts of loved ones, meek and kind.

And so on for three commonplace, sentimental stanzas. Mercifully, he couldn't remember them, though he could easily reach out to a shelf for a copy of the small collection of similar poems in which it was the first. The editor had inexplicably ('for the gratification of the public', he told him) wanted more on the same theme. He wrote them unwillingly. The poems were full of comforting nostalgia, which made the whole book sheer hypocrisy. Nostalgia and life with his uncle were not concepts easily reconciled. He sincerely hoped that Coleridge would never see them.

Even so, when finished copies of *Thoughts from Long Ago* by George Scrivener arrived, he felt the pride of his first published book, even though he thought it was trash. To celebrate, Charles and Mr Porson took him to the Sally Cat, fed him with jellied eels, meat pie, potatoes and carrots, bought endless pints of stingo and finished off the evening with a bottle of Irish whiskey so that he had a pounding headache lasting nearly a week – but it was one of the best nights of his life.

After that, he tried writing a play in blank verse – two acts of a drama set in the time of the Jacobite rising, all kilts, sporrans and bagpipes, none of which had Scrivener ever seen. *Macbeth* as written by a ten-year-old. He had sent it to a few theatre managers a year ago but heard nothing. He rejected a career as a playwright.

However, sensational Gothic novels were still all the rage and to try them might be promising. Now he was catching up with reading them and was loving it. Walpole's *The Castle of Otranto*, Ann Radcliffe's *The Mysteries of Udolpho*. Horror, sinister villains, mysterious castles, ghosts, damsels, murders, sometimes unspeakable matters like incest – he loved them all. Three above all. Mary Shelley's *Frankenstein* – these books could be serious as well as entertaining. John Polidori's *The Vampyre*. He was Byron's doctor and everyone supposed that Byron really wrote it. There should be more vampires so why shouldn't he join in? On the other hand, Irishman Charles Maturin's *Melmoth the Wanderer* chilled him to the marrow. John Melmoth, a student, finds a portrait of himself dated 1646 in a forbidden trunk in his dying uncle's house. 1646? How can this be? He realises he must somehow exist outside time. He has committed some terrible crime long ago and is sentenced to wander the world for ever, like Cain and Ahasuerus. His loneliness is complete. He ranges through the world and time seeking companions who have hidden guilts to share them with him and those he selects are haunted by him until they are consumed into Melmoth's darkness, from which there is no escape because now he can destroy them.

Scrivener was so frightened by this notion that he turned to Jane Austen and *Northanger Abbey* and saw a wonderful writer making fun of these Gothic tales. Yes, sensational novels in some form or another might be a quick way to fame and fortune. And still *The Monk* remained his favourite.

Then he remembered something disturbing. All these books were just entertainment and cheap thrills. But Coleridge had written a story which had all the features of Gothic novels, 'Christabel', even though it was a poem which had taken only half a day to copy out all those years ago. But when Scrivener tried to emulate it he found a sinister difference. The horror was real: the destruction of a soul was cold-blooded and intentional and Geraldine was the destroyer from a nightmare who had frightened him even as he read the poem for the first time. He did not want to be seduced down that way again.

No, he would just provide the pleasurable *frisson* of fear and no more. Entertainment would be the aim. And if he failed, he would have lost nothing but time and pride.

Recently he'd had some success with essays rather like those of *Elia*, with Charles's permission and approval. Several were published in periodicals and he had been invited to put them all into one volume, together with new ones. He had started a new essay only the day before.

He sat at his desk and checked what he had written.

ON BEING SENT DOWN FROM THE UNIVERSITY
It seems generally agreed that there are two types of sending down. There is that of the humble sizar, cast away for some

trivial reason such as slacking in his work or sometimes for being accused of slight dishonesty caused by sheer penury. Such disasters lead to shame, disgrace, mockery and the end of ambition for escape to a better life.

The other is that of the rich fellow commoner, sent down for romantic, spectacular transgressions, which bring fame and admiration for his daring. —Something grand to dine out on for the rest of his life. But, just now and again, the fortunes are reversed. The sizar may fight against his misfortune, persevere and find himself with a better life than might have been his had he stayed the course. While the fellow commoner might be so seduced by pride as to assume immunity from the vicissitudes of life as lived by the rest of us. He may overreach himself and his hubris will bring him down to humiliation and contempt.

Scrivener had no idea whether any fellow commoner that he had known had been sent down from Jesus, though he thought there was a good chance that one or two might have been. He had hopes for Raggett as well. He scoured the public prints every day hoping to see a news item that the Honourable Mr Copperthwaite-Smirke had been sentenced to ten years hard labour for embezzling funds from Coutts Bank.

Such an event would make satisfaction with his new life complete.

*

Ten days later, Charles said, 'George, I think it's time you met your first mentor.'

Just for a moment, Scrivener wondered who he meant. When he realised, he was frightened. *Grow up, Scrivener, for heaven's sake*, he said to himself.

'Yes,' he said. 'You're right. Except that...'

'Except what?'

'Please don't mention *Thoughts from Long Ago*.'

'Why ever should I? This won't be a discussion session. It's a friendly chat between three writers who respect each other. If Sam wants to have a discussion, it won't be about anyone in the room.'

Scrivener was content with that. Three days later they journeyed northward to Highgate and the clearer air of Hampstead Heath.

The Gillmans' maid opened the front door and took them upstairs to Coleridge's spacious, book-lined room. Scrivener's unobtrusive survey of the shelves did not reveal a copy of *Thoughts from Long Ago*.

Relieved, he switched his survey to Coleridge himself. The great man sat in an armchair. He was portly, with thinning, greying hair. Remembering all he had feared for so many years, Scrivener was surprised that *mellow* sprang to mind as the best word to describe him.

Coleridge was in a reflective mood. Scrivener listened in rapt admiration. At first he was overawed, but then realised that there was no display of knowledge to impress. Every subtle argument that appeared was fired new from the mint, straight from a mind imbued with the human 'secondary imagination' he had proposed in *Biographia Literaria*. It left Scrivener breathless.

When it was time to leave, Scrivener was exhausted but elated. The long friendship between Charles and Coleridge had shone through. 'Gentle-hearted Charles.' And today it had been manifestly true.

'He was impressed with you,' said Charles on their return to Colebrook.

'But I hardly said a word.'

'We've been friends since we were schoolboys and I know him well, so believe me. By the way, I've noticed all the novel-reading you've been doing lately. A whole shelf full of Gothic horror. Well, here's a word to the wise. Lewis's *The Monk* is one of dear Sam's favourite books.'

That night, Scrivener had two satisfying feelings. He had found a new friend and a long story was finally over.

And another one. Charles hadn't given him a hint but an instruction. An action-packed 'Christabel' without the danger. That was where his talents lay and he was going to fulfil them.

*

'Three writers who respect each other.' Charles's words. On the way home, Scrivener realised how grotesque they were. One, a poet who had changed the way poetry was written, a thinker who had changed the way it was read. Two, a writer of more limited power but prince of his genre. And Scrivener? Author of a miserable collection of worthless poems, a few undistinguished essays. All he had to show for four years of striving.

Was there hope for him? The Gothic novel? Charles had been very persuasive about STC's opinion of *The Monk*.

When they returned to Colebrook Row, Charles found Coleridge's review of *The Monk*. Scrivener took it home and studied it carefully.

The author everywhere discovers an imagination rich, powerful and fervid. Praise indeed. But then came the damning consequence.

With how little expense of thought or imagination this species of composition is manufactured.

'Manufactured'. The word stung with its truth. No imagination needed.

Then he remembered *Melmoth the Wanderer*.

It had all the usual Gothic features. But they weren't manufactured. They were stark, horrifying, real.

Melmoth's profound loneliness had pierced Scrivener like a dagger. He thought of a lifetime with his unforgiving uncle and his friendless existence in Cambridge. Yes. He knew what loneliness was. Samuele had been the first true friend of his life. So he,

George Scrivener, was Melmoth. Charles Maturin had shown him that he was not alone. A simple truth, but it had taken Charles Maturin to prove it to him.

He thought back over the past and remembered, for it was always lurking in his mind, the fateful journey to Woodstock in search of a dream. A significant time. He recalled treachery, violence, deception, anger, startling insights, utter stupidity, instinctive understanding, unforgiving meanness and sudden generosity packed into three short days. Characters not easily forgotten. He would write it out as a story. It would be a novel.

Except, he knew at once, that it wouldn't. It would be just an account. So where would he find new stories to tell?

The account of the journey would be about real people. 'Real' was a slippery word. He suddenly remembered the day he and Charles first discussed being his mentor and he told Charles about the sort of writer he wanted to be. One who would 'share life's experiences so we know that what's true for one may be true for another. To know we are not alone.'

Fine words. He had spent three years not living up to them. So why had he spent those years writing rubbish? It was because he hadn't thought carefully enough what his own words had meant.

And only now did he begin to realise his true talent. Ordinary people in all their uniqueness. The stuff of stories, the stuff of life.

The true writer creates real people. And real people can change their minds. Who knows where this might lead them? The true writer will sit back and let things take their course. And the result will be life in all its bewilderment and chaos. And the true writer will want to explore it.

He would try to write novels, letting his characters take what course they would until they found a sort of resolution for themselves and, what was more, a resolution for the structure of the whole book so that readers could say as they put the book down,

'That ending was inevitable' and 'That ending was a complete surprise' and mean both equally.

That would be hard. He knew he risked failure, perhaps even humiliation. Nevertheless, he knew what he wanted to do now. It had taken him a long time. But now his course was set and his long search was over.

Chapter 42

Samuele's Homecoming

London–Monreale, June–July 1824

Oh! dream of joy! Is this indeed
The light-house top I see?
Is this the hill? is this the kirk?
Is this mine own countree?

—'The Rime of the Ancient Mariner',
Samuel Taylor Coleridge

Samuele watched Scrivener walk away, carrying his travelling case and crossing Southwark Bridge into a new life, possessing nothing.

Suddenly, his mind was aflame. Bringing a companion would have meant forgetting his mad plan to persuade Sara Coleridge to marry him. It was founded on a lie. The law said Bernardo was his father and he could not change that. So Sara, the law said, could not be his half-sister.

Another lie, like his excuse for being here at all. Charles expected a copy of the book his dead father was supposed to be writing. Southey had said, *Your father is a man of insight and generosity. I think I would like him.* If the truth were ever known he would be disgraced for ever.

But the image of Sara was too strong. The choice was clear. The glorious prospect of one of the world's great loves which would be either the stuff of legend, or a humiliation that would kill him? He didn't care. The prize was too great. *He would stake his life on the legend.* He called the sailor who had put his luggage on board to bring it back, picked it up and started his risky journey into infinite happiness.

Then he stopped. Where was he going? People lived all over the country who knew him now. He could keep no secrets here and, when they found out, not in Sicily either. He could be a pariah for ever. Eloping to America? Madness.

There was no argument. He did not call the sailor back; he carried his luggage up the gangplank himself.

The dream was gone. But Sara's image stayed and always would.

*

The voyage to Gibraltar was dismal and dangerous. At first, Samuele stayed on deck as they headed out down the Thames. All seemed well. The sun shone, the water was calm and Samuele took his last glimpses of England with a sense of relief. But a heavy swell in the North Sea awaited them. He retched and was violently sick. When the vomiting stopped, he staggered down to his cabin. He threw himself on one of the two tiny, hard bunks, and retched. He found a chamber pot and was sick again.

Thus began weeks of misery.

*

At last they rounded Cape Finisterre and into the Bay of Biscay. The sea of storms. Samuele cursed himself, knowing he should have come home by coach after all. This was no calm sea and prosperous voyage.

He dared not go outside. Twice a day he was brought unappetising food, mere slops, and his chamber pot was taken away to be emptied overboard. Twice the sea was so rough that he thought they would founder. And all the time, fevered thoughts of Samuel Taylor Coleridge's only legacies to him overwhelmed him. Pantisocracy and Sara. And while he tried his best to imagine Pantisocracy, images of Sara kept wiping those thoughts out.

The sea calmed as they left Biscay and sailed down the Spanish coast. He ventured to go on deck.

The ship was sailing serenely through blue sea flecked by little wavelets. The sun was bright. His violent emotions in the cabin had calmed with the sea. He looked ahead and dreamt of a better future.

*

Next morning it was still calm and he could think rationally. No, you didn't have to go to America to make an ideal society. It could happen in Sicily. Yes, good would come from Bernardo's petty tyrannies.

He spent the next hour excitedly working out how he would do it. He was bringing home something entirely good. Coleridge's real legacy.

*

The *Arethusa* finally docked in Gibraltar. Samuele called at the shipping office and was offered a berth on a navy merchant ship bound for Malta three days later. He found a boarding house, explored the Rock and fed the monkeys. He felt almost lighthearted. In Malta he stayed in Valetta for two days waiting for a ferry to Sicily. He explored the tiny city and wondered if he was following in Coleridge's footsteps.

The ship to Sicily skirted the south coast and round to Siracusa, up the east coast and finally into Palermo, twenty-seven days after leaving Greenwich. And as he prepared to disembark he had ominous thoughts about his final homecoming.

Nobody knew he was coming. He had to let them know. He found his way to the Custom House, asked for paper and pen and wrote a note to his mother asking her to send Salvatore with the trap to bring him home. He did not tell her that he was alone. Then he enquired if a messenger could be hired to take the note to Monreale.

'Of course, signore,' was the reply.

Samuele paid the fee and the messenger left. He was offered a chair and realised he had not sat down comfortably for a month. That alone said his journey was finished. It also told him that an unreal fantasy was over and hard reality was taking its place.

Salvatore arrived an hour later, took the luggage and put it on the trap. Samuele clambered up to the seat next to him and they trotted smartly into Palermo. They passed the Duomo and the Archbishop's Palace, and under the Porta Nuova. He saw the narrow street leading to Mr Calvert's lodgings and resolved to speak to him soon. They started the climb up Monte Caputo. He could see the familiar outline of the villa in the fading light. They entered the orchard. His heart beat fast as he looked for the sight of Giulia picking oranges. Perhaps it might rid him of Sara's image. But Giulia was not there and Sara's image remained. He tried to damp these feelings down. He needed a clear mind for this difficult meeting. His mother would be waiting just as when he had brought Bernardo's body home.

There she was. He had no companion – but she did, indistinct in the dusk.

The trap came closer. He got ready to jump out. And then he recognised the companion. Giulia, standing close like good friends. He remembered his mother berating Giulia for eavesdropping. The great lady of the house scolding a menial. What had happened?

Samuele jumped out and Salvatore lifted down his luggage, bowed, said, 'Good evening, signore,' and drove the trap away.

Samuele faced the two women.

'You seem surprised,' said Cecilia.

'Yes,' said Samuele.

'So you should be. Where is your companion?'

'He didn't come.'

'You've been away for months. There's been no word from you, until you wrote about a companion. One letter and it told a lie.'

'It wasn't Mr Coleridge,' said Samuele.

'Thank God,' said Cecilia. 'Who was it then?'

'My friend George Scrivener. He was coming with me to start a new life. But he changed his mind.'

'You seem discomfited to see us together,' said Cecilia. 'You needn't be. I have had much time to think. I've looked at my life and have not liked what I've seen. I needed a friend and now I have one. Giulia has become my constant companion. One of Bernardo's legacies was that I am woman of substance and the wife of an important man, and must behave like it. So I believed him.

'But that's not who I am. I'm a working girl from the slums. My voice took me into the opera company. But what did that make me? We were famous. But men think opera singers are easy meat, no better than prostitutes.' She saw Samuele's look of horror. 'No, Samuele, I was never a prostitute. I looked out for myself and kept safe. But old habits die hard. I was horrible to Giulia when she tried to help me. Then I saw we were the same. Working girls together. We became friends. I know that she loves you. And I believe you may love her. And I am glad.'

Samuele felt a burden fall from his shoulders. 'Thank you, Mother,' he said. He turned to Giulia. He said the only thing he could. 'Yes, Giulia, I do love you. You've been in my mind every moment since I left.'

'And I love you,' said Giulia. 'There, at last I've been able to tell you.'

'And I'm so glad for you both,' said Cecilia. 'Now tell me about my dear Samuel.'

'Mother, when you first told me about him you seemed a young girl again. Everything was vivid as if it was still happening. He seemed a god, a free spirit, a great genius, without fault. I longed to be his son. I wanted to let him know who I was, even bring him back with me.

'Then Mr Calvert gave me another version. A wastrel, a traitorous seditionist, an opium-sodden wretch. Who was right? I went to find out. But how you'd react if the news was bad scared me. That was why I couldn't write to you.'

'So what is the truth?' said Cecilia.

'You must hear me out,' Samuele replied. 'I spoke to those who knew him best. I saw his wife but we never talked together. I saw his daughter and she did talk – just for a little, but what she said was the most important of all. Admiration for her father's achievements, desolation because she had hardly seen him since she was born. The highest love, the deepest misery.' There, he had mentioned Sara and felt enormous relief.

'I saw his best friends. Two still were his friends, though he'd treated them badly; two were not. I believed them equally.'

At last Cecilia spoke. 'Why didn't you speak to his wife?'

'One look at her told me she wouldn't talk to me. But others told me quite enough.'

'Did you meet my dear Samuel?'

Samuele noticed the 'dear'. 'I meant to. But my nerve failed. What would I have said but what I've told you? What use would that be?'

'Is that all?' said Cecilia.

'It's enough,' said Samuele. 'I don't want him to be my father. If he had stayed with you or taken you to England, he would have treated you just as badly as Bernardo did but in a different way. He would have deserted you, and me as well. I don't want either of them to be my father.'

He looked intently at his mother. How would she take this?

'Oh Samuele,' she sobbed, 'What have I done to you?'

Giulia moved suddenly. She went to Cecilia and embraced her. 'Be strong, signora,' she said. 'Samuele spoke as he did because he loves you. The truth can be hard. We've waited so long hoping all would be well. Now we know we were wrong. Believe me, signora, this will heal. And I will help you. And so will Samuele.'

*

Cecilia had been appalled when Samuele suggested they should sell the villa in Monreale and move to Floridia. Samuele was the master now. But for her, the exorcism of Bernardo's ghost meant she could appreciate the villa as the beautiful place it was.

'But, Samuele, you hated Floridia,' she said. 'You said everything growing there should be uprooted and burnt.'

'Yes, and I still do.'

'So why should I uproot myself? I shall not go.'

'Hear me out, Mother. If everything is uprooted and the soil is cleansed, we'll restore it with virgin tilth and start afresh. Out of all the things I learnt about Mr Coleridge there is just one which inspires me and which I want to make real as he never could. He had a dream. It's his legacy to me. I want to follow it and Floridia is the place for it to come true.'

Cecilia, wide-eyed, said nothing.

'We will turn the estates into a vineyard,' said Samuele. 'We will spread joy and well-being all over Sicily. In time we will produce the finest wines in all Italy. And then, the man who might be my father will see the ideal society which he never saw created. Alfredo and all Bernardo's so-called tenants will no longer be slaves. Everybody will be equal, every voice heard; everybody will share equally in the winery's success but also accept its failures. A common enterprise.'

Cecilia listened to all this and her mind was befuddled. She looked back nearly twenty years and thought she remembered her Samuel telling her something like that, but not much.

In the end she acquiesced and Samuele felt Sara's image grow a little fainter.

*

That night he thought about Mr Calvert. He should see him. At breakfast next morning he told them that he would go into Palermo.

'Why?' Cecilia asked.

'To see Mr Calvert.'

'But Mr Calvert said Samuel was an opium-sodden wretch.'

'Yes, he did,' said Samuele. 'But his last words to me were: "He may be a fool to himself, but he is a fine writer. What justification for existence can be greater?" Exactly what Charles Lamb, Tom Poole, Wordsworth and Southey said. Mr Calvert is a fair-minded man; I trust his word.'

Next morning he saddled up his horse and rode to the grim building in which Mr Calvert lived.

Peregrina opened the door. 'Samuele, welcome,' she said. 'Giulia told me you were home again.'

'I should have been here before,' he said. 'I'm sorry.'

'Mr Calvert will be so pleased to see you,' she replied.

Mr Calvert was sitting in the familiar book-lined room, reading. He rose at once and came straight to the point. 'Ah, Samuele. You said you were going to England on a quest. Was it successful?'

'I don't know.'

'May I ask what its object was?'

Samuele hesitated.

'Well, tell me if I'm wrong and berate me for being a presumptuous old fool if you want, but here's what I think. I have friends in Siracusa and about twenty years ago they came here to tell me a great poet was visiting them. I thought I'd go back with them and see for myself. They were all patrons of the opera house who regularly went back stage. One night I went with them. I recognised Coleridge there and wanted to speak to him but he and the prima donna seemed taken up with each other so I never did. I wasn't alone in noticing this and rumours were spreading until about the time of that episode with the French privateer in the harbour, where Mr Coleridge did well.

'And then we heard that the prima donna was getting married to a rich man from Palermo. In a hurry, they said. And now, nearly twenty years later my maid Peregrina tells me about you and I realise that your mother is that prima donna. Then you arrive and the first time I see you, you are reading Coleridge and I give you my honest opinion, which seems to upset you. When you said you were going on a quest to England, can you blame me for thinking it was to meet Coleridge and tell him you are his son? Or have I miscalculated and made two and two make five? Is he your father?'

'I don't know.'

There was a pause and then Mr Calvert said, 'Samuele, tell me what you found and I will give you my honest opinion.'

So Samuele recounted his whole experience, where he had been, who he had met and what he had heard. And when he had finished, Mr Calvert said, 'And did you meet Mr Coleridge?'

'No. I got as far as his front gate but I couldn't bring myself to open it.'

'Why not?'

'I was frightened. What could I say? He'd have had me thrown out.'

'Of course,' said Mr Calvert.

'Everyone told me the same thing. Somehow he was still loved even by those who hated what he did. Because they all thought he was special, a rare talent, a flawed genius.'

'And they are right.'

'I know. I began to hope he isn't my father after all. But I hope my lawful father wasn't either. I don't want either of them.'

'That is very sad, Samuele.'

'I know. I owe only hatred to my lawful father. But I have two legacies from Coleridge. One is his daughter.' Samuele thought he had better say this to get it over with. 'Sara is the most remarkable woman I have ever met.'

Leave it at that and move on.

'The other is Pantisocracy. That is a noble idea. I want to build it here in Sicily.'

'Tell me what you think Pantisocracy is.'

Samuele described this wonderful ideal society where all would be kings. When he had finished, Mr Calvert said, 'And what do you mean by building it here?'

When Samuele had told him, Mr Calvert was silent for a moment. Then he said, 'It would be wonderful to grow a vineyard. But where is Mr Coleridge's Pantisocracy now?'

'Nowhere,' said Samuele.

'Why not?'

'Robert Southey let him down.'

'But you say you spoke to Southey.'

'Yes. Until I met him, nobody mentioned it much. But he told me what it was and about the beginning of their friendship, and I saw tears in his eyes because he was sad about their friendship ending and the death of their great idea.'

'I know how he felt – everybody my age will. It's not crying for Pantisocracy. It's crying for lost youth, broken ideals. I remember the feeling so well. One day, so will you. It's wonderful to be young. But one day reality breaks through. However, if you make a vineyard which works well, where people are happy to be and are treated fairly and nobody feels badly done by and you produce fine wines then I think that you will have done all that human nature can possibly aspire to. Call it a commonwealth; that suits it better.'

Samuele did not protest. Mr Calvert had given him much to think about. 'In fact,' said Mr Calvert, 'I'm half inclined to ask if I can join you.'

Samuele smiled. 'I shall remember that,' he said.

'Now,' said Mr Calvert. 'It's time to get the Marsala out.'

*

The vineyard near Floridia had started well. The new vines were planted as the sun grew warmer and the rain gentler, and the weather seemed set fair. The changeable, cold, wet weather of the previous decade seemed gone. The vines took root and flourished.

The refurbishment of old dwellings and the building of new ones had gone well, too. As the vines grew before the first vintage, Samuele read books, visited other vineyards and worked with the vignerons and the workers. He learnt quickly. He was on the way to becoming as good a vigneron as his neighbours were.

And more. Cecilia told him how Giulia was not just an orange picker. She had responsibility for the whole orchard. She tended the trees in winter, pruning them to keep their shape, she got rid of blemishes before they spread. She loved the trees and understood them. When summer came she tended the fruit so that picking them was not just a job but a final fulfilment. And she had asked Cecilia whether, if she was now her companion, she could keep that responsibility.

'Samuele, I never knew,' she said. 'Bernardo believed servants were incapable of anything else.'

'I never knew either,' said Samuele. He was unaware of the true capabilities of the woman he would soon marry. But, he realised, as for orange trees, so for vines. Living, loving and working together.

So when he visited other vineyards Giulia came with him. If he was the vigneron, she would be the vigneronne. He was supremely happy.

They were married soon after. It crossed his mind that Coleridge had married Sarah because of Pantisocracy and he might have married Giulia for the commonwealth as well. He pushed the thought firmly away.

*

One day he asked Alfredo what he thought about the common-wealth project.

'Well, sir,' said Alfredo. 'I don't quite know what to make of it.'

'Alfredo, why are you still calling me "sir"? We are all equal now.'

'But how can we be? You are the master just as your father was. I don't doubt that you'll be a fairer master than he was. But that doesn't make us equals. I still do what you tell me and the labourers do what I tell them. Otherwise nothing can work and I won't know what I'm doing here.'

'But you're the bailiff.'

'Yes. And I have to do the bailiff's duties. But if we are all equal I can't. I like being the bailiff, I'm proud to be. Take away what I'm supposed to be here for and what am I?'

Samuele did not want to think about this for now. 'Come on, Alfredo. We'll inspect the vines together.'

'Where's the mistress?' said Alfredo. 'She knows as much about vines as we do. We'll need her here, too.'

Suddenly, Samuele felt that Alfredo knew more about Pantisocracy than he did.

They fetched Giulia over to join them and together they spent the morning with the vines. Samuele realised that, though he was learning so much about how to make wine, Alfredo and Giulia knew a lot more about plants then he did, how they grew and what to look for. It was strange. This morning, Alfredo had insisted that Samuele was now the master and he gave the orders. Watching how Giulia and Alfredo examined the vines and listening to them discuss what they saw made him feel that he had no right to be called master. They had knowledge far greater than he had and he must catch up with them. Not least because they were talking in the old language.

Now he knew that Mr Calvert had set him a puzzle. This was not a wine problem. It was a philosophical problem and he did not feel able to solve it.

He saw a labourer whom he knew by name, Cristofuru, a man who had worked hard and uncomplainingly when Bernardo was alive. He knew Alfredo thought well of him.

'Giulia, would you and Alfredo excuse me for a moment? You'll do better without me. I'll catch you up later.'

'Of course, my love,' said Giulia, and Alfredo nodded.

He slipped away and followed Cristofuru through the vines. When he was out of earshot of Giulia and Alfredo, he called out, in the old language, 'Cristofuru, may I have a word?'

Cristofuru gave a him a weary look which plainly said, *What have I done wrong now?* and answered, 'Yes, sir.'

Samuele knew better now than to query the 'sir'. 'Cristofuru, why do we never see your wife, and the wives of the other labourers, helping with the vines?'

'It is not their place to,' Cristofuru replied.

'What do you mean?'

'I mean that Sicilian men keep their wives under control. We are their masters. Without us they starve. They bear our children, they prepare the food which we have grown so that we stay fit to do our work. When times are hard, it is for them to go without. We earn the wages we receive so the money is ours to use. If they have money it is because we say so. Some are generous, others not. That is our business, nobody else's.'

'But isn't there a better way?'

'This is how it's always been and always will be. It will take a stronger man than you to change it.'

His voice was almost insolent. Bernardo – and Alfredo too – would have told him to watch his tongue.

'And another thing,' said Cristofuru. 'If we didn't control our wives they'd run off into the town where there are plenty of men waiting. If they come home pregnant, everyone knows. The husband would lose his honour. Honour is a man's greatest possession. Lose it and he is nothing. Murder has been done here because of honour, but no one pays the penalty.'

Samuele merely said, 'Thank you, Cristofuru.'

He didn't join the others. He stood deep in thought.

The workers who were once Bernardo's slaves are now the most important people in the vineyard. Without their labours, the vintages would fail. They speak in their own Sicilian language. Italian is the language of the masters. Alfredo has to translate the Italian orders into their own language. Thus the masters will keep their power. That is not right. It goes against all that Coleridge intended.

He thought about this for some time until he came to the only possible conclusion.

Without the workers, this vineyard would be impossible and our project would fail. It is they who make it possible. So, they should own it. There is only one way for this to happen.

From now on the old language will be the only one spoken in Floridia. Italian will be banned. If we all unite in the language we speak, it will bring us as close as we can be to Coleridge's dream.

At last, he was fully content.

*

'Where have you been?' said Giulia when he rejoined the others.

'Talking to Cristofuru,' he replied. 'I asked why we never see the wives.'

'And what did he say?'

'Don't ask him,' said Alfredo. 'I know already. But it's better that Samuele hears it directly from a labourer who worked under Bernardo than reported by me.'

'But there's more,' said Samuele. He explained his decision about the languages. 'You both speak it. I can speak it. There's only my mother who doesn't. I fear she may feel excluded.'

Giulia laughed. 'She asked me to teach her. We've been working on it for months. She learns fast.'

Now we truly are a commonwealth. We're as near to my father's Pantisocracy as we can get. Except for the wives.

That night, as he lay in bed beside Giulia, the image of Sara was sharp in his mind and he was racked with guilt. What would she have made of Cristofuru's views on the womenfolk? He remembered what she had said outside Greta Hall about Aunt Lovell, dependent on Southey for her very existence. 'I know that is the lot of too many women in this world.'

This afternoon he had heard more about the woman's lot, even crueller than Aunt Lovell's. And he vowed that some time, somehow, in his new commonwealth he would do something about it.

Sara's image faded. He reached out and touched Giulia's shoulder. She was his future now and he would make his perfect society just for her.

*

Next morning, he made a decision. Mr Calvert was probably right. Yesterday had shown that. Who better, with an experience of different places and different people and the worldly wisdom he had gained, to be his adviser? Besides, a vineyard would be paradise to him and he deserved better lodgings than that gloomy building surrounded by priests.

He broached the subject at breakfast.

'I'd like that,' said Giulia. 'Especially if he brought Peregrina. He will need looking after.'

'You all speak well of him. So yes, of course,' said Cecilia.

Next day, Samuele travelled to Palermo again, told Mr Calvert about his setbacks and asked him to join them.

'I'd be delighted to. There's nothing here to keep me,' he said. 'My old friends in England are probably dead by now.'

'You'll have work to do.'

'Thank you. It's what I need. But I must finish things here first.'

'And we must give you somewhere decent to live in.'

'Better than this, I hope!'

'You will have to learn the old language. It's a condition of joining us.'

Mr Calvert laughed. 'But I can speak it already. When I arrived in my new country I had to understand it through and through. I teach language, I love language. If I didn't know the language most Sicilians speak I might as well have stayed at home.'

'Will you bring Peregrina? Giulia would like it.'

'Only if she wants to.'

If only George were here.

*

He travelled back to Floridia happy. A difficult future ahead with a marvellous outcome. Not the magnificent ideal form Coleridge had imagined, but a place as fairly run as possible, in which every man was valued equally and shared a common language. The true Sicily. But what about the women?

It would take time to shift attitudes. And it would be three years until the first vintage was ready, so he would have to keep the vineyard going himself. Well, he had inherited a fortune so he could afford to. And, he thought daringly, he could pay wages to the labourers' women for what they did for their husbands. Would that spark a rebellion?

Time would tell.

But it would happen. He would carry out Samuel Taylor Coleridge's legacy as well as he could. His quest was over and it was worth it after all. He might have lied and cheated his way round England but perhaps the ending justified it. Sara Coleridge's image appeared in his mind again. *Thank you, Samuele, for what you have done for my father. I knew I could trust you.*

Then she disappeared, never to come to him again.

Coda

Highgate, late summer 1820

Cast your bread upon the waters
—Ecclesiastes 11:1

Coleridge sits alone in his rooms in Dr Gillman's house. He is answering a letter from Charles Lamb accusing him of taking away without permission a book which someone else had lent him. So perhaps he would like to dine with the owner and him next week, return the book and give them each a free copy of his own latest book.

He loves giving books away, especially his own. He will take a few for them to choose from. In the end, readers matter more than money.

His eyes light on a little pile of the single volume containing 'Kubla', 'Christabel' and 'The Pains of Sleep' which Byron had persuaded John Murray to publish. Surely everyone he knows has a copy of that by now? Then he remembers an important recipient to whom he has not sent one. Jesus College, Cambridge.

Might they have one already? He'd bet a pound to a penny that they wouldn't. He hasn't been to Cambridge for twenty years and he is probably forgotten – or disowned.

Very well, they shall have a copy. Should he sign with 'Compliments of the author'? That would defeat the purpose. It must be anonymous with no provenance. Or should it? Perhaps an anagram of his name. He tries a few possibilities. Not easy. Besides, it would be recognised.

He will think about it. He is pleased with his little project and will work it out before he sleeps.

*

Next morning he finds that a good night's sleep has brought an answer. No signing, no dedication. His brain divides in two and starts a conversation with itself.

It should be a message. To whom?

Not a named recipient. The *first* recipient.

But you don't know who that will be.

Of course not. But it doesn't matter.

Why not?

Because the main recipient will be the whole college.

Are they all going to read it at once, then?

No, the first reader will stand for all of them.

I don't understand.

Well, in a college there are two main classes of people, the Fellows and the undergraduates.

You mean you will send two messages.

No, only one.

And how will you do that?

Fellows are old, undergraduates are young. Fellows are cynics, they've seen the world and disapprove of most of it. Undergraduates are young and idealistic. Fellows have formed their opinions, mostly negative. Undergraduates are fluid, seeking new experiences, craving novelty. The old despise the young; the young defy the old. To appeal to both, my dedication will be ambiguous. It must both encourage the young searching for the ideal and for adventure and confirm the prejudices of the old.

Is that possible?

Leave it to me.

He considers the poems. 'The Pains of Sleep' does not qualify. The old will say, 'Serves him right,' and the young will be afraid of suffering similar torments. 'Christabel'? The young might merely see a wild romantic tale, the old might see deeper and be disturbed, both for the poet and for themselves.

It has to be 'Kubla'. A poem with many interpretations, all of them wrong, except perhaps Byron's. It is about opium. The confrontation is clear. Sleep versus wake.

How to put the two together in a way which does not mean what it seems to?

The answer soon comes.

The writer of the above had much better have kept his sleeping thoughts to himself, for they are, if possible, worse than his waking ones.

The first person to read it may be old. The reaction might be, 'Yes, that's clear enough. I agree. The man is contemptible.'

But what if the first reader is young? He might think it's a matter of opinion. Sleeping thoughts may be worse, may be better. Read the poem and find out, and then they might say, 'Yes, sleeping thoughts are better.' And they might start the same journey to enlightenment as his, although, he concedes, perhaps not quite as far.

He carefully writes it out, in a hand as little like his as he can manage. He doesn't want the writing recognised. As an afterthought, he adds *Perfect nonsense* above the main inscription, as if it's a signature to the poem. That could be taken two ways as well.

Yes, he likes it. Time to parcel the book up and leave it out for the post.

He is about to do this when he thinks again. No, this must not be on any accessions list. It must just appear, to be found by accident. A mysterious arrival with another mystery wrapped inside. A magical incarnation.

Magical incarnations are not easy. But there will be a way.

*

He makes some breakfast and thinks as he eats.

He could go secretly to Cambridge, sneak into the college, slip the book onto a random library shelf and sneak out again.

No. His sneaking days are over. Besides, the college's watchful porters are proof against sneaking by undergraduates and older ones have long memories, as he well recalls.

He needs a messenger. Who?

Then he remembers one of Dr Gillman's medical colleagues, Dr Holyoake, who has a son at Jesus. The son will be his messenger. How to ask him?

Later that morning he approaches Dr Gillman. 'We haven't seen much of Dr Holyoake recently. Is he well?'

'He is indeed. Why do you ask?'

'I'd like to see him again, and his wife and son. I wonder if we might have them over for dinner one evening.'

'Yes, it would be pleasant. I'll ask Ann. Of course, if you want Tobias to be there, we must choose a date in the university vacation.'

'Thank you, that would be good.'

*

The dinner takes place in late September. Tobias is quiet but attentive. The conversation ranges wide. Coleridge is on form and delights the guests.

When the meal is finished and they gather in the drawing room for more conversation and a bottle of port, Coleridge takes Tobias to one side.

'Tobias,' he says. 'Would you undertake a small task for me which concerns the college? It must remain secret, so this is just between you and me.'

'It depends what the task is,' said Tobias.

Coleridge has a copy of the book sealed in an envelope.

'I would like you to take this. It contains a book. It is for the college, a secret gift. I would be very grateful if you could slip unnoticed into the library, place the book on a shelf, any shelf will do, and slip out again. I want the book found one day, so that people will know that there is a secret benefactor. They say that the best place to hide a book is in a library. This will test the hypothesis.'

Tobias takes the envelope with a smile. 'I would be happy to,' he said. 'I love secrecy. You can trust me completely.'

'Thank you,' says Coleridge. 'I will be eternally grateful. Now let us rejoin the party.'

He follows Tobias into the drawing room. As he goes he cannot resist a quotation from his beloved Shakespeare.

'*Mischief, thou art afoot. Take thou what course thou wilt!*'

Postscript

...Beneath this sod
A poet lies, or that which once seemed he –
Oh lift a thought in prayer for S.T.C!
That he, who many a year, with toil of breath,
Found death in life, may here find life in death.

—Inscription for his own gravestone written by
Samuel Taylor Coleridge

The 1830s are here. STC's heart is failing and he knows he is dying. But he is content, calm and happy. His demons seem slaughtered. Sarah and Sara have left the Lakes and taken up residence nearby: he is on good terms with the woman who is still his wife and he loves and admires his brilliant daughter. He looks forward to her marriage to his nephew Henry, of whom he approves highly.

He finishes and publishes his last small books. Troops of friends come to Dr Gillman's house to listen to him in wonder as he holds court in his rooms. Old enmities are settled. Wordsworth realises he will soon lose 'a wonderful man'. Southey is reconciled. They recall old and better times. But the radical ideals are gone. They now crave a stable State and a settled Church. Evolution, not revolution. *Calm of mind, all passion spent.*

The year is 1834. His decline is rapid but his memories are clear. On 25 July, he dies. His last words are to John Green, his legal executor. His mind, he says, is unclouded. His very final words are, 'I could even be witty.'

Had he lasted another half hour, he probably would have been.

*

Father, no amaranths e'er shall wreathe my brow,
Enough that round thy grave they flourish now

—'To my Father', Sara Coleridge

Author's Note and Acknowledgements

The Second Person from Porlock is a riff on Samuel Taylor Coleridge's life with supernatural overtones which I think are justified by his many dreams, hallucinations and the evidence of his greatest poems.

The plot has two mainsprings. First, the handwritten comments on 'Kubla Khan', which in real life are there for all to see in a collection of Coleridge's poetry belonging to the library of Jesus College, Cambridge. I first heard of these inscriptions in Dr Frederick Brittain's book *It's a Don's Life* (Heinemann 1972), and I was so intrigued that I visited Cambridge to see them for myself. My visit was made possible by the kindness of Dr Hilary Woolnoth, college archivist.

The second mainspring is the affair with Cecilia Bertozzi in Siracusa, the truth of which is more doubtful. That they met is certain. What happened afterwards is not. For many years it was dismissed as a brief flirtation. However, later writers have suggested there was much more to it. Richard Holmes in *Darker Reflections*, the second volume of his wonderful biography, quotes the extraordinary entry in Coleridge's notebooks which is quoted here in Chapter 15 and as the epigraph to Intermezzo 1. In *The Friendship: Wordsworth and Coleridge* (HarperCollins 2007), Adam Sisman suggests that if the relationship had gone the full distance it might have done Coleridge a power of good.

While Cecilia Bertozzi's encounter with Coleridge is real and documented, what became of her after that is unknown; there is no mention of her in any history of opera. I have therefore felt justified in giving her an alternative life.

Simon Hatley is real. I first found out about him in Robert Fowke's lovely book *The Real Ancient Mariner* (Travelbrief Publications 2010). You can even see the Hatley family's house in the High Street, Woodstock, with an inset stone saying *The Home of the Real Ancient Mariner*. It is not open to the public.

To avoid having too many Saras I have followed the example of Kathleen Jones in *A Passionate Sisterhood* in standardising on 'Sarah' for Coleridge's wife. In any case, 'Sarah' may have been her original name but Coleridge insisted that she drop the 'h' because he thought 'Sara' was more 'literary'.

*

I'm very grateful to many people who have helped me write this book. First of all to Jane Spiro, who allowed me to quote from her beautiful dramatic poem 'Song of the Saras'. Then to my two assiduous beta-readers, John Cannon and David Jago, both of whom, like me, read English at Cambridge. John was at Emmanuel and David was at Jesus, Coleridge's own college, as was I. They have been unstinting in their comments, criticisms and suggestions and I learnt much from them.

Kathleen Jones has been helpful and encouraging for a very long time and her book *A Passionate Sisterhood: The Sisters, Wives and Daughters of the Lake Poets* (Virago 1998) was a real revelation.

I want to thank all at Fairlight Books, especially Louise, Laura and Bradley. Louise and Laura for their support, understanding of what I was trying to do and with unerring judgement and editorial skills pulling me up short when I wasn't delivering it. Bradley guided me through the process of providing information, especially about the genesis and research which went into the writing of this book, without which I would have been thoroughly confused and which compared well with other publishers with whom I have worked. A great team!

And last but not least, Kay, my wife, who not only made sure I conquered my inbuilt laziness (not unlike Coleridge's) but sorted out the many slips and typos in my earlier drafts.

I have read many books, articles and academic dissertations about Coleridge, all of which have helped me enormously. But two stand out. First, Richard Holmes's two volume biography, *Coleridge: Early Visions* (1989) and *Coleridge: Darker Reflections* (1998), both published by HarperCollins. The two together constitute a monument to careful and thorough research and inspired insight. The other is *The Making of Poetry* by Adam Nicolson (HarperCollins 2019), a truly superb account of a year spent in the Quantocks following in the footsteps of Wordsworth and Coleridge in their 'year of marvels', which produced Coleridge's 'Kubla Khan', 'The Ancient Mariner', 'Lime Tree Bower' and 'Frost at Midnight', and Wordsworth's 'The Prelude' and 'Tintern Abbey'.

Two wonderful reading experiences.

About the Author

Dennis Hamley grew up in Kent and Buckinghamshire. After completing his National Service in the RAF, he read English at Jesus College, Cambridge and then pursued postgraduate studies at Bristol, Manchester and Leicester, where he earned a PhD. After a career in education as a teacher, lecturer and adviser, he retired early in 1992 to write full time. His first young adult novel was published in 1974 and he has written over sixty books, both educational and for children. These include four 'crossover' novels, *Spirit of the Place*, *Out of the Mouths of Babes*, *Ellen's People* and *Divided Loyalties*, all now reissued by his imprint Joslin Books.